Lord OF SHADOWS

TANYA ANNE CROSBY

OLIVER HEBER BOOKS

 Created with Vellum

PRAISE FOR TANYA ANNE CROSBY

"Crosby's characters keep readers engaged..."

— PUBLISHERS WEEKLY

"Tanya Anne Crosby sets out to show us a good time and accomplishes that with humor, a fast-paced story and just the right amount of romance."

— THE OAKLAND PRESS

"Romance filled with charm, passion and intrigue..."

— AFFAIRE DE COEUR

"Ms. Crosby mixes just the right amount of humor... Fantastic, tantalizing!"

— RENDEZVOUS

"Tanya Anne Crosby pens a tale that touches your soul and lives forever in your heart."

— SHERRILYN KENYON #1 NYT
BESTSELLING AUTHOR

SERIES BIBLIOGRAPHY
A BRAND-NEW SERIES

ELEMENTAL MAGIK

*A most strange creature will come from
    the sea marsh of Rhianedd;
As a punishment of iniquity on Maelgwn
    Gwynedd;
His hair, his teeth, and his eyes being as
    gold,
And this will bring destruction upon
    Maelgwn Gwynedd.*

— TALIESIN

PROLOGUE
LLANRHOS, WALES, 547 A.D.

The tribes were all at war, brother scheming against brother...

The Dragon Lord of Anglesey sat beside his queen, watching a party of dancers as he brooded over the state of his realm.

So, it seemed, men no longer needed whips nor chains to sway the masses. All they needed was a bit of gold and a lot of empty promises.

The Romans might be long gone but having left behind their jeweled yokes to be donned by the people of Wales, the weight of their harnesses now grew heavy. For love of those winking jewels, the free all remained oppressed, patting their sated bellies as they toasted from sour casks of *vin*.

Now, the worst had come to pass...

But all was not lost. The spirit of the world was alive and well. It was here, in this hall, in every turn of the dancers' lithe bodies, and if anything hardened his cock, it was this: Against the taming of a nation, there was a certain beauty to be found in the old dance. Amidst their graceful motions lay passion and truth, a raw honesty that fired his spirit and stirred the blood. In every revolution the dancers made, he spied the Goddess face of the moon and heard the voices of the *faefolk* singing bard songs to the wind. It stirred a song in his own blood that made him long to strip to his boots and howl at the moon.

Alas, these were times for the changelings—those who would convert, or those who would create. But sadly, not for the ones who would cleave to the Old Ways. Still, he resolved to enjoy it while he could.

The *Gwyddon*, or *wise one*, clad in her fine white robe (to symbolize purity and light), twirled at the center of his hall, whilst twelve young disciples danced about her in a circle...

One dancer stood out amidst the rest—Sanan, his nephew's young bride. With her soft pink lips and her darkly burnished hair, the girl was striking, but, like her betrothed, there was a certain falseness about her that made Maelgwn feel she could be anyone's for the taking—even his, if he so desired...

It was that come-hither look in her jade eyes—a sultry glance that roused him, even against his will.

She dipped, then spun, raising her hands in thanksgiving to the Mother Goddess, only with a backward glance to the throne, smiling a smile intended only for him.

"You like her?"

Maelgwn slid his wife a careful glance. "Sanan?"

Nesta nodded, and he swept away the notion, no longer willing to sew his seed indiscriminately. Together they had created a beauteous daughter, and he still had one son by a previous marriage. "She's too young," he said.

And, besides, there was too much strife in his kingdom to steal his nephew's bride and then lie abed like a sated boor. The last thing he needed was to become a fat, happy emperor like those he'd despised.

"Mael," she said gravely. "I have not conceiv—"

"It matters not," he said firmly. "I am well pleased with the daughter you gave me and my son. What more could any man ask for in life?"

"Only think on it," she argued. "What if something should happen to you? Einion—"

"She. Is. Too. Young," Mael persisted, and though his tone brooked no argument, his wife was not so easily silenced. Her temperament, like her *faekind*, was wild as the wind.

"Maelgwn, please... you know that Igraine cannot inherit these lands, nor I—"

"Nay!" he snapped, and still, she persisted.

"It *must* be someone. So much as I loathe the thought of sharing you, my sweet husband, you *must* consider a new bride. Sanan comes from a good line."

"She is promised," he told her, and Nesta laughed without mirth.

"To your nephew? What has the fool ever done save to pit himself against you?"

Silence.

Because it was true.

And yet, Maelgwn hadn't any stones to throw, because he too, in the name of these lands, had slain his uncle—for Wales.

"She's as good as any, and—"

"Nay," he said, and this time she gave him respite, although he knew she would resume her campaign in good time.

She was on a mission, and he frowned, because he feared she could be right. The spirit of unrest was growing. The Roman prelates were wagging their silvered tongues. Little by little, the Old Ways were being abandoned. Nesta herself was the last of a dying breed—those *faefolk* who'd once inhabited the hills overlooking the Drowned City. Cauldron born, she was descended of the acolytes and he trusted her without fail. She was a gem among women, and though he didn't love her as he longed to love a woman, he still wasn't in the mood to collect more wives. As it was, he had a nest of vipers...

Some of them were here tonight.

Unfortunately, it was a king's duty to entertain foes.

From the dais, he studied the hall's newest guests —Uther, that golden child of the Empire, and his equally golden mage, who indeed, was quite golden. Everything about the man shone, from his pearlescent skin to his fine-gilt hair. Goddess blessed, so 'twas said, and it must be true. The mage was as fair as any druid Mael had ever beheld, and there was, indeed, an aura about him that put Mael in mind to the gods.

Both men sauntered into his hall with an arrogance born of privilege and, rather than take up a plate and find themselves a proper seat at one of the lower trestle tables, the pair approached his dais, and Uther—the sodomizing bastard—unsheathed a blade from his scabbard as he came.

Beside him, Nesta gasped, leaping up from her seat and sheltering herself at his back as three of Maelgwn's guards rushed forward to impede Uther's approach.

Undeterred by the guards, the warlord grinned,

slippery as an eel, as he tossed up a hand, as though his men were Uther's to command.

"Uther," said Mael in greeting, and he too waved to his guards, urging them to fall back as his nemesis approached.

The mage remained by his side as he bowed before Maelgwn and said, "My friend."

Friend?

May the gods rip out his tongue and cast it to the wolves. Uther was no man's friend. He was, as they claimed, a wolf in sheep's clothing.

The cords in Maelgwn's neck tightened, though he smiled and said graciously, "Welcome."

"Our King... on this holiest of nights, we come bearing felicitations from the Senate," said Uther. "And a gift..."

And then, with a flourish, he presented a strange sword, laying it gingerly atop Uther's palms, so that the inscription could be read on the shining blade.

Maelgwn blinked with sudden lust.

It was only once the revelry resumed that he realized the breath of the world had come to a pause... waiting to see how these foes would meet.

As the musicians began to play again, and the dancers' feet kicked up more dust, his favored guests brought bits of nuts and fruit to their lips. Maelgwn leaned closer to inspect the blade... Intricately crafted serpents lay entwined about an elegantly fashioned hilt.

Fascinating.

On the blade itself, glowing faintly blue in the most ancient of languages, lay inscribed, "Take me, but turn the blade, and we will see." But the runes were faint—indeed, so faint, that the inspired words might have been a chimera.

Incredible.

There was still another word etched betwixt the serpents, and this one could be read more easily: *Caledfwlch*, it said.

Cut steel.

Excellent craftsmanship, and no doubt a bribe, but Maelgwn was nevertheless bewitched. "Remarkable," he said.

"Indeed," said Uther with a knowing smile, and he flicked a short glance at the mage by his side.

No longer quite so concerned over Uther or his mage, Maelgwn longed to caress the blade.

"Who forged this work of art?"

It was Taliesin who replied. "It was crafted by the *Dynion Mwyn*, Your Grace," he said, with a respectful bow.

The Fair Men.

"It was forged from blooms of steel mined from those Ancient Hills before Avalon's doom."

Maelgwn blinked, his heart suddenly thumping with lust unlike any that might be inspired by a woman.

The blade was, indeed, a fine, fine work of art, expertly crafted, and glowing like a piece of the moon.

Every carving on the hilt seemed to shiver and come alive under the play of light and shadow; the serpents themselves appeared to writhe before his eyes.

Astounding.

Shining like tourmalines, Maelgwn's eyes fixed drunkenly on the sword, wanting it with a fervor not only born of greed. It was as though its essence called to him, beguiled him...

"'Tis a gift," repeated Uther, with a smile in his voice. "For you. We are asked to sue for peace."

Taliesin added, "It bears a druid blessing. He who wields the sword will not bleed, and he who possesses it will e'er reign as Dragon Lord of Wales."

Behind him, Nesta hissed like a cat. "Old man! Begone with your gift and your forked tongue!"

She stayed Mael's hand as he reached for the glittering prize, whispering for his ears alone. "The gifts of your enemies are not gifts, my love. Have you learned naught from our past? Better to send them away."

"Nay," said Maelgwn, silencing her with a lift of his hand. "I shall not forswear a victory gift." And then, ignoring his wife's counsel, he reached for the sword, utterly enchanted by its essence and form.

Try though he might, he could see no reason to turn his head from such a beautiful concession—and it was clearly a concession, delivered by the hands of a well-respected druid and a prelate of the Empire.

It was the mage who placed the gleaming sword in Maelgwn's hands, lifting it carefully from his master's palm and placing it into Mael's hands with the care and love of a father handing over a firstborn child.

He who wields the sword will not bleed, and he who possesses it will e'er reign as Dragon Lord of Wales...

Desire coursed through Maelgwn's veins with such vigor that he shivered. He accepted the gift, and for a moment, simply tested its weight... fine, fine, cold steel, precisely calibrated by the hand of a master. It was his now, and he could already envision himself wielding it, unsheathing it from his scabbard...

The hiss of metal was like a song to his ears.

It was only belatedly that he realized the mage still had possession of the blade, and when Mael tried to turn it to inspect it a little better, the druid turned it and slid it back, nicking Maelgwn's flesh, drawing his blood...

"It's only a scratch," he said to his wife when she gasped.

In truth, Maelgwn was too entranced to care. Enjoying the feel of the sword in his hand, he sent the druid and his master away without so much as a rebuke, and then sat back in his throne, admiring the fine cut steel.

He who wields the sword will not bleed, and he who possesses it will e'er reign as Dragon Lord of Wales...

And yet, he did bleed...

Studying his prize, he was hardly aware that Nesta abandoned his side, or that the dancers continued long into the night, performing without his regard.

Wine flowed generously. Laughter rang loudly, abundantly. And all the while, Uther kept his grin.

Unfortunately, Maelgwn was well into his cups before he realized that something was dreadfully wrong.

Sweat formed upon his brow, then trickled down his burnsides. His vision swam like a drunken otter, and still, for so long, he blamed it on the wine. Only once he took the sword and draped his hand over the arm of his chair, then dropped the sword with a clang, did he realize...

Nesta was right: The gift of an enemy was no gift at all.

The sword was cursed.

That was his last conscious thought as the room swam, then faded to black. He awoke in his bed many, many bells later, shivering to his bones. His wife was kneeling by his side, and the chamber was filled with all her ladies, weeping and praying...

"Mael," she whispered softly, her throat thick with spent tears.

"Shhh," he said, because he already knew what it was she would say, and he didn't have the heart to hear of betrayal on his death bed. "How... long?" he rasped.

She choked past a sob. "Three days... three days and three nights..."

That was not what he wished to hear. "How long?"

There was so much to be done—and what of his son?

Nesta did not immediately reply.

Maelgwn closed his eyes.

"Mael," she whispered, and Maelgwn tried hard to reopen his heavy lids. "My love," she begged, and this time she shook him very gently, till his eyes again opened. But his vision remained hazed, so the figures standing before him morphed into caterwauling banshees, summoning him from his bed to the darkness beyond. "Mael," she said, again, and the single word was so full of agony that it twisted his heart.

"Uther?" he asked weakly.

Nesta's lips quivered with grief. "He and the mage have withdrawn from our halls till the day breaks on the morrow. His armies remain camped beyond our walls.”

“My son?”

Nesta shook her head with grief, and Maelgwn felt a sob well from his breast to his sore throat. Einion ap Maelgwn was his only true heir. If his son was... dead...

If Uther lay waiting...

“You are dying,” she confessed between tears. “And yet you do not have to.”

Nesta, sweet Nesta was a child of the Goddess, cauldron born, and cauldron raised. Her knowledge was the knowledge of the Ancients. He trusted her without fail.

“My love... you must agree to allow it...”

“Dearest,” Maelgwn said with regret, and he tried to lift a finger to her cheek, falling short of her face. It fell limp beside him on the bed. Indeed, he could feel his life slipping away... like sands in a glass.

“Mael!” she cried. “Only speak the word, and I shall gift you my life! True love’s tears might save you!”

Oh, yes... They would spend eternity together, he and his beauteous wife, whose glorious bosom was the pillow of his choice. He could learn to love her properly and give Nesta her heart’s desire—a prince of her womb. “You and I,” he said. “Forever... and ever... and ever...”

To bloody hell with thrones and crowns. So long as he had her love, he would be happy evermore.

“Yay,” he said weakly. “Yay...”

His wife rose at once, her tall, lithe body towering over him, her shining gold mane surrounding her like a halo. She spilled her tears into the palm of her hand,

and then he heard her words and recognized the gleam and slash of her ceremonial blade. But even as she worked, he fell in and out of shadow, somewhere at the back of his mind, understanding the rite she was speaking...

> Here, with my blade, I take your
>   former life,
> Here, with my art, I still your beating
>   heart,
> Eternal thy flame, Lord of Shadows
>   thy name.

And then she knelt once more by his side and said her final good-bye. "Rest in shadow, my beloved, till you are once more summoned to the light."

Invoked perhaps by the sultry nature of her words, shadow and light danced before his eyes like fornicating lovers.

Shadow and light converged, again and again, until, with a violent clap of thunder, a rush of wind rose from the casket of his body, and for the sweetest interminable moment—he and his wife were caught between worlds, their souls united as one, until the torrent died like a winterbourne in summer... devoid of life, but not quite dead.

At the end of her ritual, Nesta's body lay lifeless on their chamber floor. Maelgwn could see it as though in a dream. Her maids lifted her up, then laid her beside the empty shell of her husband—his own body. When Uther arrived to claim the banner and crown, he was told the Dragon Lord's queen ended her life with her husband's last breath. No one noted the reliquary in the hand of her maid. She gave Uther the message with a nervous curtsy before quitting the chamber, rushing away with a heartfelt promise for the Lord of Shadows: "I shall keep you in secret till The One arrives, and someday, my lord, you must avenge my lady's death! A pox on the house of Pendragon!"

ONE

BLACKWOOD CASTLE, JULY 1153

He should have died.

He *did* die.

And still, here he was, flesh and blood, and it was Morwen who'd freed him. For that alone, he owed her a debt of gratitude.

Pensive and mirthless, the lord of Blackwood sat behind his escritoire, studying a small reliquary on his desk.

So, he'd been told, there were three of its kind remaining in the world—one his, one belonging to Mordecai, and the last he presumed must be Morwen's...

Presumed, only because she kept it about her neck on a chain, the same way he kept his own.

Exquisitely etched, cylindrical in shape, his was about a half inch in diameter, and one and one-quarter inches long, with a strange, blue-veined crystal fashioned at one end, the fit so seamless it was impossible to remove. The metal was intricately inscribed with runes that, to his knowledge, could no longer be read.

He met a priest once who'd called it a reliquary, although, in truth, it was nothing like those receptacles they used to hold the bones of saints. It looked like one, perhaps, but it wasn't.

If he shook it, there was nothing inside, and if he put it to his ear, he heard a hint of wind... like a seashell.

Admittedly, he didn't know how it worked, nor did he dare disassemble it. This was all he knew: It alone was the key to his existence—a ridiculous little bauble that Morwen had called a *grisial hud*. In his Welsh tongue, it meant, quite literally, magic crystal.

Lifting the pendant from his desk, he turned it slowly, examining the strange metal and markings, perhaps for the thousandth time since acquiring it.

Puzzling.

Only to see it was to imagine it an impossible sepulcher, and yet... what dimensions should one expect to provide for the totality of a human soul?

It was everything... and yet...

Nothing.

Cael d'Lucy was a creature of shadow, a man with far more to lose by dwelling in light than he did in darkness. He had more secrets than most, and too much to lose—including his life—should they ever come to light.

He was confused.

He'd come to know Rhiannon Pendragon well, and, indeed, his heart wept for Uther's heir. Still... whenever he thought to pity her, he was forced to ask himself: What was five years compared to six hundred?

Six hundred and six, to be precise.

Six hundred and six years during which his only conscious thought had been to avenge his beloveds.

Now that he had his chance, he dared not rest until the task was done. Then, and only then, could he hope to find peace.

Regretfully, the matter had become... complicated.

Almost daily, he had to remind himself who she was. Lovely though she might be, in her delicate blue veins, she bore the sins of her fathers. And, in truth, no matter how many years had gone since Uther's betrayal, his sorrow was fresh as the loam over a day-old grave.

Thinking of Nesta, his jaw worked angrily. Faded by time, an image arose from the dusty depths of his memory—her lifeless form prone on the chamber floor, her sacrifice to save his damnable soul.

Was it worth it?

Nay, he thought.

It was not.

And still, for every moment of these past six hundred and six years, he'd been acutely aware of his losses, feeling their pain like limbs plucked from his body.

He was the Pendragon.

Not Uther.

And what had the Judas gone and done?

He'd settled himself on Cael's throne, then eaten the meal from his larders.

The image sent a torrent of hatred rushing through his blood, for his true name was not Cael d'Lucy. He was Maelgwn ap Cadwallon, High King of Gwynedd, Dragon Lord of Anglesey. He was *not* the cousin of some paltry English lord, but the firstborn son of Cadwallon

Lawhir, great-grandson to Cunedda, who, by order of Governor Maximus, led the Votadini against the Pechts. And for his part in the campaign, his forebear had been awarded the entirety of Gwynedd—the Jewel of Wales, so 'twas written by a contemporary of Maelgwn's time.

And the true Dragon Lord... felled by a creature with golden eyes and hair who'd cursed him with a yellow death.

He, who'd fought and won the dragon throne, only to lose it all... over what?

Lust for a sword?

Perhaps *she* was not the sole heir to Blackwood; still she bore the blood of his nemeses in her veins. That alone should keep him from coddling her.

That alone should force him to remember.

Remember!

Fool. She's not simply some hapless maid whose mother is cruel.

Unlike her sisters, she was not the progeny of a king. Hers was a... distinctly maculate conception, and her father was a reincarnation of the man by whose hand his life was taken—that druid who'd once called himself Merlin to Britain.

God's blood, it galled him that she looked like him —all save for that wild, copper hair. She bore those same chiseled cheeks, the same fair skin, the same shape of her brows—perpetually arched, as though she alone were privy to the mystery of creation.

And, God's blood, her eyes... blue and stormy as a winter sky, while Taliesin's had been deepest amber, imbued with a cunning that few could forswear.

Not that *she* wasn't cunning, mind you.

She was certainly wily enough to sense every

chink in Cael's armor… and therefore, why should he care whether her hands were weighted with the burden of manacles?

Why should he care what became of her?

At least she still had lungs to breathe and hands to carry a child of her womb.

To the contrary, Nesta's arms were empty in death, and he himself might never see an heir to his legacy—such as it was, a decrepit old castle in the Black Mountains, not at all the kingdom he'd been promised.

Certes not his beloved Anglesey…

And what now?

He would risk even this for a beauteous witch…

"Rhiannon," he said aloud, testing the weight and feel of her name on his tongue.

Rhiannon.

He couldn't help but remember the way she'd faced him the day he'd met her, straight from her prison tumbril… with her hair disheveled, and her dirt-stained cheeks, her shoulders back and high… like a witch queen in her own right.

Even then, she'd had a fire in her eyes that matched the flame of her hair.

But now… that blaze was diminishing day by day, and there was a joyless turn to her lips…

Still… he owed her mother.

He owed for his life… and if he did not keep his promises, Morwen would collect her due.

She was a necessary evil.

A means for revenge.

And aye, she might use him as well—as she used everyone—but he would gladly allow it because… in the end, his goal was her goal: a reckoning for the Pendragon's heirs.

"Ah, Nesta," he said, with a heartfelt sigh, and then he attempted with some difficulty to summon her golden visage... all that materialized was a flame-haired beauty, whose words cut like diamonds and whose eyes, like a mirror, reflected the same sense of fury as his own.

Rhiannon.

Very, very gingerly, he set down the reliquary, considering the irony that he would now aid and abet the very institution whose gold once sought his ruin.

Indeed, with Maelgwn ap Cadwallon's death arrived a new day for the Empire. Uther himself became the new Dragon Lord, whose son later ascended to his throne...

And where was Maelgwn's heir?

Dead and buried mere days after his—

Startled from his reverie by the blast of a horn, he peered back at the door, suddenly discomposed.

This time it would not be *her* messenger; it would be the Witch Queen herself. Two months ago, she'd given him an ultimatum—wed Rhiannon, or wed her. No matter what he chose, the consequences were considerable: force Rhiannon and he would lose her evermore; marry her mother and he'd risk his own goals; defy the Witch Queen and he would lose more than his life...

And... he suspected... deep in his heart... she wouldn't be satisfied until her daughter was dead.

Knowing this, something other than common sense spurred Cael from his seat.

No doubt Rhiannon had heard the horn blast as

well. Even without her *magik*, she must sense her mother's presence.

It would take Morwen and her company another interval to ascend to the gate. Once admitted, there would be no turning back. If, in truth, these were the End Days of her prophecy, it must be now or never...

TWO

News of the outside world was scarce, though even in the confines of her plush apartments, without the use of her *magik*, Rhiannon sensed a growing darkness, a shadow that, left unchallenged, would creep over the land and swallow it whole. For weeks now, she'd had a terrible premonition—a sense of foreboding she couldn't shake. It multiplied tenfold when she heard the horn blast.

Minutes later, when she also heard footsteps ascend the tower, she braced herself for a confrontation.

Was it Cael?

Please, let it be Cael.

Sweet, sweet fates—let it be Cael!

What if it was Morwen?

After all this time, would he hand her over?

Glowering down at her shackles, she acknowledged that if she were whole, she would know who it was. But nay, nay... she could only wait... and hope...

But why should she care?

After five long years with only Blackwood's mysterious lord for company, she must confess she barely knew the man. Oh, yes, they made some pretense at flirtation, but no matter how many witty jests he made, or how long they spent in each other's company, like the castle itself, he was a fortress filled with secrets, and his truest self remained locked away no less securely than he kept her.

Four long years without answers or speaking to her sisters. Four years without practicing her Craft.

Four years!

The footsteps came closer... louder... faster.

Once again Rhiannon peered down at her manacles—impossible contraptions that defied logic. By order of her mother, they'd clapped them upon her wrists, and with the turn of a key they'd made her into a worthless bag of bones. Her lack of ability was infuriating.

Mercifully they were no longer bound together— a kindness served by the lord of Blackwood, who'd painstakingly reworked the metal over long, long hours to gift her the freedom of movement. And despite the fact, it was difficult to be thankful for his effort, when she knew good and well that he could free her with a word if he chose to.

Until such time as her mother returned to claim it, Cael d'Lucy was still lord of this demesne.

It was him, thank the gods!

By now, she recognized his footfalls—soft and sure, like a wolf on the prowl. Her heart skipped a beat, and she cursed herself for the weakness. Nearly every time she saw him, she waged a battle in her heart, one she would never, ever confess—it was true; she thought him beautiful, clever, and thoroughly impossible.

Unfortunately, whatever good she sensed in Cael d'Lucy, it was tempered by the fact that she knew him to be an agent for darkness—a scourge to England and Wales.

Indeed, he might well be respected in Stephen's court, and perhaps even throughout Wales, but Cael d'Lucy was no less a servitor for darkness than the rest of her mother's minions. And, in the end, he bowed, not to justice, nor to England's King, but to a destroyer of realms.

Morwen.

Nay, she reminded herself, *not* Morwen.

Cerridwen. The Dark Goddess, the Shadow Crone, the Shapeshifter of Legend...

And now she was here; Rhiannon could feel it in her bones. It gave her a shiver.

What now, sweet fate?

There was so much she longed to say to her sisters.

Goddess only knew, whatever perfidy Morwen was planning, Blackwood was at the center of her plans. It was that cauldron, she realized—that holiest of grails. Life was born from its belly and Rhiannon knew intuitively that it was the cauldron Morwen wanted. But it was not so simple as taking it, else she would have done so long ago. King Stephen wasn't so witless as to allow a great fortress to slip from his grasp. Instead of returning it to her family, he'd awarded it to the commander of his Rex Militum, and if Morwen tried to usurp it, he would mount an army to retake it.

No, her mother wasn't stupid either. Rather, she meant for her daughter to take it for her. But no matter how Rhiannon felt about Cael, she would be damned if she'd allow Morwen to win this game—never would she take d'Lucy's name!

But this was something she didn't comprehend: *Why?*

Why was Cael so indebted to her?

Why was he so willing to turn a blind eye to all she did?

What precisely did her mother have to leverage over Cael?

Considering all these things, perhaps for the thousandth time, she fingered the etching on one of her manacles, still sharply inscribed no matter how many years had gone by...

> Hic est Draco,
> Ex undis,
> Tenetur in argenteas
> A capite ad calcem, tace, et sile
>
> Here be the dragon,
> From the waves of the sea,
> Bound in silver,
> From head to toe, silent and still

Rhiannon was not *the* dragon, but she was *a* Pendragon, and so it seemed that whatever *magik* had been imbued into the words, it was strong enough to endure.

The footsteps stopped abruptly in her antechamber. Ready to do battle, she spun to face the door, watching through the crack as her guards silently dispersed.

And there he was... lingering in the shadows, hesitating, and she knew why. After all they had professed, he fully intended to betray her at her mother's behest.

"What are you waiting for?" she said acerbically.

At long last, the lord of Blackwood revealed himself, sauntering into her chamber with a turn of his lips that revealed the barest trace of a smile.

"Ah, my dear Rhiannon, don't tell me you missed me?" he asked, with his usual mordancy, though it wasn't a question, and even if it were, Rhiannon suspected he had long ago surmised the truth—devil take him!

She *had* missed him, though she'd be damned if she'd ever say so, certainly not to him.

"Hardly," she said. And no matter that the timbre of her voice seemed laden with contempt, her heart did a telltale leap at the familiar glint in his eyes.

He had no right to be so beautiful, and now she understood Lucifer's lament—no man with a heart so dark had a right to shine so bright. There were no half measures where he was concerned; his shoulders were impossibly wide, his hair was dark as coal, his lips were sinfully full.

And truly, for a blackguard, he had a very endearing, but telltale habit of holding his chin and brushing a thumb over his mouth when he looked at her, as though he would love to kiss her. It never failed to steal Rhiannon's breath.

"How sad," he quipped, and Rhiannon lifted her brow.

"So says the lord with a smicker."

He regarded her a moment longer, still brushing that thumb across his lips, and then he frowned. "Have I not treated you well enough?"

He had, and so he had.

Far better than her mother would have liked. Had she had her way, Rhiannon would have remained chained to a wall in the tower, deprived even of a window.

"Have I not provided your every desire?"

"Everything but my freedom," she said easily, never at a loss to remind him.

Clearly, he was in no mood to banter. She saw his countenance darken, and winced. And suddenly he approached her, and Rhiannon took a defensive step backward—not that she was afraid of him.

Rather, it was that she no longer trusted herself in his presence. Having spent so much time alone together, playing Queen's Chess, supping and drinking, sharing wit and words, she had by now developed very disturbing feelings for her *gaoler*—feelings that thoroughly confused her.

In truth, Blackwood's lord was ever gentle, showering her with gifts. And still, she remained a prisoner. No matter whether she be draped in scarlet, or that her bed was piled high with ermine, she could not for one minute afford to forget what he was: at best, an opportunist; at worst, a murderer—and perhaps even worse than that.

And yet, when she should utterly despise him for aiding and abetting her mother, she found she could not. Instead, she suffered a pang of longing whenever he wasn't near, and she loathed herself for the inexcusable weakness.

Today, his eyes glinted strangely.

"Is anyone truly free?" he asked, still assessing her. And then he came closer yet, and said, "With the absence of constraints should come great restraint;

without it, the strong are said to enslave the weak. It is, as they say, a conundrum."

Rhiannon frowned. "Ever with the posturing, my lord! Make no mistake, I am *not* weak." She lifted her right arm, proffering the right wrist, returning his canny smile. "At least, I would not be without these. Care to test me?"

The familiar timbre of his laughter threatened to warm the cockles of her heart.

"Alas," he said, standing before her, so desperately close that he could have reached out to brush a wisp of hair from her face, as he ofttimes did. "There has never been aught about you I've found to be weak, Rhiannon. In fact, I have come to fear you will be my ruin."

"*Your* ruin?"

Sweet fates. He must be jesting!

"Aye," he said, and Rhiannon took yet another step backward, unnerved by his proximity. "What do *you* want, Lord Blackwood?" Her nerves were frayed, and she was tired of his posturing. It was easy enough to speak drivel whilst he held her in shackles. As for *his* ruin, there was little about Cael d'Lucy that one could ever mistake for fear, but neither would she cow to him, or apologize for whatever sense of distress he was feeling.

"Your mother is here," he confessed, at long last, and it was just as she'd feared. Rhiannon's heart tripped painfully.

"And?"

"And," he said, without further ado, because, in truth, what more need be said? They both knew well enough that her mother despised her. Whatever the former Lady of Blackwood had in mind for her second eldest daughter, it would simply not behoove Rhiannon.

She swallowed hard, uncertain what more to say.

No matter how lightly she and Cael bantered, no matter how much consideration he gave her, in the end, he was still her mother's minion, and all she knew for certes this moment was that her time had run out. If Morwen was here after so long an absence, she was returning because it was time to put her plans in motion. Once more, she cursed the manacles for blocking her *magik*. Without the *hud* she was hapless as a babe, and it galled her that she felt reduced to begging for freedom—still, she would not.

CHAPTER

THREE

Proud and utterly defiant.

Cael's jaw worked furiously as the key's iron teeth cut into his palm. This was not what he had planned.

Having heard the horn blast, here he was—*and why?* Because he was listening to his bloody heart.

Nay, he thought.

It was not true.

His heart was cold.

It was simple human decency not to wish to see a woman suffer, and whatever he'd become, he was still flesh and blood like any other man.

And yet, because he was flesh and blood, he burned. Even now, he longed to pull Rhiannon into his arms and kiss her fiercely, especially now that their time was so short.

Not once during their time together had he ever felt the desire to rush their wooing. He'd enjoyed their verbal sparring and hoped to win her for life.

But now the stakes were higher, and the time was gone.

28

Waiting until the last of his guards dispersed, he anticipated the ebbing footfalls...

No matter that these men were loyal to him, he didn't intend to have an audience. He had a good sense of what Morwen was capable of, and, whether out of fear, love or greed, few men could deny her. She would compel them if she so chose, and she would do her worst if she suspected treachery.

At any given moment, he could not afford to forget that everything he possessed, he possessed through her good will. He had returned to this realm as vulnerable as a babe, and she'd been his benefactor since.

If it weren't for her recalcitrant daughter, he might already have had all he desired. And somehow, even after five long years, this was where they stood...

Rhiannon was willful and noncompliant.

Much like that first day, she stood facing him now, hands upon her hips, her blue eyes glittering fiercely.

"Well?" she asked. "The guards are gone. Will you speak now, or did the cat get your tongue?"

Cael laughed, though ruefully, wishing for a shot of Marcella's new brew.

Originally, her mother had intended for him to wed Rhiannon's eldest sister. It was Elspeth, not Rhiannon, who was the rightful heir to this estate, and her husband should own this demesne. Once that possibility was removed from the table, Cael had steadfastly refused a change in plans. Why, he didn't know, but he had a sense of it now...

Knowing Rhiannon would never succumb to pressure, he'd protected her all this time. If Morwen realized that she was the only reason they weren't yet wed, he wasn't certain what she would do. But he had never coveted Elspeth—not for an instant since meeting Rhiannon. With her dark copper tresses and those feral eyes, she'd stood up to him from the first, and even whilst her gaze was still afflicted, he could harbor no pity for her at all. She'd asked for no quarter and gave none.

Perhaps, in truth, her sister was Blackwood's heir, but Rhiannon was *the* Pendragon at heart, and even now, with a shadow of fear clouding her storm-blue eyes, she could set him afire with only a glance. And yet the one thing he knew for certes was that he would never take what Rhiannon would not willingly give, and he understood very, very clearly now: She would never give her heart to anyone.

In the silence that followed her question, his gaze moved to her window. Already, the sun was beginning to set. The torches along the pathways were not yet lit. Even so, he surmised they had few minutes remaining before Morwen presented herself in his hall.

Blackwood's defenses consisted of several safeguards. Surrounded by woodlands, the castle was built atop a craggy hilltop. And though it was small in terms of fortification, it was easily defensible and completely impenetrable, unless one knew of the narrow path that led to his postern gate.

The climb up was steep, and the barbican was designed to restrict access to the castle's interior.

Even beyond the first wall, there was a series of narrow bridges built over pits, all filled with pikes. It was carefully designed so that persons seeking entrance to the inner bailey were forced to travel along a narrow path.

On a good day, even in broad daylight, it was impossible to traverse more than one-man deep, and at any time, those bridges could be withdrawn.

Knowing Morwen, she had arrived with pomp and ceremony, escorted by her lackeys—all those Welsh kings she'd gathered to her side, men she'd inveigled with promises. Owain Gwynedd, the self-proclaimed King of Wales; Madog ap Maredudd, Prince of Powys; Maredudd ap Gruffydd, Prince of Deheubarth. The latter ruled with England's support, though he'd gladly put a blade through Stephen's eye.

No doubt she would expect Cael to greet her with Rhiannon at his side, but not because she cared to lay eyes upon her estranged daughter; merely so she could test the girl's resolve.

Squeezing the key in his hand, he realized that wedding Rhiannon per force would not gain him what he truly desired...

Her heart.

Alas, he must confess: He had loved Nesta dearly. He'd adored her sweet, kind heart, and he'd valued her counsel, but he'd never hungered for her body... not the way he lusted after Rhiannon. Even now, despite their circumstances, his body trembled with desire, and he longed to push her back onto the bed and pillage all she had to give—all that he had been promised.

Only what then?

Then she would loathe him.

And yes, he *could* force her to marry against her will, and hope to God that he could change her mind. But... after five long years of trying and failing, he had a feeling deep down... he would regret the decision for the rest of his days.

Even now, she glared at him as though she would plunge a dagger into his breast, and he believed in his heart that she would if she could—no matter how much he'd risked serving her. Knowing this, tendrils of anger clutched at his heart. Closing his fist about the key, he placed his hand behind his back, and with the other hand, he reached out to seize her wrist above the manacle, drawing her close, forcing her to endure his proximity if only once in her damnable life.

"Cael," she protested.

RHIANNON SWALLOWED.

For the first time since their meeting, the look in his eyes thoroughly disturbed her. There was something new and terrible in his demeanor that gave her pause—something angry and desperate.

"W-What are you doing?"

The sound of his voice was achingly low, filled with torment. "The time for games is done," he said darkly, pulling her closer, and not gently. His arm slid about her waist, pulling her against him, so Rhiannon could feel the hard contours of his body. And even as he restrained her, she felt the evidence of his arousal. "Cael," she said, though she wasn't entirely certain it was a protest.

In that terrible, terrible instant, the shocking feel of him awakened something deep inside her that she'd hoped to deny—her nipples pebbled embarrassingly, puckering against his leathers and she swallowed convulsively. "Please..."

"If your mother has her way, you'll soon be my bride."

"Never!" she spat, with far more conviction than she felt.

In truth, had the situation been different, she might have welcomed a match with this man.

There was something about Cael d'Lucy that tripped her heart and fired her soul. Never in her life had she met a man who was so much a man—strong, and crude betimes, filled with surety. She lifted her chin defiantly and lied.

"No matter what you do or what you say, you'll *never* force me to love you."

He laughed then, the sound mirthless. "Love?" he asked. "Love? What has *love* ever had to do with a contract of marriage, Rhiannon?" His black eyes shone. "Do not mistake me, lady, there is only *one* woman I have *ever* loved, and she is *not* you."

Rhiannon swallowed her words. *Why did that bit of truth wound so deeply?*

Like a chimera, his emotions morphed between hatred and... something else...

And regardless, despite the obvious disdain he felt for her in that instant, his gaze found her bed, and she noted the unbridled heat that crept into his storm-ridden eyes. Her voice faltered. "C-Cael... w-what do you mean to do?"

In all these years, he'd never even once given her a reason to fear him. Oh, she understood well enough why men cowed before the lord of Blackwood; there was a certain darkness that permeated every room he entered. No less so than any Pendragon before him, he was a dragon lord, inscrutable and cunning, treacherous and exacting. This was one thing Rhiannon never, ever dared to forget. And yet, despite this, though he lusted for her body, he'd never once acted upon his desires, and, yes, she knew—had always known—this was all it ever was for him: a man's lust.

She reminded herself that there was a good reason he'd never caved to her mother's demands.

She must not fool herself into believing this man held any measure of affection for her, even if betimes he did look at her with such incredible longing that her flesh prickled beneath his gaze—the way he was looking at her right now.

He inhaled a slow breath, then let it out, as though trying to master his rage.

Was it rage?

Or was it pain?

He said calmly, but angrily, "Once your mother arrives, you *will* join me in the chapel for our much-delayed nuptials—"

"Never!" she cried. "I will not!"

Ruthlessly, and without apology, he pulled her tighter against his body, quieting her with the force of this gesture. "Aye, Rhiannon, you will," he said low, and with unmistakable menace. "Already, I've sent for the prelate. Once he arrives, you and I—" He squeezed her again when she opened her mouth to protest. "Will stand before him and graciously accept our vows, with your mother and the Welsh kings as witnesses."

Rhiannon blinked away tears, hoping against hope that he might at least give her some sense that he wanted this too. "To please my mother?"

His smile thinned. "Ask me no promises, I'll give you no lies."

"I—"

He squeezed her one more time, silencing her

with the ferocity of his gaze. "You *will* marry me, Rhiannon," he said, with quiet menace. "You will be *my* lady. And I shall speak no more of my fealty to your mother—never again! Do you understand?"

Angry tears filled Rhiannon's eyes—until he found her hand and pressed something small and sharp into her palm. It took her a full moment to make out the small object... a key?

To what?

He lifted his brows. "Do you understand?" he reiterated.

Dumbfounded, she lifted the key to examine it and blinked in shock. She hadn't seen this key for five long years, and yet she knew precisely what it was. She knew it because it bore that same odd glimmer as the metal of her shackles. Lifting her eyes to Cael's, she swallowed convulsively, finally understanding. He released her abruptly.

"My bride's gift to you," he said, searching her eyes for comprehension. "Only do me the inestimable favor of waiting before you use it. Speak your vows when the time requires, bide your time. Later, when the time is right, I'll see you have the opportunity to escape."

Vows?

Go?

"When?"

There was nothing gentle about his dark look. His jaw worked furiously. "You're an intelligent woman. You'll know," he said. "And, in the meantime, put a smile on your face and pretend that wedding me is the one thing you most wish to do."

After all this time... Rhiannon would be the lady of Blackwood... and then she would be free.

Dumbfounded, she closed her fist about the precious key. "Why?" she asked.

His lip turned cruelly. "Why do you think, my lovely termagant? The more your mother believes we are aligned, the greater your chance to escape."

"No, I meant, *why*—why are you helping me?"

It dawned on her suddenly how much this would cost him. *Everything*. And still, he meant to do it.

"*Why* is not important."

Her brows collided. "Aye, but it is."

His gaze softened now, his expression incongruous to his words. "If you must know, I do not take kindly to being told what to do. You are not the only one averse to sharing a marriage bed, my beautiful harpy."

Rhiannon winced. *Sweet fates.* As much as it pained her to acknowledge it, she sensed the truth of his words, and still there was more that he seemed disinclined to say.

"Thank you," she said, bewildered.

Did he believe her mother would kill her once their vows were spoken? Some part of her searched for a hidden motive she could live with.

Or did he truly not want her?

Unfortunately, she waited too long to speak.

Another horn blast sounded from the ramparts, and the lord of Blackwood turned on his heels and marched out the door, leaving Rhiannon alone, for the first time without guards. She stared unblinking in the direction he'd gone, and then she peered down at the key in her hand.

The key to her shackles.

CHAPTER

FOUR

R hiannon's guards did not return.

She stood alone, listening to the distant echo of Cael's footsteps, ebbing swiftly as he made his way belowstairs.

She could leave, she realized.

Go!

Flee!

As though to emphasize this truth, her wrists burned with new awareness of the enchanted metal that bound them.

The key in her palm seared her flesh like a burning ember.

Until this instant, she hadn't had any inkling there were varying degrees of "alone." Alone without companions or visitors, and alone without guards were two wholly different things. Once Cael was gone, silence rang in her ears—an endless silence that left her confused.

No shuffling of feet outside her door.

No sniffles.

No quiet laughter.

No idle chatter.

No taunts, or jeers.

Although, truth be told, these past two years of her confinement, they had all begun to treat her with a modicum of respect. And, of course, she understood why: After all this time, they must assume she and Cael were lovers.

After all, why wouldn't the lord of Blackwood avail himself of the woman who was meant to be his bride?

The simple fact that Rhiannon had never once wept nor shouted against his advances could easily have been because she'd welcomed his hands and his lips upon her body.

Except she had not, and Cael never once afflicted himself upon her person—not once.

To be sure, the man was a conundrum.

He was her enemy, in truth, but he was also her friend—and never was she more aware of this dichotomy than she was now.

Morwen was here.

How in the name of the Goddess could she face her mother after all Morwen had done?

How could she pretend for even an instant?

Now that she possessed the key, how could she maintain these shackles upon her wrists when her hands ached to squeeze her mother's throat?

Two of her sisters were dead because of Morwen, and there was nothing anyone could do to remedy that fact, nor bring Morien or Arwyn back, though she could leave here at once and make certain her living sisters remained safe.

She blinked down at the key.

Aye, it was true. She could take off the shackles...

here and now. Be free of this cruel binding. But Cael had asked her to bide her time...

Dare she trust him?

Aye... she did.

The lord of Blackwood might be many, many things—a villain, perhaps, no less than her mother—but Rhiannon had never once witnessed him to be a liar.

What if she refused his dictate and walked away—down those stairs, out the door—would he prevent her?

There was only one way to find out, but the longer she stood gaping at the unguarded doorway, the more ambivalent she was.

Her mother had arrived.

To see her wed?

If so, what would be the impetus for Cael to release her now? Did he so much loathe the thought of wedding her?

Perhaps so, but she realized that merely wedding her would never assure him the stewardship of Blackwood. Cael must realize this as well. And if not, he was deaf, because she had told him so at least a thousand times. Blackwood was always meant to go to King Henry's favorite, Elspeth. Certainly, King Stephen might be inclined to ignore his uncle's decree, but Rhiannon was neither the eldest Pendragon, nor was she herself of any royal blood—leastways not English.

And yet, she had no doubt about Cael's ambitions. He coveted Wales, and Stephen had already promised the duchy to him, so long as he maintained Blackwood in good standing. Whether Rhiannon was elder born or nay, she was Welsh by blood, and with the strength of their alliance, he might, indeed, continue to keep the Welsh rebels at bay.

The last thing Stephen needed was to bleed his coffers dry putting down unnecessary rebellions, and the last thing anyone needed was for the Welsh to resume their hostilities. As it was, her mother kept them appeased with her promises.

Thus said, Cael shouldn't be so quick to release his best claim to Blackwood, a daughter of the Pendragon line. After all, Blackwood belonged to *her* family, and if Cael couldn't manage to secure the eldest Pendragon as a bride, Rhiannon would be the next best thing.

So, then... was it a trap?

A show for her mother?

Or perhaps a ruse to convince Rhiannon to speak those loathsome vows, and then afterward he meant to lock her away in that tower. Only, what would that gain him that he didn't already possess?

Naught, she realized; it would gain him *naught*.

Nor did she like to think that everything they had shared was meaningless...

At any given point during these past years, Cael might easily have marched her back up to the tower and locked her away, but he had not. To the contrary, he'd moved her into this suite intended for the lady of the castle, and he'd showered her with gifts that were all fit for a beloved wife—perhaps yet another ruse to soften her resolve?

He didn't need to cajole her. He could very easily have forced her to wed. By Welsh law, Rhiannon couldn't be forced to marry against her will; but Cael d'Lucy was not beholden to Welsh law. He answered to England's king. Although Stephen had his troubles with the Papacy, they would never take Rhiannon's side—a known Welsh witch, a daughter of their mortal foe. If Cael should happen to bring her before an ambassador of the Church, her protests would fall upon deaf ears.

Utterly confused now, she closed her fist about the small key and stared into the darkening hall...

Had he left her door unguarded only to prove a point to her mother—that what?

That he'd finally won Rhiannon's heart?

That guarding her was unnecessary because she was so pliant?

So, he could give her the freedom she would need later to escape...

The notion accosted her as swiftly and fiercely as did the certitude that Cael d'Lucy was assured little through his marriage to her, but far, far less if he set her free.

So, then... *why*... why would he help her escape in the final hour, when doing so would only earn him her mother's wrath?

Never once had he given her any cause to believe he might waver in his allegiance. In fact, he'd always made his intentions very, very clear: He was aligned with Morwen.

His goals—whatever their extent—were bound to hers as well.

So, then... dare she believe that he'd made this decision with his heart, not his head?

It was the look in his eyes before he'd left that convinced her it must be true. For all these years, she had so desperately longed for some proof that his soul was not so black as it seemed. Was this the evidence she'd sought?

Her embittered heart could not believe it!

And perhaps with good reason, because, in truth, releasing her might not be entirely altruistic.

If Rhiannon abandoned Blackwood, he would have one less obstacle in his way.

And, if by chance she were slain during her escape... well, then, he could wash his hands of the entire affair, and call himself blameless. For all intents and purposes, he would have done precisely what her mother expected of him—marry Rhiannon for better or worse.

There is only one woman I have ever loved, and she is not you...

Clasping her fist to her heart, with the key nestled in her palm, Rhiannon sank down on her bed, reminding herself that all things in life bore consequences: Stay or go... she would pay a price...

Tears brimmed in her eyes as she remembered a night so long ago in their cottage at Llanthony—that night she'd convinced her sisters to summon a brume to help Elspeth escape the priory. She'd known then that she would be destined to trade places with Elspeth as Blackwood's bride. She'd known it with all her heart.

Effectively, her sisters had agreed to the bargain only because no one ever supposed that Rhiannon, with her afflicted eyes, could make an agreeable choice for the great lord of Blackwood. After all, he had bargained for Elspeth, whose pale violet eyes were soft and gentle and whose birthright could provide him Blackwood without contest.

And yet... knowing what she knew about fate, Rhiannon had never doubted her vision. She had known then that this day would arrive, even despite that for all these years it had been all too easy to deny Cael.

For so long they'd played a game of cat and mouse, neither entirely committed to catching a prize. But here they were... precisely as her vision foretold. In scant few hours, she would be wed to the lord of Blackwood—a loveless match, with a single purpose: *To bind him to Blackwood.*

But Rhiannon had never anticipated this—not *this.*

If she did as Cael asked, she would become a fugitive, if not from the law, then most certes from her mother. And knowing her mother as she did, Morwen would *never* stop searching until she found Rhiannon.

Arwyn learned the truth of that the hard way, and so, too, would Rhiannon, if Morwen ever caught her.

Their mother hadn't a single bone of compassion in her body, and the blood they shared only gave her more cause for enmity.

No matter... how could she not seize this opportunity to escape? Even now, with scant hope of seeing her sisters again, she felt a quickening joy.

What was more: Her heart leapt with anticipation over the return of her *magik.*

Oh! What glee to feel it coursing through her veins!

Oh! How she missed the tingle beneath her flesh.

The inspiration of power in her breast!

Bide your time, Cael had said.

Bide your time.

And so, she must, despite that she suddenly longed for freedom even more than she did her next breath—oh, what a cruel, cruel jest it would be if he'd purposely given her the wrong key!

Fighting a nearly overwhelming urge to slide it into her shackles and test the lock—because if she removed the shackles, she would never put them back on—she slipped the key into a hidden pocket of her dress.

As children, she and her sisters had learned the value of sewing hidden compartments into the seams of their gowns. All the while living at court, they'd used them to hide foodstuffs from the kitchen—a bit of bread from the table when no one was looking... a grape or two from the King's plate. A bite of cheese, or length of salted meat. And they had done so without remorse, because even then, they'd been forced to fend for themselves. After all, who should have cared for Morwen's brats?

It didn't matter that they were Henry's daughters as well. And perhaps Henry had honored them well enough by giving them a home in his palace, but behind his back there was no one who would willingly share a morsel with the Welsh witch's eldritch brats. Her mother was as despised then as she was now, and no matter; that woman lost no sleep. She certainly never once let a thought of hungry bellies stop her from doing her worst, and if they dared complain, she would remind them of their blood, and bade them to figure it out. And so they had. All together they had "figured it out."

To this day, no matter that Rhiannon hadn't Seren's skill with a needle or thread, she fashioned a pocket into every new gown. Although her stitches left much to be desired, the pockets were nearly indistinguishable from her seam—three small threads to keep the material from gaping. The tiny key slid easily between the folds.

Come what may, she would make the decision to trust Lord Blackwood, and not once would she dare peek out of her room, no matter if her guards did not return—mostly because she was afraid that if she went to the door, she might keep going and never return.

But neither did she dare gather her belongings. If her mother should appear in her doorway, she didn't intend to be caught packing. Therefore, she realized... when she left this place, she would be departing with nothing but the clothes on her back... that and her *magik*.

Come to think of it, maybe not even that.

She worried whatever *magik* had been cast upon these shackles, it had depleted her, like darkness banishing light.

Fortunately, the one blessing of these shackles was this: Whilst it allowed no *magik* to leave her person... neither should it allow any within—at least that's what Rhiannon presumed, and soon she would put it to the test, because if her mother suspected treachery, she would unleash the worst of her *hud du*, and not even Cael would manage to survive it. She prayed to the Goddess that he knew what he was doing, and then resigned herself to wait...

It wasn't long before she was summoned belowstairs.

To her surprise—and to her dismay—along with the summons arrived an unexpected gift: a gown unlike any she'd ever beheld. It was a silvered surcoat, dyed purpure, with a snow-white *chainse* to wear beneath. Only, no matter how desperately she searched the folds, there was no place to hide a key, and no time to sew a pocket into the dress.

"My lord sent me to help you dress," explained the girl who brought it—a maidservant Rhiannon hadn't met before now.

Perhaps noting her confused expression, the girl added, "He said he needed Aelwyd in the kitchen and sent me instead."

Aelwyd was the only maid who'd ever served Rhiannon, though even Aelwyd had not been altogether companionable. She did her lord's bidding, and kept her distance, perhaps frightened of what and who Rhiannon was.

"Oh," said Rhiannon. "Well... no matter. I'll dress myself."

"Oh, nay, *meistres*! What of these?" asked the girl, showing her a fistful of ribbons. "I am bidden to weave them through your hair."

There were no fewer than twenty ribbons, Rhiannon noted, and she winced over the time it would take to braid them—time she desperately needed to prepare.

"Very well," she relented, smiling, but her eyes scanned the room, alighting upon an empty ewer. "Oh, but please... I am thirsty. Might I trouble you for a bit of mead?" And then she lifted her hand to show how it trembled. "Nerves, I suppose."

Eager enough to please, the maid curtsied at once. "Of course, *meistres*. I'll go fetch a cup." And then, smiling still, she rushed out of the room, tossing her ribbons upon a table, leaving Rhiannon alone for the moment.

The very instant she was gone, Rhiannon rushed over to pluck up one of the silver ribbons, lacing it through the eye of her key. She then tied the key firmly to her ribbon, and when that was done, she rushed back to the bed, shoving the ribbon, along with the key, beneath her pillow, scarcely in time to turn and greet the maid, who'd returned too soon with a sheepish smile.

"Owen says I'm not to leave you. He'll go fetch it."

Rhiannon frowned, realizing belatedly that her guards must be watching belowstairs. So much for Cael trusting her to do the right thing. And, aye, indeed, so much for believing she could leave if she chose. Although she should have anticipated as much, the revelation disheartened her. Perhaps because it dispelled any notion that she had been given a choice in the matter. And, aye, she would wed Cael d'Lucy, because he demanded it, and she knew that if he set her free, he would do so at his own discretion.

Rotten, misbegotten cur.

Mistaking her downcast expression, the maid tilted Rhiannon a look of compassion. "Oh, please, *meistres,* don't worry, you'll be lovely," she said. "I'll see to it myself, and ye'll make your mam proud."

Rhiannon winced.

The thought was unthinkable.

Retrieving the ribbons, the maid brought them over and tossed the entire lot onto the bed, lifting one, then catching a thick lock of Rhiannon's hair.

"Used to be I lived here when I was a little girl," said the maid conversationally. "We went away when King Henry took the castle, but your sweet mam brought us back. She cured me and my mam of leprosy."

Leprosy? Rhiannon's eyes were drawn to the hands the maid moved so deftly—hands that were devoid of scars. "My mother cured you?" she said with surprise.

The maid smiled warmly. "Aye, *meistres.* She did. I

swear, no matter how terribly they speak o' her, I know what I know, and I will ever be grateful."

"Oh," Rhiannon said, because it explained so much—most notably why Cael had never allowed this girl to serve her before. Only he knew who to trust in this wretched pile of stones. And if he'd sent her here, he must have needed the aid of a servant he trusted. *That* lifted Rhiannon's hopes.

She didn't bother to tell the poor girl that Morwen never did anything for selfless reasons. If she had cured the woman and her mother, she would only have done so to enthrall them. Morwen cultivated sycophants—by whatever means she could, be it *hud du,* or lies. Therefore, she kept her mouth shut and allowed the maid to plait her hair, taking comfort in the fact that if all went well this eve, she would be long gone from this place by the cock's first crow.

Newly returned from negotiations, Giles de Vere was home long enough to see his newborn son, wash, sleep, fill his belly, and then get himself an earful from his wife and his sister by law, then he was back in the saddle, with his brother at his side.

Evidently, the King's son had desecrated the abbey at Bury St. Edmunds, pillaging the Church coffers and destroying holy relics. Giles was commanded to locate the fool and return him to London to treat with his father, although Giles half hoped someone would put an arrow through the dastard's heart and save everyone the trouble.

Eustace was a menace to the realm. By now, the King's son had abused his state in more ways than anyone could count. Not only had he burned Warkworth to the ground, merely to appease his puerile sense of importance, but he injuriously taxed his counties until they complained to the bishops. It was no wonder the Church steadfastly refused to consecrate him, and now that his bear of a mother was dead, he hadn't many allies remaining, not even his father.

However, the winds of change were blowing in one final tempest and his warrior's heart anticipated the worst...

All it would take to change the course of history was the death of two *very, very* mortal men. If Stephen and Duke Henry should happen to find themselves murdered, and if Eustace remained the last man standing, with that witch by his side, the kingdom would come undone.

By now, Giles had come to understand this was not truly the tale of a usurper, nor the uncle betrayed, nor even a grandson so eager to reclaim his birthright.

Rather, it was a story about queens.

Three, to be precise.

First, the Empress Matilda, whose mother kicked up her toes when she was only sixteen, and whose father left her with an uncertain legacy.

The Queen Consort, whose husband was a usurper, and who, no matter how hard she tried, never outran her cousin's shadow, even in death.

And lastly, the Witch Queen, who, spurned by a young maiden who'd resented her father's paramours, grew spiteful and treacherous.

But so, it seemed, if *politiks* were akin to a game of Queen's Chess, for the time being, the queens were no longer in play on the board: one defeated, one deceased, one now missing.

A few years ago, on threat of excommunication, the Empress Matilda abandoned Devizes Castle and returned to her court in Rouen, leaving her son to assume her battles in England.

Last year, consumed by fever, the Queen Consort died, leaving her sovereign husband to rule without his greatest ally.

Alas, sadly for England, the last queen standing was the most treacherous of all… older by far than Wales, more elusive than a will-o'-the-wisp, more deadly than a fork-tongued adder, Morwen was out there… somewhere, though she'd yet to resurface after Maude's death—not because she was aggrieved, Giles suspected. Those two were enemies more than allies, despite that the Queen enabled Morwen as much as her husband did. After all, it was the Queen's indefatigable desire to see her son consecrated that had kept the Welsh witch by her husband's side, whispering like a viper into his ear. Mercifully, the one thing Morwen no longer had was Stephen's ear. Nor was his son the heir apparent.

At twenty, Duke Henry was now favored for succession. As the true heir to England's crown by virtue of his father and grandfather, the Vatican preferred to see Matilda's elder-born consecrated over his mother or Stephen's son.

As it stood, barring some unforeseen catastrophe, King Stephen would retain his throne until the event of his death, and thereafter, it would fall to Duke Henry.

At long last, after nineteen years of anarchy, the nation was prepared to settle. Only, naturally, there was one person who was not so pleased by the recent arbitration…

According to the missive, the King's son left Wallingford in a rage, with a handful of barons who couldn't stomach the thought of seeing an Angevin on the throne.

Much to Giles's disgust, at six and twenty, Stephen's elder-born was no more than a spoilt wretch, and this latest tantrum was yet another example of why no one with half a brain should ever trust him. Add that to his affiliation with Morwen, and it was a dangerous brew.

But this was the true danger of Morwen; her agenda was not Eustace's agenda, nor was it King Stephen's. Hers was a far, far more nefarious scheme, and if there was one thing Giles had come to understand, it was that she would do nothing that didn't serve her purposes.

The King's son was only a distraction.

Hoping to seize the fool before he did more damage, he and Wilhelm rode south with all due haste, stopping only now and again to rest their horses.

It was dusk on the seventh night, when they arrived at Bury St. Edmunds, greeted by the scent of charred grain and earth.

Mercifully, the stench of blistered flesh was absent from the milieu. Black-faced with ash, the entire flock could be found in the fields, salvaging what little remained—spring crops that would yield no ale, but at least the fire, far from prescribed, would improve the health of the field.

Abbot Ording rushed to greet them. "My lords," he cried. "Welcome! Welcome!"

Giles alone dismounted, swinging one leg over his saddle to plant his feet on the ground. "He's gone?"

There was no need to say who.

Ording crossed himself and kissed the tip of a thumb. "Aye, my lords. He took to his mount in a fit of rage after he realized most of the coffers had no keys."

"No keys?"

"Well, my lord," he said, his cheeks blooming red. "There *are* keys, of course. However, only one brother may ever be apprised where they are kept. We... er... locked him in the silo when the King's son arrived. Verily, 'tis far simpler to make away with a single pricket than coffers full of gold." The man crossed himself again. "Even so, he took a cartload, but we hadn't another cart available for use—we burned them all in the barn," he said behind a hand. "So, he set fire to the fields in retribution, all the while cursing over Angevin hell spawns."

He was referring to Duke Henry, whose father was Angevin by birth. Giles re-examined the fields, his gaze finding the barn, which was also destroyed. It was difficult to say who'd wrought the most damage on this abbey—the monks themselves, or the Prince and his cronies.

Mounted and silent, his brother studied the blackened fields, swallowing visibly—no doubt recalling the burning at Warkworth, where Wilhelm, alone, had hauled out their dead. "Bastard," his brother said low. "I'd like to set fire to his arse."

Abbot Ording started over the blasphemy, crossing himself again. "My lord! You mustn't say so: two wrongs do not make a right," the priest scolded. "You wouldst do far better to pray for the prince's soul."

"*You* pray for his soul," countered Wilhelm. "I'd sooner give the stupid cunt something to pray about."

At six-foot-five and weighing more than sixteen stone, Wilhelm's threat was hardly innocuous. Abbot Ording shuffled closer to Giles, although in truth, he should have worried more over Giles... if only he knew.

Erudite though he might appear, Giles was a paladin—a polite title for his post to a company of what amounted to no more than a troupe of assassins.

Perhaps it might seem odd that the King would hire one of his kind to retrieve his wayward son, but this was a true testament to the state of the realm. Giles understood why Stephen had called for his help instead of one of his own. Firstly, Giles was bound by his faith to exercise every option before dispensing "God's justice." But far more importantly, if Stephen had to call upon his own Rex Militum, his son wouldn't survive the day. At the instant, Eustace was the most hated man on the continent, and no less so by the King's personal guards.

"You came so swiftly," said Ording, endeavoring to change the subject. "We thank you! Alas, though, there is nothing more to be done." His demeanor changed now. "I... I'm afraid we haven't much ale remaining, and in truth, we haven't much of anything. The prince emptied our larders as well, though we could offer you a warm bowl of gruel if you like—or if you hurry, you might still catch him at Edwardstone."

"Is that where he went?"

Abbot Ording lifted a shoulder. "We cannot know for certes, my lords, but he did hasten away with the name of that abbey on his lips. If you hurry, you may catch him."

It was clear enough that the good Abbot didn't relish the notion of either of them remaining to sup. "Fret not, Good Father," said Giles. "Keep your gruel for your weary men. By the looks of your flock, they'll need it more than we do."

"Oh, thank you, my son!" said Ording, with a grateful bow. "Thank you so much!"

"Miserly Benedictines," groused Wilhelm.

With a lifted brow for Wilhelm, Giles turned to reclaim his saddle, assuring the priest, "I'll send word to Warkworth to dispatch more supplies. You'll have more than enough to replenish your larders within the fortnight. Take it as our gift to God."

"Oh, thank you! Thank you!" said Ording. "God bless you—" He cast a wary glance toward Wilhelm, and said again, "God bless you both!"

"Keep your blessings," groused Wilhelm. "Save them for Eustace. The bastard's going to need every prayer he can get if I get my hands around his throat."

"Nay, my lord!" chided Ording. "That is treason! He is still the King's son." He crooked a finger at Wilhelm. "Remember... as he hung on the cross, our Lord said, 'Forgive them, for they know not what they do.' I tell you true, no man may pass judgment in this realm." Abbot Ording lifted his chin, scarcely able to meet Wilhelm's gaze. "'Vengeance is mine, I shall repay, sayeth the Lord.'"

Giles smiled faintly. Little did the man realize... *he* was God's vengeance on this earth.

"'If your enemy be hungry, you must feed him,'" continued Ording, heedless of the ire his words were inspiring in a man whose faith had died the night Warkworth burned. "'If he be thirsty, give him drink; for by doing so ye shall heap burning coals upon his head!'"

"So, I see," said Wilhelm, sardonically. "You feed your enemies, but not your allies. 'Tis quite enlightening, Good Father. Thank you for that clarification. I see now that you follow your scripture to the letter." He patted his empty belly to make a point, and thankfully, the Abbot was silenced by the rebuke, though his cheeks bloomed red.

Wishing Wilhelm would shut his gob, Giles cursed softly beneath his breath as he gave the Abbot a farewell nod and a wave good-bye, then a final warning glance toward his brother. It was only after they were away that he dared to rebuke Wilhelm for his churlishness.

"God's bones! The years have yet to mellow you, brother. One of these days you'll say the wrong thing to the wrong person, and we'll both find our necks in a noose."

"That man is a greedy cur," Wilhelm said defensively. "We came more than eighty leagues to his rescue, and still, he cannot spare a measly mug of ale?"

Giles sighed. "If 'tis true what he claims, he may not even have enough for his own men. Wouldst you have him share with you his last bowl of gruel when we have more than enough in our satchels to fill our bellies for a *sennight*?"

Wilhelm grumbled loudly. "I warrant he's got more'n he claims. You heard him: He managed to save 'coffers full of gold,' so he can pay for more supplies, still you gift him more?"

"The time for hoarding is done," said Giles. "We've more than enough to share, and a siege of Warkworth is no longer likely."

"Says who?"

Giles slid his brother a sideways glance, realizing how worried the man must be. Edwardstone was nowhere near Warkworth, and neither was the castle any longer vulnerable, but he couldn't precisely allay his brother's fears.

For one thing, he couldn't yet tell Wilhelm anything about the envoy due to arrive at Warkworth soon, with its precious cargo. If he knew, he would immediately return, for fear of his wife's wellbeing. For another, who was to say in this current clime, and with Eustace's current state of mind, that he would not find just cause to avenge their support of his father. After all, it was at a time precisely like this that he'd ridden south from Aldergh to burn Warkworth.

Furthermore, it was no secret that Giles had fervently lent himself to the negotiations at Wallingford, and that he'd lobbied vigorously in defense of Duke Henry. And everyone also knew that Warkworth enjoyed the support of the Vatican, the very entity that so long denied Eustace his confirmation.

Therefore, in truth, Eustace had more than enough cause to attack Warkworth, and despite this, Giles sensed he would not—not yet, at any rate. If ever he returned to Warkworth, it would be with Morwen by his side, and they would come for the Pendragon sisters. But this was why they must locate Eustace with all due haste and return him to London. They must find the fool before Morwen found him. And then they must hie back to Warkworth to meet their guests.

Reaching back into his saddlebag, he snatched a bit of salted meat and tossed it over to his brother. "Fill your belly," he demanded. "We've another five leagues to ride, and I'll warrant the prior at Edwardstone will find you less churlish if you settle that demon in your belly."

With a scowl on his face, Wilhelm caught the length of salted meat.

"Our battle is not with God, Wilhelm, nor with those poor monks. They, too, have suffered because of

Eustace. You would do well to remember what it feels like."

His brother all but snarled as he shoved one end of the salted meat into his mouth, and said, with a mouthful, "Betimes you're an imperious ass."

Giles's face split with a toothy grin. "Only betimes?"

Reluctantly perhaps, his brother's lips turned up at one corner, revealing a hint of a smile that betimes mirrored Giles's. But the smile didn't quite reach his eyes. "I'll wager five marks he's not gone to Edwardstone," said Wilhelm as he chewed.

"You think Ording lied?"

"Nay," said Wilhelm. "I just think he wanted us gone and it was the first thing that came to his lips."

Giles arched a brow, intrigued by the conjecture and the wager. "Silver or gold?"

"Gold," said Wilhelm as he chewed.

An entire month's wages.

"Where to?"

"Darkwood."

"Darkwood?" asked Giles. "What makes you so certain, brother?"

"Well... consider it... that mean little shit might not give a damn that he's defiling God's lands, but I warrant his men will. See how you rush to chasten me for words alone? After Bury St. Edmunds, they'll abandon him for fear of God's wrath."

"Probably, but why Darkwood?"

"Only think on it," suggested Wilhelm. "Money will not gain him what he wants, but Morwen could give it to him yet. And where would *you* go if you meant to seek that Welsh witch?"

Darkwood Inn was more than a den of thieves. It

was Morwen's enterprise, so they'd discovered some years ago. She, alone, was Darkwood's patron, and though she might not be in residence, that inn keeper would know how to reach her. Giles gave his brother a nod, and without another word, he turned his mount.

His brother followed suit.

SIX

The former lady of Blackwood arrived with, all things considered, a small retinue. Thankfully, none of the bunch happened to be Mordecai. For that much, Cael was grateful. Her manservant was nosy, intrusive, and the first thing he seemed to like to do, every time, was pore through the castle to see what he could find. Preventing Mordecai from gleaning their plans would have been nigh impossible, and there was no way Marcella could finish her task in the courtyard with Mordecai milling about. As it was, he sent Morwen's Welsh "guests" with escorts to see to their quarters and personally kept Morwen preoccupied, so she wouldn't run to admire her Unholy Grail. Hopefully, in the meantime, Marcella would find a way to mask the scent of her potion, because Morwen had the nose of a bloodhound.

He cringed now as she sniffed the air, like a dog following a scent, and he moved quickly to distract her. "I see you managed to wrest Owain from his throne of twigs."

She arched a brow. "Art jealous, my pet?"

"Hardly. He's cocksure, no doubt, but he's already made himself an enemy of the one man who helped him take his throne."

"Cadwaladr?"

"Aye."

"If I have my way, he'll be driven into exile. Don't worry. We'll dispose of Owain soon enough," she said. "You'll take his island then. For now, we need his armies."

"Even the best of Welsh bowmen won't stand against Stephen."

"He's weaker than you think," she said. "And besides, we only need one."

"So, then, you have news from Wallingford?"

"Nay," she groused, removing her gloves and snapping them with annoyance. "You?"

Cael shook his head. "Nay. Apparently, whatever compromise they've agreed to is now only privy to those who were present in the marquee. I've not heard a whisper."

"Your... *spy*?"

"Nay," said Cael, again. "Not a word."

"Pity," said Morwen, though her tone seemed hardly disturbed. "Really, my lord, how am I supposed to plan my revenge if I haven't any notion what that fool means to do?"

Cael didn't bother to point out that had he remained with the King as was originally intended, he would have been a witness to the entire negotiation. But that was a moot point now, because here he was, and so was she.

"Don't worry," she said again. "Without Maude to temper his tantrums, he is prone to maudlin fits of pride. For all we know, he may have already refused

Duke Henry's demands. After all, we know how arrogant that little whelp can be, and if such is the case, Eustace shall remain his heir."

"Doubtful," said Cael, and because it had never been his way to mince words, he didn't intend to begin now. "Unless you have something momentous planned, you ought to begin wooing Duke Henry. Despite that the news has not been made public yet, I know enough to know he *will* walk away with the spoils. If not today, then later."

Morwen clucked with disdain, lifting a hand to silence him. "I weary of speculation, Lord Blackwood. If you cannot provide me facts, speak naught at all."

A muscle ticked at Cael's jaw, though he nodded, ceding to Morwen's will, for the moment. He wasn't always so compliant, and he knew she valued his unbridled advice, but today was not the day to test her. In truth, he would like to have told her naught at all. He was growing ever so weary of her brusque demeanor, and the prize at the end of this journey was beginning to look like no prize at all. It could well be that, in the end, their affiliation would bring him naught but grief, and Owain would keep Anglesey.

"What of my daughter?" she asked, contempt dripping from her tone.

"She has agreed."

Morwen tilted him a glance. "So, you have said, but I cannot rightly conceive it. My daughter is a shrew if ever I met one. Tell me, you must have fucked her?"

Cael forced a smile, ignoring her rude question. "You will see," he said, and hoped his tone sounded appropriately optimistic. "She has changed."

"I hope so," she said, and shrugged off her fur

cloak, laying it into the hands of one of her attendants. The man dusted it off, then departed without so much as inquiring as to which room she would be assigned.

"Wait!" said Cael, not wanting him to pass through the courtyard. "Take it to the lord's chamber," he commanded the servant, and pointed to the stairwell.

Morwen offered him a coy smile. "How lovely. You would provide me your bed chamber? Do tell, my lord... will you be joining me as well?"

"On my wedding night?" he asked, with a well-calculated wink. "Alas, nay," he said. "For the purpose of this evening, I will happily share my lady's bower. 'Twill be easier that way, and perhaps it may afford us more... privacy."

"You must know I have talents my daughter does not."

"I'd never disrespect you, *meistres*."

She cast him a sideways glance. "You are ever a spoilsport, my lord. And you bore me, in truth."

"Aww, well. I'm quite certain you haven't any use for an old goat like me," he said, and then he added, "You'll be comfortable in the lord's chamber and I presume you'll enjoy a view of tonight's celebration from the inner balcony."

Built adjacent to the tower, joined by an ancient, ivy-tangled courtyard, the great hall consisted of two levels—the great hall itself, and the lord's apartments on the second floor. The kitchens were nearby, attached by a loggia. No doubt, Morwen would enjoy a good glass of mead as she surveyed her minions in the comfort of a robe—or at least, the thought of it should please her...

The reality would be somewhat removed from this plan. Fortunately, he knew she coveted the lord's chamber, and it suited his purposes to put her off her guard.

Like Mordecai, she rather enjoyed a good snoop, and, after all, if a man had anything to hide at all, he would keep it in the privacy of his quarters. Still, Morwen found a reason to grouse. She was as distractible as she was irascible today. Hopefully both would work in his favor.

"Since when have you allowed my daughter the use of my suite in the tower?"

"Some time ago," Cael confessed, his shoulders tight as he braced for Morwen's displeasure. "You must admit, I could scarcely have expected to win Rhiannon over by keeping her in a cell, so I thought it prudent to give her a place of honor. She's in many ways her mother's daughter."

Morwen huffed in response. "Naturally," she said, as they arrived in the main hall, and moved toward the dais. "But you needn't have wooed the bitch. If you were half the man you are purported to be, you'd have dragged my ungrateful daughter before a prelate long before today. Instead, here you are playing nursemaid and catering to her every whim."

"Hardly," he said.

"I have my little birds," she reminded him, and Cael tensed, wondering if her "little birds" had already told her about their moonlight brewing. Marcella had been working all night long to prepare the potion, and though she'd finished early this morning, she spent the entirety of the day trying to cover up the smell. Thankfully, Morwen didn't ask to see her cauldron—though whether this was a good or bad thing was yet to be determined. Instead, she led the way to the dais, comporting herself as though she were already mistress of Blackwood, which, to some extent, she probably was.

Half his denizens he did not trust. The other half he trusted with his life—and that was a good thing, because tonight, that's precisely what he had to lose. "Have you any wish to refresh before the feast?" he asked politely.

"Nay," she snapped. "Worry not, my lord. The journey here was not too arduous. And, really, I care nothing for my daughter's nuptials—leastways not beyond the rewards I will reap. You did your job well enough, and, as promised, I will reward you in turn. Too bad you don't seem particularly inclined to take your payment in my bed."

Cael stiffened. "Not if you mean for Rhiannon to believe I have given her my heart," he said. And then, because curiosity needled him, he dared to pry. "By the by... you never said *where* you have been sheltering, *meistres*. Much has trans—"

"I can be found when there is need," she replied, and then she said no more. The woman was as cunning as her "little birds." In fact, wherever she'd kept herself these past three years, she'd kept her whereabouts entirely secret. But Cael suspected she must be close—somewhere she could keep a wary eye on her precious cauldron. She had not kept her head all these years without keeping a few secrets. According to his own "little birds," she'd not called upon Darkwood in quite some time.

"You brewed my honey wine!" she cried at the top of her lungs. "I thought I smelled mead."

It was her preference of drink. And while it was

not Cael's, he nodded to a servant girl waiting to serve them. "I'll have some as well," he told her.

Only then was she appeased. Without bothering to ask which seat to take, she assumed the seat to the immediate left of the lord's chair—the one that, according to propriety, should be left for his bride. "Let us talk," she demanded, with a satisfied smile. "We have much to discuss."

SEVEN

"And then, once the vows are spoken, I—"

All chatter ceased abruptly as Rhiannon floated into the hall amidst a billowing cloud of gilded purple. Thereafter, it was all Cael could do to keep his attention on the woman seated beside him—his means for revenge, like that sword that once doomed his soul. And yet... no longer was the object of his lust a spellbound blade, but a flame-haired beauty draped in silvered thread. She was lovely—more so than he could ever have imagined after greeting her fresh from that tumbril five years ago. But the dress...

Dyed a true purpure, the long flowing sleeves and surcoat were dark and rich. By contrast, the sendal *chainse* was paler than the palest shade of a new moon.

Moreover, she'd plaited her thick tresses into lovely braids that fell to each side of her flawless face, completing the look with silver ribbons that were each interwoven throughout the plaits. Altogether, the metallic threads glistened, reflecting the torchlight in such a manner that it appeared she glowed like the sword his hands once ached to hold.

Enchanting...

Even her damnable mother was gobsmacked by the sight of her, though she covered her shock with a discreet little cough. "How... beautiful," she said.

Morwen herself was stunning for her age—a greater feat than most realized since no one had any notion of her true age. Not even Cael knew for sure, though he knew *who* she was and *whence* she'd come, and that was shocking enough, though not as shocking as the envy that was so palpable in a mother's voice—as conspicuous as the silver threads so masterfully woven throughout Rhiannon's attire.

"I... have... never seen... anything... so... exquisite."

"Indeed," said Cael, though she was speaking of the dress, he presumed. He himself was enamored of the woman, and he found himself bitterly envious over the way the shimmering fabric clung so possessively to her curves.

To cover his stupefaction, he leaned close to whisper into Morwen's ear, and he had no need to feign the admiration he felt. "A wedding gift from my *cousin*. So pleased you agree."

"Of course," she said, though Cael could hear envy dripping from her tone. And then she found and grasped a thread of joy, "Didn't I tell you that dolt would prove useful?"

"It's not from Graeham," he said quickly. "It's from Marcella. She's come to pay her respects."

Morwen's smile vanished. "Marcella?" She inspected her fingernails, her expression turning grim. "Really?" she said. "Is she tired of the shrew already?"

Cael shrugged. "Apparently so. She has assured me that her loyalties are no longer with the Empress, but to the people of Wales. She claims she doesn't care how the King's negotiations end, so long as they benefit the realm."

"The realm," Morwen scoffed. "More like, she longs to return to your bed."

"Or perhaps yours?" he suggested. "It was never mine that brought her such joy."

Her eyes glittered fiercely. "I really don't care about that! All I care to know is this: Do you trust her?"

Cael shrugged. "So much as I trust you," he said easily, and the implication wasn't entirely lost to Morwen. He watched a veil fall over her eyes and smiled.

"Take care," she said darkly. "Marcella will bring trouble." And then her gaze returned to her daughter as she added, "Though, in truth, you might be more concerned about Rhiannon." Her shrewd gaze shifted to the reliquary that lay hidden beneath his tunic—a relic that stung his flesh, and yet, he never removed it. He peered down to discover it was emanating a strange glow, and his brows knit. He'd never noticed that before. Then again, it was the first time in Morwen's presence that they'd dared speak of the artifact, calling his attention to it... *odd*.

"You would be wise to keep that out of *her* sight," she advised. "Indeed, she seems content enough for the moment, but she is no fool. You haven't any notion how much hell she will unleash if she learns what that is."

Cael smiled tightly, unable to constrain himself.

"Like mother, like daughter," he agreed, and then he returned his attention to his beauteous bride, who was now making her way through the aisle, greeting vassals as though she knew them all by name—she did not. Her time as his ward had not been so reckless as that. Blackwood was full of Morwen's spies, and he'd made good and certain Rhiannon knew it as well.

One by one his *guests* rose from their seats to greet the future lady of Blackwood. The Lord Rhys and his father, Maredudd ap Gruffydd, rose and hailed her as she passed. Rhiannon stopped to greet the man, taking the elder's hand, and offering him a courteous bow.

Good girl, he thought.

It would serve their ruse all the better if her mother believed she came to him willingly, and that she honored the alliance.

He was entirely relieved to see she'd heeded his advice. Had she attempted an early escape, there would be nothing he could do to prevent her mother from doing her worst—not so long as she held Cael's fate in her hands.

Indeed, Rhiannon was a wise little bird...

Perhaps wiser than her mother could possibly know.

But he knew.

She was passionate, brave, loyal and intelligent, and so much as he'd resisted the bent to admire her, he nevertheless did.

Never once had he allowed her to win at a game of Queen's Chess; she'd matched him point for point, and gave no quarter, pursuing him as artfully as a courtier, sealing his fate time after time. She was as cunning as she was lovely, and neither did she need *magik* to best him.

Nay, indeed, she was here because she, too, was playing a game, and he wondered... what did she consider to be the ultimate prize?

The obvious answer was her freedom, but some tiny part of him hoped...

Would she take some small pride in taking his name?

"Excuse me," he said, rising abruptly, intending to play the part of the smitten groom—nor would it be particularly difficult ... so long as he didn't consider the evening's conclusion.

God's bones, he would miss her—far more than he was willing to confess.

"Of course," said Morwen, though he felt her eyes boring into his back as he abandoned her upon the dais. *Good.*

If she was already warning him about his misplaced trust and affection for her daughter, everything was going according to plan. For everyone's sake, it was crucial that Morwen believe he, too, had been betrayed. But he was no fool. If she suspected aught was amiss, this was not the time or place she would reveal her hand.

THIS WAS NOT the greeting Rhiannon had anticipated. Inconceivably, there were looks of adoration as she passed, although she couldn't help but wonder how much of the pageantry was an act. For all that the hall seemed to abound with laughter, she sensed vipers coiled beneath the tables, waiting for her to pass to strike.

How many of these guests had arrived with her mother?

How many were loyal to Cael?

Whatever the case, none of them were Rhiannon's allies, and precisely as the maid who'd dressed her had made so perfectly clear, no one attending this evening would take her side against Morwen—except Cael.

Cursing Cael for leaving her to parade herself alone through this hall, she held her breath as she made her way to the dais, encountering a sea of curious gazes—blue eyes, green, brown... only she was acutely aware of one very canny pair of golden eyes, watching every move she made. And regardless, her gaze was drawn, not to Morwen's, but to the steely pair of eyes of the man who'd risen from his seat and now wended his way toward her...

Cael.

Dressed in an elegant black surcoat, his eyes glinted mercurially, begging caution. Clearly, he understood, as she understood, that one wrong word would force an end to their charade, and perhaps to their lives as well.

Behind Cael, her mother sat very still upon the dais, watching, like a spider waiting to see what prey would wander into her web. But, of course, she was nothing if not clever, and Rhiannon was infinitely grateful that Cael was brave enough—or witless enough—to defy her.

Surely, he must have some ulterior motive; it simply couldn't be that he cared for her...

Catching her by the arm, he drew her close to whisper in her ear. "Kiss me as though you mean it," he demanded, and then took her face into his hands, as a lover might, cupping her cheeks with such tender ferocity that Rhiannon was momentarily stunned by the gesture.

Never in her life had she been kissed by any man, but the dark look in Cael's eyes before he possessed her mouth effectively silenced her protest. For an interminable moment, she was too stunned even to nod.

Sweet, sweet fates!

The instant his mouth—hot, wet and persistent—found hers, in full view of so many witnesses, it stole away her breath.

No one present could call this a lie.

No one had any true inkling what transpired in the privacy of her bedchamber. For all they knew, this was merely one of many kisses that came before it. "Cael," she breathed, though she wasn't sure it was a protest. To all watching, there could be no question; they must be lovers.

"Cael," she whispered, again, as he grinned, breaking the kiss to peer at her with an odd glimmer in his eyes that could only be mistaken for affection. He caressed her flushed cheek with a thumb and Rhiannon hadn't any clue how long she clung to him, only that sudden and raucous laughter erupted amidst the courtiers and guests. Rude jests were made.

"He can't even wait for the vows," said a man very gleefully.

"Look at the lance in his breeches!"

"I warrant he'll stab her and good," said another.

"There's no time," Cael whispered. "Play the part of a besotted bride, and all will go as planned."

"When?" she asked.

"You'll know," he promised, and then, what seemed a full eternity later, he finally released her, and then took her by the hand, a beloved lord performing for his audience.

"Please... forgive my lusty greeting. I am a man too-long deprived," he said, and then he laughed, and leaned toward Rhiannon once more to say, "Forgive me." But he pecked her on the cheek.

More cheers resounded, and now, at last, Rhiannon chanced to look at the dais where her mother remained seated, smiling very tersely. After a moment, she, too, rose from her seat. "A toast!" she shouted, her voice silencing the revelers. "To my beauteous daughter and her dutiful champion!" She tilted her head ever so slightly and smiled disingenuously. "At long last, a daughter of Avalon returns to Blackwood!"

"Hear! Hear!" echoed the crowd, and Rhiannon swallowed a knot of fear that rose to choke her.

Morwen was a master at mindspeaking. She could betimes read minds as well—did she know?

The absence of her mother's voice in her head was heartening. But, if in fact the shackles effectively blocked her *magik*, then it was still quite possible she could read the truth in Cael's mind, no matter if she couldn't read Rhiannon's. Forcing her lips into a tremulous smile, her heart remained confused by the man whose hand she held.

Goddess, please! she begged. Wasn't it impossible to kiss a woman so profoundly and not have some measure of feeling behind it? Could it be that Cael cared for her? After all these years had he discovered in his heart some measure of compassion for Morwen's second eldest?

It was Cael's turn to speak. "Friends!" he said, grinning proudly. "My lady and I—" He gave Morwen a discreet nod. "Will go speak our vows in the privacy of our chapel, and then return... to celebrate alongside you."

Another hearty round of cheers erupted.

Up on the dais, Morwen took this as her cue. She laid her glass of mead down on the table and made to join them. Still, her golden eyes slitted suspiciously, and Rhiannon's heart prickled with fear.

"In the meantime," Cael added, his voice carrying like thunder through the hall. "Please, stay! Enjoy libations."

Without warning, he jerked Rhiannon's hand very rudely, turning her so that they preceded Morwen into the courtyard. All the while smiling at folks, he spoke between his teeth. "Guard your words as I will mine. Endure the ceremony with a smile, and you will soon be shed of me."

He lifted her hand to kiss it gently, and Rhiannon felt another prickle rush down her spine— only this time it wasn't fear. But, nay, could it be anticipation?

And then a thought occurred to her...

Did he mean to collect her virginity before setting her free?

If he did not, would they still be wed in the eyes of the law?

Did she want a bedding?

Surely not!

Goddess, lend me strength, she thought. No matter what he said or what he did, Cael was still her mother's ally, and simply by virtue of this fact, he was still her mortal enemy.

How in the name of the Goddess could she crave another shocking taste of his traitorous mouth?

Plagued with thoughts she ought not be thinking, she allowed him to lead her out the door, into the courtyard, and mindlessly toward the chapel, all the while her mother followed behind.

EIGHT

The scent of decayed lilacs filled the courtyard. Even as they trampled sunbaked blossoms, the perfume brought a sting to Rhiannon's eyes. It was perhaps meant to be lovely, but the effect was cloying—an opinion clearly shared by the pinch-nosed prelate awaiting them inside the windowless sanctuary: No doubt he was incensed to be called from Abbey Dore to preside over a ceremony for "heathens," only to suffer a megrim over the decor of this Roman-style chapel, with its arched entries, fat pillars and half-finished wooden apse.

Perhaps the church was meant to be grand in its day, but it was bleak now and hardly equipped to be used in modernity. With cracks in the mortared stone and a pocked and rubbled floor, it was not even so well-kept as the ivy-tangled courtyard that harbored her mother's cauldron—an *eglwys* so much as this was, though its ceiling was not vaulted between pillars, but rather an open sky, and its altar was a pagan relic of bygone days. That, too, must have annoyed the Cistercian, judging by his downturned lips. She recognized his order by his robes—crude, undyed wool to proclaim his penury before God. His order also rejected the black robes of their fellows, and his shoes were made of cowhide, not Cordoba leather. However, like most monks, he was tonsured—the crown of his head shaved, leaving a band of hair below his ears, to symbolize his crown of thorns.

Why her mother did not call upon Llanthony, Rhiannon didn't know, but she wondered if it had something to do with a rumor she'd heard that the old goat Ersinius was finally dead.

Reminding herself that no one attending today could possibly guess at the bargain she'd struck with Cael—or that he was aught but a besotted lover—she drew a smile on her face to hide the trembling of her lips.

Her betrothed was solicitous throughout the entire ceremony, holding her hand and making room for her beside him on the chancel, smoothing a loose strand of hair from her face.

For her part, she found herself heartily confused by his ministrations—and perhaps her mother was, as well. Morwen's disgust was writ plainly upon her face. Although, in fact, she coveted this alliance, she clearly didn't relish the notion of her daughter winning her husband's heart—little did she realize.

"Is there any man here who opposes the union?" asked the prelate, and for an instant, Rhiannon thought her mother would speak—and so she did, but they were not words anyone anticipated.

"You sack of bones! There are three witnesses in attendance. Do you believe we're standing in this joyless crypt for our own pleasure? Nay! Get on with it, you lout!"

The expressions that flitted across the prelate's

face were entirely laughable. Anger, followed by fear. Though he daren't even look at Morwen to chide her, and one of Cael's guards coughed loudly to cover a choke of laughter.

The prelate cocked his head to plead his case with Cael, but the lord of Blackwood's expression remained sober. "Go on," he commanded the man.

They finished in short order—Christian vows only, though Rhiannon was not of that order, and she doubted Cael was either. Certainly, Morwen was as far from being a good Christian as any woman could be. In fact, standing amidst the shifting light inside the chapel, her mother's starkly beautiful face twisted under the play of light and shadow, making her appear very much like the demon she was.

All the while, as the prelate sniffed with disapproval, her mother's lips curled on the verge of a snarl. She remained silent thereafter, looking this way and that, studying the priest, then Cael... then Rhiannon.

Even Cael seemed tense, though he gave her a reassuring squeeze. But the gesture only managed to confuse her more. Throughout the entire ceremony, she stood, deaf and dumb, the moment passing like a dream—good or bad remained to be seen. Although if Morwen thought anything of Rhiannon's uncharacteristically quiet demeanor, she mistook it for nerves, because after the ceremony was done, and their vows were spoken, they quit the chapel forthwith, and made their way back to the hall uneventfully—all but for one instant, when her mother swept to the fore, preceding them into the courtyard. She cast an impatient glance toward her cauldron, then turned away, and Rhiannon thought she heard Cael sigh in relief.

And no matter, he oughtn't rest so easily... not yet. Now was the Golden Hour when her mother's *hud* would be at its strongest. Even wearing these shackles, Rhiannon could feel potential rise in the air like tension. That woman was the scourge of Wales, and the bane of men—not to mention a murderer of her own kindred.

Her sisters were dead now because of her, and if Morwen had her way, she would slaughter the remainder of her daughters, beginning with Rhiannon.

Verily, if her mother turned on her now, she wouldn't be strong enough to defend herself. Even as she acknowledged the truth of that, her shackles weighed heavier. Therefore, she kept her mouth shut, and guarded her thoughts, all the while the silver key stung her flesh where it fell between the curves of her breasts.

Soon.

Soon she would be gone.

Bide your time, as Cael suggested.

Hatred tempted her tongue, but prudence kept her gaze fixed upon her mother's back. And even so, she could feel the witch's presence as surely as her lips could feel Cael's very passionate kiss—sweet fates, every time she thought of that kiss, she felt a strange ache in her bosom that teased her all the way to her womb.

He has branded me, she thought.

In all these years, she'd never once dared to think of him that way—not like that! —and it was as though that damnable kiss somehow shone a light on a dark place in her soul where she'd hidden all her feelings.

Now she could no longer lie to herself and claim

she didn't love him… because… against all odds… she did.

Sweet Goddess, how?

How could any sane woman love a man who'd kept her imprisoned for so many years?

And yet…

Swallowing, Rhiannon dared to cast a glance at the man who was risking so much to free her. His hair, dark as coal, glistened by twilight. His cheeks and nose were chiseled hard in profile, and the color of his skin, unlike her own, was sun-kissed and gold. If he sensed her scrutiny, he didn't look to meet her gaze…

It didn't feel like a celebration, more a funeral procession. Side by side they re-entered Blackwood's vestibule and hall, and once there and reunited with their guests, their solemnity ended forthwith. Cael's lips broke into a hearty grin. He lifted their joined hands as though to display them for their guests. Rhiannon's ever-present bracelet glinted inauspiciously against the flickering torchlight. "Behold!" he said. "The new mistress of Blackwood!"

A round of cheers erupted throughout the hall, and the musicians began to play, and then, and only then did Rhiannon dare to assess her mother…

Morwen's eyes glinted wolfishly…

As though she knew.

~

In the name of King Stephen, Lord Protector of England, Wilhelm and Giles searched every room at Darkwood, including a dirty kitchen, two storerooms, and a "workshop" containing little more than a stained and foul-smelling cot, a rusty brazier and a soiled chamber pot. That room smelled sourly of sex, but there was no one within, nor was there anyone in any room they encountered, aside from an elderly cook, and an impossibly skinny, pale-faced tavern boy.

Considering the innkeeper's tensions—as though he feared being discovered—and hoping against hope that he might encounter Morwen herself, Giles pressed on, one hand firmly on the hilt of his sword.

Sour-faced, the innkeeper led them, complaining over the imminent displeasure of his benefactor. "She won't be taking to it kindly," he said.

"Morwen?" inquired Giles, as he opened one last door, and peered into another empty room.

It was Eustace he was tasked to retrieve, but he wouldn't turn away the opportunity to return the Welsh witch to her prison in the White Tower—for what, precisely, he didn't know yet, because so far as anyone knew, Morwen had done naught recently save to eschew Stephen's court. That was no crime, but for the sake of his wife and her sisters, he would endeavor to think of something. And, if he could not, he'd take the bitch's head, and accept whatever consequence arose. Unfortunately—or perhaps fortunately, as the case might be—it was not a decision Giles would be forced to make. In the end, there was no sign of Eustace, nor his guileful benefactress—or at least no indication she'd been there in quite some time, or even that she was meant to return. "I don't know any Marwen," said the innkeeper, purposely mispronouncing her name, but there was something in his shifty eyes that called him a liar.

"Who then?" demanded Giles.

"None o' yourn," the man retorted.

Removing his hand from the hilt of his sword, Giles narrowed his gaze, considering his options...

Burly as the innkeeper was, he had enough arrogance and mettle to stand up to a lord bearing the King's seal. Sweaty though he might be, and shifty as he was, there was naught about the look in his eyes that betrayed any fear. So, then, he must feel quite reassured by the influence of his benefactress "Marwen."

"What of Eustace?" snapped Wilhelm.

The innkeeper snapped back, "I don't know 'im!"

"So, you've never heard of the King's son?" pressed Wilhelm.

"What makes ye think our good Prince would lower himself to come here?"

"So, you admire the man?" asked Giles, turning on the innkeeper at the end of the upstairs hall, giving his brother a quelling glance. As strapping as Wilhelm might be, the innkeeper was bigger yet, with shoulders as wide as a barn door, and legs as thick as tree trunks. "You seem well fed," remarked Giles. "Your benefactress must be generous?"

"I do well enough," he said with a mealy-mouthed smirk, and then hitched his chin. "Now that ye've turned the place o'er, why don't you be awa' now like ye said?"

Weary as Giles was, and weary as the horses must be, there was nothing about Darkwood that made him feel like testing the night. And yet, he sensed down in his bones that his brother was right: The King's son might not be here this moment, but it was only a matter of time before he would seek out Morwen. Darkwood was the best chance to catch him before he caused more trouble. But perhaps there was no need to wait. There was a look of impatience in the innkeeper's gaze that made Giles feel the man was itching to send a message.

He nodded politely. "Apologies, good man," he said, more respectfully. "We had word that our Prince would be traveling these parts. But I can see they were mistaken."

The burly man's arms uncrossed, relaxing.

Giles continued. "In fact, I can see you're a man of enterprise," he said. "Perhaps you'd be willing to feed our horses and grant us a bed for the evening?"

Giles could see the man's thoughts churning behind beady eyes. Thankfully, Wilhelm had by now become accustomed to his sophistry; his brother said naught. Moreover, if the innkeeper was surprised by the change in Giles's attitude, his body language conveyed only relief.

"We've been traveling for weeks, dead on our feet. I'd kill for a cup of soup and a pillow." He produced a single silver coin, and the man's eyes glinted greedily. "Grant us a boon, and we'll be asleep quick as you please, then gone by first light."

"One mark for each o' ye?" the man dared.

That was shameless robbery.

"You bloody—"

"Shut up, Wilhelm," said Giles, producing a second coin. "One now, one when we go?"

The man eyed both silver coins, looking from one brother to the other, and then back to the marks.

"Please, forgive my brother," said Giles. "He sometimes speaks out of turn. He's baseborn and lacks the manners God granted better men."

God's bones. Later, when they were alone, he

would pay for his high-handedness, but Wilhelm must be made to understand. The innkeeper grudgingly reached out to snatch the coin nearest to him. "Aye, then," he said, glaring at Wilhelm. "Take this room at the back. There's only one cot between ye but ye'll have to make do."

Giles smiled evenly. "You drive a hard bargain," he said, and Wilhelm snorted his disgust. The innkeeper took the coin with a greasy hand, and Giles had little doubt he would go away now and do whatever it was that he must do to contact his benefactress, reassured that his new patrons would soon be fast asleep in their beds. No doubt, given the chance, the man would slit both their throats without a backward glance.

"Dinner ain't served at all bells," the innkeeper groused as he marched away. "Eat when I call ye, and if you ain't down in the tavern to get vittles, ye won't eat."

"Fair enough," said Giles.

"Bugger ye both!" the innkeeper said, then grumbled beneath his breath. Still clutching his silver mark in his fat fist, he left them without another word—at least none that were immediately discernible.

Wilhelm waited until the innkeeper turned the corner before he exploded. "Are ye daft, brother? What in the name of Christ makes you believe I'll shut my eyes in this den of wolves?"

Giles lifted a single finger to his lips as the innkeeper paused at the top of the staircase, the boards creaking beneath his feet. "Later," he mouthed, inclining his head toward the stairwell. Out loud, he said clearly, "Never. Again. Speak so insolently to me in the company of strangers." He cuffed

Wilhelm atop his head, hard enough that he knew the sound carried to the man's ears.

"Ouch!" said Wilhelm, glaring at him.

"Brother or nay, I'll horsewhip you myself," Giles added, as he reached out to grasp his brother's arm to prevent him from punching him. "Now, go settle our horses, and bring in the packs," he demanded.

Snorting, clearly amused, the innkeeper hurried down the steps, his footfalls far lighter than they should have been for a man his weight and size.

After he was gone, Giles reassured his brother. "Don't worry; I don't intend to sleep in this Godforsaken hellhole," he said, whispering. "Rather, I mean to see what that drudge does to call for his benefactress."

"Horsewhipped?" said Wilhelm, shaking his head. And then, he added, "Please, don't tell me you're going to pay that idiot another silver mark?"

Giles grinned, then clapped his brother lightly on the shoulder. "Why not? 'Tis a small price to pay when I've suddenly found myself with another month's worth of your wages."

"Bloody bastard," said Wilhelm, though without much heat. "I'll double my wager right now if you'll let me rack the bugger, and Eustace as well once we find him. And, by the by, if you do, I'll ignore the shite you were saying about me. Else I'll gi' ye a trouncing when you least expect it."

Giles shook his head, smiling. "What a vicious mongrel you've become."

"Clearly not vicious enough!" countered his brother. "You've bloody sharp knuckles and the next time you do that to me, I don't care what the cost, I'll break your fingers one by one."

Halfheartedly, the brothers elbowed one another, then started down the stairs. Once outside, Giles spied the innkeeper's brown *sherte* as he disappeared into a garner.

Halting with a hand to his brother's chest, he eyed the nondescript, windowless shack, realizing that they'd somehow missed it before, hidden as it was amidst woody shrubs. "What is it, Giles?"

"Go on... do as I said... make ready to ride," he demanded, hitching his chin in the direction of the garner. "I'll go give a gander inside."

But it wasn't necessary; before Wilhelm could move to comply, the man re-emerged from his storehouse with a large black raven perched upon his arm. Without the least concern for an audience, he removed the bird's black hood, then unshackled its talon. He spoke to the bird, then dispatched it, and the raven spread its long, blue-black wings and took flight... displaying a patch of white at its neck as it turned to clear the trees.

A chill rushed down Giles's spine. "Let's go," he said.

"What about our pretense?"

"We have what we need. We'll follow the raven."

A talented trio of musicians performed in the center of the room—one with a lute, one with a harp, one with two reeds betwixt his lips. Rhiannon would dearly love to steal one of those reeds and shove it none-too-gently down her mother's throat, silencing her once and for all. Her nerves were stretched taut as the strings of the minstrel's lute, and every word Morwen uttered plucked them raw.

Clearly, her mother's rudeness was not reserved for the prelate. Rhiannon had no choice but to sit and wait as the Golden Hour came and went. By now, her sense of anticipation had long dimmed, and she was beginning to fear that Cael's offer of freedom was nothing but a cruel jest—or worse, that he and her mother were secretly amusing themselves at her expense.

Moreover, he was behaving very strangely.

No doubt these two had been planning this wedding for quite some time. That became more than apparent as trays laden with foodstuffs whizzed past from the kitchen and fresh pitchers of ale and mead swept through the hall. There was no way—not even through *magik*—that they could have baked so many trenchers to serve so many guests, not without time and planning. Doubtless, they had been scheming now for weeks, and Cael never once deigned to warn her.

Had he presumed she would balk and hadn't wished to invite argument when they both knew very well that she hadn't any choice?

Or perhaps he'd always known he would offer her this bargain she couldn't refuse?

If, indeed, it was a bargain at all.

"Somehow you've managed to win his trust, even with your foul mouth and temper," said Morwen, the instant her husband quit the dais to approach a young woman Rhiannon didn't recognize. Morwen watched them both with an undisguised look of disgust, all the while clicking her nails on the chair.

Who can it be?

Whoever it was, her husband was quite pleased to see her, Morwen not so much...

Her manner of dress was not at all that of a servant's. Fashioned of a beautiful celestine, nearly diaphanous sendal, her gown was trimmed generously with miniver, and despite that it wasn't so fine as Rhiannon's purpure, it was, indeed, very, very lovely. So was the woman besides—dark haired, dark eyed, she looked like a Welshwoman, though she certainly didn't dress like one. She dressed more like a French courtesan.

Jealousy reared unexpectedly, though Rhiannon forced a smile.

"Envy is not your color, my dear."

Gritting her teeth, Rhiannon ignored her mother's barb. Her gaze remained fixed on her *husband* and the strange woman he was speaking with. With one hand behind his back, he bent to lend an ear to some idle chatter, and, in response, the woman laughed—open-mouthed, showing a string of pearly white teeth.

Another stab of envy cut through Rhiannon's heart.

Sweet fates. In all these years she'd never once entertained the notion of Cael with a paramour. Now, she had to wonder...

But why should she care?

Gods willing, she would be away from this place before sunrise.

Anyway, he'd said so himself: *There is only one woman I have ever loved, and she is not you...*

Was it her?

Was it that lady?

Distracted, Rhiannon picked at a thumbnail and worried the inside of her lip. Perhaps gleaning more than Rhiannon was comfortable revealing, her mother affected a sympathetic tone. "Poor dear," she cooed. "You see... this is the problem with men... Once they catch you, they'd sooner let you go."

Rhiannon stiffened.

Did Morwen know?

Nay, she reassured herself.

Nay. She did not.

She couldn't possibly, because, in truth, if she did, she would not be taking such unbridled joy in the possibility that Rhiannon might have to share her husband.

In fact, she seemed quite gleeful over the fact—in this, her mother was utterly predictable. She loathed all her daughters that much. Swallowing her disgust, Rhiannon strengthened her resolve. She could not bear the sight of the woman seated at her side. And truly, considering all that Morwen had done, it was all she could do not to murder the hateful bitch where she sat—wrap her manacled hands about Morwen's elegant throat and squeeze till her eyes bulged and her tongue lolled.

The image pleased Rhiannon immensely, unkind as it must be. Morwen Pendragon was a murderess at best, and no one in this realm could imagine the worst. Rhiannon herself could scarcely conceive it and she knew the truth...

Nay, the woman beside her was not the woman she claimed to be, although *when* she'd ceased to be Morwen Pendragon, Rhiannon didn't precisely know. She only knew that the real Morwen was long gone, and what remained in her place was an evil sorceress that not even Rhiannon was prepared to deal with.

Oh, she realized her mother was keeping her alive for some purpose, and perhaps it was this... merely to bind herself to the lord of Blackwood, and once the deed was done... there was naught to say she wouldn't be well-disposed to kill her. In fact, it was entirely possible that this was her plan all along, and Cael only meant to keep Rhiannon quietly appeased until such time as they were wed...

But, nay, she refused to believe it. Deep in her heart, she sensed a better man in Cael—had always sensed that man, although he fervently denied her claims. There *was* something good in him; she sensed it in her heart and saw it in his aura as well. No doubt, it was dark—darker than anyone's she'd ever known except her mother's—and still, it wasn't black, and there was a thread of crimson besides. This could signify anger, though it could also be love...

Rhiannon chose to believe in love.

Pleading silently for her husband's return to the dais, she kept her gaze trained upon him, and said, "Please... do not pretend there is love betwixt us, Morwen. You are not my mother, and I am not your daughter."

"Oh, my dear," Morwen exclaimed, utterly amused. "But you are, Rhiannon! My dearest, I can assure you: You were dragged squealing from my womb, and you are more like me than you will ever care to confess."

"Nay! I am not!"

"I beg to differ."

At long last, Cael cast them a glance. His dark eyes were smoky with unspent passions, and Rhiannon's heart squeezed painfully. Would he satiate himself once she was gone? With that woman? The thought pained her more than she might have realized.

"I wouldn't worry," said Morwen, as though she'd read Rhiannon's mind. "The eyes have but one language, my daughter. Judging by the look he's giving you now, I'd say the man is hopelessly besotted. In truth, 'tis more than enough to put me off my dinner."

He is?

No, he wasn't!

Not with Rhiannon.

Surely her mother meant that he was besotted with that woman he was speaking to?

She frowned, because he did seem to like her

overmuch, and to the contrary, she and Cael fought far too oft. And then she sighed, because she didn't know what a besotted man should look like, and it galled her that her own *mother* should find the notion so utterly appalling. It would seem that on a day like today she might dredge up some small shred of good will in her awful bag of bones. But she didn't sound pleased when she said, "I've known that man a long time, and let me tell you, I've never once seen that look in his eyes. Take care if you are not already deflowered, my daughter. I suspect he will pound you till you bleed."

Startled by the brutality of that image, Rhiannon winced, and despite her resolve not to be affected by anything Morwen said, she blushed hotly. "He's never touched me inappropriately," she said in defense of him.

And it was true.

Whatever else he might be, Blackwood's lord was a gentle man. She couldn't even imagine him "pounding anyone until they bled"—most certainly not a woman who was his wife.

Oh, she had no doubt he'd done far worse to those men he was sent to "hunt," but Rhiannon was not his enemy.

Oh, yes, you are, a small voice argued.

And perhaps she was.

Morwen snorted. "Grimace all you like but remember this: My daughters were not bred to be prudes."

It was the wrong thing for Morwen to say. All caution flew out of Rhiannon's head. "Really, *Mother*? How would you know? You were not there!"

Not even whilst they were together in London

while King Henry was still alive. Rather, it was always Elspeth who'd nurtured them, and then Isolde once the nursemaid arrived. Morwen was scarcely ever about, and even when she was, she was utterly blind to her daughters. "Not all men are so foul," she suggested. "Nor is every bargain to be made in a bed."

Morwen laughed brutally. "And yet," she said. "That is precisely where this bargain will be sealed tonight, in a bed." There was a smile in her voice and Rhiannon swallowed her disgust—not that she wasn't attracted to Cael. She was. But she would not be used so meanly.

"Only remember this, my dear, all the while his tongue tickles your bits... your husband's ambition is the same as mine. Today, you did not merely align yourself with the lord of Blackwood, you have bound yourself to me. Trust me when I say... that man cares less for what lies betwixt your soft thighs than he does for what else he has to gain."

Rhiannon's gaze slid to her mother's face, and she knew the bloom in her cheeks had little to do with the impropriety of her declaration. Morwen was furious, she realized, but good! At least Rhiannon was not the only one who was nettled, and if her mother's intentions had been to give Rhiannon worry over the possibility of a physical union with her husband, well, she'd struck her mark. The entire ordeal was disgusting, and no matter what she'd been taught, she was repulsed. Nay, she was not a prude, but she was still a maiden—not because she feared the coupling. She and her sisters had been taught to revel in all that made them women. Their ancestors had been pagans, who, rather than find shame in the act of procreation, had been taught that the greatest gift a woman could bestow on the world was a child of her womb.

Not that Morwen ever valued such gifts.

Despite that she had, indeed, borne the world five daughters—all "squealing from her womb"—she was a very poor excuse for a mother. Even so, the images that accosted Rhiannon now filled her with chagrin. No matter what, she would not allow any man to "pound" her.

Goddess forgive her if Cael reneged upon his promise...

If he dared try to force her...

If he left her in shackles...

She didn't think she could bear it.

Her mother was crude and cruel—not that Rhiannon had ever hoped for more. Where Morwen Pendragon was concerned, hope was only another tool for that woman to abuse. "I see you are unchanged by the years," Rhiannon said, her loathing beginning to creep to the surface, though she somehow held her aplomb. "How comforting," she added very drolly, her gaze again seeking Cael, who was still speaking to that damnable woman.

If only to cover her unease, Rhiannon reached for her cup of mead and took a small swig—too sweet, she thought. *Over-spiced.* And, for the first time in all her years at Blackwood, she considered how she might improve their kitchen—*if* only this were a union in truth. Too bad she wouldn't be staying.

Her mother was also watching Cael and that woman, her displeasure in plain view. "Well," she said. "You needn't be overly concerned. He could have had that tart long ago if he'd wanted her, and besides, she's his *cousin*. Though... I do wonder... why he's not introduced you?"

Cousin?

Swiftly on the heels of that thought, Rhiannon had yet another, and a prickle of fear stabbed at her heart. If, in truth, this were some grand scheme to deceive her, it wouldn't do for Morwen to become suspicious.

What could she say to deflect?

And then it came to her, and she said, affecting an air of confidence. "He means to give us time. If you must know, *Mother*, my husband has some idiotic notion that you and I will reconcile. Alas, he cannot possibly understand that no matter what my heart feels for him, it will *never* soften toward *you*."

"You wound me," Morwen said, completely without feeling, and Rhiannon cast her mother a withering glance.

Despite her untold years, the woman was still uncannily beautiful—not a wrinkle visible on her face, no loss of sheen in her hair. The gleam of her eye was still sharp enough to wound. Much to her dismay, Rhiannon felt a new surge of hatred so intense that it threatened to discompose her—that she should be seated here, forced to converse with this creature whilst her husband flirted with his cousin!

Morwen smiled thinly. "One day you'll learn to forgive your enemies. Nothing, and I do mean *nothing*, vexes them more."

"Alas, I will *never* forgive you," Rhiannon said behind clenched teeth. "*You* are the reason my sisters are dead—or needst I remind you?"

Of course, she would never address Morien—that

sweet child she slew in the womb. "Arwyn was a full-grown woman with a mind of her own. She made her own choice."

"Because *you* forced her," Rhiannon countered, fury heating her cheeks. If only to calm herself, she took another sip of her mead and then put the goblet down, realizing how dangerous it was to imbibe in her present state of mind and mood. She mustn't let down her guard at all.

Her mother turned to assess her then, and it was all Rhiannon could do not to flinch beneath her hateful scrutiny—not because she was afraid, mind you, but because she had never felt so exposed as she did at that instant.

Her mother's gaze was savage; her lips curled. "No one told that little knob to set the ship ablaze."

Her very stature seemed to grow before Rhiannon's eyes, and her eyes slitted vengefully.

"In truth, *I* should be the one so furious that my own daughter preferred to toast herself rather than reunite with her mother! Rejected, I am! By all of you! I gave you birth, and you share my blood, still you forswear me!"

Discomfited by her mother's loss of temper, although she'd certainly sought it, Rhiannon averted her gaze, secretly pleased that if she must lose her temper, she still had the means to make Morwen lose hers as well. Even so, she wished to the Goddess that she could do what she longed to do: How delightful would it be to thrust her poniard straight through her mother's wicked heart?

If indeed she had one.

And still, against her better judgment, she couldn't hold her tongue. "Mark me, *Mother*. In the end, Duke Henry *will* win the day, and you *will* lose everything." She averted her gaze. "I only fear for my lord husband. He will come to regret having put in his lot with a treacherous bitch like you. I know you have bewitched him!"

Morwen snorted. "*Me?* Bewitch *him?*"

She sounded furiously amused.

"Cael d'Lucy?" She laughed again, a bark that resounded throughout the hall. "Nay, daughter. Much to my bother, the lord of Blackwood is his own man; he *cannot* be ensorcelled—which is a very good thing for you, since you no longer have the means." She flicked a glance at Rhiannon's manacles, then sneered, although Rhiannon blinked in surprise at her words. "Good thing he hasn't lost his wits so soundly that he removed *those*, and yet I see he's discovered a way to lessen the burden. How thoughtful. I shall have to speak to him about that to see if we can remedy it."

Rhiannon blinked again.

Despite the overt threat, it was not that which gave her pause... Cael could not be ensorcelled?

Everyone could be ensorcelled.

Except for *faefolk* or *dewinekind*.

Rhiannon narrowed her gaze.

"Why can't he be ensorcelled?"

"Because, you stupid, piteous girl, he's been to the Other Realm and once that Veil has been crossed, a man's eyes cannot unsee what they have seen."

Rhiannon blinked again. "What?"

Her mother flicked a hand, dismissing the conversation once and for all. "Never mind, stupid wench! These things are none of your concern. If you care to know more, ask your beloved—that is, if you can pry him away from his cousin!"

Rhiannon sat upright, stunned, uncertain how to respond. *Cael had crossed the Veil?*

When?

How?

Was he *dewine*?

Nay... nay... there was naught about Cael d'Lucy that had ever led her to believe he was aught more than a mortal man. He was an executioner for the King, she realized—feared by many, but still only flesh and blood.

Yet so was Morwen—for the most part—so was Rhiannon. They were *all* flesh and blood. They were born and bled like everyone else. So, then, who was Cael that he should cross the Veil, and live to speak of it? So far as she knew, not even Morwen had ever done so...

And yet, Morwen was stronger than ever. Even wearing her shackles, Rhiannon could sense her mother's force.

Alas, after five long years of wearing these shackles, Rhiannon felt drained. As beautiful and vivid as her dress might be, she felt drab in comparison. The best she could hope for would be to survive this day without Morwen discovering their plans, and with that thought, she turned to find Cael returning to the dais. His eyes found and held hers. "Forgive me," he said, turning to regard her mother. "Did you ladies miss me?"

Though he and Morwen shared a meaningful glance, neither Morwen nor Rhiannon responded. Both sat long faced and sullen. Cael twisted his lips, and reached for his cup, then without another word, turned the goblet, downing the contents, and called for a serving girl to return with her ewer.

"Drink up!" he said, with forced gaiety. "Tonight is a time for celebration! Tomorrow will be soon enough to resume all our petty squabbles." And then, very discreetly, he hitched his chin at the woman he'd been speaking to—his cousin—before resuming his seat at Rhiannon's side.

Rhiannon sat, furious now.

The one thing her fury was not, was *petty*.

She wanted to shout a demand that he explain himself in regard to his cousin. She wanted to ask him why the devil he had not yet introduced them. She wanted to smack him right on the cheek, and demand he kiss her... *why?*

By the cauldron, this wedding was a sham!

Annoyed by her husband as well as her mother, Rhiannon shoved her goblet toward the serving woman when she arrived to refill their cups.

If Cael wasn't going to set her free tonight—well, then, he was going to have to carry her insensate to consummate their vows, because she was *not* going to submit to him willingly!

"By the rood! 'Tis no wonder spiders consume their young," Morwen said snidely, and then she, too, reached for her goblet, putting it fast to her lips. "Ungrateful little bitch."

It wasn't entirely clear to whom Morwen was referring because her gaze followed Cael's "cousin" until she removed herself from the hall without a backward glance. Still, Rhiannon gloated, feeling as though she had won some small victory, because Morwen's face was now flushed, and her eyes sparkled with unmistakable fury.

Truly, if she could accomplish that at least once per day for the remainder of her life, she might not entirely mind having to remain at Blackwood, enduring Cael and his cousin as well. Her mother's misery made her unexpectedly glad.

Alas, there was no guarantee her mother would remain at Blackwood, which meant her sisters would be in danger.

Nor would Rhiannon ever best that creature whilst she was wearing these infernal shackles.

Nay, if ever she was going to go, she must do so now...

All three musicians continued playing at intervals, while Morwen held her tongue, quietly seething, drinking one cup of sweet mead after another.

All the while Cael whispered love words into Rhiannon's ear—all for show, she realized. "Art even more beautiful than your mother," he said once, loudly enough for Morwen to overhear, and her mother growled, then clapped her goblet down upon the table.

"*If* that is the sort of woman you prefer," she said, beginning to slur her words. "As they say, beauty is in the eye of the beholder!" And then she remanded a pitcher from a passing maid, seizing the vessel from the poor woman to pour herself another drink, and then, just for good measure, she hoarded the entire pitcher, rudely waving the girl away.

If only to annoy her, Rhiannon reached for the pitcher, as well—after all, it was her house.

Cael caught her hand. He smiled warmly, lifting her hand to his lips to kiss it ever so sweetly, his eyes spoke words that never found purchase on his tongue. *No*, they said, and he shook his head, almost imperceptibly.

No.

And just that swiftly Rhiannon's sense of anticipation returned.

Something was happening.

Morwen was incandescently angry, oblivious to all but her fury, and she was, in truth, so livid that her guard came down.

With a nod, Cael laid down their joined hands, pinning Rhiannon's firmly beneath his own, and then slowly, very slowly, Rhiannon peered over to discover that her mother's chin began to wilt...

She blinked as Morwen's cup tilted precariously, although her mother seemed perfectly unaware. In fact, her eyes drifted shut, and her fingers relaxed on the stem...

Stunned, Rhiannon's gaze shifted to the ewer of mead—a ewer no one else had drunk from yet. And now that she considered, the kitchen maid had not been passing by. She was waiting close to Morwen... waiting. Once her first pitcher was consumed, it was the same girl who'd replaced it with another.

Poisoned?

By the time it dawned on Rhiannon what must be happening, she saw Cael gesture to Aelwyd, making a discreet circular motion with his finger.

Mead for all?

Indeed, within moments—as though they'd been awaiting a cue—a horde of servants emerged from the kitchen, all cradling ewers.

As Morwen's head lolled, they made their way down every aisle, filling goblets and mugs as they passed.

After a long, surreal moment, Cael reached over to gingerly shove at her mother's shoulder, to which she responded by slumping listlessly to one side of her chair, eyes closing and mouth agape, suddenly drooling.

At once, Rhiannon dragged her gaze about the hall...

CHAPTER

TEN

The goblet in Morwen's hand crashed to the floor, spilling its contents. Still, it didn't faze Morwen, though it startled Rhiannon. For better or worse, the deed was done.

There was no telling how long they had.

Cael waited only another moment for good measure, and then, none-too-gently tugged Rhiannon to her feet.

Already, the draught was taking effect. Most of his guests were following suit, laying down their heads, some in their trenchers, others beside it...

A few toppled from their benches, and Cael made a mental note to secure his own position once the time arrived so he wouldn't end up with a knot on his head, although perhaps if he did, it would better serve his cause.

"You poisoned her?"

Rhiannon sounded horrified.

"Not precisely."

"What then?"

"A sleeping draught."

"How did you know it would work?"

"I didn't," said Cael.

"That was your plan?"

"Aye," he said. "But don't worry, Rhiannon, she'll wake in good time."

"Oh, you mistake me!" she countered, and Cael smiled over the rueful tone of her voice. If any daughter had a right to despise her mother, Rhiannon had more cause than most.

He led her quickly from the dais, dragging her through the hall. "I'll warrant, she'll wish she were dead once she wakes, and she may see to it I am."

"That is not amusing!" Rhiannon said, hurrying along behind him as they made their way through the guest-littered hall. They were dropping like flies amidst a cloud of smoked camphor. Only a few people remained awake—a handful of men and women he trusted. Everyone else was innocent of his plans, and he meant to make it clear they had no part in his ruse. Once the plan was fully orchestrated, those who'd helped perpetrate it would have to leave Blackwood. Already, they were gathering their numbers to flee.

By now, even the musicians were drowsed. Together, they sank to their knees, and collapsed, their instruments banging across the rough stone floor. The lute played a hollow note and one of the pipes rolled beneath a table.

As *drogued* as everyone was, no one paid any attention to the lord and his lady rushing from the hall. Cael doubted anyone could see further than the tips of their noses.

"I cannot believe you did this!"

"Oh, but *I* did not," he countered, turning to wink

at her. "You did it. I am but the besotted old fool who dared to trust his beautiful bride."

"Beautiful?" she repeated dumbly.

"Infinitely so. And, in the eyes of the world, I am not the first husband to be betrayed, and neither will I be the last."

She sounded terrified. "But Cael... she'll not believe you."

"Too late, Rhiannon. 'Tis done. You'll be gone ere she wakes, and even if she does suspect me—and she won't—she needs me. Without me, she has very few allies remaining."

"It doesn't appear this way to me! What of those Welsh lords she brought?"

"What about them?"

"Wait!" she protested and tried to resist.

Cael wouldn't allow it. There was no turning back, no matter how many Welsh kings she'd brought. For better or worse, Morwen was now *drogued*, and come morning, Rhiannon must be gone. Daring to waste no time, he led her out of the hall, through the courtyard, past the cauldron her mother cherished above all else, and straight toward the hidden portal at the back of the chapel. He wondered if Morwen even knew it was there, it was so well hidden.

Perhaps the child she had been once knew, but he was hoping the creature she'd become had long forgotten.

"Remove your manacles," he demanded, releasing Rhiannon's hand to clear a path through the tangle of underbrush...

• • •

RHIANNON FROZE, but only for an instant, realizing that, in truth, this was happening exactly as he'd promised. Only now she was terrified to go.

Why?

Because... suddenly it mattered more than words could say that her mother wouldn't wake and punish Cael for deceiving her.

"Don't worry," he said, mistaking her hesitation. "You'll be safe very soon. I've engaged the services of a capable guide."

"I am not worried for me," Rhiannon confessed.

He was moving too quickly; she daren't fall behind. Removing the ribbon holding the key from about her neck, she took care not to drop it in the weeds. She called out after him, "How can you be so sure she'll not suspect you?"

She heard the levity he tried to impart, but it didn't ring true. "Because... I, too, will be drooling in a trencher once she wakes, and you will be long gone. Only for good measure, I'll be wearing your manacles."

"Nay!" she exclaimed and shook her head. "I'll not leave without them. Anyway, why would I use them on you?" she reasoned. "For anyone but a *dewine*, the shackles are no more than a pair of bracelets. I beg you! She knows me well enough to know I'd never leave them to be used again—unless you intend to use them on her?"

"Nay," he said, stopping if only for a moment. "You take them." And then he ducked beneath a small tree, forcing Rhiannon to follow.

"Cael!" she pleaded, using his given name. "Please, come with me!"

"Nay, Rhiannon, but don't worry. She'll not blame me. She'll blame you."

"She'll blame both of us," Rhiannon persisted.

The foolish man couldn't possibly know what she knew, and perhaps he didn't understand the danger he was in.

Alas, he was moving too swiftly through the tangle of brush and she was already out of breath. Having been shut away so long, she hadn't much stamina, and no strength to continue arguing with such a stubborn, foolhardy man.

"Be damned!" she said, pausing for breath, and then, as best she could, in the darkness, whilst following, she scratched the small key near the aperture of the lock, and her heart did a wild leap of joy when the key sank into the metal.

Like a lover waiting to be kissed, she savored the click.

One manacle fell away, and she immediately felt a surge of energy return to her from the *aether*.

Gleefully, hoping her feet would meet even ground as she stumbled through the underbrush, she sank the key into the other manacle, unlocking it as well, and her breath hitched with relief as the second bracelet fell away.

"At last!" she exclaimed.

Only now she saw stars swimming before her eyes as the *hud* returned to her full force—not merely to her limbs. She felt the lift like an inspiration of breath through her lungs, a wellspring of vitality that lifted her feet and gave her the sensation she could fly—she couldn't of course. She could barely even keep up with Cael. Tripping herself rudely, she followed through the underbrush, her limbs awkward and all her pleas sticking in her throat.

"Here it is," he said, somewhere ahead. He grunted, then struggled with something large in front of him.

Rhiannon could spy the outline in the dark. It grew in clarity as she came closer, her eyes growing accustomed to the night. With a final grunt, he shoved open a portal, and to Rhiannon's utter shock, she found that woman from the hall on the other side...

His "cousin" smiled, and Rhiannon faltered in her step.

"Marcella will guide and protect you."

"Well met," said the lady, though Rhiannon suddenly had her doubts as to whether the woman was any sort of lady at all.

"Halloo," said Rhiannon, staring.

Marcella was wearing a man's tunic and chausses. Her hair was caught in a messy plait. Clearly, when she'd quit the hall, she'd done so to change. "Please, allow me to take those," she demanded, plucking the manacles out of Rhiannon's hands without permission, and offering them to Cael.

"Nay," he said. "She means to keep them. Put them in your satchel." And then, his tone softened with unmistakable affection. "Art certain, Marcella? She'll flay you alive if she catches you."

Marcella arched a brow. "As she will you if she discovers the truth."

"But she won't," he said.

"Neither will she catch me."

"Godspeed, sweet cousin."

Marcella cursed softly beneath her breath—

words Rhiannon didn't comprehend—and then she said, "God be with you, Lord Blackwood." Then, she made to leave with the manacles, but before Rhiannon could turn to follow, or even protest, Cael caught her by the arm.

"Rhiannon," he said hoarsely, the sound guttural and anguished.

Rhiannon winced over the strength of his grip, lifting her gaze to meet his dark, unfathomable eyes.

"We are not aligned," he said meaningfully.

Rhiannon frowned, then swallowed uncomfortably. "I know."

The torment in his gaze was indisputable, and yet it couldn't possibly match the pain in her heart. "You must understand... if I am forced to pursue..."

Rhiannon nodded, understanding. "I know."

And she did.

She truly did.

She knew full well that if he caught her again, he could not afford to give her a second chance. "May the Goddess keep you," she whispered, tears scalding her eyes.

He nodded soberly. "And you."

Then, without warning, he drew her into his arms for one last kiss, only this time he kissed her with a fervor born of the moment, tasting and plundering her mouth in a manner she'd never imagined a man would wish to taste a woman.

Sweet fates.

This was not the simple imparting of a kiss, and in retrospect, the kiss in the hall couldn't compare...

In her heart of hearts, Rhiannon understood... this was farewell.

She was his wife in name only.

From this day forward, she was his enemy, as well...

So much regret squeezed through her heart—so many years of pretending!

Good-bye, Cael, she thought.

Good-bye!

Unbidden, tears stung her eyes.

She couldn't help herself—every word she'd ever longed to say flew to her lips, and she spoke them, but not with her mind, or with her voice, but with her tongue... answering every forage of his with a taste of her own, exploring his mouth as wildly as he did hers, until the kiss left her dizzied and breathless. It was all she could do to remain standing on her own two feet. Of their own accord, her hands moved to his shoulders, and any ambivalence she'd felt before was gone. When he might have moved away, she clung to him desperately, never wanting the moment to end...

Yegods...

If she dared to stay, she would know it was because of this kiss—betrayed by her own heart!

If she left... this kiss would haunt her for the remainder of her life. Only, what possible good could be wrought by staying? Already, he'd warned her that they were not aligned. She really must believe him!

Neither could he love her.

It was all a sham.

Except... it didn't feel like a sham with his arms around her, and his mouth possessing her, his tongue exploring the depth of her mouth, as though he were committing the feel and taste of her to memory, his tongue lapping and tracing, like an artist rendering.

Cael, she tried to say.

No words emerged through the tightness of her

throat. The only sound to escape was a desperate moan. But why in the name of the Goddess, would she deign to reconsider?

Why, indeed?

For a tumble in his bed?

For another kiss like this?

What new demon had possessed her?

Cael d'Lucy was his name.

Only, now that freedom was so close at hand, the last thing Rhiannon needed—or wanted—was to find a reason to stay when she really needed to go.

Rosalynde needs me, she reminded herself.

Elspeth needs me.

Seren needs me.

Go! a small voice commanded.

Flee!

Goddess, alive! There must be a reason he was releasing her now. Clearly, he feared what would happen to her more than he feared her mother's wrath. Still, this did not mean he loved her.

Nor did it mean he would continue in this vein—kissing her so passionately, whispering love words into her ear.

'Tis a sham, she told herself.

At long last, he tore his lips away from her mouth and Rhiannon felt the separation acutely. "I lied," he said, reaching for her face one last time, caressing her so tenderly. "I've loved you from the moment you opened your mouth, Rhiannon Pendragon... disheveled and lovely, proud and fierce!"

"Cael," she cried, because now it was impossible to deny she felt the same—only how could it be?

"Take good care," he said soberly, and then he turned, and pulled the portal closed, shutting her out, and Rhiannon was left mute, with her hands fumbling in midair, feeling for the lingering warmth of his body like a specter.

"Rhiannon!" Marcella called out. "Time to go!"

She couldn't tear her gaze away from the portal. "What will he do?"

"Whatever he must," said his cousin. "And you must believe his warning. He will do what he must if he catches you again."

Rhiannon swallowed convulsively.

Her mother would see her dead.

Only now, it wasn't only Rhiannon who would suffer Morwen's wrath if she woke to find them lingering.

Swallowing again, Rhiannon conceded, though she gave the portal one final beleaguered glance, her hand begging to test its weight. Some part of her longed to shove the door and run after Cael... beg him to understand: Her mother would kill him if she suspected.

"Do. Not. Test. Him," Marcella warned. "You stupid, stupid girl. Count yourself fortunate that he loves you enough to betray himself... if only this once."

Already, Rhiannon's *magik* was strengthening. She was free—free, at last! All she had to do was turn and walk away. Accept the gift her husband had offered her.

I lied, he'd said. *I've loved you from the moment you opened your mouth, Rhiannon Pendragon...*

Goddess only knew, there was *one* reason to stay... and too many to flee... Three very, very important reasons awaited her in England.

Resolved to do what she must, knowing in her heart that it was the right thing to do, Rhiannon turned her back on Blackwood's portal, making her way down the narrow path after Marcella. "Take these," Marcella said, turning to hand Rhiannon a pile of clothing. "Tunic and breeches," she explained. "Leave your gown." Then, before Rhiannon could object, Marcella's hands were disrobing her in the woods.

"Won't they find it?" Rhiannon protested, feeling oddly sentimental about her wedding gown. It was the loveliest dress she'd ever possessed—a bride's gift from Cael, though not nearly as precious as the other gift he'd laid in her hand early this afternoon: the key to her shackles. If she lingered now, that gift would be squandered and England itself might be doomed...

The sound of her gown renting made Rhiannon wince. "That is precisely the point," said Marcella. "They'll send out the dogs first and they'll find the gown with your true scent. The tunic I gave you has been treated with another."

Tears scalded Rhiannon's eyes as she stepped out of her ruined gown, faltering in her step. She was only vaguely aware that Marcella produced a vial and sprinkled the substance over her discarded gown.

Benumbed, and breeze kissed, Rhiannon donned the sour-smelling tunic, and once it fell over her hips, she stopped to tug on the leather chausses, lacing them quickly, never bothering to step out of her slippers.

She was dressed none too soon. As they reached a promontory, they found horses waiting, and Rhiannon noted a second companion, presumably her guide. The lad waited with the reins to their horses in his hands. He handed one to Rhiannon, and said, "I am Jack."

Marcella wasted no time. She placed Rhiannon's shackles into her own saddlebag—perhaps realizing that even within proximity the bracelets would siphon her *magik*. "There are boots, as well," she said, pointing to a dark spot in the grass. "Put them on, toss your slippers into your bag."

As soon as that was done, they were away, on foot, leading the horses down a narrow path by a sliver of moon. Only for good measure, Rhiannon whispered a prayer, but it wasn't for freedom she prayed—she prayed with all her heart that Morwen wouldn't wake to harm Cael.

ELEVEN

In slumber, her face was... serene.

The frown lines about her mouth, eased, the creases between her brows, softened. A thousand years may have been erased from her countenance by the curative power of sleep, and in the truest sense, she was, indeed, a sleeping beauty.

And yet, Cael was very aware that, like a viper, she was equally as dangerous. One wrong move and she would sink her fangs into his flesh, and never let go until her venom sucked the life from his veins.

Very, very gingerly, he eased the witch goddess's limp form from her chair, to the floor. Somehow, her position in the chair had prevented her fall.

Once on the floor, he rolled her over to inspect her more thoroughly.

Clearly, Marcella's potion was more powerful than she'd anticipated. He had his own vial ready in the palm of his hand, but he paused to assess her face.

It was true; Morwen did resemble her daughter. As with Taliesin, they had the same almond-shaped eyes, the same full lips. The only differences between them were the coloring of their hair, and the contents of their hearts.

And still... here and now... it was so easy to see her as the woman she had once been: Nay, not his master, nor his mistress, but his emancipator, and... at one time... she'd been a friend. As shocking as that might be to some, he hadn't any outrage in his heart for Morwen... only a burgeoning sense of unease for the cancer in her heart—that hatred that consumed her day by day. But she wasn't always this way...

In the beginning, there had been moments of reason between her bouts of fury. She'd sat with him on many occasions, baring her heart and woes. Like Cael, she'd returned to this world with a heart full of grief and a drive for vengeance... and, very much like him, she'd also faltered in her mission, every now and again regretting the path that drove her to this end.

In fact, he remembered when she'd first met Henry—the longing in her heart for a love of her own. Contrary to the belief of some, she did not scheme to rule in those days. She'd only wished to be his lover, and she'd tried to befriend Matilda and William, as well, but to no avail.

Alas, she might be a goddess, in truth, but she had a woman's heart, and the fury of a woman scorned—not once, but thrice.

In fact, in the beginning, she'd been so different that Cael had doubted the rumors he'd heard—most notably, the sinking of the White Ship to murder the King's heir. But now... he knew her well enough to believe it. And no matter that he felt conflicted, he knew in his heart that he shouldn't be. His decision should be clear: He should remove the *athame* from around her neck—slowly, circumspectly, he reached for it now, slipping it from beneath her gown.

He should take the weapon in hand, and plunge it through the bones of her breast, into that cold, cold heart.

What then would be the consequences... for him?

Considering that question, he wrested the chain from around Morwen's neck, perhaps only to inspect it...

The dagger was quite ancient, made of the same alloy as *Caledfwlch*. It glowed faintly blue whilst in her presence, and yet... the reliquary she kept on the same chain did not. He studied it now, considering the bauble more closely. It looked like the one he wore about his neck... except...

He drew out his own to compare, startled to discover his glowing blue... like her *athame*.

And yet, the one she'd worn about her neck did not... *why*?

Once, long ago, she'd confessed to him that her soul was bound to a *grisial hud* like his. Could his belong to her... and hers to him? Was it possible that she'd given hers to Cael, knowing full well that he would protect his own sepulcher with his life... because his soul depended upon it.

He placed both reliquaries in the palm of one hand, side by side—presumably his, presumably hers —and then stood, moving away from the listless form on the floor, watching the glow of one fade, if ever so slightly.

Neither of the stones had ever glowed for him.

Down in his gut, he sensed the truth: For some reason, Morwen had kept his *grisial hud*, entrusting him with hers... though she'd allowed Mordecai to keep his own.

Why?

Cael didn't know precisely how they worked.

He didn't even know if he had to be in its presence to make use of it—specifically, whether his soul would locate his sepulcher outside proximity if it should separate from his body.

What was it she'd said?

His soul was bound to the crystal. So long as the reliquary remained undestroyed, wherever he was, his body could be slain, but his soul could endure and be summoned.

Presumably, this was how she'd returned Mordecai to his body some years ago, with a ritual at the Widow's Tower. He wasn't there to witness it, because Cael had begun to question her motives, and shortly before then, they'd quarreled over her method and madness. Little by little, he'd hardened his heart against her. Now, it was growing more and more difficult to see the good in her—more difficult yet after watching the enmity she held for her own daughter.

She'd brought him back to this world, and for that, Cael would always owe her a debt of gratitude, but the fury in his own heart had blinded him to the evil in hers, and perhaps even some small part of him had relished her vengeance.

After all, he, too, had been betrayed—and by none other than those folks who'd played the Witch Goddess false...

Taliesin and Uther.

He stepped closer to her body, staring down at the twin reliquaries in his hand... one cold and tarnished, one warmer and glowing blue.

Trying to understand, he stepped back again, further and further, watching the glimmer fade, until the one nearly matched the other. Without the luminesce they were indistinguishable, even to the crystal.

Once again, he moved closer, watching the return of the glow, knowing in his heart it was hers—it *must* be hers!

The fact that she was lying so still... it must be proof that, in mortal form, she was as vulnerable as he was.

If he took her life...

If he dared...

Rhiannon, he thought.

It would bring an end to the bloodshed and violence.

But...

Very carefully, he removed the dagger from the chain, and then bent to lay the athame atop her breast. Still kneeling, he opened both fists to examine the contents of both hands. In one he held the vial filled with Marcella's potion; in the other he held both reliquaries.

If he kept her *grisial hud* and threatened to destroy it, could he persuade her to his will?

He didn't know, but for all that had passed between them, he couldn't kill her—not here, not yet. At the instant, she was naught but an insensate, vulnerable woman, and he couldn't kill her, but... he suddenly couldn't see the wisdom in remaining to see her wake. He had betrayed her by setting her daughter free, and Rhiannon was right: She would not forgive him. Rhiannon was the last of her daughters to be bartered, and Cael had effectively taken that away.

Decided, he flung both chains around his neck,

then examined the vial in his hand, realizing what it was that he should do...

If he stayed, she would inflict her anger on the innocents in this hall, if only to punish him. She would test him, and she would test them, stopping at nothing to extract the truth. On the other hand, if he left... she might leave them be, realizing they were as much a victim in this as she was. None of those remaining would deny the Witch Queen what she sought. She would ask them if they knew, and some might even tell her they remembered him escorting Rhiannon from the hall...

Kneeling by her side, Cael plucked the stopper from Marcella's vial, placing the bitter, foul-smelling liquid to his nostrils and wincing.

Would another dose kill her?

It very well could, and if he gave her an overdose, he would have to live with it, he supposed, because, suddenly more clear-headed than he'd been in years, he knew what must be done...

Sliding an arm beneath her shoulders, he lifted Morwen so that her head tilted back, naturally parting her lips, and then, more resolved, he emptied the contents of Marcella's vial into her mouth, and gently laid her back.

Now it was done.

Now, he must go, and when she awoke, she would find him gone. She would know he'd conspired with Marcella to betray her. And she would pursue them both. The very least he could do for Rhiannon was to free the hounds. Shaking his head with disgust over the present circumstances, he hurled the vial across the room, although he should have laid it by her side. She would know anyway, and she would curse him for it, and if he was wrong about the reliquaries, she would stop at nothing to destroy him.

Turning from the woman to whom he owed his freedom, and his second chance at life—the Lady of Avalon, the mother, mage and crone—he made his way to the stables to prepare his horse, with a name on his lips and in his heart: *Rhiannon.*

TWELVE

All Rhiannon needed to do was keep walking, put one foot in front of the other.

Why, then, did it seem to take such effort?

It wasn't only the physical exertion. Wearing the manacles had been akin to suffering a five-year malaise. By contrast, she felt as though she were walking out of a fog. But she was leaving without Cael, and this was her greatest ambivalence. She worried about leaving him at her mother's mercy.

And yet, wasn't he the same as she?

His goals were her goals—isn't that what he'd said?

On the one hand, he'd been Rhiannon's willing *gaoler*.

On the other, he'd kept her sane in a world where all seemed hopeless. Somehow, he'd managed to renew her faith, even despite everything.

Still, why should she worry about a man who'd kept her imprisoned?

She was as confused now as she ever was—perhaps even more so.

The truth was that she had always had a single-ness of purpose from the moment she was born. She'd vowed then to avenge Morien's death, and she still meant to do it. But here was her dilemma now: Cael was her husband, and her husband was also her enemy. Unfortunately, no matter how she willed it, her heart couldn't seem to harden against him.

Pausing for the hundredth time since their flight from Blackwood, she cast a glance over her shoulder, hoping to find he'd changed his mind and decided to follow.

"Rhiannon," Marcella begged. "You mustn't tarry!"

Rhiannon's heart squeezed with grief.

Some fool part of her longed to rush back, even knowing that would be unwise. Why, oh why hadn't she put her poniard through her mother's black heart whilst she still had the chance?

Because she hadn't been thinking; that's why.

Only feeling.

So stunned by Cael's actions, she'd allowed him to lead her mindlessly from the hall. And now, she couldn't stop thinking about everything she should have done differently.

She couldn't stop thinking about him...

Morwen would kill him.

Even if he took the draught and lay prone at her feet, her mother wasn't a fool.

Wracking her brain, Rhiannon tried to remember their discourse at the table.

Morwen had been so sure Rhiannon didn't know Marcella because it was true. She'd smelled Rhiannon's envy like a hound sniffing *merde*, and she'd gloated over it. Only now, Rhiannon tried to remember exactly what she'd said—had she confessed that, in truth, she'd never met Cael's cousin?

If so, would Morwen believe she was lying?

She prayed with all her heart that her mother would believe Cael's ruse, else he would pay a terrible price.

In fact, he might pay anyway, because Morwen had all the same gifts Rhiannon had, only far more attuned to the *aether*: If she sensed lies, she would turn him to dust where he stood. But that wasn't the only thing Rhiannon was worried about; she was worried about this: That draught was bound to work differently on Morwen than it did on Cael or his servants... What if they'd misjudged its potency and Morwen had already roused to find him gone?

What if she was only waiting for Cael to return?

What if she'd killed him right then and there and came flying after them, and even now was hot in pursuit?

In the darkness, every sound conspired to defeat her nerves—the breeze hissing through the trees, startled conies dashing across their paths, nightjars trilling from their perches. The suspense of it left her shivering, wondering if her mother's minions were already here. Brave as she believed she was, her heart tripped as many times as she did, and the one thing she took comfort in was the absence of barking hounds. She knew Cael kept a stable full, though she'd rarely chanced to see them. Still, she'd often heard them from her bower.

"How long till they wake, do you think?"

"I don't know," said Marcella.

As it happened, the draught they'd used to sedate the entire hall had been concocted by none other than Marcella, using, of all things, Morwen's cauldron in the courtyard. All the while Rhiannon had been forced to endure Morwen's company at table, Marcella and Cael had been in the process of orchestrating the *drogue's* administration. As potent as the philter was, only a few drops in each of the ewers had been enough. Just to be certain, they'd waited until Morwen was affected, then sent kitchen maids to administer the rest to the guests. Only Aelwyd had known what they were planning, and she was sent away for her own protection. If everything went according to plan, Morwen would wake with the castle aslumber, and no one the wiser. Then, it would be up to Cael to convince her that he hadn't had any part in the ruse, but was he clever enough to beguile a woman with the power to read minds?

Only the Goddess knew.

But if Rhiannon knew her mother at all, she wouldn't wait about for explanations. She'd sooner strike him down than ask questions. There was no way her pride could withstand losing yet another daughter. She would be out here forthwith, combing the woods, with Mordecai and her ravens at her side...

"How did you know the draught would work?"

"Because," Marcella confessed. "I tested it on myself."

"How does that signify?"

"I am *dewine*."

Rhiannon blinked. "*You?*"

"Aligned to earth, alchemy my calling. Apparently, you are not so attuned with the *aether* as you'd like to believe, Rhiannon. Even unshackled, you did not read my aura."

Rhiannon bristled, though it was true. It was only

then, in that instant, that she perceived the faintest trace of pink in Marcella's aura—so faint that it was no wonder she'd missed it before.

Pink, you see, was the color of Rhiannon's kindred —those who bore the blood of Taliesin. Although it seemed that, by its measure alone, Marcella's blood was much diluted—that, or the ill effects of wearing those manacles might be permanent.

"*Dewine?*" she said, again, because so long as she'd lived, Rhiannon had never once encountered another *witchkind*, much less a sister of Taliesin's blood. Certainly, she'd suspected there were others, but if Marcella was a *dewine*... what then was Cael?

Not *dewine*.

Even with her manacles, Rhiannon would have sensed it. And so it would appear... the more she knew about Cael, the more of a mystery he became— a mystery she fully intended to solve once they were out of Blackwood's shadow.

~

WARKWORTH CASTLE

It was the crow on the windowsill that woke Seren.

Again.

Silent, watchful, it sat perched on the sill, its lustrous blue-black feathers catching a hint of moonlight. "I'm awake," she groused to the bird, giving it a thankless glance. It was impossible not to sense the beady-eyed gaze, even under a veil of slumber.

Alas, with the gargantuan bed so painfully empty beside her, she was finding it more and more difficult to rest.

Rising with a breathy sigh, she swung her feet over the edge, searching for her slippers. She didn't intend to remain here in this bed—not tonight, with her mind scattering all her thoughts to the winds.

No one had heard from Morwen, but that didn't mean she wasn't out there, somewhere, scheming. Now, more than ever, Seren felt time slipping away, like sand through a glass. Over and over, Isolde's warnings kept ringing in her ears: *You will be the Regnant—you and only you, and if not you, no other in this day and age. Earn your laurels. Find your true self. Only then will you find your answers.*

The problem was... Seren didn't know how to find her true self. Neither did Rosalynde or Elspeth. And neither did Isolde, for all her cryptic words.

Sometimes it seemed to her that only Arwyn, for all her lack of affinity, had ever truly understood her true purpose in life. Once the occasion had presented itself, her sister had done what she'd known she must, without hesitation.

To the contrary, she, Rose and Ellie were all like blind women leading the blind.

And Rhiannon—where was she? For all her promises, Rhiannon was silent as the grave.

Muttering crossly, she found and donned her slippers, sliding her toes inside, before making her way across to the dressing table to find a taper.

Not bothering with a fire steel, she lit the wick with her will and sighed again—at least her fire affinity was growing stronger.

The wick flamed to life with a deep, amber glow, startling the crow. It took flight from her windowsill and vanished into the night, and Seren took the taper and shoved it into a pricket. "Good riddance," she said, though she knew she should be grateful for any sort of champion at all, even a puny little crow.

This bird had appeared weeks ago, around the same time Isolde came to call, with all her cryptic stories and all her mysterious divinations. As it happened, the old woman and that crow were never in the same place at the same time, and every time Isolde went away, that damnable bird returned. Even so, Seren had never actually witnessed a transformation, so for all she knew, it was only a stupid little bird taken to loitering in her window—night after night after night.

It was a good thing Wilhelm was gone, because he'd already threatened to take a sling to the bird.

Shaking her head, she made her way down the hall, holding a hand beneath her pricket, lest the wax mar her husband's perfectly polished floor.

Indeed, shapeshifting was a rare talent, one most practitioners of the *hud* did not know how to perform. It was, in fact, a form of *hud du*. Her grandmother had said that all knowledge of those dark arts—if ever they'd existed—passed away with the fall of Avalon. But this was not precisely true. Morwen was a practitioner of the dark arts, and if, in truth, Isolde was a shapeshifter, as well, then she too was a student of *hud du*. Alas, the old woman was nearly as mysterious and elusive as their mother, arriving without announcement, then taking her leave without goodbyes.

Whenever she was about, she rambled on and on about prophecies, giving more than enough warnings, but answering all their questions with riddles that left Seren scratching her head. Without the *gri-*

moire, how was she supposed to learn if Isolde wouldn't teach her?

By now, Seren had all but given up asking that woman for help, because it seemed she was disinclined—or else she'd forgotten everything she'd ever known. How fortunate for Morwen if that be the case.

At least Elspeth and Rosalynde had had the opportunity to skim the *grimoire* at their leisure. That was how they'd learned to concoct a form of *witchwater* for the motte—a strange brew for transmutation that was made mostly from spoilt mushrooms. It was that very concoction that was responsible for turning a visiting merchant into a thief, and several small stones into fish. By now, the poor motte was filled to capacity, and the fishes were jumping about for air, though at least the villagers had their fill of smelt.

Looking back on it now, the simple fact that they'd managed to thwart their mother at the Widow's Tower seemed more of a miracle than it was any sort of achievement. To their good fortune, fate had intervened that day, bringing all three sisters together by chance. Seren had discovered her true destiny only because of happenstance. In the end, they'd won the day simply by virtue of the fact that they'd survived—no small thing to be sure, but they'd lost so much that day, most notably *The Book of Secrets*.

Alas, that tome harbored centuries' worth of *dewine* histories and receipts—summoning spells, banishing spells, transmutation spells and more.

Ages and ages of trial and error and painstaking documentation by all her *dewine* sisters. Sadly, all those histories were a loss beyond telling.

No doubt, she and her sisters could craft all new

spells, but those histories were another matter entirely.

For her part, Isolde had only snippets to share, and Seren had a terrible, terrible suspicion that the key to defeating her mother lay hidden in their past.

One way or another, even without the help of the *grimoire* or even Isolde, Seren must persevere. She *must* find her "true self" so she could imbue the sword—but *what* did that mean?

Did it mean that simply knowing oneself as Regnant wasn't enough? Did it mean she must come to know herself experientially? Or rather, should she pray to the Goddess for bestowal of her gifts? Or perhaps it was so simple as discovering some way to remove the *glamour* spell that had been cast upon her as a child?

The answers to these questions eluded her, and Isolde was no help at all. Instead of offering clues, she came to pester Seren whilst she slept, cocking her silly little bird head and stealing her sleep like a mean old hag.

Carefully now, so as not to drip candle wax, she made her way down the darkened hall.

At this late hour, the entire castle was abed, but since Seren hadn't any babies to wake and feed, she found herself drawn to the workshop she shared with Rose. Elspeth was here as well, to witness the birth of Rosalynde's firstborn child.

Removing the chain from around her neck, she unlocked the heavy banded door, then pushed it open, entering cautiously, half anticipating pixies.

Not a soul stirred.

In the dead of night, the workshop was eerily

silent. The ancient sword remained precisely where she'd left it on the herb-littered bench.

Approaching it reverently, Seren took some comfort in the lack of blue shimmer on the shining steel. She had only witnessed that effect once... a chemical reaction to her mother's *magik*? A warning from the *aether*?

Find your true self.

Only then will you find your answers.

Isolde's words accosted her again as she gnawed at the tip of her thumbnail. Trying to remember all she'd learned over these past weeks, she stood studying the ancient weapon—a sword originally imbued by the father of their coven and gifted to the Dragon Lord of the Anglesey.

He wasn't a witch, but his wife was. And merely because Maelgwn had valued his lady's counsel, the Church pronounced him an enemy. Plotting against him, they'd sent Taliesin and Uther under the guise of friendship, and one night, after drinking his wine and supping at his tables, they'd slaughtered the Dragon Lord, murdered his son, captured his daughter, and stole his pennants. Thus, was born the new dynasty, through treachery and blood.

This was the story, according to Isolde.

But that was only part of the tale... a tale that began ages and ages before Uther and Maelgwn...

It began with Cerridwen and her hatred for her husband. For all her fury against the man, she'd brought down a wrath from the gods so fierce that the consequences were felt far and wide.

"What am I supposed to know?" she asked quietly, regarding the ancient sword. "Tell me, Goddess, lest I fail you."

Silence was her answer—a deep, abiding silence that betrayed nothing. The shutters remained closed against the night. No crow returned to her sill.

Whatever truth she must reveal, it would not come easily.

"Where the devil are you, Rhiannon?"

Rhiannon alone had the knowledge their grandmother bestowed. Without her, this task seemed daunting and indomitable. And nevertheless, Seren knew there was no time for regrets.

Everything happened for a reason—wasn't that what her sister claimed? To arrive at this place and time, there was no other path to have been taken. If Elspeth hadn't escaped from Llanthony, she wouldn't have met Malcom. Instead, she would have been trapped in a loveless marriage with the lord of Blackwood. And she would never have defeated Morwen at Aldergh, nor would Rosalynde have been inspired to leave London with Morwen's *grimoire*.

More importantly, Rosalynde's affiliation with Giles now gave them possession of this sword... the only weapon of consequence to be used against Morwen.

Sadly, if Arwyn hadn't sacrificed herself that night... Seren, too, might now be dead...

Like a window to the past, she saw it in her mind's eye—a glimpse of that moment on the *Whitshed*, when Arwyn, holding that shard of Merlin's Crystal, hurled it at the door. Like a dream, she witnessed the final moments and heard the words Rhiannon spoke before she, too, fell silent evermore: *Aye, 'tis she,* she'd said.

She.

The witch goddess whose sins doomed Avalon.

She whom her mother and uncle had summoned here from exile.

Only now, if no one stopped her, she would doom England as surely as she'd doomed her beloved isle.

How to stop her was the question... and the key... in part... was the sword.

The beauty of it was immeasurable.

Undetectable to any but *dewine* eyes, a tangle of intricately carved serpents writhed over its silver in-spired hilt. On the blade itself lay etched in the most ancient of tongues, "Take me, but turn the blade, and we will see." And still, no matter how long Seren stared at the sword, or how many times she repeated the phrase, she hadn't any clue what it meant.

Take me, but turn the blade, and we will see...

There was another word etched betwixt the ser-pents: *Caledfwlch*. Translated from her native tongue, it meant "cut steel." And in the language of the Holy Church... *Caliburn*.

Some also knew it as Excalibur.

Crafted from some alloy taken from the heart of Avalon, the blue shimmer was not its only blessing. It had another, so 'twas said—one that could only be actuated by a Regnant, which Seren was not...

Not yet.

Even so, she must find a way to fulfill the ancient prophecy, so that he who wielded the sword might not bleed. Without that quality, it was uncertain that anyone could survive an encounter with her mother.

"Take me, but turn the blade, and we will see," she said aloud, again. Unfortunately, those words meant nothing to her, and by now, she had turned the blade more times than a cake in a pan. Nothing ever happened.

She was a *dewine*, indeed, a Promised One, according to Isolde, but she hadn't any notion how to entreat the Mother Goddess for all the gifts she'd been promised.

"Seren? What are you doing at this late hour?" asked Rose from the doorway.

Seren turned to find her youngest sister peering into the workshop. "Oughtn't you be sleeping?"

"I woke to feed the babe," said Rose. "I saw the light pass my door and I thought it might be you."

Seren drew a weary hand through her hair. "I could not sleep."

"More dreams?"

"Nay. The bird."

Rosalynde hitched her chin. "Isolde," she whispered softly.

"I cannot help but feel she is trying to tell me something."

"What do you suppose?"

Seren shrugged. "I don't know. Something has changed. Nothing I can put my finger to, but I can feel it in my bones."

Intuition was itself a form of *magik*. All creatures were born with a sense of it—men, women, even dogs, cats and birds... it was imperative to listen.

"Shall I wake Ellie?"

"Nay," said Seren, without bothering to consider. "Let her sleep. She has her hands full with the boys. Tomorrow will be soon enough."

Rosalynde smiled fondly. "Why don't you come back to my room?" she suggested. "We'll snuggle like the old days."

Whilst at Llanthony, all five sisters had slept together in the same bed, and, far from being a burden, it was the one thing Seren most missed.

"I think I will," she said, abandoning the sword. At the door, she handed the pricket to Rose so she could lock the room.

THIRTEEN

The hounds were getting close.

Unfortunately, it was impossible to say from which direction they were coming, although Rhiannon feared it must be Cael.

By now, they must have found her ruined gown. She only hoped Marcella's masking potion would do its job and send them searching in another direction.

Unfortunately, they daren't mount until the terrain was even enough to ride, and much to Rhiannon's dismay, it was nearly daybreak before they climbed into their saddles. Only then, finally, they were able to gain some distance from the barking hounds—thankfully, because they were still much too close to Blackwood to take any chances. Any experienced *dewine* would recognize the scent of *magik* and intuitively follow it. To hell with those hounds, a nose like Morwen's would smell the tiniest disturbance in the *aether*.

Essentially, all things were born of the *aether*, all things returned to it, but if one had the skill to do it, the *aether* could be manipulated. Still, it was impossible to do so without some form of *residua*. Ofttimes, with smaller spells, the scent was imperceptible, but it was completely unmistakable with larger-scale manipulations. Knowing that, Rhiannon held back, even with the smallest incantations.

Silently, she followed Jack through the brambles as he cleared a path before them. Directly behind Rhiannon, agile as any man, Marcella followed with her blade in hand, riding as though she were born to her saddle. Her hooded cloak hid her ebony tresses. And her bright green eyes assessed their surroundings with a shrewdness born of experience.

How old was she? Rhiannon wondered.

She behaved as though she were a hundred and Rhiannon's elder, though she couldn't be much older than Rhiannon.

For his part, Jack couldn't be more than nine and ten, though it was difficult to say for certain, because he, too, wore the same concealing cloak. Both seemed far too young to be able protectors.

Dressed in black, the young man shouldered a darkness that belied his youthful countenance, and, even by night, the haunted look in his pale blue eyes was unmistakable. Rhiannon wondered what travails he'd encountered to make him seem so glum. Whatever it was, she suspected it must have something to do with her mother.

What else could convince strangers to aid her against Morwen? Either they owed Cael a great debt, else they loathed her mother so much they were willing to risk life and limb on Rhiannon's behalf. But no matter the circumstances, Rhiannon was grateful, though there was something about Marcella that needled her.

The woman was sullen and suspicious, curt and

mercurial—very much like a changeling. One minute she was entirely too solicitous, the next she was snappish, and it seemed to Rhiannon that no matter what she did, the woman was despotic.

Right now, it was impossible to gauge her expression or her mood for the hood she wore. "At this pace, it won't be long before we cross into England," she said aloud.

"Good," was all Rhiannon could think to answer, and then after, the silence grew thick.

Sweet fates.

They weren't even gone one night, and already she found that Cael's face hovered like a ghost behind her lids, threatening to materialize every time she closed her eyes.

I don't love you, she told herself furiously.

I don't even like you.

But it wasn't true.

She loved him with reckless abandon—even more now that he'd dared to risk his life to save her.

Aye, she knew beyond a shadow of doubt that there would be a price to be paid for this. She only hoped that Cael understood what he was doing and that he knew how to handle her mother.

Time and again, she turned to scrutinize the path behind them, trembling with fear, all the while lying to herself and telling herself she didn't care.

But she did.

And if, indeed, Cael's ruse was discovered...

The thought left her sick with fear.

"You love him, do you not?"

Startled by the impertinent question, Rhiannon met Marcella's gaze. "Nay," she lied.

The *dewine's* lips tilted up at one corner. "Ah," she

said, with an infuriating sense of certainty. "I think you do."

Rhiannon cast the woman an annoyed glance. "Why should I?"

"Why shouldn't you?"

"Oh, I don't know," said Rhiannon, with no small measure of disgust. "Perhaps because he's in league with my mother?"

Silence.

"Or, better yet, mayhap because he kept me imprisoned for five long years!"

Marcella flicked her hand dismissively. "Alas, my cousin is a complicated man. And yet, I know he loves you."

Or so he'd claimed, though it didn't suit Rhiannon to dwell on such notions—not here, not now. It would serve her far better to remember the worst of Cael—that he'd locked her away in a tower for six long months before finally affording her the luxury of a bower.

And then he'd allowed her mother's lackey to place her in shackles, then no matter how oft she'd lowered herself to beg, he'd never once considered removing them.

Until last night.

"I don't think *he* knows what love is," Rhiannon countered.

"Hmm," said Marcella, scornfully. "I wonder how he might prove it?"

Nettled, Rhiannon met her question with stubborn silence, though Marcella persisted.

"Perhaps by setting you free at peril to himself and to all he holds dear?"

Rhiannon fought the urge to fly at the woman and

scratch out her eyes. She didn't like Cael's "cousin," and she liked her even less with every passing moment. She was grateful certainly, and she would endeavor to remember her gratitude, but she'd love nothing more than to enjoy a moment of silence. And even so, Marcella persisted. "Wouldn't that be proof enough?"

Rhiannon narrowed her gaze.

Was that resentment she noted in the woman's voice?

Moreover, she had the inescapable feeling that this *dewine* knew more about Cael's affiliation with Morwen than she was willing to reveal. *That* bothered her even more.

Who was this woman who claimed to be her husband's cousin? Though curiosity needled her, she refrained from asking, sensing Marcella wouldn't provide any answers.

Cael was no longer her concern, she told herself.

Even now, he might be dead, and, really, she must endeavor to harden her heart. They had a long way to go, and much to accomplish. Cael d'Lucy's decisions were his own, and she couldn't allow herself to take responsibility for his choices, or his affiliations. No one had told him to align himself with Morwen... nor did Rhiannon ever ask to be imprisoned at Blackwood.

Certainly, she'd never asked to love him.

The woman riding alongside her looked too much like a cat who got the cream.

"Why are you helping me?" Rhiannon asked. "For my husband?"

"Nay," the woman replied. "Mind you, I care deeply for Lord Blackwood, but I believe loving you will be the death of him yet, and for what? I cannot believe you ever knew his heart."

Rhiannon winced, confused, more than angry.

It was true, perhaps: There was much about Cael d'Lucy she was not privy to know. But that was *not* her fault, she told herself. He'd only ever revealed the face he cared to show. And even so... she'd spent so many waking hours in his company over these past five years; shouldn't she know him better than some woman who hadn't seen him in years? Even a cousin?

"He's not the man you believe him to be, Rhiannon."

"No doubt," Rhiannon agreed. "But then, prithee, who is he?"

The *dewine* shook her head. "That is not for me to answer, my *dewine* sister. Though if he survives your mother, you might ask him yourself." Then she laughed acerbically. "As to the reason, I'm helping you... why else? 'Tis the will of the Goddess, no doubt."

"I see," said Rhiannon. And perhaps she did—far more than she cared to. It was there in the glint of Marcella's eyes, in the tears she'd disdained to shed. Marcella might, in truth, be his cousin, but the woman might also be in love with him.

The two women shared a knowing glance, and then Marcella huffed a sound of disgust, and put a heel to her mare, moving ahead to take the lead. Meanwhile Jack fell back to ride alongside Rhiannon. "You mustn't concern yourself with Marcella," he advised. "Betimes she's abrasive, though she means well. She's quite protective of Lord Blackwood."

"So, I've noticed."

The young man grinned stupidly, then sighed,

watching as Marcella whacked at brambles. "She's not only lovely, but she's clever, as well."

Annoyance rushed down Rhiannon's spine. "So, I must presume."

Jack nodded, ignoring the telltale note of sarcasm in Rhiannon's voice, responding with unreserved pride. "She served the Empress and her house many, many years."

The Empress. Rhiannon's half-sister, though they hadn't really a drop of blood in common. Still, her interest was mildly piqued, and she said, "In what fashion?"

She never anticipated the answer she received. "Marcella is the only woman ever to be assigned to the Papal Guard."

FOURTEEN

She was a paladin?

Rhiannon blinked, surprised for the second time this morn, now seeing the woman with entirely new eyes.

Gripping her reins until her mount protested over the tension, she stared wide-eyed at Marcella's back. Riding with her back straight, head held high, with her trusty sword brandished in her hand, she wielded it with the same confidence she displayed in the saddle.

How was this possible?

Even by her own admission, Marcella was a witch. For obvious reasons, those two professions did *not* align.

Disbelieving what she'd heard, Rhiannon met Jack's gaze, only to be sure. He nodded swiftly at the question in her eyes, and Rhiannon blinked yet again.

How was this possible?

For ages, their *dewinefolk* had been hunted by paladins—and not merely in past times. From its conception, the Papal Guard had ruthlessly hunted her kind, dragging them out from their homes only to be burned at the stake—like her grandmother. Shortly before Rhiannon was born, her grandmother was sentenced to death, and executed by a company of paladins. They were, essentially, no more than executioners for the Church.

But she shouldn't be so surprised because her own forebear was said to have aided huntsmen. The great and esteemed Taliesin was Uther's mage, and Uther was said to be a founding member of the Papal Guard. There wasn't a living witch who knew their *dewine* history who didn't feel some measure of ambivalence over the conflicts of their past. There might appear to be clear sides—right or wrong—but the truth was far more complicated.

A pure blood *dewine* herself, Cerridwen should have been the one to whom their loyalties were bound. After all, she was a Goddess, and Taliesin was her child, natural born though he was not. And yet, it was her blood that made him, and in the end, he'd betrayed her—as he later betrayed their *dewinekind* by aligning himself with Uther Pendragon.

As the story was told to Rhiannon, Uther hunted *faefolk* and slew them till their numbers had dwindled. He was the reason her people hid themselves in the sacred forests and buried their *grimoires* for fear of persecution.

And yet... here was Marcella... aiding Rhiannon... at her *cousin's* behest. It was enough to make Rhiannon's head ache as much as her heart. Even with the burden of her manacles lifted, she could scarcely think to make sense of all the things she'd learned. Everything was clear as sludge.

And yet, she knew that not all paladins were agents of destruction. Proof of that was her brother by law; Giles de Vere was Rosalynde's champion and now her husband. For love of her sister, he'd turned his back on his paladin vows.

Had Marcella as well?

And what, pray tell, was Marcella's connection to Cael?

Whose side was she on?

And so, it seemed, even after so many centuries, there were still no clear lines to be drawn... Morwen was evil, perhaps because she was betrayed, and despite that this alone was no true defense, neither was Taliesin an innocent man. Their ancient feud—fanciful though the bards might make it—was as real as the nose on Rhiannon's face, vicious besides.

There was no way around it; Morwen must die. And yet, despite this, Rhiannon suddenly understood something about her mother's plight—perhaps even sympathized with her as well.

And now, if she sensed ambivalence in Marcella, at least she understood why: Marcella might, in truth, be her *dewine* sister, but she was a slayer of her own kind. Therefore, she was not to be trusted nor trifled with, and, yes, indeed, Rhiannon *must* keep her wits about her, until she chanced to discover what it was that motivated the paladin.

In the meantime, one thing was certain: It was going to be a long, long journey to Warkworth.

FIFTEEN

By the time they crossed into England, Rhiannon felt her strength nearly returned. Although her body wasn't so hale as it was before the confinement, her head felt clearer than it had in ages—as clear as it could possibly be while plagued with thoughts of Cael.

Unfortunately, there was little she could do for Blackwood's lord, and she must accept the truth. Her husband had chosen his fate. Whatever his attachment to Morwen, his consequences were his own to bear. But it still made her miserable—as miserable as she'd been over the loss of her sister, although, in truth, they shouldn't be the same.

She'd known Arwyn her entire life.

In contrast, she'd known Cael but a small portion of that.

And furthermore, Arwyn was an innocent, a good woman, who'd spent her entire life following the dictates of her heart.

Rhiannon didn't know what Cael was, but he wasn't particularly "good," and neither was he innocent.

Inherently, it was a waste of time to grieve for a man like him. And nevertheless, she was coming to realize that love was not reasonable, and neither was it kind—not if the ache in her heart was any indication.

Distracting herself from her wayward thoughts, following her guides, she idled away the hours honing her Craft, summoning water from the *aether*, then tossing it away—a tiddly little spell that didn't require much manipulation so it shouldn't call undue attention. Their proximity to Blackwood was still too precarious and she wasn't yet strong enough to cast a big enough protection spell to make the gamble worthwhile. But this spell was so simple that she performed it by rote, casting it again and again, strengthening her connection to the *hud* by virtue of the repetition. She was desperate to prepare herself in case her mother should appear, and they were far enough now that it should be safe.

On the bright side, they'd been traveling for most of the day, and still, there was no sign of Morwen or Cael. If luck remained their ally, perhaps by the time they made camp this eve, she would be strong enough to cast a proper protection spell. If not, she'd find some other way to defend herself and her companions—whether or not they deserved her protection. One way or the other, the onus must fall to Rhiannon. Only she had any true chance to prevail against Morwen, because, skilled as she might be, Marcella's sword was a poor defense against *hud du*. Paladin, or nay, her Craft left much to be desired. Bravado would take her only so far. With that sword, she might fare well enough against brigands, but Morwen was another matter entirely. Potions were weak and ineffectual, compared to elemental *magik.*

Although, at this point, the sword had returned to her scabbard, all day long, she'd been swinging it as though in warning, casting narrow-eyed glances toward Rhiannon each time Rhiannon dared perform a new spell. This was the extent of their interaction, and Rhiannon quickly came to realize how much that woman resented her.

Envy perhaps?

If not over Cael, then mayhap over *magik?*

Ready to do battle over her right to defend herself, Rhiannon summoned another palmful of water, and then cast it away, marveling over the rush of *magik* through her veins.

Only a *dewine's* eyes could spy the small points of dew that flew to her hand, each lit by a soft incandescent glow that reminded Rhiannon of tiny stars—dew lights, she'd called them as a child.

Oblivious to those dew lights, Jack rode beside her, regaling Rhiannon with tales of his days at sea with his father. He recounted all their travels, the ports they'd visited and all the commissions they'd accepted from her half-sister Matilda.

"That's how I came to know your sisters," he said, and Rhiannon frowned.

"Sisters?"

He smiled ruefully. "Seren and Arwyn," he said. "My papa was *capitaine* of the *Whitshed.* Sadly, he died in the same fire that took your sister's life, though I do not blame Arwyn."

"I-I'm... sorry," Rhiannon said, stunned.

Why hadn't she realized sooner?

This, then, was the reason for the melancholy so

evident in his pale blue eyes, ever present even despite his good humor. Apparently, he'd been a witness to her sister's sacrifice, and by no choice of his own, had lost his father as well. Only, it occurred to her suddenly that if he was there that day, he would also know if Seren survived. Because of her infuriating shackles, Rhiannon never had the opportunity to find out. Now, she was afraid to ask.

"Four years ago, last month," he said. "I miss him still." And then he crossed himself and kissed his thumb.

Rhiannon's fingers fluttered to her breast, pressing the dampness into the rough wool of her tunic. "And Seren?"

He shook his head, and Rhiannon's heart tripped painfully.

"I've not seen her in years," he said, "though I believe she and Rosalynde now reside together at Warkworth." He smiled sadly as he added, "You know, it was Arwyn who first taught me my letters, and then... Seren who held me together..."

He didn't seem able to finish, and Rhiannon's gaze shifted into the treetops, hoping to stem the flow of tears—relief and sorrow warring inside her.

Seren was alive!

"I did not mean to upset you," he said.

A well-worn grief came back to haunt her, and Rhiannon lifted her hand to her throat, shaking her head mutely. Emotion stuck in her throat.

It was not Jack's fault.

It was not Jack she blamed.

Rhiannon was the one who'd encouraged Arwyn in those final moments... That day, she'd *mindspoken*, defying their lack of proximity, earning herself a pair of manacles and her sweet sister a fiery end. Thereafter, Rhiannon had wept for days, until Morwen's lackey arrived to place her in shackles. From that day forward, she'd nourished her anger, because grief alone would have broken her entirely.

"She was a kind soul," Jack said. "Unlike my father, your sister had a way of making figures seem like the most diverting task. She made me long to read."

It had been so long since Rhiannon had had news of any of her sisters, the telling of his tale was bittersweet. Her breath hitched, remembering Arwyn...

Her sweet, young sister could raise anyone's spirits. She had loved fiercely, and in the end, had proven that love. The world was darker without her.

"She had this... crystal," he said. "As my reward for a job well done, she would betimes allow me a look at it to see what I could spy."

Merlin's Crystal.

The scrying stone her sisters had destroyed before leaving London. Older yet than the Book of Secrets, it was priceless and irreplaceable. Alas, like every scrying stone, it only revealed itself to those with the sight.

"And did you ever spy anything?"

He shook his head. "Your sister made me believe I could... but nay... never."

Rhiannon nodded, grateful for all that he'd shared. "Thank you," she said, wanting to know more, but not strong enough to ask. At any rate, he was a bit of a *blathererprater* and she didn't really need to coax him.

Throughout the day, he told her about his mother and his father. Evidently, his mother was a distant relation to Geoffrey d'Anjou, second husband to Matilda, and father of Duke Henry. Jack's father's father was a ship's captain as well, as was his great grandsire—the latter having captained the flagship of The Conqueror's invading fleet. No small feat. He said he'd once thought he might enjoy being a ship's captain, too, but after his father died, he lost his love for the sea. Relieved over his change of heart, his mother had convinced him to apply himself to the Empress's guard.

"So, you returned to France?" Rhiannon asked.

"Eventually."

That's when he told her about Wilhelm of Warkworth, the bastard son of Richard de Vere—a bear of a man whose bark was sharper than his bite. Sent by his brother to locate Rhiannon's missing sisters, he'd discovered both Seren and Arwyn hidden away on the *Whitshed*. Unfortunately, not in time to save Arwyn. It was only then that Wilhelm had appointed himself as Seren's champion. He later married her as well. "I don't remember much about that morning," Jack said. "But I vividly recall that fire." He shook his head. "It was like nothing I've ever seen—those bright, bright blue flames rose higher than the masthead."

"Witchfire," said Rhiannon. "'Tis—"

"Oh, I know," he said, perhaps hoping to spare her the explanation. "Of course, I did not witness it myself, but I'm told your sister cast the same blaze at the Battle of the Tower."

Rhiannon furrowed her brow.

"Battle... of the Tower?"

Averting his gaze, Jack sucked in a breath, perhaps realizing how little she'd been told. He then proceeded to explain: After the fire, Wilhelm escorted Jack and Seren as far as Neasham, leaving Jack there, in the care of the nuns. He was thirteen, he said, and neither Wilhelm nor Seren had relished the thought of exposing him to danger. In those days, he'd had no knowledge of witches, and he'd begged them not to leave. Turning a deaf ear to his pleas, they left him anyway, and neither did they tell him the truth, not until they returned to collect him many months later. By then, Jack had already heard the news.

Apparently, after leaving him at Neasham, Wilhelm and Seren continued to Warkworth, taking a familiar route. It was in Holystone Wood that they'd encountered Rose and Elspeth at some ruin called the Widow's Tower...

Of course, Rhiannon knew none of this, because all of it took place after they'd placed her in shackles, effectively blocking her *magik*. Naturally, nobody ever bothered to inform her—yet another reason for her to be furious with Cael.

Evidently, having been summoned by Morwen, her sisters arrived to retrieve Elspeth's son. Surrounded by Morwen's army, and far outnumbered, they'd feared the worst.

"She took Ellie's son?" interrupted Rhiannon. "I don't understand... how was she able to enter Aldergh castle? After Eustace and Morwen's attack, I helped Elspeth fortify a warding spell."

Jack shrugged.

"Because your mother's a canny old witch, that's why," announced Marcella, tugging on her reins and falling back to ride alongside them. Her green eyes glittered fiercely. "She gave herself a *glamour* to resemble Elspeth."

Rhiannon peered around Jack to better see Marcella, and asked, "So you were there?"

"Nay, I was not," said the witch-paladin. "'Tis simply my business to know."

"Did my husband *know* as well?"

The witch-paladin eyed Rhiannon shrewdly. "I cannot say what your husband did or did not know." She lifted her chin. "Would you like to feed your angry wolf, or would you like to hear the rest of the tale?"

Rhiannon's changing emotions returned to annoyance over Marcella's officious tone. She swallowed her ire and said, "I'd like to hear the rest, please."

Marcella smiled victoriously. "Deceived by Morwen's *glamour*, your sister's guards invited Morwen into the castle; there, she stole the elder boy, and took him to the Widow's Tower, threatening to murder him if they did not return her *grimoire*."

Rhiannon pressed a hand to her breast. Even all these years later, prickles of fear sidled down her spine in anticipation of hearing the rest. "What then?"

"Seren—"

"Nay," Marcella interrupted Jack. "Seren did *not* cast the *witchfire*. Rather, she was the one to put it out. It was Morwen who summoned *witchfire* and demanded that Seren pass through it to trade the Book for the child."

"And did she?" Rhiannon swallowed convulsively.

Marcella shook her head. "Nay, she did not. For love of her, and in fear for her life, Wilhelm Fitz Richard seized the *grimoire* before Seren could comply, intending to sacrifice himself to save the child.

So, it seemed, the battle would be lost, but Seren saved the day, dousing Morwen's *witchfire* with her *witchwater*, even as your mother fled, taking the *grimoire* with her."

So many questions sprang to Rhiannon's lips. "What of the child?"

"Fine."

"And Wilhelm?"

"Fine."

"My sister did that?"

"Aye," said the paladin very smugly.

"My Seren?"

Marcella lifted her brows. "Perhaps you know another?" When Rhiannon shook her head, she said with a sniff, "Seren will be Regnant, so I'm told."

Rhiannon was too stunned by the revelation to take offense over Marcella's high-minded tone.

Witchwater?

Seren had cast *witchwater?*

Seren?

With the power to heal, and cast away demons, the Church had once used *witchwater* for their sacraments. However, since the break between the Papacy and the doom of Avalon, they'd been using plain old well water, blessed by a priest. There were only three sacred elements in the world—*witchwater, witchwind* and *witchfire*. Supposedly, if a dewine grew strong enough, and her affinity allowed it, she could find within her ability to cast one sacred element. No witch in modernity had ever had the power to summon them all… not even her grandmother.

None of her sisters were skilled enough for that.

Elspeth was aligned to earth. All her *magik*— what little she'd dared perform—always hearkened this alignment. Rosalynde's affinity was water; from the time she was young she could cover a windowpane with frost in the middle of summer. But Seren?

And yet, somehow, it did make sense...

Someone had to be the Regnant, and her sister's *magik* had always been odd—as though it were bound. Her middle sister had displayed a very strange combination of affinities. Although Rhiannon had always supposed she was aligned to air, she was also gifted with the skill to charm, much like Ellie, only better. However, charm was a skillset aligned to earth, and earth was not compatible with air. Therefore, the only logical explanation should be that Seren, too, was aligned to *aether*. Rhiannon had never seriously considered this, mostly because she herself was aligned to *aether*, and the alignment to *aether* was so incredibly rare it was far more likely that all her sisters would be aligned to a single affinity, rather than to have even one aligned to *aether*... much less *two*... or *three*.

"Art certain?" Rhiannon asked, casting another dubious glance at Marcella.

Marcella lifted a black brow. "Quite," she said. "Your sister will be Regnant—Goddess willing."

"But... *I*... am aligned to *aether*," Rhiannon said. "'Tis highly improbable to have three *dewines* all in one family aligned to *aether*..."

"Nay, not three," Marcella countered, and Rhiannon tilted the paladin a questioning look. "Your mother is *not* aligned to *aether*," she said, and then she averted her gaze, staring straight ahead with her chin raised belligerently. "God's blood! You look exactly like her," she interjected, and it sounded like a complaint.

By now, Rhiannon had had enough of Marcella's icy demeanor. Ever since leaving Blackwood, she'd been moody and argumentative. She didn't know what was wrong with the woman, but why in the name of the Mother Goddess would she deign to help Rhiannon if she loathed Rhiannon so much?

"I look like her because she *is* my mother," Rhiannon said icily. "And because she is *my* mother, don't you suppose *I* should know best if my mother is aligned to *aether*?"

Marcella lifted her brow a little higher, as she slid Rhiannon a triumphant glare. "Oh, how ignorant you are!"

Rhiannon pursed her lips and longed to fill her palm with water again, only to cast it into Marcella's face. "I beg pard—"

"Oh, please!" said Marcella. "Spare me, Lady Blackwood! I know your kind!"

Rhiannon was momentarily disarmed by the vicious presentation of her title—Lady Blackwood. For the past few hours, she'd somehow been able to keep Cael off her mind—thanks mostly to Jack. Clearly, Marcella could not.

"All your life you've been blessed in your affinities, and perhaps you believe yourself better than those with less. Merely because I've chosen alchemy as my profession, and simply because I've no elemental affinity, does not mean my *dewine* blood is less than yours!"

Rhiannon opened her mouth to speak, but the paladin wasn't through...

"What I lack in my affinities, I make up for in expertise elsewhere. Unlike you, Lady Blackwood, I've made it my life's devotion to know my kin."

Rhiannon countered, "And yet, you would hunt and slay your own kind?"

Marcella's eyes narrowed till they were slits. "You know nothing, Rhiannon *Pendragon*," she declared, with the emphasis on her ancestral name, and the rebuke left Rhiannon dumb. Once again, she opened her mouth to argue that she, too, had dedicated her life to her Craft—practicing even when her sisters dared not. But she closed her mouth again, wondering...

Could it be true?

Did she believe herself better than others?

Was this why Marcella had been casting her the evil eye all day long? She had only assumed it was her affection for Cael, but perhaps it was not...

She peered over at Jack, but the young man looked like a frightened rabbit facing a wolf, and his shoulders lifted and froze.

Snapping her reins indignantly, Marcella harrumphed, hitching her chin. And once again, as she had this morn, she spurred her mount ahead, taking the lead. Only this time, as she went, she said, "When you are ready to humble yourself, Lady Blackwood, and perhaps learn something more than you think you know, please let me know!"

CHAPTER

SIXTEEN

Humble?

Sweet fates! For five years, Rhiannon had been humbled by no choice of her own.

Even before her confinement at Blackwood, she and her sisters had spent nearly every day of their lives taking whatever scraps were offered.

At Llanthony, they'd occupied a single-room cottage with a crude, dirt floor and one bed—five girls, sleeping all together in whatever corner could be found.

In this day and age, she and her ilk were ill-favored, condemned by the Church as heretics or demons. But they were far from that lot; *dewinefolk* were merely flesh and blood like anyone else.

Moreover, it didn't matter that she and her sisters were blood to a King, they'd suffered no less humility than leper-infected beggars.

Each of them had gold aplenty they'd never even once benefited from—not even her wedded sisters, because they'd married men of whom the Crown did not approve.

It was only after becoming Cael's "ward" that

159

Rhiannon had ever even owned a new dress she didn't sew herself. "Humble!" she said crossly.

How dare that woman imply she was anything but.

Jack rode silently beside her, saying nothing at all —at least not for the longest while, and then he suggested, very gently, "Some folks believe you must be poor and suffering to comprehend humility. But my father used to claim that betimes, even the poor, sometimes perceiving humility to be honorable, will borrow the cloak."

There was little rebuke in his tone, and something about his expression led Rhiannon to resist the temptation to lash out at him. She bit her tongue, considering the parable.

Indeed, she *was* prideful—had always been. She knew her faults as well as any.

In fact, her pride had more than once led her to argue with Elspeth, because, as the eldest, Ellie had so often carried herself as though she knew everything. Rhiannon couldn't bear to be told what to do, or how to think...

And yet, knowing what she knew now, if she could take back one moment of prideful disagreement with any of her sisters, she would do it in a heartbeat. Never in her life had she appreciated them more than she did right now... and clearly, she'd underestimated them as well.

Seren would be Regnant?

And Arwyn... were the situation reversed, would Rhiannon have sacrificed herself the way Arwyn had?

Alas, no one could say for certes how they might respond in any such moment, but Rhiannon liked to believe she would. And yet, she had always believed herself to be the indispensable one... so, then, perhaps she would not?

And now, as it turned out, though her *hud* was quite strong, she didn't have half the ability Seren had proven to possess. Still, no humbler person than Seren had ever lived. She needn't have seen her these past five years to know it was still true.

"I know your sisters quite well," said Jack, as though he'd read her mind. "I spent a good deal of time with all three before returning to Calais. It has been my pleasure to know them, and yet I have never encountered so much kindness."

"Indeed... my sisters are wondrous," said Rhiannon, still mulling over his parable. "It is for love of them I'm so much a fiend."

"Aye," said Jack, with a wink. "So, I'm told."

Rhiannon smiled ruefully, embarrassed, and then she cast yet another glance at Marcella's rigid back.

"I can only imagine," she said, wondering over the things Jack might have heard. Clearly, Marcella hadn't any respect for her, she and Elspeth had argued all too oft, and while the rest of her sisters had tried in vain to keep the peace, admittedly, Rhiannon was possessed of a temper.

"Only to hear them speak of you, I admired you well," said Jack. "So, I am told, you are the best, the wisest, the most talented *dewine* of our age. Naturally, I could not wait to meet you..." He shrugged. "And here I am."

Surprised by the compliments, Rhiannon shifted her gaze to meet his. "Have I disappointed you?"

The young man's golden brows lifted. "Not at all, m'lady. I can see why Lord Blackwood is so smitten." He inclined his head toward Marcella. "In fact, were my heart not already taken, I might be obliged to offer it to you."

He winked at her again, but Rhiannon's smile faded, thinking about Cael. "Not so smitten he would abandon my mother," she groused.

Jack sighed then, sounding weary.

How old was he? she wondered yet again. If he had been thirteen when he first knew her sisters, he must be no more than seventeen or eighteen—younger than the nineteen she'd first presumed. Comparatively, Marcella was easily ten years his senior, with a decade's worth of life and knowledge that would naturally leave the poor lad wanting.

What a jumble this was: Rhiannon loved Cael but couldn't have him. He claimed to love her, as well, but not enough to abandon her mother. Marcella loved Cael, Rhiannon suspected, and yet here she was left in the cold. And so, too, was Jack, because he coveted a woman who was well out of his league and whose heart belonged to another.

"Your mother is... quite... the force," he said. "In truth, she frightens me out of my wits. I see you do resemble her, Rhiannon... so, then... I must presume that while there may be something of her in you... there may also be something of you in her."

"Aye," agreed Rhiannon. "'Tis precisely this I fear."

"Perhaps... so does she," he suggested, hitching his chin once more at Marcella's back. "And yet, she must know as I know, that Lord Blackwood would never have summoned aid for you, if there was so little in you to be loved. Therefore, at least for now, you must content yourself to know that your husband is not precisely the man you believe him to be, and that is a good thing."

Rhiannon nodded.

"Neither is *she*," he added, though if Rhiannon hoped he would say more, Marcella turned to cast him a withering glance, and he shut his gob and spoke no more.

~

THERE WAS a lot to be considered, and yet, after a while, one grew weary of self-rumination. Hours later, Rhiannon was still pettish and growing peckish besides.

Now that the initial danger appeared to be over, her stomach grumbled in complaint, and, even after having appeased it with a small stick of smoked beef, she longed for more. Not having been privy to Cael's plans, she hadn't touched her supper last night.

At any rate, how could anyone eat seated next to that despicable creature?

Reaching back into her saddlebag for whatever morsel could be found, she fished out a small sack of filberts, her favorite nuts. No doubt this was Cael's doing. In fact, she had the feeling that half the reason he'd ever deigned to serve her all these years was because he'd enjoyed seeing the brightening of her countenance when he brought her special treats.

And she, of course, incensed by her eternal confinement, had resolved to deprive him even of that.

No matter, there were times she couldn't hide her joy, and betimes, when caught off guard, her spirits brightened, and she'd lifted her gaze to find him smiling too.

She popped a filbert into her mouth, considering the man's endless patience, his bigger-than-life presence. She missed his devilish smile and his glinting eyes.

Would she truly never see him again?

There had been no sign of hounds since leaving Brecknock Forest. Wales was long in their wake, and the only sounds of pursuit came from their coursers as, one after another, they trampled over heavy bracken, snapping twigs and disturbing dew-dampened leaves—that, along with the occasional thwack of an errant bough.

"God's blood," complained Jack, as another branch whipped back to slap him on the cheek, courtesy of Marcella. Evidently, she was still nursing her pique and Rhiannon munched on nuts and held her tongue, taking perverse joy in Jack's indignation. Annoyed, he called out to the paladin in a deceptively amiable tone, "Thanks for *la colée, mon patron*—the second one you've dealt me today."

"Be vigilant," Marcella demanded, unfazed. "Else you will find yourself with a *coup de grâce*, and it will not be dealt by my own hand."

Unappeased by her response, Jack argued, "Aye... well, wouldn't it be wiser to travel by night, when these stupid birds will be roosting?"

"Nay," she snapped, and then explained. "'Tis not the ravens I worry over, Jaques. They cannot follow our scent like the hounds. Coming into these woods will necessitate coming within proximity of our bows, and Morwen will not risk her precious birds. Rather, she'll use Blackwood's hounds to follow the scent and the birds to search hill and dale. This is why we washed Rhiannon's tunic with a masking philter."

Taking his blade to another wayward limb, "Jaques" muttered crossly beneath his breath, his mood a bit less affable now than it had been earlier in the day.

Rhiannon couldn't help herself; she smirked.

By now they were all exhausted, after having traveled most of the night and day without rest, and soon —*very, very soon*—they would be forced to abandon the woods.

"They *can* smell," Jack argued. "I've watched them sniff out carrion with my own eyes."

"Not very well," Marcella persisted. "In order to smell your *merde*, they would have to shove their black beaks up your adorable little arse. And besides, *grâce à Dieu,* you are not rotting nor are you bloody."

"Not yet," he persisted. "But I may soon be if you keep flinging thorny limbs in my face!"

"There are no thorns on these branches, Jaques," she said placidly. "You complain like an old woman, my friend."

"I felt a thorn," he said, though it couldn't be true. His face would have been pocked and marked if that were the case, and it was still smooth as a baby's bottom—not even marred by chin hairs.

To that, Marcella shot back without compunction, "Simply watch where you are going, Jack. I've seen you nodding. Now is no time to sleep."

Jack grumbled beneath his breath—something about stopping to rest—as Rhiannon popped the last of her filberts into her mouth, then shoved the sack back into her bag.

Marcella was right, of course. Now, when it seemed they should be out of danger; this was when they were most at peril. They couldn't afford to let down their guard. Morwen was ruthless and persistent. Still, Marcella's imperious nature was infuriating. Young as she must be, the woman behaved as though she knew *everything*. It grated on Rhiannon's nerves—and evidently, on Jack's nerves as well, even despite that he'd confessed affection for her.

Marcella was also right about the ravens. Having lost so many birds already, her mother wouldn't risk even one unnecessarily. Insomuch as birds loved trees, and trees loved birds, they were, indeed, far less useful in the confines of these dense woods. And because they weren't particularly tiny, the odds were quite high they would spy a raven before it ever spied them. Quick as they were, they weren't faster than an arrow, and if either of these two were worth their salt, Rhiannon wouldn't have to wield her *magik*, and yet... she could. Even now she itched to flick a flame into Marcella's beautiful black mane.

How, in the name of the Goddess, could a woman look so stunning without any feminine accouterments. The deep brown stained—almost black—cowl had slipped down to puddle about her shoulders, catching a waterfall of shining tresses into the back of her hood. Even tired, her skin was tawny, and her facial features so dark they appeared to be painted. In fact, in all her life, she'd never seen lashes or brows so thick and black.

To the contrary, Rhiannon felt smelly, dirty, itchy, and only thanks to the braids she'd worn last eve, she didn't have a rat's nest for hair. Her skin was pasty from lack of sun—years of lack, in fact. Next to Marcella, she felt like a faded scrap of cloth—and yet, alas, not so washed out that she would be invisible to

Morwen's ravens. At least, not until she could perform a proper protection spell.

"Seems to me, she'd be willing to lose a few, if only for the sake of expediency," Jack grumbled, as he unsheathed his sword again to hack at another tangle of limbs.

"She will not."

"How can you know?"

"Because," Marcella replied. "I heard she's having trouble breeding them. Those ravens are meant to mate for life, and so many of the mates have been slain. Whatever else they are to her, they are integral to her plan. I promise you she will not risk even one."

Rhiannon listened quietly, loathe to take the witch-paladin's side, despite that she was right. "Command the birds, command the nation," her mother used to say.

And, of course, it was true, because whosoever commanded the realm's mode of communication, commanded the barons as well. Morwen's affinity with those birds had made her indispensable to Henry, and then to Stephen as well. Ultimately, this was how a penurious young Welsh maiden was able to gain the notice of a King. Consequently, it was also how she'd kept it long after her wiles had failed her. Eventually, both kings had their fill of the witch, and when they did, she moved on to Stephen's son...

Eustace.

Scourge of England.

Bane of his father.

Puppet to Morwen.

"Is it true she can change them?"

"Aye," said Marcella and Rhiannon, both at once.

Marcella peered back at Rhiannon, giving her an

annoyed glance, though Rhiannon ignored her. Rhiannon asked Jack, "Did you never meet Bran?"

"Nay."

"I wish I had not," she said, though thankfully, she'd heard naught more from her mother's manservant since the day she saw him on the *Whitshed*.

Alas, she wished she could say the same about Mordecai. Now and again, that abomination had come to perch himself on her windowsill, in the guise of a bird. Only once had he ever ascended the stairs as a man, and Rhiannon had made Cael aware of it and he promised to never allow him to come again.

As for Bran, Rhiannon prayed to the Goddess that those flames had taken him as well—and surely, they must have, else, like Arwyn, Seren would never have lived to see the end of the day.

Poor, poor Arwyn.

Her people held a strong belief that all things were one, living and dead. If, indeed, the tenets of their faith were to be believed, nothing ever truly ceased to be. If she was lucky, mayhap one day she would see Arwyn again, though if she did, what would she say?

I'm sorry for asking you to sacrifice yourself.

I'm sorry I wasn't strong enough to save you.

I'm sorry it wasn't me.

Anger blazed through her—a righteous anger so intense that it threatened to make her combust right there in her saddle. She had allowed Arwyn to sacrifice herself, just as she'd let Morien...

Her sister Seren was blessed with infinite patience and goodwill, but Rhiannon feared she was cursed with her mother's darkness; what was more, she heartily embraced it.

Five long years of incarceration had made her more wrathful than ever—more so at herself for loving a man who'd kept her imprisoned.

Cael...

Oblivious to her state of mind, Jack and Marcella prattled on endlessly and Rhiannon couldn't help herself. Squeezing her fist tight, she opened it suddenly, and her fury materialized in the palm of her hand, a tiny blue flame she longed to cast away to set the forest ablaze, damned be the consequences!

Oh, yes, she knew there was a price to be paid, and she accepted the Law of Three as truth. Still, anger was her constant companion...

If, for example, one had summoned a brume to aid one's sister's escape... perhaps five years of imprisonment would be one's just reward.

And mayhap, rather than blame Cael for all her troubles, she should blame herself...

Closing her fist, she snuffed out the flame.

"Do you smell that?" asked Jack.

"What?"

"Smoke."

"Nay," said Marcella, although she turned to peer over her shoulder at Rhiannon, narrowing her shrewd green eyes.

Rhiannon smiled innocently and shrugged.

SEVENTEEN

The days blurred one into another...

Ride, eat, sleep, wake, listen to Marcella crow, ride, eat, sleep, wake, listen to Marcella crow...

Whatever her true allegiance, her opinion was clear as *Waldglas*: Marcella wasn't impressed by the English, nor their usurper king. But what wasn't precisely evident was where her loyalties lay—not with the Germans, neither with the French or the Normans, even despite that she'd spent so much of her adult life in Germany and then Normandy with Matilda.

At heart, she was perhaps a Welsh patriot, but that was not entirely evident either. She defended Matilda as well as the Church, and marveled that the marcher lords hadn't found a way to depose all the shambolic Welsh kings.

She was, in truth, a bit of a riddle...

"Pride is their sin," she said now, expounding on Stephen's barons and specifically their choice of war mounts. "If you ask me, they are too concerned with appearances, not enough with practicality," she said.

"Destriers are a menace on the battlefield. Meanwhile, our coursers might not put the fear of God into a man, but neither will they madden over the scent of blood. *That* is why *he* fell," she said, speaking of King Stephen. "Not because he is ill-favored by God—that, and because he's old and weak. Try putting a bit of horseflesh between your legs as an old man and see if you don't find yourself with a gob full of muck as well."

Apparently, the King had taken a tumble from his horse very recently—a few, in fact. The last time, he went face-first into the mire, causing a bevy of tongues to wag. He was "cursed," so they'd said—abandoned by his God.

But really, how could he possibly win against the anointed son of a Holy Roman Empress! Duke Henry was the rightful heir, and furthermore, how was Stephen ever supposed to keep a discontented nation when he couldn't even control his own son?

"I am only repeating what I heard," said Jack, conversationally. "Though, in truth—at least to me—he seems ill-favored as any man can be."

Marcella's bark of laughter was acerbic. "Please!" she scoffed. "He stole his uncle's throne, quite literally—stole England's treasury, as well, and then forsook an oath to Matilda. Even so, that man kept his throne for nearly a full score years. If that is not good fortune, my young friend, I cannot say what is."

Like her eldest sister, Elspeth, Marcella was clearly a loyalist for the Empress—prepared to defend the haughty woman at a moment's notice. Sadly, Rhiannon hadn't any love for the Would-be Queen. Half-sisters though they might be, in all their living years,

Matilda had never once shown any of them any affection—not even Ellie.

Oh, yes, perhaps, in truth, she'd been kinder to Elspeth, once upon a day. But that was so long ago that Rhiannon doubted Elspeth would even remember what Matilda looked like at this very late date. Truly, that woman could be standing before them, grizzle-haired and full of chin hairs, and neither would recognize the other.

So far as Rhiannon was concerned, it didn't matter to her who sat upon England's throne, so long as they weren't a poppet to Morwen—which, in fact, Stephen was.

True: He might be rethinking his alliances these days, but so long as Morwen kept his son's ear, and so long as Eustace was still the heir apparent, her mother would rule through him. Rhiannon didn't know Eustace well at all, but she knew enough about him to know that he was as weak of mind as he was of heart. But she was bored of *politiks*, and she wasn't moved to speak throughout their entire discourse. Kings, queens, emperors, empresses—they all shat the same, so far as Rhiannon was concerned. She wasn't impressed with any overlord, no matter their affiliations.

In truth, she couldn't bring herself to believe that, when push came to shove, their champions wouldn't abandon them, as well. It was what Cael had done, after all.

Hadn't he?

I've loved you from the moment you opened your mouth, Rhiannon Pendragon...

Lies!

If he did, he would be here with her, right now, defending her, as a champion should.

Moreover, if Cael truly loved her, he wouldn't keep so many damnable secrets... secrets he'd clearly shared with his know-it-all *cousin*.

Scowling at Marcella's back, loathing her more and more with every word she uttered, Rhiannon found the woman to be insufferable, and yet, regrettably there was little she ever found to disagree with.

That was annoying.

More today than yesterday, tensions were tight, but so long as Rhiannon abstained from the conversation, Marcella and Jack maintained a fine fellowship, even if they disagreed about everything. It was evident that Jack admired the lady, but not so much that he was afraid to speak his mind. They argued good-naturedly, about *politiks*, swords, armor, horseshoes, horseflesh, gold, salt, cheese, *vin*, cats, birds, dental paste, and leather. No topic was invulnerable to their debate, and, so it appeared, the one thing everyone agreed upon was a shared loathing for Rhiannon's mother.

Listening quietly, Rhiannon practiced her repetitions, minding her own affairs, allowing the two to agree to disagree as they would, time and again, with Marcella always, *always* having the last word. One would think they were in attendance at court, with barons postulating over Henry's Forest Laws. But at least they managed to divert her attention... for a while.

~

FLEXING HER HAND, Rhiannon slid from the saddle. Her hand ached from so many repetitions. But it was only when she pulled up her sleeve to rub at the soreness that she noted the greenish-black stains marring her wrists—left by the bracelets?

Only now she wondered if the discoloration was why she was having trouble restoring the full scope of her abilities, even after three days of practicing as they traveled.

Tired and bleary-eyed, she longed to fall face-first into a hump of leaves, may the midge flies bite what they pleased. But at least they were still free, with no sign of Morwen in pursuit. How in the name of the Goddess they'd managed to evade that woman, Rhiannon couldn't begin to fathom, but in retrospect, it was entirely possible the hounds they'd heard weren't from Blackwood at all.

And still, though she knew it was improbable, she hoped Cael would follow.

Alas, she was too tired to think of that or anything else right now. She longed for a good night's rest, and a belly full of victuals—not necessarily in that order.

There was a brook nearby. She could hear the tinkling of water over stones. Mayhap in the morn, she would go wash her face and endeavor to remove these stains from her wrists. The last thing they needed right now was for her to retain any of the inspired metal, especially if it could silence her *magik*. As it turned out, it was fortuitous that Marcella was carrying the bracelets—so long as she didn't intend to return them to Rhiannon's wrists. Somehow, the woman seemed determined to nettle her unto death. And, naturally, she would choose a thicket tangled with brambles. Though it was all well and good.

There was more than enough space to shelter the three of them, along with their horses. Hidden amidst a spinney of trees, the thicket was perfectly positioned to cast some sort of protection spell and, finally, after multiple failures, she was excited to try again.

Anticipating the rush through her veins, Rhiannon located a stick to draw with and made ready to cast her spell.

Marcella stopped her. "Not yet!" she screamed, lifting a hand and startling Rhiannon from the task.

As she had the past two nights, the paladin produced another set of her mysterious vials, then proceeded to open one and sprinkle her potion in a wide arc, in much the same way Rhiannon meant to do with her pentacle.

Annoyed, Rhiannon eyed Marcella's vial with a lifted brow. "How will *that* protect us?"

Clearly taking offense to her dubious tone, Marcella snapped, "You are not yet strong enough to cast any spells. If you try again and fail, and she is near, you'll risk us all—not that I will not die to defend you, Lady Blackwood. But if you should risk Jacques, I'll kill you myself."

Stunned by her vehemence, Rhiannon rocked back on her heels, as though buffeted.

Sweet fates. She didn't wish to argue any longer—not when they were supposed to be fighting for the same just cause. By now, it seemed to Rhiannon that she'd been fighting for too many years, especially with Cael—a thing she sorely regretted now that it seemed entirely possible she might never see him again.

She couldn't comprehend why Marcella was filled

with so much animus toward her, but it was time for it to cease and desist. Someone must make the first concession, and Rhiannon supposed that someone should be her. After all, she did owe the paladin a debt of gratitude.

"You must know I'd not risk *any* of you," Rhiannon said in her most conciliatory tone, tossing away her stick. "I am truly grateful for your help, Marcella. Tell me what to do and I will do whatever you deem best."

"Meek words for a high and mighty witch?" Marcella mused aloud, and nevertheless, she seemed to deflate before Rhiannon's eyes. She said nothing at all for a moment, and then, perhaps realizing, as Rhiannon had, how pointless it was to argue amidst themselves, she relented, "You know, it was Jacques who advocated for you?"

Rhiannon's brows knit. "He did?"

Marcella nodded, handing Rhiannon a vial of her own to dispense. "Aye," she said. "When Lord Blackwood came to address the Council, he was the first to testify in your behalf." She arched a brow. "He claimed your freedom was vital to England's salvation."

Already, in the short time since Rhiannon had known the young man, she could easily envision him doing such a thing. He was perhaps young, but he was quite capable of arguing his cause. She'd seen more than enough evidence of that. And yet, before they'd met here recently, he hadn't known Rhiannon at all, so why would he bother to argue in her defense? "I suppose he did it for Seren?"

"Perhaps," Marcella said, then shrugged. "Perhaps so. He tends to be easily inspired, and your sister is quite beautiful."

In fact, Seren's beauty was celebrated. There were no doubt several barons whose hearts she'd broken when she married Wilhelm.

Eyeing Rhiannon circumspectly, Marcella continued to sprinkle the contents of her vial, as she added, "I must confess I argued against him. I truly believed he was mistaken."

"I see," said Rhiannon, very carefully.

"Nay, you do not. Despite your many talents, Lady Blackwood, there is so much you do not understand." Her expression was sober, though without enmity. "In fact, perhaps there is much your visions have revealed to you, but so much remains veiled."

There was a note of sadness in the paladin's tone.

"You are, indeed, quite strong," she said matter-of-factly. "But you are arrogant and all the weaker for it, else you'd have realized long, long ago that your sister was Regnant. Consequently, you would have placed her life before yours, as did your sister Arwyn... as I do for you..."

Rhiannon swallowed. So much as she longed to object, there was a note of truth in her words, and truth was indisputable, no matter how much she wished to deny it. She had, in fact, believed herself to be the Regnant and she had placed her own life above that of her sisters' on so many occasions.

Marcella shook her head. "The boy's heart is as big as his mouth, I fear. And yes, I do believe he was enamored of Seren. Alas, after seeing how his affiliation with your sister changed Giles, I very much suspected Jack's motives. There is something about you

Pendragons," she said, with measured wariness. "Something that naturally beguiles..."

Rhiannon opened her mouth to disagree, because if that were, in fact, true, she shouldn't have spent five long years in confinement at Blackwood; still Marcella continued.

"For Rosalynde, Giles turned his back on his brethren. He was our superior, and thusly entrusted with the Sword of Ages. But then he gave the sword to your sister."

Marcella's eyes shone. "But you knew that, didn't you?"

Rhiannon nodded; she did. Her visions had revealed as much.

"Then you should also understand why I mistrusted you, particularly when, despite that I pleaded for Cael to put aside his alliance with Morwen, it was only after meeting *you* that he changed his mind."

"And yet he didn't," Rhiannon argued, overlooking the paladin's use of her husband's given name. "If, indeed, he had, wouldn't he be here with us instead of there, with her?"

There was an unmistakable note of bitterness in Rhiannon's voice, and Marcella rolled her eyes. "*Mon Dieu*, there is so much you do not know," she said, gesturing toward the vial she held. "Go on. It doesn't matter who dispenses it, but please try to scatter it evenly. Last night you tossed it all into one spot."

Eager to put dissent behind them, Rhiannon nodded, and said, "I am sorry."

Marcella gave her a tentative smile, and turned to do her work, but Rhiannon needed to know. "Marcella... I was wondering... the way you speak his name... I must suppose the two of you are not cousins, after all?"

There was no need to say to whom she was referring.

"Nay," Marcella confessed, without looking at her. "We are not."

"What, then?"

She peered up then, casting a glance over her shoulder. "Cousins so far as the world should know."

"Otherwise?"

She stopped dispensing her potion and turned to face Rhiannon directly. "What we *were* is lost to me now, Lady Blackwood. What he is now is *your* lord husband. This is not something I will ever disrespect... nor will Cael ever forsake a vow of honor. And yet, this is the rub: If you believe he would, you do not know the man at all, and I pity you this more than I pity your circumstances."

We are not aligned, Rhiannon heard Cael say, again.

So then, as Marcella had just confirmed, he would not forsake his vows to her mother, and thus, she was bound to be his enemy no less than she was his wife.

A wave of sadness enveloped her—particularly so, since it was clear to her now that the woman standing before her knew more about her husband than Rhiannon was ever bound to learn. "He made a vow to *me*," Rhiannon said plaintively.

"And yet... I did not see him kneel before you and pledge his sword."

Rhiannon's gaze shot up. "You were there?"

Marcella smiled sadly. "For an instant. I watched from the shadows to satisfy my own curiosity. Sad, is it not? That I would pledge him—and you—my life, even as he forsakes me for another."

"I... am... sorry," said Rhiannon, but she wasn't, not entirely. Some small part of her reveled in the fact that she and Cael were man and wife—even if the truth was that neither she nor Marcella could have him and he was lost to them both.

"He does love you," Marcella said quietly.

"Did he love you?"

She seemed to think about it a moment, and then shook her head. "Nay," she said. "I think not, although we were... affianced... for a short while."

"You were?"

"Aye, we were," said the paladin with a nod.

"What happened?"

Marcella lifted a brow. "Well... you could say..." She tilted her head as though to consider how best to say it. "He became... a different man."

"He changed?"

Marcella nodded. "Oh, I'd say so. Very much."

Rhiannon frowned, peering down at the vial in her hand, her throat suddenly too thick to speak.

Goddess only knew, she loved Cael so desperately, although apparently this meant something different to each of them—or did it? If their roles were reversed, would she, indeed, give up all that mattered to her... for Cael?

The answer was "nay."

She would not.

Some things were bigger than both.

Rhiannon would no more sacrifice another of her sisters for Cael than he would give up whatever it was that Morwen promised him.

Only now, she considered that mayhap, it was not greed that drove him...

Perhaps he, too, fought for something greater—something for which he'd been willing to betray Morwen and perhaps even make an appeal to the Papal Guard.

"What is this?" Rhiannon inquired of the vial in her hand.

The witch-paladin smiled faintly. "Amaranth, with a bit of asafetida to drive away demons. Also, a pinch of bryony to amplify the strength of my brew."

For many years, Rhiannon had encouraged Arwyn to pursue alchemy because her *magik* was so sorely lacking. Her sweet sister never took the art to heart. In fact, although alchemy wasn't so powerful as the manipulation of the *aether*, it did have its merits. "Interesting," she said, curiously, and lifted the vial to her nostrils, then said, "Pew!"

Marcella laughed.

"Do I also scent metals as well?"

"You have a good nose," said Marcella, with approval, as she continued to administer the contents of her own vial. "'Tis brewed with a little copper dust, agate, malachite and amber—all to summon a guardian angel."

"Angels?" Rhiannon asked, with surprise, as she began to move in the opposite direction as Marcella, carefully sprinkling the contents of her own vial.

Her sister Elspeth had oft claimed that wherever *magik* dwelt, angels did not—only why that should be so, Rhiannon didn't know, because there was nothing particularly sinister or unnatural about the *hud*, lest it be dark.

"In truth, I have never seen one," Marcella confessed, with a rueful smile. "But it can't hurt, can it?"

Rhiannon returned the smile. "We can use all the help we can get against my demon mother."

"Ah, but she's not a demon," said Marcella pointedly, and something about her tone prompted Rhiannon to stop everything she was doing and tilt the paladin a curious look.

"What is she then?"

Marcella inhaled deeply and shook her head. There was a sadness in her expression that Rhiannon didn't comprehend. "Not yet," she said, only this time there was no enmity in her tone. "When Jaques returns, I'll explain everything."

"So, tell me... if you did not agree with Jack... what changed your mind?"

"About you?"

Rhiannon nodded, and Marcella lifted a hand. "Not now," she said again, meeting Rhiannon's gaze with a wearied look. "I promise to explain all when Jaques returns."

"As you wish," Rhiannon said, trying not to be vexed.

She finished dispersing her vial, then wiped her fingers on her tunic. The gesture wasn't very couth, but considering her garments in broad daylight, she doubted one more stain could hurt them. Her own cloak was made of the crudest of undyed wools—not nearly the quality of her wedding gown. Her tunic wasn't much better. Moreover, the breeches were too snug in the most disturbing of places. Goddess only knew how Marcella managed to move about so gracefully in such unconventional attire, because Rhiannon felt... constrained.

She was only grateful that Marcella hadn't removed her cloak because she'd already surmised by the fit of her *gambeson* that there would be little left to the imagination. It was no wonder Jack was so enamored.

What would Cael think of her now?

Reeking of horseflesh and sweat, dressed like a man. She remembered the way he'd gazed at her when she'd appeared in the hall wearing her wedding dress... the way he'd risen so purposely and then came marching toward her, drawing her into his arms and kissing her so hungrily...

Don't think about him, she scolded herself.

Look ahead, not behind.

EIGHTEEN

When Jack did not return by sundown, Rhiannon began to worry. "Should he be out there, alone?"

"He knows what he's doing," said the paladin, in a complete reversal of attitude, as she led her horse back from the brook and tethered the mare to a nearby tree. "He's spent the past four years training precisely for this. As young as he is, he's even more adept than his teachers."

"At what? Arguing," Rhiannon said, with a lifted brow, although it wasn't meant to disparage the young man.

Marcella laughed, as she began to undo the straps that kept her blanket secured to the back of her saddle. "Hunting," she said carefully.

Dewines was the first thought that accosted Rhiannon, though she didn't speak it aloud, careful to maintain their fragile new peace. "Who were his teachers?"

"To begin with... Giles."

"Now you?"

Marcella's smile lit her green eyes. "Yes, of course," she said.

And with that single revelation, so much made sense.

That council where Jack had testified in Rhiannon's behalf was a council of the Papal Guard. Therefore, if Giles was a paladin, and Marcella was a paladin, Jack must be a paladin, too. Did that mean Cael was a paladin, as well?

Surely not.

A spy perhaps, though Cael didn't strike her as a man who played both sides, and regardless... the possibility left her feeling utterly bemused.

On the one hand, if it was true that he was working surreptitiously to defeat her mother, it might serve to wash the stain of guilt from his honor.

On the other hand, if he, too, was a paladin, then he was a slayer of *dewinekind*—a huntsman, according to her people. Never in her life had she ever thought to associate with one, much less two—and now, perhaps she was married to a huntsman as well?

So, it seemed... the more she discovered about Cael... the less she knew.

In fact, the more she discovered about life itself, the less she realized she knew.

How in the name of the Mother were they ever going to defeat Morwen when there were so many questions left unanswered?

As it was, Rhiannon felt unprepared for this task, particularly so when she'd once believed herself to be the Regnant, destined for this fate. But Marcella was right. She had, indeed, presumed too much, and everything she thought she knew was wrong.

Oh, she realized she had a part to play—felt it deep in her bones—but what that part was had greatly diminished just since discovering her sister was to be Regnant.

It was all very humbling.

Mulling over all that she'd learned—quite a lot during the span of these past few days—she claimed a spot for her pallet, then kindled a fire, anticipating something more to put in her belly besides nuts and smoked beef. Her sisters had always contented themselves with vegetables from their garden, but Rhiannon's appetite had more raptorial tendencies. She would be pleased enough with whatever could be foraged, but she certainly wouldn't turn down a bit of cony. Thankfully, Jack arrived with a nice, fat one, and later, over supper, whilst he roasted it "the way Wilhelm taught me," they settled back to devour the fruits of his labor, and that was when Marcella shared the remainder of her tale.

According to her, shortly after the battle at the Widow's Tower, Jack returned to Warkworth. There, he learned a bit of swordplay from Giles, after which, Giles handed him over to a Papal emissary, who then introduced him to Marcella.

Evidently, Marcella, too, had once apprenticed with Giles—and this made sense. It explained very well why Giles had embraced Rosalynde so easily. Through his own apprentice, he'd already been exposed to the Craft. But clearly, it was easier for the Church to accept Marcella's brand of *dewinity* than it was for any of them to embrace *dewines* likes the Pendragons. But she supposed it didn't help matters much that they were also kin to Morwen.

By the by, Marcella interjected—in case Rhiannon might be wondering: She'd had nothing to do with the death of Rhiannon's grandmother. That business, she explained, was a bit of misfortune that originated with the Empress herself, perhaps spurred by her hatred for Morwen—a visceral and passionate thing Matilda carried with her to this very day.

Apparently, the Would-be Queen held Morwen entirely responsible for the death of her mother, although Rhiannon had never heard a word of that tale before now—not that she doubted her mother was capable of it. Morwen was many, many things, but according to everything Rhiannon knew, Matilda was already sixteen and wed by the time Henry's first wife died. It wasn't until six years after the Old Queen's death before Morwen ever came to Henry with a belly full of child, and at least a good three years after that that he'd taken himself a new wife—Adeliza of Louvain. A sweet, but timid creature, who'd never born him any children, though she sure did whelp a few for William d'Aubigney. Still, perhaps it didn't set well with Matilda to return to England to discover a Welsh witch warming her father's bed, and a young, but barren Adeliza, scarcely older than she was, seated on her mother's throne.

Truth be told, King though he might be, Henry was a bit of a roué. He'd fathered more bastards during his sixty-seven years than most men knew how to count. That he wasn't Rhiannon's sire was no reason to weep. And yet... at least he took care of his bastards, and he'd counted Rhiannon as one, awarding her a dowry no less than her sisters.

Fortunately, only Rhiannon and her mother knew for certain who her true father was—not even her sisters knew—and Rhiannon had good cause to keep it a secret.

All this time, Marcella had been watching her, perhaps waiting for Rhiannon to put all her stories together. And then Marcella said, at last, "You know... she... was... my friend."

"Who?"

"Morwen."

Marcella tore another bite from her cony and chewed, while Rhiannon pondered the inflection of Marcella's words. A flicker of emotion—sadness?—crossed Marcella's lovely features, and then it vanished, replaced with a brand of steely temperance that was entirely her own.

"We grew up together," she said, and Rhiannon blinked back her momentary shock, because it couldn't be possible. Marcella was too young. Even on closer inspection, it would seem the paladin was no older than Rhiannon...

With furrowed brow, she examined the woman's soft, smooth face—lacking even a hint of crow's feet at the corner of her eyes.

Startling her even more, Marcella claimed to be seventy-three, attributing her "youthful appearance" to a bit of alchemy, and good *dewine* blood.

Listening intently, Jack held his tongue, his gaze alternating between Rhiannon and Marcella, though if any of this was a surprise to him, he gave little indication of it. Looking bored, he tossed a mauled bone into the flames, and watched the fire flare over the grease.

"Alas, I must confess... we were close—very, very close."

Rhiannon stopped chewing only to stare openmouthed at the paladin, wondering what it was she was trying to convey. Something about the way she said the word... *close*... gave Rhiannon pause.

"She wasn't always the way she is now. As a girl, she was... well..." She shrugged. "She was Morwen."

She said it with such tenderness that Rhiannon had to work hard to swallow the bite of food she had in her mouth.

"What... happened?"

Rhiannon had meant the question drolly, but Marcella responded very soberly. "One evening... whilst I was out with your grandmother, foraging for herbs for my potions, your mother and Emrys borrowed her *grimoire*..." She averted her gaze now, tears brimming in her eyes. "She was never the same after... and well, Emrys... neither was he." She hushed then, swiping a tear from her cheek. "We were fifteen."

"So, then, you knew her... *before*?"

Before the change that made her a Witch Goddess.

"Aye," said Marcella, with a nod. "Quite well." And then she said again, with meaning, "Quite."

Rhiannon blinked over the revelation, realizing how little she knew of her own mother. Clearly, this woman had loved Morwen—truly *loved* her. The very notion was... unthinkable. Not only because—well, she was a woman, and so was Morwen, but... because it was impossible to imagine Morwen as a maiden in love.

Really, their kind were not pietists. She'd heard many such Beltane stories about free love under the stars—maidens and stags, stags and stags, maidens and maidens... it was simply that... well... she was talking about Morwen.

Rhiannon blushed hotly, and Marcella offered a

hint of a smile. "We were young," she explained. "Both of us filled with so much wonder and love for our Craft. Alas, I was never very skilled... So much as I adored the Craft, it never came so easily to me as it did to Morwen."

She broke off then, looking angry, ripping another bite from her cony, before casting the bones into the weeds. Afterwards, she sat chewing, the tension in her body unmistakable, clenching and unclenching one fist, until at last, she pierced Rhiannon with a pointed glance. "As you already realize... she is no longer who she was. But what you cannot know... is... her true form... she's Sylph."

"Morwen?"

"Cerridwen."

Swallowing with some difficulty, Rhiannon's lips parted, then closed again, realizing intuitively what it was that Marcella was telling her: Her mother wasn't a witch *aligned* to *aether*... she was *of* the *aether*.

"So... you see... this is why there are two Pendragon sisters aligned to *aether*."

Rhiannon considered that another moment, before Marcella added, "'Tis also why it was possible to bind Seren and to deceive your mother. Even considering what she was, Morwen never suspected there could be two."

Blinking again in shock, Rhiannon felt as though she might purge the contents of her belly.

"This is also why I agreed to remove you from Blackwood... to keep you safe—not merely for Cael. But rather... because... well, in truth, neither you nor your sisters have any notion what you are capable of... and neither do *we*."

"We?"

"The Guard, of course."

Rhiannon's gaze shifted to Jack. His brow was furrowed as though this did surprise him. He stopped chewing and sat ruminating.

"Alas, you above all are an anomaly, Rhiannon. Born of *two* true-blood *dewines*, and bearing the *hud* of three..."

Rhiannon recognized truth in her words...

She and her sisters were each born with *dewine* blood, but her mother was in fact the essence from which they drew. They were demigods, like the cauldron-born *fae*... but Morwen... she was a Goddess, in truth.

"You share her blood," Marcella reasoned. "And yet, despite that your sister is to be Regnant, you are, indeed, an aberration. It could well be that, after five years, those manacles have weakened your affinities, but I cannot rest easy until I know your heart. As Jack here has said... you might, indeed, be England's salvation... but it could be that you will be its doom."

The look she gave Rhiannon was unmistakable, and the knife hilt at her boot glinted ominously against the firelight. "You, Lady Blackwood, are the reason I hunt my own kind."

Silence permeated the forest about them—a silence so complete that the flame in the pit sounded like a roar.

"And, by the by, before you think to judge me," Marcella added, "consider that before we are done, one of you—either you or your sisters—will put a blade through your mother's heart. Therefore, you are no better than a huntsman. Either you *will* spill Morwen's blood, else she'll spill yours, and for the good of the realm... I am prepared to slay you all."

CHAPTER

NINETEEN

WARKWORTH CASTLE

Exhausted from having awakened this morn to the ear-splitting sound of a babe's wails, Seren retired early, leaving her sisters to compare notes about their insatiable newborns—Elspeth's scarcely older than Rosalynde's.

Troubled by Isolde's words, she retrieved the sword from their workshop and took it into her chamber, laying it down gingerly upon the bed she normally shared with her husband. No doubt, the sword was a poor substitute for Wilhelm, though she needed its presence tonight to work through the growing turmoil in her heart.

Unlike Rhiannon, she had not spent her entire life preparing for the life of a priestess. She did not know what that should entail, nor did she comprehend what should be done to entreat the Goddess for her prophesied gifts.

She, more than any of her sisters, had been dutiful to Elspeth's mandates to refrain from practicing the Craft. Although Rhiannon had seemed to enjoy defying Elspeth at every turn—Rosalynde, as well—she and Arwyn had been less inclined to put their eldest sister into a fit of apoplexy. For Seren, it had never been worth the argument or distress, particularly when she'd thought her affinities so weak.

Only now that she understood *why* that was the case, she wished she had practiced more oft, although despite that she could do so freely now, she still didn't experience the joy Rhiannon did when she manipulated the *aether*.

Perhaps because of the binding spell, *magik* simply didn't come naturally to Seren, unless her emotions were heightened, and then, she couldn't control it. It rushed over her like a torrent and dissipated like the wind.

Practice, practice, practice, Elspeth now demanded —quite the change from the old days when she'd wagged a finger at them any time the Craft was employed.

So here she was.

Again.

But at least she didn't have to feel guilty over slipping away. Even her duties had been appropriated. So much as she had enjoyed helping Rosalynde with her chatelaine's duties, her sister's newborn babe was well cared for by a wet-nurse, and Rosalynde had insisted upon returning to her household duties so that Seren might "find herself in prayer."

But that was yet another thing Seren didn't particularly enjoy—prayer—perhaps, because, while at Llanthony, the priests had used it as a form of punishment, and never once guided them to do it properly.

Generally, once those monks were finished in the chapel, she and her sisters were ushered inside, and the doors were locked from Sext to None, while the monks were busy filling their bellies and sampling their ale. If she and her sisters couldn't manage to find peace through prayer during this time, they were encouraged to clean for three hours straight, whilst their bellies grumbled in complaint. The entire experience left a sour taste in Seren's mouth, and she had never truly allowed herself to learn to meditate thereafter.

Unfortunately, now it was imperative she learn.

Although she would like to say she wasn't frightened, she really was. She didn't have the same understanding about the Craft that Rhiannon had, nor was she born with her grandmother's gift of knowing. Rhiannon was the one who had, day after day, moment by moment, strengthened her prowess. She was the one who'd defied Elspeth to practice, and she was the one whose gifts now excelled. It didn't make sense that Seren should be Regnant, though she knew in her heart it was true. Once the truth was revealed, it was no longer so easily denied. So, then, one way or the other, she *must* find a way to fulfill the prophecy.

It was sheer desperation that led her to lie with a blade—cold steel against her warm flesh. She rested with one hand on the hilt, and hours later, eyes closed, she still lay next to the sword, as she deliberated the cryptic inscription...

There *must* be something in those words... *something*...

She could glean little from its story, no matter how many times she pored over the tales Isolde had told her. Aye, she knew the blade was enchanted. She also knew it glowed in the presence of evil. She knew it once belonged to Uther, and that it was forged by the Fair Men of Glastonbury, whose *dewinity* was bestowed, not by the Goddess, but by the Horned God of Donn, the Dark One from the House of the Dead. Whereas some people believed the Mother Goddess represented life, the Dark One represented death, and according to Isolde, his home, Cnoc Fírinne was where all souls gathered in death... beneath the Hill of Truth...

Take me, but turn the blade, and we will see...

So, then, if the sword was forged by the *Dynion Mwyn*, was *truth* the sword's most divine gift?

Could it be that *Caledfwlch* was meant to reveal the truth of her spirit?

In that vein, why did the sword glow blue in her mother's presence? But not in hers?

Why, indeed?

Because Morwen was evil?

Or because Morwen herself was truth?

And consequently, if Morwen was truth, what terrible brand of truth might she be?

Nay... this wasn't right.

There was a piece of the puzzle still missing—something Seren should have discovered in the *grimoire...*

She tried to remember everything Isolde had said...

Together, the Mother Goddess and the Horned God fashioned all things in their union, and because the Goddess herself was said to conceive and contain *all* life in her divinity, then *all* beings were divine by their birth, only without truth until it was learned.

More riddles, she hadn't a clue how to decipher...

According to the teachings of the Holy Church, if Eve was the representation of the Goddess, the snake in the garden must be the Horned God, and mayhap the apple he gave her was the incarnation of truth...

Take me, but turn the blade, and we will see...

Growing desperate, Seren concentrated harder, poring over all the things she'd learned...

A pentagram was also said to express truths about the hidden nature of existence. There was a very good reason it must be drawn in the proper order to accomplish a given task: Some spells called more to the Goddess, others to the Horned God. The five points, each aligned to an element, were ascribed to one or the other. But the fifth element, the *quintessence*, formed a marriage of both... essentially creating a divine child.

And yet, it was interesting to note that the elements were unevenly distributed, and more interesting yet was the fact that there were only three divine elements, and each of these were aligned to the Goddess.

How did these play in her role?

Or did they at all?

Take me, but turn the blade, and we will see...

According to Isolde, the gods were able to manifest themselves, either through dreams, or as physical beings, but also through the minds and bodies of a priestess or priest. The latter was essentially the making of a Regnant, whereby the Goddess must be called upon to bestow divine possession.

Only how was it done?

Compelled to examine the sword again, she opened her eyes, lifting it to inspect it, wondering that perhaps there might be a key in the artwork. Pressing, caressing, she admired the intricate design, running her fingers over the writhing serpents. But then, having found nothing, she laid the blade in her palm...

Take me, but turn the blade, and we will see...

Losing patience, she turned the blade, nicking her flesh so it bled... though not much... only a thin red line. And yet it was certainly blood. "Ouch," she said belatedly, lifting the sore hand to her lips, and lapping at a droplet of blood.

So much for imbuing the sword with divinity. Anyone who dared to face her mother with this accursed blade would be sorely equipped to survive the ordeal. She was beginning to feel like a failure. For weeks and weeks now, ever since Isolde put the thought in her head, she had been trying in vain to find her true self.

Find yourself, the woman had said, *then imbue Caledfwlch with the power of the divine.*

Then, and only then would she know what to do to save, not only England, but the Realm of the Living. It was a terrible burden to suffer for a woman who'd only ever coveted a normal life...

Take me, but turn the blade, and we will see...

Damnation.

By now, she had lain in this bed so bloody long that morning arrived, illuminating her room with a warm vestal light.

Time was her enemy.

Urgency quickened her veins.

Desperation wrenched her heart.

Outside, she could spy the first light of sunrise, and as it so happened, choosing that instant to return to her window, the damnable crow came to rest on her sill, its beady little eyes peering into her room.

"There you are," she said, annoyed. "Where have you been?"

"Caw!" it said, and then beat its shining wings.

Alas, she was going out of her mind. Speaking to a stupid little bird, who seemed to enjoy pecking holes in her sill.

Peck. Peck. Peck.

"You are *not* a woodpecker," she scolded the bird as it continued to worm its little beak into the fresh wood of her sill. Perhaps consuming insects? Or mayhap it was senile—like Isolde— and couldn't remember how it was that a crow was meant to behave?

Sighing despondently, Seren returned her attention to the blade, lifting it higher to admire the gleam of dawn light against the metal.

"I am unworthy," she said, with feeling. "Sweet Goddess, I am only a humble servant of men. Why must it be me?"

Tears brimmed in her eyes.

And then something unexpected happened.

As Seren tilted her head to better examine the reflection... the sword burst into flames, illuminating the room with its light. To her amazement, she held a raging fire in her hands, but it emanated no heat.

"Caw!" said the bird excitedly.

Mesmerized, Seren stared at the firelit sword for a moment longer, then lifted one hand into the pale golden flame, touching it with wonder. Inconceivably, it was cold, and the fire left her hand unharmed.

Drawing the hand away to inspect her fingers, she found them completely unaffected, and then instinctively, she lifted her hand again to the blade, turning the sword against the meat of her palm to nick her flesh...

This time she didn't bleed.

Withdrawing her hand again, she inspected it closely, and not only was there no second cut, the first cut was no longer present, nor was she scarred.

Take me, but turn the blade, and we will see...

A sense of quietude fell over her, a feeling unlike anything she had ever known in her life, a sense of purity that had no words. The room in which she lay faded to white, and she longed to rise—and did, though she had the sense that she did so only in her mind.

Surrounded now by a blinding array of white light, she heard a disembodied voice...

A drop of your blood to reveal,

The mysteries of life my sword conceals.

"Who are you?" Seren longed to ask, but her voice never emerged through the tightness of her throat.

The Goddess replied. "I am who I am, Seren Pendragon," she said, with a timbre that echoed throughout eternity. "You are blood of my blood, heart of my heart, soul of my soul."

A maternal face materialized from a cloud of white—eyes first, shaded the palest amber to mirror the flame of the sword in her hand. Kind and gentle eyes...

Next, she saw a perfect patrician nose. High, beautiful cheeks, like those of a Saracen's. Lush, full lips, like those of a Nubian Princess. Wings of a Valkyrie. Breasts, high, round and firm. Thighs, long and stout. Hair, flowing like a thousand rivers to the sea... She was every woman at once, and all these things rippled from the *aether*, forms in a cloud, inconstant, and ephemeral, almost as though if Seren dared to expel a breath, it would all dissipate and never reappear. Therefore, she held her breath.

"Come," the woman demanded, and Seren knew in her heart that she spoke to the Goddess. Quickly, sensing herself crossing time and space, she knelt at the feet of this exquisite creature, who seemed to embody every woman she had ever met... a heavenly body made of wind and fire and *aquavit*, all at once, though it hardly seemed possible.

The Goddess materialized fully then, her face furious and terrifying, a maelstrom of every sacred element, glowing and swirling like the eye of a storm.

"Where am I?"

Despite her terrifying visage, there was a benevolent note in the woman's voice, and her words rang like melody. "Some call it Heaven. Some call it Tween. Others call it the Other Realm. Only someday you'll know it for what it is... the dominion of the Sylph."

"Sylph?"

Your true kind.

"Caw, caw!" said the black bird from the dark recesses of Seren's mind, but it was not here in this place. It was perched on some windowsill in another world, one she no longer inhabited...

We are bound by destiny, to destiny bound,
I to you, and you to me...
Choose me or choose to be free.
As you will it, so mote it be.

"I... choose... you," Seren heard herself say.

"Caw!" said the black bird.

Art certain, child?
You do not sound certain.
The path you are destined to travel is perilous,

Only truth may light your way.

Wander into shadow and your soul will be the price you pay.

"I am certain," said Seren, and she felt the woman's smile like an ember burning through her breast.

Art willing to die for truth?

"I am."

"Caw!" said the black bird.

Will you shed your blood for love?

"I will."

"Caw!" said the black bird.

Will you sacrifice the fruit of your womb?

"I..."

"Caw!" said the black bird insistently.

Will you?

"A-Aye," said Seren, yet not so quickly.

The woman's voice, which had been soft and soothing before, filled with empathy, now boomed with the fury of thunder and the promise of retribution. Her face twisted so that Seren could no longer tell if she was male or female. Horns grew upon her head—horns like those of a stag.

The voice reverberated across the universe itself.

Now is the revelation of truth.

Now is the light of our kind born in you.

Now is the seed of all lies revealed.

Now is the verity of your words made known. If, indeed, you choose me, turn the blade, and we will see...

"Caw!" said the black bird, as an unseen wind stirred, growing now in intensity, whipping Seren's hair about her face, so that even in her dream state it stung her flesh like whips of fire. To her dismay, the longer she stood without making a true decision, the more violent the wind grew, and the tendrils of the Being's hair grew long, and fiery, like the appendages of a She Dragon in a raging lake of fire...

"I choose you!" Seren shouted above the din, fearing she'd angered the creature, but uncertain how.

The voice demanded, "If you choose me, turn the blade, and see..."

"Caw, caw!" said the black bird.

It was only belatedly that Seren realized she was still holding *Caledfwlch* in the palm of her hand—the Sword of Ages, the ancient blade of Uther and Taliesin. In that instant of realization, the sword erupted more violently with flame, only this time the flame turned as blue as the Endless Sea.

Arising from her knees with great difficulty, Seren dragged up the heavy sword along with her. Whereas before she'd felt weightless as a feather as she'd drifted to the Goddess, she now felt heavy as a lump of iron, anchored to the very spot where she stood, constrained as though by a thousand chains of steel. And yet somehow, though she wondered if she'd drifted back to sleep in her own room, on her own bed, she felt in the marrow of her bones that dream, or no dream, whatever choice she made here and now... whatever the result of this vision, she would carry the consequences in life... and death.

The voice was furiously insistent. *If you choose me, turn the blade, and see...*

In a moment of terror, Seren understood what He was saying. The creature meant for her to prove the veracity of her words with a willing sacrifice... only a sacrifice of her person... a sacrifice of her womb.

If you choose me, turn the blade, and see...

"Caw, caw!" said the black bird.

Only now, she understood, and once again, despite the angry face that glared down upon her, the same sense of quietude arose within her, and she knew... deep in her heart... if the Goddess was life, then, as her lover, the Horned God must be the one to light the spark of truth in her to create the Divine Child. She was the Divine Child. The Chosen One of her Age. The Regnant of her Day. But only if she gave herself to this sacrifice... and the sacrifice she now knew was a child of her womb. And yet if she chose this, she would be barren for the rest of her days. She would never, so long as she breathed, give Wilhelm a child of his blood. She would never know what it was like to be a mother...

Why? Even her grandmother had known the joys of childbirth. Why must *she* make this choice before ever having conceived?

Every path is different, my daughter... your child is every child...

The booming voice was gentle again, although it buckled and twisted against the wind, breaking like the voice of a youth on the verge of becoming a man.

Male. Female. Child. Mother. Father. Indistinguishable.

We are bound by destiny, to destiny bound,
I to you, and you to me...
Now you may choose or choose to be free.
As you will it, so mote it be.

Tears brimmed in Seren's eyes, but she steeled her heart and wiped her face. Now was no time to weep.

If she did not choose this now, it could be that no more children would be born to the realms of men.

If she did not choose this now, her sisters might die, as well...

So, too, would Wilhelm—the man she loved more than life itself.

If she didn't choose this, her mother's shadow would descend over the realm, extinguishing the light of this world, and the hearts of men would lie stillborn in a cradle of night.

With a defiant scream, Seren lifted the Sword of Ages and turned the blade—but not within her hand.

Understanding what was required of her now, she turned the blade so that its point was poised to enter her breast, and then with a sob, she fell upon it with all her might.

The sword pierced her flesh, filling her body with excruciating pain. It found her heart, and she screamed, sobbing over the death of her body, and suddenly, as the wind died, the clouds dissipated, all faces vanished...

She lay very still upon her bed... in the morning's first rays.

The black bird flew away.

For a long, long moment, she lay prone on the bed, confused, wondering how in the name of the Goddess she'd come to lie face down on the Sword of Ages.

"Seren!" said Rose as a flash of light illuminated the room and they saw her lying so still on the bed. "Seren!"

"Sweet loving Mother!" said Elspeth.

Seren heard the rush of feet to her bedside, felt her sisters shove her over, and lift her gently off the sword. She felt hands sweeping over her body, her breasts, her limbs...

The sword went clattering to the floor as someone hurled it from the bed, and the voices that surrounded her now sounded a bit less frantic.

"Was it another dream?" pressed Elspeth.

"I-I don't know! I heard her scream and thought it must be one of our babes."

A warm hand slapped Seren upon the cheek. "Seren?"

"Is she ill?"

"I don't know," said Rose.

"Wounds?"

"I see naught. Seren, wake up! Seren!"

"Look at her hair," said Elspeth, expelling the words with a gasp, as Seren opened her eyes.

CHAPTER

TWENTY

S leep eluded Rhiannon.

For the love of the Goddess, Cael hadn't freed her; he'd put her in the hands of a fellow executioner.

Didn't he know?

But, of course, he did.

We are not aligned, he'd said.

We are not aligned.

Tears pricked at her eyes as his words needled her heart, far, far more painfully than did any of the brambles she'd slept near. He'd kissed her good-bye, perhaps forever, and now it seemed that instead of saving her, he'd given her over to be murdered for the good of the realm?

Marcella claimed she was taking Rhiannon to her sisters—or at least, this was what Rhiannon had presumed. Only now that she considered it, *no one* had ever said they were taking her to Warkworth. *Had they?*

Nay.

Marcella had merely said she'd been tasked to "remove" Rhiannon from Blackwood, and yes, perhaps to keep her safe, but only so long as she didn't deem Rhiannon a threat to the Realm...

By the by, before you think to judge me... consider that before we are done, one of you—either you or your sisters—will put a blade through your mother's heart.

Therefore, you are no better than a huntsman.

Either you will spill Morwen's blood, else she'll spill yours, and for the good of the realm... I am prepared to slay you all.

Frustrated, Rhiannon turned on her pallet, peering into the treetops. By now, the fire had long since died, and she was cold, but she hadn't the wherewithal to cast a warming spell. Her teeth chattered viciously, perhaps more from nerves than from the chill. Every time Marcella or Jack turned in their beds, disturbing bracken, it made her heart leap painfully against her ribs.

She was afraid, she realized.

Terrified.

Perhaps for the first time in her life.

During these past few days, Marcella had managed to strip Rhiannon of her pride. She gave her a true glimpse of her own vulnerability. Rhiannon wasn't anyone's savior, nor anyone's protector. She was merely a woman, surrounded by uncertainty, who missed her husband... desperately.

Using her cloak for a blanket and her arm for a pillow, she tossed and turned, doing her best to avoid brambles. Alas, the more she fidgeted, the more they clawed at her, even as worry pricked at her belly.

She could leave, she realized.

Now, whilst they were still sleeping...

Like her sisters, she was a child of the forests. She might have a chance alone. She didn't know precisely where Warkworth was, but she knew it was north and close to the sea. She also knew how to gauge direction by the position of the sun. Whatever she didn't have in her saddlebag, she could forage from the land.

She didn't need these paladins...

Unfortunately, the horses were weary from so many long days. Like Rhiannon, they hadn't rested properly since leaving Blackwood, and if she left now, her poor horse would pay the price of her impetuosity.

So, then, she could travel afoot... concealing herself with *magik*, though Marcella was a *dewine*. She would know what signs to look for.

Anyway, Marcella would have use of the horses, and she also knew precisely where Rhiannon was going. Doubtless, they would pursue her till caught.

Going back wasn't very wise either. Although they'd managed to slip away, by now, Morwen was no doubt in pursuit. She would push her band to their limits to make up for lost time.

Nay, in the end, it simply wouldn't be wise to waste more time trying to escape a woman who, according to her own word, had been assigned to protect her. She *must* believe that Cael would never put her in the hands of a mercenary who meant to kill her. And yet, she lay there, confused by all she'd learned—one shocking revelation after another from the instant she'd left Blackwood.

Sylph...

Her mother was Sylph.

How was this even possible?

Sylphkind were beings Rhiannon had only ever heard of in legend—children of the Gods, so they said, formed of moon dust and spirit, ethereal as air. Said to be *skyspeakers*, they were able to communicate with creatures of the air—and this perhaps rang true, though it was unfathomable.

Moreover, how was it that something purported to be so exquisitely lovely could be so base?

By all accounts the *Sylphkind* were lauded to be creatures of beauty and love... untouched by the guile or greed of men.

They were said to be so fiercely beautiful that to look into the eyes of a Sylph could, in fact, blind like the sun.

Like Avalon, *Sylphkind* were like chimeras... here one instant, gone the next... ephemeral and without constant form. And yet, Morwen *did* have a physical form.

Sylph?

Truly?

Nay, it couldn't be... and yet... she knew the ring of truth when she heard it.

In the darkness, she was moved to examine her own hands— solid, with distinct human form. She had never once—not once—had an inkling she could shift her form. And yet, she, too, must have Sylph blood running through her veins—her sisters as well —though Rhiannon bled like anyone else.

More to the point, so did Morwen.

A memory filtered into her mind—her mother slicing a finger, not on accident. Using her dagger with the obsidian handle, she'd bled herself for a spell —*blood magik*, so she'd said. Only now that Rhiannon recalled... that dagger also glowed blue in Morwen's presence, like Rhiannon's manacles... and the key. The glow for Rhiannon was faint, more like a shimmer, but it was nevertheless there.

She tried to remember what her mother had said about the glow when asked… Rhiannon was four, watching, as her mother's blood dripped into a chalice. "What are you doing?"

"Can't you see I am busy, child? Go away!"

Much to Rhiannon's detriment, the *athame* had already captured her attention, and curiosity compelled her. She couldn't tear her gaze away from the ancient blade.

"Why does it glow?"

Her mother's sigh was disparaging. "Because it sees my true soul," she'd said, annoyed.

"Does it see mine?"

"Nay."

"Why not?"

Morwen's amber gaze sought her then, eyes slitted, and burning like coals. "Because you are imperfect," she'd said meanly. "Plain, ugly. Have you never looked into a mirror, child? Only a blind man will ever claim you with that affliction."

Disheartened, Rhiannon's lips had turned down at the corners, but even then, she'd refused to weep. One did not show weakness in front of Morwen.

Instead, a four-year-old's burgeoning fury had welled up inside her as her mother shouted for Elspeth. "Elspeth! Get this brat out of my sight, right now! Else I'll think better of it and drain her pitiful body of the blood I need for my spell."

Elspeth had rushed over at once, removing Rhiannon from her mother's proximity, whisking her out of the apartment and down into the castle kitchen to pilfer a sweet cake from the cook.

It sees my soul.

Did the *athame* leech from Morwen, like those manacles?

Nay. Nay.

Somehow, those two were the same, but not the same, because her mother still carried the *athame* on a chain about her neck. Therefore, the manacles must be changed by the binding spell etched into the metal.

Tenetur in argenteas

A capite ad calcem, tace, et sile

BOUND IN SILVER,

From head to toe, silent and still

Something about those words spoke to her sense of knowing, just as something about the blue shimmer of the metal seemed relevant to their cause.

It sees my soul.

Will it see mine?

Nay.

Why not?

Because you're imperfect.

Tears stung Rhiannon's eyes.

Sadness permeated her heart—sadness and anger.

In truth, she had never been a lovable child. Ellie used to claim she was born angry, and it was undeniable. And yet, why shouldn't she be furious? She'd suffered the death of her twin in the womb. Both had been close to death—poisoned by their own mother —and Morien had given up her life force to save Rhiannon. Her death gave Rhiannon the strength to be restored, and whilst her own heartbeat had strengthened over time, her sister's body began to decay in the womb. Most people might not recall events before their birth, but Rhiannon was not most people: She was a *dewine*. She remembered *everything*. She had a blood sister no one—not even her living sisters—had ever chanced to know. Only *she* understood the sacrifice Morien made for her that day. Only she truly knew the heart that stopped beating only for her—no less a sacrifice than the one Arwyn had made at twenty.

Pushing aside the pain of her reopened wound, she tried in vain to rest, resigning herself to her current path and realizing that they would have another long day. She bolstered herself with surety: No longer was she a poor, pitiful child dependent upon a cruel beast for a mother. She was a woman, grown, married for whatever good it might do her.

And Cael... he *did* feel something for her...

Something...

He'd kissed her much too passionately, his longing betrayed by the smoke in his eyes—eyes that made love to her despite that his hands and body never would.

Nay. She *must* believe Morwen was wrong: Someone did love her, even if their love was doomed.

Where are you, Cael?

Are you alive?

Please, please don't die.

Live.

Those gloomy thoughts held her transfixed. And then, at long last, when finally, she drifted into a fitful slumber, she heard Marcella rise. But at least the woman didn't immediately attempt to wake her. Rhiannon watched through slitted eyes as Marcella tapped her protégé with the tip of her boot. Jack rose at once, without complaint, and set about to righting their camp, but his demeanor, too, seemed changed this morn. Perhaps he, too, had come to understand something of his own fate, after the stories Marcella had shared by the campfire.

When they were ready to go, Jack came over to gently wake Rhiannon. "Time to rise," he said.

Rhiannon opened one eye to his winsome smile.

In the bright morning light, he didn't appear particularly sinister, and she was glad now that she'd remained.

She saw everything through new eyes. Knowing what she knew now, nothing would ever be the same.

Nodding sleepily, Rhiannon sat, then stretched—taking simple pleasure in the fact that she could do so without lifting heavy manacles. Even bone-tired, and riddled with midge bites, she must at least be thankful for that much, and this was proof that Marcella didn't intend to kill her—at least not yet. The paladin had left her free to defend herself, and there was no doubt in Rhiannon's mind that Marcella knew precisely what Rhiannon was capable of, even despite her dire words last night.

Without a word, she rose, still mulling over the night's deliberations. She led her mare to the brook to drink, and there, she knelt to lave the metallic stains from her wrists and refresh her face.

Peering into the water, she spied her own visage. The girl who stared back was sorely unkempt, though she was not plain or ugly. She was fierce, to be sure... dark copper hair, her features dark, as well—all but the bright blue eyes.

"You look exactly like her," Marcella had said.

And she did... only to be fair, her mother was more beautiful, even if her heart was black as a raven's wings.

Even if her gaze was so full of loathing that hate was *all* Rhiannon had ever gleaned from her.

It was no wonder Rhiannon had always despised her own reflection.

Plain. Ugly.

Have you never looked into a mirror, child?

Only a blind man will ever claim you with that affliction.

And yet, her eyes were no longer afflicted; they were blue... no longer crossed.

She could no longer deny the truth: She was not to be Regnant. And more, whether it be from the manacles, or nay, neither was she so strong as she liked to believe.

She would not grow up to slay this demon, not alone...

Everything she'd ever believed of herself mightn't even be true now that Seren was Regnant... beautiful, beautiful Seren... whose eyes... had always been blue... although she must have been *glamoured* by a spell so strong that not even Morwen had been able to see beyond the visage displayed.

Rhiannon sighed.

Life was not fair.

And no matter, despite that she'd like to be angry for having borne the brunt of a disfigurement that wasn't her own, she couldn't truly be angry at Seren.

Neither was Seren's beauty a lie; she was lovelier yet on the inside, and this is where it counted most.

Rhiannon had learned so much since leaving Blackwood... and yet, no revelation had shocked her so much as the knowledge that Marcella once knew her mother so well.

Loved her, in truth.

That was more than evident by the shine of her tears. They'd spoken louder than words. And yet, so much as Rhiannon wished to know more... she feared hearing more "truth."

How much more could she bear?

Heaving another sigh, she swept a hand across the visage of her face, dispersing the eerie likeness to a watery grave, and then, resolved to rise and face whatever the day might hold—until she heard a voice at her back, a voice she didn't recognize, and froze.

"Well met," said a man.

"Well met," said Jack, appearing behind her.

Marcella, too, crept into the vicinity, although she said nothing and Rhiannon came to be acutely aware that the paladin had moved into the space betwixt her and the newcomer, as though to defend Rhiannon.

Rhiannon daren't turn... not yet.

She stood slowly, reaching for her mare's reins as the animal continued to drink from the brook.

"Di' ye hear the news?" the man said joyfully.

"What news?" inquired Marcella.

Rhiannon heard only one man dismount, his feet landing in the bracken...

Was he traveling alone?

"At long last! We have peace!" When nobody spoke, he continued. "The King and Duke Henry have formed a new treaty."

"Before witnesses?"

"Aye," said the man, excitedly.

"Signed?"

"Not yet, though Duke Henry is withdrawing from Wallingford as we speak."

"What of the King's sons?"

"Bugger'em both," said the man.

Rhiannon brought herself to her full height, although for some reason, she was still afraid to turn and face the man, instinct warning her to keep her face hidden.

She could hear him walking his horse to the brook to drink, and wary though she might be, Marcella let the man pass. He was directly behind Rhiannon now, his horse stretching its long, shining chestnut neck to drink from the brook beside Rhiannon. In her periphery she saw that the stranger gave her a good, long look.

"What about Eustace?" Marcella inquired, perhaps to distract him.

"Ah, well," he said, turning to answer the paladin's question. "The fool's gone mad."

"Mad?" asked Jack. "How so?"

"Fool. He fled the King's marquee in a rage. Accused his father of ruining his life and swore to avenge himself. He took several barons with him, though most returned, falling to their knees and begging forgiveness. Seems Prince Eustace took it upon himself to relieve Bury St. Edmonds of God's due."

"God's due?" inquired Jack, moving closer to where Rhiannon stood.

"Gold, jewels, he took a bloody cartload."

Directly beside Rhiannon, the man's horse lifted its head and slid Rhiannon a long, black-eyed glance. She sent a calming spell to settle the mare, if only for good measure.

"Only Prince Eustace remains at large," the man

continued. "A few have been sent to locate the moron and return him to his sire, before he does more harm."

The man inhaled a long breath, and then slapped his belly. "If'n ye ask me, I believe that fool means to seek his Welsh witch."

Morwen.

"We mean to find her before he does," said the man, untying his breeches, and despite being in the company of women, he pulled out his cock and began to piss in the brook, yammering all the while.

"We?"

"A few of us. If you ask me, I don't know why the King would trust those Warkworth brothers to do his bidding when neither has ever had any love for him."

Silence.

"No matter, while they're preoccupied, we'll find that Witch and put her daughters down, as well— else we'll see them all packing to Rome, let the Church do their worst."

The silence persisted.

"If'n ye ask me... the Empress had the right of it all those years ago, burning that elder bitch at the stake. You know, I was there that day... she never screamed... not once... but those eyes... I felt cursed just the same."

Rhiannon's blood began to simmer.

Nobody had asked the man a bleeding thing, though he seemed to know everything. Sweet fates, she wanted to reach a hand into his throat and twist his tongue into knots.

All sound abated as the man continued to speak and the breath of the world came to pause... only the sound of his piss tinkling into the brook sounded at all.

Rhiannon swallowed her words, anger searing her veins. She had to hold herself back, because she longed to pounce on the man like a wild cat and scratch out his eyes.

"Wicked witches," he said. "I'll put a blade to their throats sooner'n they blink, and I'll do it right if I ever see one. Believe me, I will…"

Very, very slowly, Rhiannon turned to face the man, and everything happened so quickly. His eyes widened with recognition at the sight of her.

"You!" he spat, mistaking her for Morwen. Dropping his cock, his hand moved swiftly to the hilt of his sword, drawing the weapon from its scabbard as his breeches fell to his knees. "Vile, disgusting bitch," he spat.

Jack moved at once to stand in front of Rhiannon, and everything happened with a blur of motion.

The man spat another round of curses, but Marcella was quicker than he was, unsheathing a knife from her boot. She tossed the blade so hard, the thunk it made when it penetrated the man's skull was akin to the sound of an arrow piercing hard wood.

He didn't even realize what was coming. With the blade embedded in his forehead, he fell backwards into the bracken, with an arm dunked into the brook, and Marcella moved swiftly to cuff him with the heel of her boot, just to be sure. Satisfied, she cast one glance over her shoulder at Rhiannon, then bent to pluck the knife unerringly from the man's face. She wiped it on her tunic, then said calmly, "Let's go. It's not safe."

TWENTY-ONE

Abandoning the man's corpse, with his breeches trussed about his ankles and a pit in his forehead, they sent his horse traveling south, with an empty saddle, in hopes that it should distract anyone who came searching for him.

Jack took the lead, as Marcella took stock of her arrows, counting them and inspecting them one by one, then returning them to the quiver she kept on her horse.

"Where are we going?" asked Rhiannon after a while, at long last breaching the silence.

"North to the Pennines, then west," provided Jack.

"Your sisters are at Warkworth," said Marcella. "'Tis my duty to reunite you."

Rhiannon breathed a sigh of relief as the witch-paladin reached into her saddlebag and took out a sack full of something Rhiannon assumed must be filberts. Plucking a nut out of her sack, she popped it into her mouth, crunching very loudly, and swallowing before she said, "You appear relieved, Rhiannon."

Rhiannon averted her gaze from Marcella's shrewd eyes. "I-I thought—"

"I know what you thought," she said, and Rhiannon recognized amusement in her voice. "Apparently, it was agreed upon by all: Seren must be Regnant, but Rhiannon Pendragon is the hope of England."

"I thought you said—"

"I know what I said," Marcella interrupted. "But, truly, do you believe I'd be here if I hadn't come to believe it as well?"

Rhiannon turned to look at the woman, and Marcella proffered her a nut. Rhiannon shook her head, and Marcella placed it into her own mouth.

After a while, she said, "By the by, I've kept the manacles in my satchel, not to keep *you* away from *them*, or to save them to use later, but to keep *them* away from *you*... a subtle difference. Knowing what I know, I'd not have your energy siphoned when we need you most."

Rhiannon slid the paladin another glance, and Marcella said with a wink, "Cast away, *mon amie*. You need all the practice you can get."

"So, then... are we friends now?"

"Of a sort," Marcella said, with a crooked smile, and just at that moment, a small, bent-legged crow came to perch upon her shoulder. "Well, hello there?" she said, not at all surprised. She handed the bird a nut, as though it might take it, and when it cawed in protest, she put the nut into her own mouth, and said, "Suit yourself."

"You speak to ravens?"

Marcella's green eyes glinted. "*Paranoos* does not

suit you, Rhiannon. Does she look like a raven? Nay, *mon amie*, 'tis only a wretched old crow."

"Caw!" said the bird in complaint, and Marcella laughed.

But there it remained, seated atop her shoulder, watching Marcella eat her nuts, and all the while, Marcella chatted with the creature—a one-sided conversation that didn't make a bit of sense.

"So, 'tis done?"

"Aye?"

"Good."

"'Tis a relief, I tell you. I was beginning to believe it all in vain."

Rhiannon listened intently, but there was nothing at all said to enlighten her. Overtired from a night's lack of sleep, she decided to mind her own affairs, leave the daft girl to talk to herself. After a while, the crow flew away, and the trio continued in silence.

~

Warkworth Castle

After having spent most of these past four years fortifying Warkworth Castle in the event of a confrontation with Morwen, the Pendragon sisters now prepared to abandon their sanctuary. For the time being, their children would remain inside the curtain wall, and this time, Elspeth hadn't a single complaint over the state of their fortification. Indeed, it was better defended than Aldergh, and, really, more so than Westminster as well.

As a matter of practice, they kept two years' worth of rations inside the main fortification, and a second, smaller wall—also warded with complex enchantments—prevented anyone from entering their village.

Like the *witchwater* in the motte, anyone entering the general vicinity simply forgot where they were and wandered away.

Using each of their affinities to the best of their abilities, the sisters then cast separate defense spells.

Rosalynde enshrouded the castle with a mist that rolled for two miles beyond the outer wall.

Elspeth warded the interior with a spell that should keep all but its denizens at bay—and this time, no one would be allowed to enter.

Finally, Seren enchanted all the animals in the surrounding woodlands. Anyone approaching would discover themselves sorely abused by great, tusked boars.

Considering the circumstances, there was no rest for the weary—not even for a mother fresh from the birthing table. Rosalynde hadn't the luxury of time to nurse her newborn babe, so she gave the duty to her wet-nurse, and only now, as she stood peering down into her son's face, she couldn't help but recall her sister's desperation and fear when their mother had threatened her eldest child. Anxious to leave him, even despite all the precautions, she clung to young Richard with a new mother's desperation, kissing him very gently upon the forehead, before handing the babe back to his nursemaid.

Named for his grandsire, the boy went without protest, although his dark eyes, so like his father's, never left his mother—not till she vanished amidst a sea of armored men.

It was not normally a woman's place to lead armies, and yet, it was always presumed that, no matter how capable their champions were, in the end, it would be the Pendragon sisters who must challenge their mother.

After all, what good was cut steel against *hud du*?

Fortunately, all three sisters were wed to men who understood their lot in life, and who not only accepted their fates, but prepared them with all the skills and knowledge they would need to prevail.

Day after day, for four long years, Seren and Rosalynde had sparred with swords. Elspeth came now and again—nearly every time Malcom was meant to be away.

And finally, as a gift from the Holy Church, the sisters were each afforded ringmail suits, all blessed by the Pope and fitted to their precise measurements, complete with coifs, chausses, sturdy boots and gauntlets. Moreover, each sister rode a courser trained by the paladins, and the horses were lightly armored as well. Each sister wielded a finely honed sword, calibrated precisely for her weight and height... with one exception: Seren carried *Caledfwlch*, though *Caledfwlch* was meant for another.

Now, as Warkworth's army prepared to ride, messengers were dispatched to Malcom Scott at Carlisle, another to King Stephen at Wallingford, yet another to Duke Henry in place of Matilda. For all her years of battling Stephen's barons, the Empress Matilda seemed content enough to remain in Rouen and tend to affairs in Normandy.

Sadly, there was no guarantee anyone would answer their summons. After twenty long years, England was finally at peace. For all intents and purposes, their days of war were behind them. But little did anyone realize that the greatest battle of their day was soon to be waged... but not at Wallingford.

Sweet Goddess have mercy if this battle was lost.

If it was lost...

It wouldn't matter what peace Stephen and Duke Henry had wrought; England would face certain doom, dark days would descend on the land...

God save the realm.

Seren saw it all now.

She'd witnessed the tapestry of time weaving itself through the ages: the brotherhood of twelve kings, their *dewine* imbued swords; the bloodshed that ensued betwixt them; the betrayal at Llanrhos, where her forebear, Taliesin, conspired with Uther to take the life of the true Dragon Lord.

And, aye, she knew now what *he* was, as well—a Shadow Beast, whose soul was bound, and whose eternal life could only be ended by destroying the reliquary his soul was bound to.

And, more importantly, she knew what and who her mother was. Morwen had lived by many names: The Dark Goddess, the Shadow Crone, the Shapeshifter of Legend, the Mother of Avalon, Keeper of the Cauldron and Defender of the Grail. But there was only one true name for her: Cerridwen, destroyer of realms.

And still she was more: She was a true-blood daughter of the God and Goddess, who'd created all realms. She was, as Lucifer was, an angel fallen from grace, and in her true form, she was a Sylph—she who was tasked to protect the realms of men, and who, in her fury, betrayed her promises to the coven and was banished from Heaven and earth.

Morwen's soul, like Cael's and Mordecai's souls,

was bound to a reliquary, but for one very crucial difference: Hers was the soul of a goddess and could never be fully destroyed.

At best, they might hope to put an end to her mortal form.

As it happened, gods and goddesses did not die the same way mortals died, and the crux of it all was that, despite their immortal blood, a *dewine* was only a demigod, and therefore bound by mortal laws. They bled as men bled. Their hearts beat as all hearts beat. They were merely more attuned to the *aether*, which was, in its essence, the breath of life.

The day seemed bleak as ever.

The sun refused to shine.

At the end of July, there was a pall over the land that lingered, despite the season.

In truth, there was no reason to believe they would prevail. There were no more favors to be called upon from Scotia, or anyone else.

And, aye, the Church had sent its company of paladins, but it would never dare confess its true relation to the company of assassins, and neither would they ever acknowledge a preternatural threat to this realm that was directly opposed to their doctrine. No matter the truth, to their specifications, witches were not angels, or natural beings. They were aberrations of nature, to be feared and reviled.

And neither would they acknowledge any but the "One True God" and put no others before him, not even the woman who was his mate. England was a patriarchy in the truest sense.

Truth itself was a weapon to be feared, and therefore, a call for banners would be raised in the name of

England, but it could be that Warkworth's would be the only army to bear the King's standard.

As though to add insult to injury, the skies parted about midmorn, pouring down over the troops—a wet, cold deluge that dampened the spirits as surely it did the infantry, and even hope itself.

But this was no time for weakness in spirit.

No time for despair.

Every able-bodied warrior was conscripted to ride, and once the sisters were ready, they moved together to the head of the line, preparing to lead their warriors into battle.

Taking his cues from Rosalynde, Warkworth's seneschal rode to the helm. Loyal to his lord and lady, Edmund cried out to the gatekeeper. "Gates!" To his troops, he said, "Prepare to ride!" And then, if only because he insisted, he rode ahead of his mistresses to secure the way.

"Art ready?" asked Rosalynde of Elspeth as Edmund passed them by.

Elspeth nodded, and then both sisters looked to their Regnant—wholly transformed by her recent consecration.

White hair flowing at her back, face and skin radiant as a pearl, lips red as an apple, and cheeks rosy with color, Seren Pendragon moved to ride directly behind Edmund, with the sword Excalibur in her belt, and a small, bent crow riding atop her shoulder.

Their destination: Amdel.

TWENTY-TWO

First, they discovered the riderless horse.

Then, traveling in the direction from whence the horse had come, they happened upon a man's body lying next to a brook. Caught unawares with his breeches down, there was a bloody hole between the man's eyes where a sharp blade had once rested. The wound was deep, penetrating the skull, and to inflict such a wound, the assassin must have been very, very close, or very, very precise and skilled.

Since it didn't appear there was any sort of scuffle, Giles presumed the latter.

He knew only one woman who could wield a knife with such deadly precision: Marcella le Fae. But, if, indeed, she had passed this way with her charge, then everything was going according to plan and he must let them go. The sooner they found Eustace and returned him to his father, the sooner they could return home.

At his back, Wilhelm busied himself inspecting the boot and hoof prints surrounding the carcass. "These tracks are fresher than the rest," he said.

"Boot or hoof?"

"Both."

"How many?"

"One man, I believe. No less than fifteen stone, riding a courser, so it appears."

That was not Marcella. She was tall for a woman, not heavy. "Fresher than the rest, you say?"

"Aye," said Wilhelm. "'Tis as though he came lately and stopped to investigate."

"Same direction as the rest?"

"Aye," said Wilhelm, again.

"This one's a King's man," said Giles, examining the livery of the dead man. He wore Stephen's standard on the front of his gambeson. However, nothing on the horse they'd found, nor on the corpse had been pilfered, even so near to Darkwood. In fact, the horse's satchel still contained all his travel supplies and there was a small gold purse, filled with coppers, tied to his belt.

It was only by a stroke of luck they'd encountered the horse, standing beneath the shade of a tree, so they'd first thought, waiting for its master to return for it. It was a good-sized destrier of the sort normally conscripted for the King's army, and thinking it might be Eustace, Giles had put Wilhelm in charge of tracking. His brother could scout better than any man Giles had ever encountered, and for the most part, he trusted Wilhelm's instincts without fail. When they'd spied the vultures circling over this woodlot, they knew they'd found their man.

"How long do you suppose he's been dead?"

"Half the day, no more." Giles had seen more than his share of dead bodies to know. "How many traveling altogether?" he asked his brother.

Wilhelm shrugged. "Looks like four, mayhap, not including the dead man." He hitched a thumb at the corpse. "Appears to be three women traveling together, else three young men. The one following behind is more than twice their size and weight."

"Hmm," said Giles.

"Whoever the fourth rider is... he didn't linger long. He took a gander, then moved along."

"Neither did he bother to inspect the body," said Giles, pointing to the sack of coppers. "Else he hadn't much interest in coins."

"So, he's in pursuit of the others?"

Giles nodded. "That's what I gather. Can you tell which direction they are going?"

Wilhelm examined the woodlands, then peered up into the trees at the sun in the sky. "They came southwest, more or less, traveling northeast."

Indeed, they were traveling in the direction of Warkworth. Instinct told him that it must be Marcella, and if that was the case, she was coming from Blackwood, and the extrication had gone according to plan. He'd yet to reveal the plan to her sisters, because he hadn't wished to raise their hopes. In fact, he hadn't even told Wilhelm, because Wilhelm could keep no secrets from his wife. He didn't know who the fourth rider could be, but it wasn't Morwen. That witch wouldn't be traveling alone unless it was her manservant. But this was a big country, and, in fact, it could be anyone—Eustace, included.

He didn't say so, however. If, for an instant, Wilhelm thought there might be danger en route to Warkworth, God himself couldn't keep the man from returning home. Nay, he had long ago learned to follow his gut, and his gut said to let this go, and continue their mission.

It went against his sense of propriety to steal a dead man's coins, so he left them where they were, knowing good and well that they would be gone with the next passerby.

So be it. Better it should go to someone in need. He had plenty of his own.

"Do you know to whom these lands belong?" asked Wilhelm, still studying the landscape.

Giles peered about, and said, "I'd gander 'tis a Royal Forest, perhaps Morfe, south of Wellington and Amdel?"

"Beauchamp's seat?"

"Perhaps," said Giles as he nodded. "The idiot. Word came whilst I was still at Wallingford... he met his end at the end of Blaec d'Lucy's blade."

"Will he be punished?"

"D'Lucy?" Giles shook his head. "Nay. To the contrary. He's been raised to Earl by order of King Stephen. His brother renounced the seat."

"Will Duke Henry honor it?"

Giles shrugged again. "Who knows, brother."

Wilhelm scratched his head. "What of Beauchamp's land?"

"Haven't a bloody clue," said Giles. "He's survived by a sister, who's, in fact, wed to Blaec, so I don't know how it will reconcile. What I do know is that Stephen will take his counsel from Duke Henry, and Duke Henry will not welcome the opportunity to reward Stephen's barons. Rather, he'll award lands to those who supported him."

Wilhelm pointed down to the corpse. "Think he's one of the men who rode out with Eustace?"

Considering everything, Giles peered over at the dead man's horse. The animal might slow them down, but it would be cruel to leave it to fend for itself. "Could be," he said. "But if so, I'd warrant it wasn't Eustace who killed him. That greedy bugger would have taken his coins."

"Probably," said Wilhelm, with disgust. "Could be this one left him and met a poor end on his own. With Darkwood so close, there's no telling what skamelars lay in wait."

"Very true," said Giles, and then both their gazes slid one toward the other. "Are you thinking what I'm thinking?"

"Amdel lies empty?" asked Wilhelm.

Giles nodded. "Aye."

"Do you think Eustace might be there?"

"I don't know," said Giles, lifting his brows. "Let's go see."

~

Dinogad's shift is speckled, speckled,
Made from marten pelts.
'Wee! Wee!' Whistling.
We call, they call, the eight in chains.

Marcella's Welsh lilt was a trace more apparent now as she sang. But it wasn't only the diction of her words... the song was oddly familiar, leaving Rhiannon with an inexplicable note of dread...

When thy father went a-hunting,
A spear on his shoulder, a club in his
hand,

He called the nimble hounds,
'Giff, Gaff; catch, catch, fetch, fetch!'

"That song," she said, trying to place it.

Marcella shifted her dark eyes. "'Dinogad's Shift,'" she said, and sang the verse again in their native tongue—far more eloquently than Rhiannon could ever have.

Pan elei dy dat ty e helya;
Llath ar y ysgwyd llory eny law.
Ef gelwi gwn gogyhwc.
Giff gaff. Dhaly dhaly dhwg dhwg.

The paladin smiled then, and for the first time since meeting Rhiannon, that smile lit her lovely green eyes. "My mother used to sing it to me when I was a girl," she explained.

"Seems to me I've heard it before."

"Aye, well... no doubt you have, Lady Blackwood. Your mother enjoyed it, too."

Rhiannon tapped a finger to her breast. "*My* mother?"

The paladin nodded, though it was impossible to imagine Morwen as a wee girl enjoying anything so achingly sweet as a lullaby. *That* was *not* the woman Rhiannon knew, and if Morwen had ever even once sung Rhiannon a song, the memory was long overshadowed by all the atrocities she'd committed since.

Nay, indeed, there was nothing tender in her memories of Morwen. But Rhiannon supposed she still could have heard the song through Elspeth.

Of all her siblings, Ellie was the only one who'd ever really known their maternal grandmother, and for all that Rhiannon had received Morgan's gifts, she'd never once met the good lady face to face—a fact she was sorely aggrieved by, if not for the blessing of a hug, then for the sake of her Craft.

There were few souls remaining who'd studied the Old Ways. People no longer believed in *faefolk*. Or even the wonder of ordinary *magik*—the birthing of a babe, the life-giving warmth of the sun, the gathering of dew in the curve of a leaf, or in the metamorphosis of a caterpillar into a moth.

Magik, in truth, was not so uncommon as people were accustomed to believing. All living creatures had some ability within them, be it a simple sense of knowing, or the ability to heal (far less extraordinary than people presumed). The minds of men, whether they knew it or not, were very attuned to the *aether*.

Rhiannon sighed heavily, only to find that Marcella was still watching her—always watching, as though she were a specimen under a philosopher's glass.

All the while, Jack rode behind them, silent and thoughtful—as he had been since departing the brook.

Marcella turned for an instant to regard him, and then, after a moment, returned to her tale.

"The song was written about a warrior of the Britons led by Urien ap Cynfarch. Do you know him, perchance?"

Rhiannon gave the paladin an impish smile. "Alas, I never had him for tea," she jested, and Marcella laughed, a nice sound that filled Rhiannon with something like joy.

It was the first time in all her life that she'd had a confidante besides one of her sisters, and she was beginning to discover that she liked it. Marcella was brusque betimes, but no more so than Rhiannon, and she was most definitely the sort of woman someone would want on their side—fierce, loyal and smart. "'Tis a widow's lament?"

"Nay, nay... not so much a lament, as her praise. In the song, she fashions her babe a beautiful smock made of pelts that her husband hunted for her before his death."

"Because, definitively, that is all a man should ever be remembered for," quipped Jack at their back.

Ignoring the barb, Marcella continued. "When she discovered her husband had perished along with his lord and king, she offered the verse to his bard..." Marcella slid Rhiannon a meaningful glance. "Whose daughter also happened to be Urien's widow."

"I suppose the poor lady meant to commiserate with the widow through song? It makes sense she would give it to his bard."

"Perhaps." Marcella nodded. "Else... it could be that she simply wished to have the bard publish her song. He was very well regarded. In fact, after Urien's death, his daughter made a far more prodigious match."

"Aye?" said Rhiannon, only half listening now. It was a little difficult to concentrate because Marcella kept looking back over her shoulder, as though someone might be following. "Who did she marry?"

Marcella's brows lifted. "Well... of all people, she married Orkney's King Lot, who... by the by... also happened to be a vassal and half-brother to Uther Pendragon."

Rhiannon's eyes shifted to meet Marcella's. She

opened her mouth to speak, but closed it again, realizing that this wasn't idle chatter.

Clearly pleased by Rhiannon's response, Marcella continued. "You see... all of Urien's brothers were quite ambitious. Another one, Angus, ruled Moray and Scotland. Twelve brothers in all, every one of them granted swords that were forged by the *Dynion Mwyn*, each imbued with properties meant to ensure their victory against foes. Together, they formed a Fellowship of Twelve, whose sole intent it was to rule Britain altogether, including Alba and Wales."

"Blood brothers?" asked Rhiannon.

Marcella turned a palm. "So 'tis said. But there, as they say, rests the fly in the ointment. Each of the brothers claimed to be sons of Ambrosius, the old Roman Emperor, and meanwhile, the High King of Gwynedd was not a son of Ambrosius. Rather, Cadwallon was a grandson of Cunedda's, and his claim to the throne was stronger than any of Ambrosius's sons, even despite that Ambrosius led and won so many battles against the Saxons.

"Only then, to make matters worse, Cadwallon urged his son to slay his uncle so that Cadwallon could seize his brother's lands. It was a fair share of Wales, mind you. Afterward, Maelgwn was so aggrieved by his part in the scheme that he put himself into a monastery, and the Fellowship presumed he'd forfeited his father's lands. Later, when the old man died, Maelgwn was called to return, and, naturally, this set the Fellowship's teeth to grinding. They formed a plan to murder Maelgwn. But Urien and Maelgwn were close allies, and Urien objected. Later, when Urien, too, was found murdered, it was believed to have been perpetrated by none other than the bard in his court—coincidentally the same bard who'd plotted with Uther to kill Maelgwn."

Rhiannon experienced a chill as Marcella slid her another meaningful glance.

"That bard… was Taliesin," Marcella said, and then cast another long look over her shoulder.

"My—"

"Aye," said Marcella quickly, though she frowned, and rushed to say, "Apparently, King Urien had the misfortune of allying himself to the Dragon Lord, and Uther coveted not only Maelgwn's territories, but Maelgwn's daughter, as well."

"So, then, if Urien's wife was Taliesin's daughter—"

Marcella nodded again, and said, "Precisely. But she was Morgan le Fae, not Yissachar. As it so happened, Yissachar was wed to Uther, and, later, after Maelgwn was murdered, Uther took the Dragon Lord's daughter as his concubine. She, as you know, gave him Arthur."

"Igraine," said Rhiannon, leaning forward to pat her mare's withers. "But these are all my forebears," she said. "Why have I not heard these tales before now?"

"In truth lies power," suggested Marcella.

And then she snorted inelegantly. "Really, in a sense, what happened in those days is not so different from what has happened between Stephen and Henry. History is ever destined to repeat itself, and so, it seems, man is not content to abide; he must always rule."

Rhiannon liked the way Marcella thought; they were very well-aligned. "Goddess forbid that any man should ever bow to a woman! Matilda never had a chance."

In fact, her half-sister had spent most of her adult life trying in vain to win her father's barons. Even with the help of their cousin, Robert of Gloucester, few of them had ever championed her. She'd gone to battle beside them, and it didn't matter. After her last stand at Devizes some years ago, Rhiannon heard she'd departed England. And, so much as Rhiannon had never had too much love for the half-sister Ellie liked to champion so much, she did feel sorry for Matilda. She also suffered righteous anger over the fact that anyone would be denied their birthright simply because she was a woman.

"How utterly painful it is to sit and listen to women speak of men," complained Jack. "You must realize it is not only men who aren't content to abide. The Empress fought tooth and nail for twenty long years to regain her father's throne. Now, do you believe she'll be content to abide, as you say?"

"Aye," said Marcella, casting a sharp glance over her shoulder. "Prithee, Jacques, where is she now? I'll tell you where she is: Home, tending to her house, supporting her son from afar. That is what women do when they lose."

The younger paladin lifted a brow, and said, "I warrant ambition is not only a man's vice, *mon patron.*"

Marcella curled her lip at the youth, and offered him her back, and Rhiannon gloated over the endless, but amusing, contention between them.

She could easily see that the two were oddly enamored of each other—only like children vying for supremacy. Indeed, it seemed to Rhiannon that Marcella considered herself well beyond Jack's years, and therefore, beyond his reach as well. But Jack wasn't content to let it lie, even after Marcella had confessed her true age.

No doubt he'd been brooding ever since, but Rhiannon noted the way he looked at her whenever Marcella wasn't looking. He loved her, in truth, and age didn't matter to him at all.

Dismissing Jack, Marcella returned to her tale, and this time Rhiannon was far more attentive...

"So, now you have both Taliesin's daughters wed to brothers—Yissachar to Uther and Morgan to Lot.

"One day," she continued, "the sisters learned their husbands were brawling over Igraine. Yissachar became convinced that it was all Igraine's fault, and in a fit of rage, she took Uther's sword and slew his concubine... spilling Igraine's blood with the very same sword that once slew her father."

"*Caledfwlch*," Rhiannon surmised.

Marcella nodded again. "Aye."

The two shared a knowing look, and Marcella continued again. "So, now, fearing to lose his beautiful bride, Uther defended Yissachar to the Church, saying it was all the fault of the sword. He claimed it was cursed, and thus Yissachar was spared, banished to Blackwood for her crime."

Rhiannon nodded, then sang...

"Blackwood, Blackwood, there she remains,
All through the dark and light of day.
Eyes o' fire, and bright-silver mane.
Summer to winter and summer again."

Marcella nodded as Rhiannon finished her verse. "That's the one."

"So, what happened to Uther's sword?" Rhiannon asked.

"The Church confiscated every weapon that Taliesin had forged with the *Dynion Mwyn*—twelve altogether—and they established an elite Guard, awarding each paladin with a sword that formerly belonged to the Kings of Briton."

"The Papal Guard," Rhiannon surmised. "And whose sword do you carry?"

"I believe it was Urien's."

Rhiannon turned to ask Jack, "And yours?"

The young man coughed indiscreetly. "I'm not yet worthy to carry a Sword of Power."

"You will in time," returned Marcella, without looking at the young paladin.

"When?"

"When I die," she said matter-of-factly, after which, another length of silence ensued.

It was, perhaps, a prospect Jack didn't relish, but to Rhiannon it made perfect sense. If, in fact, there were only twelve swords altogether, unless an officer of the Guard should perish, there were no more swords to hand about. She knew Giles had given his sword to Rosalynde, but that was another matter entirely. Naturally, such was the nature of these things; someone would have to die before another sword was granted.

"Who else possesses a sword?"

Marcella smiled forbearingly. "That is not something I'm at liberty to say, but I can tell you this much: One sword never left Alba."

"David of Scotia?" Rhiannon said.

Marcella confirmed nothing, but she said, "You're

quite astute. It took me years and years of investigations to put all these stories together."

"To great avail," allowed Rhiannon. "You know your histories far better than anyone I have ever met."

"Well, I made it a point to know," Marcella said, "all for the sake of a man I once loved." And then she averted her gaze, into the woods, and Rhiannon sensed intuitively that she must be speaking of Cael, although something in the paladin's expression kept her from inquiring.

"So, what happened to the other sister?" inquired Jack. "The one called Morgan."

It took Marcella a while to respond.

"Well... it was Yissachar who slew Igraine, so they let her be. In keeping with our kind, she grew to be a very, very, very old woman. She escaped the fate of many of our kind, simply by virtue of the fact that her husband was conscripted to the Guard. Meanwhile, Yissachar languished in her tower, and, by decree of the church, they purged the remainder of *dewinekind* from the realm."

Jack sounded incredulous, and perhaps a little incensed. "Uther allowed it?"

Marcella lifted a brow, casting Jack a backward glance. "Allowed?" she said. "My dear, Uther *led* them. Do you not pay attention to your studies, ever?"

Rhiannon frowned.

In all her years, she had never heard their story told so succinctly and so candidly. So, it seemed, her kindred were a bloodthirsty and treacherous lot—including Taliesin.

It left much to be considered—particularly Taliesin's entire role in Cerridwen's tale. Verily, if the man they'd been led to admire and emulate, was, in fact, a thief and a murderer, then what else could be expected from a man who'd steal a mother's curative? Of course, she was speaking of the potion Cerridwen brewed for her son Morfran... that boy whose fate Rhiannon had always believed she'd shared.

Of all people, Rhiannon knew well enough what it felt like to be reviled for the way she looked. Only now that her face was altered, it didn't eradicate the pain of her youth. In her mind's eye, she was still that wretched little girl, with the crossed eyes, and a temper as wild as her hair.

So much of what she'd come to know was utterly wrong.

In the stories she'd heard about Taliesin, he was the one who was pursued and persecuted. He was the golden mage whose wit and wisdom united kingdoms. He was the wise druid, whose name was known and respected by the Romans. He was the falcon who'd guided them.

But, in reality, there was another way to perceive the tale, and in this new light, he wasn't the least bit flattered.

It was not enough that he'd stolen from those less fortunate, but he'd also befriended the man who'd stolen the Witch Goddess's daughter, and then he'd turned her against her own mother, only to marry her as well, even amidst their mother's bitter protests—an incestuous relationship that purportedly enraged Cerridwen. And it was all because of her fury that Avalon was ultimately destroyed. Considering all this, it didn't seem entirely fair that Taliesin somehow escaped the wrath of the gods.

In fact, now that Rhiannon considered it, she understood why, after being possessed by the Witch Goddess, that Morwen had bedded her own brother—an eye for an eye, she supposed. After all that had been done to her, her heart now burned with an ember of hatred that could no longer be extinguished. She was the sum total of her life, Rhiannon supposed, and now she also knew why the Witch Goddess was so bent upon revenge—if only she didn't also have the grave misfortune of knowing that the Witch Goddess was also Morwen. And therefore, whatever Morwen was in theory, it was hardly what she was in the flesh...

Still, she was a daughter herself, cast aside and forsaken.

She was a wounded creature, dangerous and resentful.

She'd lost everything throughout her life—husband, son, her beauteous daughter, her precious isle, and her standing with the gods... Naturally, all Rhiannon and her sisters were to her now were bitter reminders of the betrayals she'd suffered throughout her life. And really, since she was only borrowing Morwen's body, in her eyes, they were children of Taliesin's, not hers. They were ungrateful half-breeds, who shouldn't be allowed to wield the gifts of the Chosen Ones.

So much made sense now.

And yet, it didn't make the pain of her mother's existence any less difficult to bear. Morwen's pain had become her daughters' pain, and now she hadn't any more mercy to give—not if you also understood that it was mercy for Taliesin, the babe, that allowed him to live. And then he grew up to be her ruin.

Alas, so it seemed, there were no true heroes in

this tale—none save the innocents who'd found themselves in harm's way.

"Rhiannon," said Marcella, gently, perhaps realizing how difficult it must be to accept all these truths—one terrible revelation after another since departing Blackwood. She was like a *hud du* doll full of pins, scarcely able to bear the thought of another. Slowly, pensively, Rhiannon lifted her gaze to her new friend.

"There is one lesson you *must* take from this tale…"

"Me?"

Marcella nodded portentously. "Of all the swords that were forged by the *Dynion Mwyn*… only one was forged in the spirit of betrayal; it might yet lend itself to this game."

Rhiannon furrowed her brow. "What are you saying?"

Marcella's voice was sober. "What I am saying is that, indeed, *Caledfwlch* is cursed. 'Twas made to beguile Maelgwn ap Cadwallon, and with that sword, Uther slew him. Later, Lot slew Urien—again, with the same sword. And then, after, Urien's wife slew Maelgwn's daughter… Do you understand what I am saying?"

Rhiannon thought she did, though it seemed to her that Marcella was trying to say something more.

"If Taliesin's own daughter was not immune to *Caledfwlch's hud du*, neither are we."

"My sister Rosalynde has the sword now. Are you saying she will betray us?" Rhiannon was horrified by the prospect.

Marcella gazed at her mournfully, and Rhiannon shook her head adamantly. "Nay! She would never.

My sisters would not. Arwyn died to protect Seren—she *died*!"

The look in Marcella's eyes was full of pity. "Calm down... all I am saying, *mon amie*, is that when the time comes... there is one among us who could be swayed. And..." She shook her head. "That is all I can say; because to say more wouldst be a betrayal."

"To whom? My mother?"

Marcella laughed bitterly. "Oh, my friend, you cannot betray someone you are not aligned with."

"Cael?"

"Ah," she said, lifting a finger, then wagging it. "There's the rub... Lord Blackwood's part in this tale is his alone to tell. But now I shall truly say no more, because the Law of Three does not only apply itself to the Craft of the Wise, I fear."

Rhiannon's mind whirled. What role in this pageantry could her husband possibly play?

And then suddenly, another thought occurred to her. "If you and my mother were..."

"Lovers?" Marcella finished.

"Aye. Then why didn't she remember you at Blackwood?"

Marcella pursed her lips. "Oh, believe me. She remembers. She's the one who introduced me to Cael, and no matter what we once were to each other, she was all too willing to use me to her service. She was merely too arrogant to—"

"What?"

Marcella reined in her mount suddenly, sidling about to face Rhiannon. "Never mind," she said quickly, sliding from her saddle. "None of that is important."

"Then why have you told me these things?"

"Because," she said, "it could be there won't be another opportunity."

"Why not?"

Marcella nodded toward the bright sunlight at the end of the forest lane, and said, "We've kept to the woodlands as much as possible. Soon, we'll be leaving Cannock and we'll not encounter shelter again until Macclesfield or High Peak. But that is not our immediate concern."

"What is?" asked Rhiannon.

"We're being followed," said Jack.

TWENTY-THREE

Whatever awkwardness existed between the paladins, it vanished in that moment. They moved deftly together, like a choreographed dance, as though teacher and student had already rehearsed their parts.

Jack responded by moving forward to sweep up the reins of Rhiannon's mount, drawing her off the road.

A glance about revealed that Marcella had chosen a spot to their advantage, with ample shelter on either side of the lane.

Even as Rhiannon dismounted, Jack was already down from his mount, unsheathing his dirk.

For her part, Marcella stood squarely in the middle of the lane, defiant and fearless, preparing to face their pursuer alone—a single rider who revealed himself without delay.

Rhiannon gasped aloud, her heart kicking against her ribs as she realized who it was...

Cael.

It was Cael.

No longer dressed in the finery of their wedding

ceremony, he looked like a dark lord emerging from a mist.

Dressed in the accoutrements of war, he and the horse came trotting up the narrow path, his slow but purposeful gait deceptive in its casual affectation. Beside him traveled a lone, gray hound, eyes as yellow as a wolf's, the head nearly as tall as the belly of his mount.

But though his pace was easy, there was little about him that was carefree. He moved fluidly with his destrier—a monstrous beast unlike any Rhiannon had ever beheld, and he wore his great sword tucked behind his back, with the pommel rising over his head so he could easily grasp the hilt. He appeared larger than life, and only for an instant, her knees went weak as pudding.

Fortunately, Jack caught her before she fell, but then he put a small blade to the tender flesh of her neck, as though to threaten her. Shocked by the sting of cold metal, Rhiannon unleashed her *hud du* and the knife in Jack's hand heated swiftly, glowing red like fresh hammered steel straight from a forge. Jack yelped and dropped the knife.

Casting him an annoyed glance, Rhiannon rushed into the lane to stand beside Marcella, but here, again, the elder paladin seized her by the tunic, dragging her back behind her. "Damnation!" complained Rhiannon, but Marcella ignored her, her attention affixed to the approaching rider.

"I'll not allow you to return her to Morwen," said Marcella, and lest anyone mistake her meaning, the paladin withdrew the sword from her scabbard and held it at the ready.

Calm as ever, Cael kept his saddle even after he

halted, his dark eyes looking past Marcella to Rhiannon.

"I do not intend to," he said, with a half-smile that materialized only for her.

"Bedamned! If that is true, then love for this woman has compelled you where I could not, and now you have endangered everything!"

"Indeed, I suppose I have," he said without much concern, leaning forward in his saddle, with a shrug.

Still nursing his hand, Jack emerged from the thicket, and if Cael had witnessed Rhiannon's act of defiance, he must have approved, because he glanced at Jack with lifted brows, then turned a devastating smile toward Rhiannon and winked.

That small gesture of approval sent heat surging through Rhiannon's veins and a slow burn crept into her cheeks. Even so, she kept her feet planted behind Marcella, uncertain what to do. *"We are not aligned,"* he'd said.

So how was it possible they suddenly were?

They were not.

So why is he here?

To return her to her mother?

Never!

She daren't believe a word he said.

He stabbed a thumb over his shoulder. "I'm guessing this was your work I spied by the brook?"

He directed the question to Marcella.

"The bloody fool recognized her," said Marcella, though she didn't lower her sword. "What else would you have me do?"

Cael's grin widened, and Rhiannon watched the pair closely. Cousins, they most definitely were *not*. She recognized the heated look they exchanged, but

Cael's gaze cooled at once, and Marcella groaned as he swung his leather-clad leg over his mount and slid to the ground. Still, he made no move to unsheathe his sword, and finally, Marcella lowered hers.

"I meant every word I said, Cael. I am tasked to keep Rhiannon safe, and I wouldst do so on pain of my life—no matter what you say, I'll not be swayed!"

"I warrant she can take care of herself," said Jack darkly, sucking on a finger.

Cael approached them, still making no move to retrieve his sword. "As I've said, I'm here to help."

"Why?"

"Because she's my wife, lest you forget."

And with that, he met Rhiannon's gaze, begging her to... *what? Understand?*

Her heart did a little leap in her breast, though she didn't know what she was supposed to say, much less feel, or do.

Indeed, they were man and wife, but in name only, *and yet...*

And yet...

And yet...

She lifted a finger to her lips, remembering his impassioned kiss, and Cael grinned like a well-satisfied cat.

"Why should I trust you?" persisted Marcella.

Hardening his voice, his gaze returned to Marcella. "Ever once, have I lied to you?"

Marcella's tone was rueful. "Nay."

"Why would I begin now?"

For a long, long moment, the pair glowered at one another, and then Marcella conceded. "Swear to me you are not here in the service of Morwen!"

"I am not here for Morwen," he said calmly. "I am

here…" His black eyes met Rhiannon's again, as he said, "For her."

Apparently satisfied—or as much as she could be under the present circumstances, Marcella re-sheathed her sword, and said, "Then you are a stupid fool. Then, again, from what I know of you, you have always been a fool, Cael d'Lucy, and far be it from you to ever listen to the advice of a woman."

THEY DECIDED TO MAKE CAMP, but not for the evening, only to rest the horses and sup, then prepare a new strategy.

Now that Cael had joined them, with news of Morwen, it was perhaps wiser to take stock of their circumstances.

Accordingly, whilst they waited for Jack to return with a stitch of firewood, Cael perched himself on a fallen tree to share some of the details of his return to Blackwood.

Apparently, it was Cael who'd loosed the hounds. One lone wolfhound refused to leave him and re-mained stubbornly by his side. The enormous beast sat quietly behind him, his eyes never leaving its mas-ter. He was like Rhiannon, she supposed—painfully loyal, invisible, besides.

Like that hound, she listened quietly as he dis-cussed his *politikal* matters with Marcella, only now and again sliding Rhiannon a black-eyed glance.

Marcella relayed the news they'd heard from Stephen's man this morn—a happenstance that Cael was apparently already aware of. Evidently, he'd been privy to some of the negotiations while he was still in attendance at Wallingford. Perhaps perceiving what was to come, Morwen had summoned him home some weeks past, with demands that he marry Rhiannon once and for all. As of that time, the King and Duke Henry hadn't yet reached any agreement, although it was apparent they would soon.

Stephen no longer had the will to fight. His eldest living son wasn't fit to rule. Nor did his youngest have the mind for *politiks*, although Cael suspected William simply wasn't bold enough to claim what he wanted. Unlike Eustace, who was brazen and stupid, William would be the sort to skulk about in the shadows and steal what he wanted through cunning.

The King's sons had inherited much from their mother, because even despite usurping Henry's throne, there were many who claimed he was only complicit because he'd believed it was for the good of the realm. Greed was not his sin. Doubtless, he no longer considered this to be the case, and his actions spoke volumes. He was already distancing himself from Morwen, and, with his wife dead, he could far more easily confess the iniquities of his elder son.

As for Morwen, evidently Cael had given her the draught that was intended for him, and this was why she hadn't given immediate pursuit. In fact, according to her husband, she could be sleeping still, though Rhiannon doubted it. The laws that applied to others did not apply to Morwen. She was, indeed, a force to be reckoned with; the time to face her was growing nigh. Even now, there was an impending sense of doom in the air—a prescience that manifested itself like an ague in the bones, a damp chill that raised the small hairs on her nape.

"By the by," said Cael, with a wink for Marcella.

"Well done. She never once thought to inspect her cauldron."

The paladin blushed, a rare hint of color appearing in her high cheeks. She looked softer and more vulnerable than she had since Rhiannon met her. She smiled coyly. "Doubtless it was the sweet rot of lilacs," she explained.

"Brilliant suggestion," he said. "I only hope she directs her anger accordingly when she wakes." He exhaled sharply. "I left her with a hall full of sleeping guests."

Rhiannon grimaced, hoping her mother would be in too much of a hurry to waste time with punishments. Still, it was impossible not to consider the worst-case scenario—that she would wake and slaughter all those innocents, whose worst crime it was to try to curry favor with the lord of Blackwood by attending his wedding.

In any case, she was relieved to know Cael wasn't there to suffer whatever fate her mother deemed appropriate.

"They are safer without you," suggested Marcella. "I warrant she would have abused them only to spite you."

"I considered that," admitted Cael.

"Any news of Mordecai?"

"No sign of him. He did not arrive with Morwen, nor did anyone mention him thereafter. She must have put him to another task."

"Clearly, she trusts you," said Rhiannon, acerbically.

Cael merely shrugged, ignoring the veiled accusation in her tone. "She trusted my greed and my desire for vengeance," he readily confessed.

But Rhiannon wasn't prepared to leave off simply because he'd confessed his sins.

"You should have killed her when you had the chance," she said sourly. "I know my mother well enough to know she'll not return the favor when she faces you again. It was stupid and why? What possible reason would you have to spare her? You left her insensate, and vulnerable—precisely as you'd want her to be to vanquish her once and for all. Now, not only will she never let down her guard again, but you've lost the opportunity to save more bloodshed."

He didn't answer, though he sighed, and then produced the twin reliquaries from about his neck to show them. Side by side, they were indistinguishable.

"That's it?" asked Marcella. "*That's* what she's been holding over you all these years?"

He nodded. "This is it," he said, casting another brief glance at Rhiannon. Marcella, too, slid Rhiannon a careful glance, and Rhiannon realized there was more to this story—inconceivably so, as there was so much she'd already learned.

How many secrets did one man keep?

How complicit was he in her mother's machinations?

And nay; she didn't like it that he confided so much in Marcella—shouldn't Rhiannon be the one to know her husband best? Even if her marriage wasn't a sham, she'd spent these past five years with Cael, and clearly, there was a lot he'd never bothered to share with her.

And yet, he'd shared everything with Marcella...

The realization made her burn with envy—envy she ought not be feeling, considering the circumstances.

Nothing was as it seemed, and now, with her sweet sisters still in danger, what Cael did or did not share with a woman of his past shouldn't concern her... and still it did.

They were all silent a while, waiting for Jack, mulling over the things Cael had already revealed.

Eventually, the silence grew too heavy to bear. They returned to their stratagem, drawing out maps on the ground.

Considering the distance between Cannock and Macclesfield, Cael and Marcella discussed taking a new route. It was agreed that they should rest till eventide, and then, when night fell, they would set out across the moorland.

Morwen's birds could see well enough by night, but by then, they might be roosting. Her mother would use them wisely, positioning them at intervals to watch where they emerged from the woods. That would be their most vulnerable point, but everything would depend wholly upon how intent Morwen was to push those birds to their limits. Already, they had determined she would not. Her birds meant more to her than did any of her daughters. She would not dispatch them when they were at their most vulnerable. She would use them when they were at their best and rest them otherwise.

On the other hand, she would and could send Mordecai to scout these woods. It was entirely possible he was already in pursuit. Lamentably, no one knew what he was capable of.

Her sister Rosalynde had witnessed his transformation in that woodlot south of Whittlewood and Salcey, but what he was, precisely, nobody but Morwen knew.

His form had been that of a dragon-like creature, with a beak and speared tail. Rhiannon had never in her life even imagined such a creature existed, and all she had known to do was warn her sister to run. In the end, the Goddess had intervened, offering Rosalynde words to bind its mortal form, and yet, despite this fact, Mordecai had somehow returned.

"He can't change at will," said Cael. "He'll come as a man, with all a man's weaknesses."

"And you know this how?" ventured Rhiannon, annoyed yet again, though she knew her ire wasn't entirely rational.

Cael had yet to embrace her, and what should she expect? That he would rush into her arms and beg forgiveness?

Nay.

He wasn't that sort of man.

And yet... he hadn't bothered to answer her question, and the simple fact that he and Marcella were still so familiar didn't set well with her. Instead, he and Marcella continued their discourse. Therefore, once Jack returned with his kindling, Rhiannon did to the kindling what she longed to do to both Marcella and Cael.

The fire blazed to life even before Jack could fully retrieve his hand from the pit, and he gave her a beleaguered glance.

Oblivious to their exchange, Cael and Marcella continued to talk.

Jack sat down beside Rhiannon, and said, "I'm sorry." Perhaps he'd mistaken the reason for her self-indulgence. "I didn't intend to harm you with the knife." He cast a surreptitious glance at the lord of

Blackwood. "Rather, I only meant for *him* to think I might."

"I'm not angry, Jack, don't worry."

"You sound angry," he said.

Rhiannon cast him a pointed glance. "Did you find dinner?" she asked, changing the subject.

"Nay. But I tell you true, if *they* want something other than what's in our saddle bags, they'll have to go get it themselves. I'm weary of being everyone's errand boy."

Rhiannon knew precisely how he felt, although she didn't wish to confess it.

"Alas, I'd like to say I know how you feel," said Jack, leaning close. "But I don't. In fact, I can't say much about your husband's debt to your mother, but—"

Rhiannon shot him a furious glance. "Because you are sworn to secrecy, or because you do not know?"

Sweet fates. Did everyone but her know about her husband's debt to her mother?

"Well... I do know his life depends on her good graces," he finished.

Didn't everyone's?

It wasn't enough of an explanation—and neither had it come from the right person. Incensed beyond measure, Rhiannon tossed a pebble into the flames.

"The fact that he's here says a lot," Jack persisted. "Take heart in that."

Rhiannon offered the young paladin a cutting glance.

Was she so transparent?

Were her feelings so near to the surface that he could read her so easily?

Why couldn't Cael?

He sat there, discussing ancient relics with Marcella, both their heads together, whispering feverishly, scarcely aware of anyone else in their proximity.

"So, you do care for her?" she asked Jack, a little petulantly.

"Aye," he confessed. "Sadly, she fancies herself more of a sister to me."

"Why don't you tell her how you feel?"

He shrugged, then hitched his chin. "Why don't *you* tell *him*?"

Rhiannon frowned. "Because *I* don't feel *that* way," she persisted.

"And yet... you do," he argued. "There's no mystery in the way you two regard one another, Lady Blackwood."

"Nay, Jack," she contended. "Art mistaken."

"Oh? In that case, how about I attempt to kiss you and see how it is that your *husband* responds?"

"I'm his wife," she hissed "How do you think he'll respond? He's like any other man. He may not want something for himself, but he won't give it away."

"That's not what I see," Jack argued, and perhaps to prove his point, he leaned closer to Rhiannon, as though to whisper in her ear... so close that she could feel the feathery heat of his breath tickle her flesh.

Before Rhiannon could push him away, her husband stood, unsheathing the sword at his back, deftly and with purpose, then drove it into the ground between them. "Altar boy," he said. "Get your smooth little arse away from my wife."

Jack complied at once, with a knowing smirk, and when Cael sat back down to continue his conversation with Marcella, he chuckled and said, "I told you so. That man is so aware of all you do, I can scarcely imagine how he's keeping his attention on their discourse."

Much to her consternation, Rhiannon couldn't hide her answering smile.

For the past few hours, it was all Cael could do to keep his attention on Marcella. That man-child was trying his patience—sitting so close to his wife, mumbling things he couldn't hear into her ear—good Christ, she was *his* wife, and still, he could scarcely believe it!

Only a week ago, he'd feared she would never agree to the bargain. Considering that her eldest sister was to have been his betrothed, he'd expected Rhiannon to continue to deny him out of spite, or in defiance of her mother.

For all these past five years, he'd tried in vain—or so he'd thought—to win her over; and she was no easy mark. In the beginning, the wooing was no more than a diversion, but one night, whilst he'd lain abed... he'd realized... it had been years since he'd last thought of Nesta. It was no longer her face, but Rhiannon's that appeared to him in his dreams, and it was Rhiannon's name he oft breathed in the throes of pleasure—self-served, mind you. Much to his bother-ation, after meeting Rhiannon, he could no more con-sider a romp in the hay with some nameless wench than he could remember the way it felt to be touched by a woman he loved.

For a while, guilt had plagued him, because Nesta had sacrificed her life to save him, and the least he could have done was to honor her memory. Instead, he'd found himself hard as stone with thoughts of a red-haired termagant whose tongue was as sharp as her wit.

God's truth. Even weary from travel, she was beautiful, with her dark, copper curls as wild and free as she was.

No doubt, he'd wanted to cheer her when she'd burned that man-child's hand, and with his own blade to boot. It served the wretch right for testing her so stupidly.

In fact, now that she was free from her manacles, there was no telling what powers Rhiannon possessed, but if that was a small inkling...

"Are you listening?"

Marcella's eyes impugned him.

Cael shook his head. "Apologies," he said, his gaze returning to the pair of reliquaries in her hand. "The problem is... now that we are no longer in her proximity, there is no way for me to tell which is mine. They are precisely identical, save for that odd glow in her presence."

"Even the crystals," Marcella agreed. "The veins are precisely the same."

"Aye."

"So, then... what is the worst thing that could happen if we destroyed them both?"

Cael shrugged. "The worst? I haven't a clue. Perhaps nothing at all? Or it could be that I would cease to exist. I haven't any notion how they work. Every time I inquired, Morwen was adamant I not concern myself with specifics. She merely bade me to care for them as though my life depended upon them, because, she said it did."

"Aye, well, if it is any consolation, I don't believe you would cease to exist," Marcella argued, still examining the reliquaries. "If what you say is true, she gave you the means to destroy her, and kept your reliquary, for herself. This tells me that she mustn't be overly concerned about its destruction." She placed one crystal between her teeth, and bit down to test its solidity. "Rather, I believe she knew you would keep it safe from others, and she must have presumed you would guard it better than she could amidst so many enemies."

"We've now proven she's not immune in her mortal form," Cael said, casting Morwen's daughter another glance, watching her interactions with Jack.

The man-child was goading him, he was sure of it, but why? He hadn't any sense the lad was stupid, nor had there ever been any rancor between them. Perhaps it was only to prove a point. He hadn't missed the lad's good-natured chuckle, nor Rhiannon's answering smirk once he'd planted his sword between them. It remained there now, a reminder to both that he was watching them still.

"Cael?"

Cael nodded, then realizing he didn't hear the last thing she said, he peered back at Marcella. "What?"

"I can see you are too preoccupied for this discussion. Should we remain here tonight, or press on?"

Cael could think of nothing so sweet as to lie with his wife in his arms, but this was not the time nor the place. "Press on," he said, and suggested, "but mayhap not straight to Macclesfield."

He lifted the stick Marcella had been drawing with and poked it at the etching already made in the soil—a crude map of their intended route and destination.

"'Tis roughly eleven or twelve leagues to Macclesfield. But... I happen to have learned that my cousin recently dispatched the lord of Amdel."

"Beauchamp?"

"Aye."

"Dispatched?"

Cael arched a black brow. "Aye, as in... relieved him of, not only his worldly possessions, but his life as well."

"How does this serve us?"

"Well... I warrant that with Stephen so preoccupied with Duke Henry at Wallingford, Amdel's disputed parklands are the furthest thing from his mind. I must presume the castle lies empty still."

"But isn't your cousin wed to Beauchamp's sister?"

"'Tis a complicated matter, but aye. Yet not the brother you presume. Graeham d'Lucy has forsworn his lands; he ceded them all to his brother."

Marcella's brows rose. "With the King's blessing?"

"Indeed. He appealed to Stephen some months ago, right before he left London, and Stephen agreed. Although he might well trust Blaec well enough to give him another parcel, there's no way Duke Henry will ever concede to the granting of Beauchamp's lands to a man who already holds a powerful seat, not when he can award them to another of his loyal barons."

"I ask you again, how does that help us?"

"Because, in the meantime, Amdel remains empty... and unguarded."

A once, Marcella relieved him of the stick, then poked at her etching, at a location that appeared to be somewhere behind them. "Correct me if I am wrong, but Amdel lies here." She poked at the drawing again, and again. "We are here, and we must go here." Then, she poked the stick far to the right and north of her drawing. "This is where we must end."

Warkworth.

"Aye," said Cael, relieving her of the stick once more. "So, this is what I propose... we backtrack a bit, go here." And then he drew another small cluster in the dirt. "From Amdel, we travel through Kinver, then pass to Wellington, and through the parklands at Drakewich. From there, we will still end in Maccles-field, although without having to cross the moorlands."

Marcella sat, silently poring over Cael's proposal. And then, she asked, "Art certain Amdel lies empty?"

"As certain as I can be. Worst case, we pass by and travel on to Drakewich—another three or four hours thereabouts."

"I don't know if she can endure." Marcella hitched her chin in Rhiannon's direction. "We've been trav-eling endlessly."

"She's strong," he said with a note of pride. "My guess is she may very well outlast both you and me."

"Nay," Marcella said. "You overestimate her. She's vulnerable. After five years locked away with those manacles, I'm surprised she's made it this far without so much as a complaint." There was a note of admira-tion in the paladin's voice, though Cael didn't remark upon it. Finally, Marcella nodded, perhaps beginning to see the wisdom in his plan.

Not only would it circumvent the need to travel so far under open skies, but it might also further serve to confuse Morwen, because she would, no doubt, anticipate the distance they would travel since leaving Blackwood, and chances were that her birds would be circling that area, waiting.

Ultimately, she must already have discerned their intended destination, and that's where she would concentrate her search efforts. Nobody could anticipate they would double back—for what reason?

He tossed the stick away, and Marcella leaned forward to brush at the dirt, erasing the proof of their stratagem. "Go on," she said, following his gaze. "See to your wife. Far be it from me to keep you from your greatest desire."

Besotted as he was, Cael didn't need to be told twice.

He stood at once, brushing off his breeches as he considered the woman he was once involved with. It hadn't lasted overlong, and though neither of them had any true love for the other, he realized Marcella's feelings ran deeper than his. Alas, though, he had never anticipated that his heart would be free again, or that he could ever love anyone so deeply. He'd told her the truth all those years ago—that his heart belonged to Nesta. It simply was impossible to compel a heart to love anywhere but where it wished. He understood that Marcella must feel tormented by his change of heart, but he'd also never foreseen how Rhiannon's presence in his life would affect him.

Like her mother, she was an irresistible force.

"I am sorry," he said, after a moment.

"For what, Cael? For discovering that you are still capable of love?"

He stood silently, wishing for Marcella's sake that he could deny it... but he could not. His one point of comfort was that he knew he was never Marcella's true love either.

She peered up at him then, her green eyes soft with affection. "The heart must love who it loves," she reasoned. "And I, too, have my own cross to bear."

"Jack?" he said quietly, and when she nodded, he said, "It's obvious."

"Indeed," she said. "Alas, though... I remember a time when my heart was so easily led as well."

This, he realized, was not a reference to him at all, for their relations had been anything but simple, or easy. He knew who it was she was speaking of, and it wasn't him, nor was it Jack. And this, too, was something they'd shared, because, though his love for Morwen wasn't Eros, Morwen was a poppet master of the greatest degree, expertly pulling her strings. Terrible though she might be, she knew how to engender loyalty, and... yes, even affection. Those who followed her, followed her devotedly, knowing the venerable lady behind the veil. In her weakest moments she bled like everyone else, and Cael had once cared for her as well.

How could he not?

But then, again, love was not the proper word for what he'd felt for Morwen Pendragon. He'd never once shared her bed, nor, until recently, had she ever invited him.

There was only one woman he had ever truly loved, and not even Nesta had inspired in him the passion that his beautiful *dewine* bride could inspire.

Rhiannon was very much like her mother in some ways, but in every way that mattered, she was nothing like her at all.

During his time in this realm—at least this time around—the few times he'd fallen into another woman's bed, it had been joyless and uninspiring. No other woman, save Rhiannon made his cock so hard that he walked around in a state of constant arousal, like some beardless youth with more seed than sense. Even now, he could think of little else but having her... undressing her, at long last, dragging her beneath him, and drinking from the font between her thighs.

Somehow he understood that what he now felt for Rhiannon—this wildly impassioned fire—Marcella had once felt for Morwen. They'd been friends before they were lovers, at a tender age when love must have seemed sweet and new—two gloriously pagan young women unashamed to explore. Some part of him envied her doughtiness, to love where she willed. He lingered a moment longer because he felt compelled to speak aloud what they both knew.

"In the end, she must be destroyed," he said.

Marcella nodded gravely, averting her gaze. "I know," she said, and a single tear slid down her cheek. "The only true question remains... who will be the one to do it?"

TWENTY-FIVE

Cael could barely concentrate on the business at hand for all his lusty thoughts of his wife. Therefore, he slipped away when he could, to find himself a quiet spot, thinking everyone would be better off if he could only reduce a bit of tension.

He couldn't do much about their current circumstances, nor the travesty hanging over their heads, but there was something he could do to relieve a bit of stress—or, at the very least, settle the beast in his breeches.

Devil take him, he wanted naught more than to drag his new wife into these woods and consummate their vows at long last, but this was not the time for that.

Moreover, he should have enough bloody sense not to choke his cock alone in these woods, with his travel companions not more than twenty yards away and a wolfhound sniffing at his heels. But evidently, he didn't, and there was only one small comfort he could embrace—that he was still human enough to have a man's desires, even amidst the chaos surrounding them. But it was a youth's appetite he enjoyed of late, and this was nothing to crow about. He was a besotted auld fool, whose modicum of good sense now faltered whenever faced with his beautiful, willful bride.

Such as it was, Cael couldn't even begin to conceive why it was that he was compelled to make excuses in broad daylight, or why he thence put his back against a tree, or why he then unlaced his trews, or pulled out his cock—only to piss, he reasoned. But that wasn't true, because he stood there with the beast in his hand a moment too long, and then he stroked himself a few times for good measure, moaning with pleasure over the feel of the hot, tight flesh in his hands.

But there was that bloody hound, with its bright wolflike eyes fixed upon him...

Still, intent upon his pleasure, he shut his eyes, envisioning Rhiannon's face—not the way she appeared tonight, with that mile-long scowl—the way she oft looked when she trounced him at a game of Queen's Chess, her soft, sultry lips curved ever so slightly with that beauteous smile, and her steel, blue eyes glinting with bravado...

The dog whined and Cael opened his eyes.

"Truly? Are you going to do this to me?" he inquired of the wolfhound. "I allowed you to come along, and I fed you."

Scowling at the dog, he once again tested his own bravado, stroking himself a few more times, his skin hot and engorged. But the dog whined yet again, and his manhood wilted in his hand. Finally, he let his hand fall away, and growled at the dog, nonsensical as the gesture should be.

Shaking his head, still half mad with lust, and completely unsatisfied, he tugged up his breeches and laced up his trews. "Bloody hell," he said, scowling at the hound. "I thought you were supposed to be man's best friend. God's truth, you're no friend to me!"

The dog whined pitifully, and Cael bade him to follow with a snap of his fingers. Together, man and dog started back in the direction of their camp.

Evidently contented with the outcome, the animal scampered up beside him, wagging its tail, and peering up at Cael with an unmistakable look of admiration. And, despite himself, it melted his heart precisely as it had when he'd first tried to shoo it away after leaving Blackwood.

God only knew, the rest of the pack had been pleased enough to run free, and Cael knew that they would eventually return home, as they always did after a hunt; hopefully not before Morwen departed. Clearly, this one had a soft spot for Cael, as he did for it. He was getting soft in his old age.

With a sigh, he reached down to scruff the animal's thick fur. "Mayhap you can find a way to soften your lady's mood," he conspired with the animal. "It's the least you can do."

~

LONG BEFORE THERE WERE *GRIMOIRES*, or even words for that matter, the *hud* simply was. Therefore, even despite lacking a true *grimoire*, there was no spell Rhiannon shouldn't be able to cast, given the will to do it.

Even before her mother had clapped her in irons,

she'd already begun to understand this experientially: that spells didn't require words, nor did they necessitate herbs or rites. Rather, all these things only helped the caster cast: words for focus, herbs to facilitate manipulation of the elements, rites to channel the energy of the *hud*, and to honor the Mother Goddess by whose grace all things were made possible.

Essentially, all things were summoned or banished, created or destroyed, transformed or reformed. And while it might seem there should be many, many nuances, or that, by virtue of these differences, it left too much to be explored, she had also come to know that all spells essentially belonged to the same two classifications, and that each had a genesis in either acceptance or denial. Therefore, if one viewed the world under these simpler terms, it was easier to channel the proper energy for a given spell.

Fundamentally, belief opened up all possibility, and emotion was the energy's source.

So, then, theoretically, she shouldn't even need to know *what* was possible in casting, she only needed to believe it was possible and to put heart and soul into the spell.

At least she hoped these things were true.

The time was coming soon to face Morwen—not a month from now, nor a year, but any moment...

Considering both protection spells and offense spells, she tried to open her mind and her imagination.

She only wished she could discuss such things with her sisters, because in the end, she needed their help—a truth she hadn't ever considered before realizing how wrong she was about her role in the world.

In the meantime, she was grateful to have Marcella. The paladin was as close to a dear friend as Rhiannon had ever known, complicated though their relationship might be—and despite Marcella's obvious affection for Cael.

And yet, truly, one could not control who they loved. Simply because Marcella held some strange affection for Cael, it didn't mean they couldn't be friends. Intuitively, she trusted the paladin's word. She would never betray herself, nor her word, and no matter how she'd felt about Cael, she was still willing to put an arrow through his heart in defense of Rhiannon. This was proof of her honor.

Considering these things, Rhiannon stood checking her cinches, after returning her supplies to her satchel.

Marcella and Jack were both busy repairing the campsite, and all together they were preparing to depart.

Supper had been mean, only a bit of salted beef, and a bite of *pan*. Evidently, Jack had meant what he'd said, and the memory of his rebellion made her smile.

Only when Marcella had asked where the cony was, he'd shrugged and told her she must have forgotten to procure it. Then, he'd offered to go find her a proper butcher, but his tone was so acerbic that it was impossible to mistake his meaning. There wasn't any butcher around for leagues, and neither did he intend to go searching.

For his part, Cael had made some excuse, then disappeared into the woods, perhaps to tend to his ministrations. No one dared follow him, except for that wolfhound, who, like Rhiannon, clearly longed for some attention.

What a silly fool she was, yearning for Cael's embrace and his kisses.

How was it even possible that she was so concerned with something so ridiculous as kisses when the fate of England was now at risk? At any instant, Mordecai could descend upon them—and God help them all if it should happen to be Morwen. None of them were prepared to face her mother yet—not even Rhiannon, and certainly not Jack or Marcella. And nay, most especially not Cael. Morwen would tear out his heart sooner than she would listen to a word from his mouth.

"Rhiannon…"

She turned to find her husband emerging from the woods, with the wolfhound at his heels.

He stopped, and the dog stopped beside him, and Cael immediately buried a hand into the animal's thick fur—as tall as it was, he barely had to stretch.

Still rather annoyed, even despite having discovered that he wasn't so immune to her as he might like her to believe, she turned her back on him and continued repairing her saddle. "Am I supposed to forget everything you said to me at Blackwood simply because you are here?"

"Nay," he said.

Rhiannon continued to repair her gear. "We are not aligned, you said. And what is more, you gave me every indication that if you were made to pursue, you would do your worst."

"Aye, Rhiannon, but I also said—"

"You said a lot of things," she interrupted.

"I said I love you."

Rhiannon stiffened.

"I truly meant it."

Tears pricked at Rhiannon's eyes and she daren't turn—so easily did he melt her heart.

Nor did it help much to see a grown man traipsing about with an overgrown pup—like an endearing little boy.

No one in all her life had ever said they loved her.

Not even her sisters, because the sentiment was always understood.

"Rhiannon," he said again, gently, and Rhiannon swallowed hard as she sensed him moving near. He reached out to touch her elbow. "I am here... because it occurred to me that, whether I live or die, I must do so for you..."

Rhiannon swallowed again, uncertain how to respond.

There wasn't time to stand on ceremony, she realized. Death would come for them all, and much to her dismay, she had desperately feared Cael's time had already come—only fate had intervened and given them another chance.

She couldn't help herself. She turned to fling herself into his arms, tears burning her eyes, even as she buried her face against his gambeson.

"I thought you were dead," she said, and he placed his arms around her, holding her close. "I thought—"

"What?"

Rhiannon shook her head, not wanting to say what else she'd thought—that he'd pursued her only to return her to Blackwood... to her mother... and worse.

We are not aligned, he'd said.

Together, they stood, embracing for the longest moment, and finally, at long last, he acknowledged what Rhiannon was only thinking. "Did you believe I intended you harm? That I could speak my love for you, kiss you so passionately, then harden my heart enough to come and slay you?" She nodded brokenly, her throat too thick to speak, and he squeezed her tighter. "I suppose I did imply so much, did I not?" He laughed then, ruefully, as he smoothed the tangles from her hair. "In truth, Rhiannon, I thought I must. I considered it a matter of life or death, and yet... once I returned to face your mother... I realized then and there that there was only one good reason to die... It wasn't for her."

Rhiannon still couldn't find her voice to speak, but there was so much she wished to say...

"I meant every word I said, Rhiannon. 'Tis true, though I didn't know it until I said it; I loved you from the moment you first opened your mouth—so brave and true. But you must have suspected so much? Did you not? Why else would a grown man eschew his duties for hours on end to sit in a lady's bower over a game he could never hope to win?"

Rhiannon choked on her laughter. It was true. He was miserable at Queen's Chess. "I assumed you let me win," she said with a watery laugh. "After all, you're the commander of the King's Rex Militum. Stratagem should come easily to you."

He sighed heavily, as his hand continued to caress her hair. "Aye, well... I must presume our King is a poor judge of character."

Rhiannon laughed again, and though often she would have continued to spar with him—cutting him with her words, because a sharp tongue was the only weapon she'd ever had—she embraced him fully, laying her head over the spot where his heart beat strongest.

"Rhiannon," he said again, and this time her name sounded more like a caress.

Hapless to do aught else, she lifted her eyes to meet Cael's, and her breath caught at the intensity of his gaze.

"Before witnesses, and before God, I have pledged you my troth," he said. "But here, now..." His hand slid from her waist, tickling her back, appearing between them to lift her chin. "I pledge you my loyalty and my life. Where you go, I will follow. Every moment of the time we have remaining, I pledge these to you."

Rhiannon didn't know what to say.

There was naught in the fathomless depths of his eyes that called him a liar, and yet, she couldn't speak those words herself. She would not choose him over all, nor risk her sisters' lives for him. "Thank you," she said, at a loss. And then, her husband did, what she sorely hoped he might do: He ceased with more words, lowering his mouth to hers, and thoroughly kissed her—not with the fervor of his first kiss, but tenderly, and full of promise, coaxing love words from her lips, as urgently as his hands held her.

Still, she could not say them, though she didn't know why. The need to speak aloud what was heartfelt was nearly as potent as the burn of *magik* through her veins.

And still, she refrained...

"Time to go, lovers," shouted Marcella.

Cael ended the kiss abruptly, smiling down at her.

Rhiannon felt the separation like the rending of a

limb. "Little does she realize," she quipped, scarcely aware that it sounded like a lament.

He winked at her. "We'll remedy that," he said, and Rhiannon shivered over the promise in his eyes.

She wanted to say that it wasn't what she'd meant, but wasn't it? Even now, her body thrummed where he'd touched her and... more. Deep down in her womb, she felt a desperate need to be filled. Sweet fates, her desire was as potent as Marcella's philters.

TWENTY-SIX

A rising mist obscured the forest floor—naturally, else Rhiannon would smell the manipulation.

They could barely see the full moon through the lush canopy of summer green, but the night was still bright enough to lend a modicum of light as Cael scouted the path ahead with his wolfhound by his side.

Like its master, the overlarge beast moved stealthily through the woods, padding through a pillow of composting leaves.

Jack assumed the rear of their cavalcade, Marcella's normally amiable apprentice silent and taciturn—more and more so as the night wore on.

By now, everyone was tired, and it was a dangerous proposition to double back through these woods, effectively countervailing the lead they'd attained.

For her part, Marcella rode beside Rhiannon, tirelessly scrutinizing their surroundings, her sword at the ready should anyone emerge from the shadows.

If everything went according to plan, it was estimated they should reach Amdel's parklands by Lauds, or thereabouts—a full seven bells in the saddle, stopping only now and again to tend to the mounts.

For the sake of their horses, the pace remained easy; even so, Rhiannon was bone-tired, and by now, her lids were heavy. Still, she found little enough to complain about, particularly considering that whatever discomfort her companions were suffering now, they were suffering it for her. Her gratitude was boundless, and her heart was full. So much had changed over these past few days.

Scarcely a week ago she'd been imprisoned, with no hope for escape. Now, she was free, and no longer alone.

In fact, not only was she surrounded by men and a woman who'd sworn vows to protect her, but she also found she rather enjoyed Marcella and her painful candor.

She enjoyed Jack, as well.

And she loved Cael, though she couldn't seem to say it aloud.

Despite fearing the worst, he was alive and well... here, with her. And soon, very soon, she would be reunited with her sisters as well—perhaps a bit longer than anticipated, now that they were doubling back so far, but everyone had seemed to agree that this was the best laid plan.

Ellie, Seren, Rose... it won't be long now.

Together, they would find a way to defeat Morwen.

Together, they would endure.

Had Seren already realized her destiny?

She wanted desperately to *mindspeak* but didn't dare.

How strange the fates.

Her sweet sister was simply not the sort that Rhiannon would ever have imagined in such a role. Goddess knew, if there was anyone in this realm less ferocious than Seren, Rhiannon didn't know them. She had always envisioned the Regnant as a warrior queen, more like herself, truth be told.

How wrong she had been.

And what of Rose?

Was she still the same? Prickly as a thorn, and wily as a fox—slipping away from the priory every chance she got. It was inconceivable to imagine that only five years ago, Rose had been a young girl, who'd enjoyed stealing men's clothing. She wore them to slip into the woods to forage for herbs.

Of all her sisters, Rose had been the most like Rhiannon, and Seren and Arwyn had been most disparate —both sweet and gentle, with voices that never carried.

And then there was Elspeth—dearest Elspeth— she and her eldest sibling had locked horns so oft they both ought to have beat each other senseless.

Oh, nay, they never came to blows, but Elspeth had been equally as willful as Rhiannon, only far more self-righteous. And yet, she supposed Ellie had earned the right. She had been the one who had to defend them against Morwen.

Seeking Cael, taking comfort in his presence, her gaze traveled unerringly through the shadows, finding him tall in his saddle, looking like a venerable champion... her very own.

She couldn't wait to introduce him to her sisters.

She wanted to assure them she was free and on the way, but daren't *mindspeak* with Morwen in pursuit. Now that Rhiannon understood more about what her mother was—a *Sylphkind*—she realized it would be impossible to keep her from intercepting anything she put into the *aether*.

Nay, she decided. It was safer to keep her thoughts to herself, although, apparently, she couldn't manage to conceal them all from Marcella. The paladin, with her limited abilities was able to glean the truth about what was lurking in her heart —else it must be a woman's intuition. "I was right," she said, with a little smirk in her tone. "You do love him."

Resigned, Rhiannon gave the paladin a tentative nod, though she wasn't even certain that Marcella could see the gesture in this inky darkness. Thankfully, Cael rode far enough ahead that he couldn't overhear.

"It pleases me to know it," she said. "He's risked so much to join you, I hope you realize."

"I do," assured Rhiannon, although she knew he hadn't told her everything yet, and it still annoyed her that he was keeping secrets. "Alas, you seem to know my husband better than I do," she said, though she didn't intend it as an accusation, and thankfully Marcella didn't take it as one.

The paladin laughed softly. "It took me years to cut through his armor," she said. "But never fear, I've no doubt he'll tell you everything in good time. Perhaps even tonight when we are safe at Amdel?"

The tiny hairs at Rhiannon's nape prickled—anticipation?

The thought of being alone with Cael sent a

frisson down her spine—not fear precisely, but not entirely delight.

For one thing, she hadn't the first notion how to do a woman's duty in the bedroom. Oh, she knew *how* it was done, and, in fact, she'd pleasured herself a time or two in secret. She understood it could be pleasant for a woman as it was for a man. But she desperately wished to please her husband, and as bold as she liked to believe she was, she blushed like a nun merely at the thought of undressing in his presence.

Would he find her lacking?

Would he regret having embroiled himself?

After all, he didn't have to wed her, and in truth, he was promised little for the effort. If in fact King Stephen meant to cede his crown to Duke Henry after his death, he hadn't any reason to keep his Rex Militum, since the entire purpose of that commission— by all accounts, Rhiannon had heard—was to find and exterminate all threats to his reign. So, then, Cael might yet have to forfeit Blackwood, after all—not that she cared, mind you. Though she could certainly find it in her heart to love that pile of stones, she would be content enough to simply *be* with Cael, wherever that may be.

She wondered then... were they truly wed if they hadn't yet had a first night?

Did men still have the desire to lie with a woman in the midst of war?

She considered that, and thought perhaps the an- swer must be yes, because she was a woman and even she thrilled over the barest possibility. More- over, she'd heard about those women who followed troops, sometimes traveling along with them. They wouldn't be doing that if men didn't enjoy them, therefore the answer must be aye, but then, she frowned over the thought, wondering if Cael had ever availed himself of their services. She didn't relish the possibility.

Something inexplicable had changed since he'd joined them—something Rhiannon couldn't begin to construe.

It was as though she might be two people now—one, naught but a silly, blushing bride who longed for nothing more than to be touched by her lord husband. The other a dauntless soldier, ready to do battle for the sake of the realm. Neither of these two women had any likeness to the other, and somehow she was both.

And really, considering the circumstances, she shouldn't even allow her head to be so filled with thoughts of kisses and caresses, but she couldn't help it.

Even the steady trot of her mare left her wiggling in the saddle, and she felt like a doxy, exposed, even in full attire. No one was watching her, but she felt as though everyone one must be. She longed to ask for Marcella's advice, but didn't know how to broach the topic, and then it occurred to her that, normally, this might be something a maiden would ask her mother —more's the pity, because she'd never had one.

"You speak so fondly of your mother," Rhiannon ventured. "And yet you've never spoken her name."

"Isolde," said the paladin after a moment.

"Isolde?"

"Aye."

"The same—"

"Indeed, she is one and the same," Marcella said,

and once again she heard rather than spied Marcella's smile.

Goddess, alive, it didn't seem there could be any more surprises, but here was yet another.

Isolde was the old woman who'd tended them for a while at court, whilst they were still very young. She was also the same woman who'd delivered Rhiannon and her sisters to Llanthony the year King Henry died. She was the one who'd roused them from their slumber in London, and spirited them away to the Vale of Ewyas, where she'd placed them in the care of those monks. Only then, she'd gone, and they never saw her again, and Rhiannon had only assumed she had abandoned them to their misfortunes. After all, who wanted to attach themselves to five penurious young maids.

Rhiannon didn't know what to say.

"We parted ways after an argument over your mother," said Marcella.

Rhiannon shook her head. "So, it seems, my mother is the cause for so much discontent. I'm so sorry to hear this, Marcella. Have you seen her since, or are you still estranged?"

She sensed Marcella's gaze, even through the darkness. Her face became visible only in glimpses as moonlight pierced the foliage. "My mother is dead," she said. "She died a few moons after Henry died. There was a bout of leprosy at Blackwood when I was young, and despite that she was healed, she was twisted and ravaged by her illness. After she left court and deposited the five of you at Llanthony, she wasted away and died. God forbid she should ever humble herself enough to appeal to me—not in life. Though I do still see her now on occasion."

Rhiannon blinked. "You still see her?"

Silence was her initial response, and then, Marcella asked, "'Tis odd how we can know something in our hearts, and still not know it experientially."

"I don't under—"

"As you must know already, all things are one, living and dead. If the stars align, you might still connect with loved ones Beyond The Veil, but you must wholly believe it."

Rhiannon considered that a moment, and then Marcella added, "If you look and listen, you'll see signs of our departed in so many forms."

Rhiannon wondered how Arwyn would appear—in a glorious explosion of flames, she decided with a smile. Her youngest sibling may have been gentle at heart, but she was dazzling in spirit. She found the thought comforting and tucked the knowledge away for further exploration.

"How much longer to Amdel? Do you know?"

Marcella peered up at a sliver of sky through the trees. "I would suppose by now we have passed into Darkwood, so perhaps another bell."

Rhiannon stiffened.

"Never fear," Marcella said, correctly reading her unease. "We are far north of the inn."

Rhiannon shivered, although it had little to do with the evening's damp or chill. "I have never been there, but I know enough from my sisters to know it is nowhere I wish to be."

Marcella agreed. "No man, lest he have some death wish, ever rests at that inn."

"My mother is the patron, did you know?"

"Of course," said Marcella. "And I must confess I made good use of that knowledge."

"Hunting?"

"Aye."

Rhiannon arched a brow. "*Dewinekind?*"

"Nay," said the paladin, sliding her a glance. "I know what you think, Lady Blackwood. Fortunately, 'tis been an age since *dewinefolk* were the sole concern of the Guard, or even the Church. Mind you, we've far worse enemies now, and the greatest being your mother."

Rhiannon peered back to find Jack loitering at a distance, and she wondered how much he knew. "If you don't mind my asking, what precisely is Jack to you?" Rhiannon asked, taking advantage of Marcella's forthcoming mood.

"He's only my apprentice."

"And Cael? I know his commission is nearly the same as yours."

"Not quite. He answers to your King. I answer to my Church."

"*Your* Church," Rhiannon mused aloud. "How odd to hear you say so, though I suppose one creed is the same as another."

"More or less," agreed Marcella. "Some call it prayer, others invocation. Still, these are one and the same, and how sad to know it and still find so much discord."

"I did wonder... how came you to be a paladin?"

There was a long, long pause, and then Marcella said, "Interestingly enough, because of your mother. She charged me to spy on Matilda whilst she was still wed to the Emperor. And, of course, this was precisely the reason for the discord with my mother. She begged me not to do it, and I... well... as you know, I forsook her advice."

"Did you do it to please my mother?"

"I did," Marcella confessed. "I would have done anything for Morwen in those days."

"Anything?"

Marcella didn't immediately respond, and Rhiannon afforded her a small change in topic. "So, you said Cael came to supplicate my case to the Guard? Did he oft have business with the Church?"

"Ah, Rhiannon... there is so much I am not at liberty to say, but I suppose he did. Often, our dictums were... shall we say... very well aligned."

"So, then, he answers to both the Guard and the Rex Militum?"

"Alas, my dear Lady Blackwood. 'Tis not so simple as that."

"Please... call me Rhiannon. I haven't any notion how to behave as the lady of a great house. But, at any rate, I consider you to be my friend."

"As you wish," said the paladin dutifully, but there, again, was a smile in her voice.

Rhiannon smiled as well, and they rode for a while longer in silence. She felt, for the moment, content. But it was important to her that Marcella understand exactly how she felt, and she wanted the paladin to understand she was at peace with her past with Cael, whatever that might be. "He cares for you, I think."

There was no need to say who she meant.

Marcella sighed impatiently.

"May I inquire something of you?"

"Of course."

"Do you love him still?"

"Nay, Rhiannon. I do not. Not the man he has become."

"But I don't under—"

"Please," Marcella interrupted, "suffice to say that not every wetted wick is worth keeping lit."

Heat suffused Rhiannon's cheeks, and Marcella turned to peer over her shoulder to see where Jack might be. Finding him well out of hearing range, she confessed, "Alas, your husband was not my only mistake; there is Jack as well."

Rhiannon lifted a hand to her lips. "Sweet fates!" She giggled nervously. "Who haven't you lain with?"

The paladin snorted. "Not you," she jested. "Care to remedy that?"

Rhiannon's blush burned hot. "Nay! Sweet fates! I-I did not mean that to be so disparaging... 'tis only..."

"Promiscuity is unnatural for a woman?"

Rhiannon nodded quickly.

"Alas, *mon amie*. A woman's desires are not so different from a man's. And besides..." She eyed Rhiannon's attire. "If you wear a man's breeches long enough, you'll find it affords you liberties you never imagined."

Rhiannon laughed softly, though she tugged at her leathers, and then, confessed, "You know... I... I... was wondering. I have... never lain with a man..."

The whites of Marcella's eyes widened visibly. "Not even—"

Rhiannon shook her head, embarrassed.

"I assumed—"

Rhiannon shook her head again, her face burning so hot now that she was grateful for the cover of darkness.

"Oh, my," said the paladin, and then she grinned at Rhiannon until Rhiannon could spy the whites of her teeth as well. "Well then... please allow me to do you the honor of explaining the joys of congress."

And then she did. And out of everything Rhiannon had heard so far, this was the most shocking of revelations—not because she didn't already know what should transpire between a man and woman, but because there were so many ways to accomplish the task.

TWENTY-SEVEN

Late, late into the night, as a misty rain began to drizzle down, Rhiannon found herself struggling in the saddle.

Pulling her woolen cloak more tightly about herself, she donned the hood as well, tugging it down over her face.

Compelled to despite her resolve, her eyes closed of their own accord, and not even the dampness soaking through her cloak was enough discomfort to keep her from teetering in the saddle.

Forsooth. If her mother should appear right now, she would be ill-suited to do aught more than fall at her feet, face down in the muck—like King Stephen.

How embarrassed he must have been—the sovereign of England with a gob full of mud.

Rhiannon might have enjoyed seeing that—though not more than she would have enjoyed the sight of his sour-faced wife lying there beside him.

Deliriously, she thought, "That's not very nice, Rhiannon." *The poor lady is already dead.* But then again, because that was so, she already had a gob full of muck, now didn't she?

That wasn't Rhiannon's fault.

Half insensate, Rhiannon seized a handful of her horse's mane only to help steady herself, refusing to complain. If everyone else could endure so long, so, too, must she.

"Just a little further," she coaxed herself.

Like a black-clad guardian angel, Cael appeared by her side. With barely any effort, he plucked her from her saddle, dragging her into his arms, where he tucked her against him and said, "Rest, my love."

My love...

My love...

Was she really his love?

Could one truly love despite being aligned elsewhere? Every day of her confinement, he had reminded her of the debt he owed her mother. And more... that he'd desired everything Morwen desired —most importantly, an end to the regime that answered to an unscrupulous Empire. Betimes he spoke as though he had a personal grievance against the Church, and Rhiannon oft wondered why.

He wasn't a *dewine*—never the hunted, always the hunter! He was an executioner, a man to be feared. And yet... Rhiannon didn't fear him, and she never had.

Aside from those first few months that he'd kept her in the tower, Cael d'Lucy had never once mistreated her.

Even then, he'd come to keep her company, talking with her for hours, standing outside her *gaol*, even without a chair. Conversely, at least Rhiannon had had a cot to sit on, and betimes whenever she'd wept, he'd opened her cell and come to sit by her side, gently wiping the tears from her cheeks. She'd known then that, deep down, where it mattered, Cael d'Lucy's heart was good. In fact, before her mother had delivered the shackles, she might easily have found a way to escape, still she never tried.

Why?

Because of him.

It wasn't only because she'd had a vision of their fates. Admittedly, some small part of her had lived for each moment when he'd come to console her.

In the beginning, she'd believed it was pity that compelled him—pity for her affliction, pity for her circumstances.

The child in her had clamored for some simple human connection, and the woman in her had laid her tear-stained cheeks in the crook of his neck and inhaled the very masculine scent of him—a scent that to Rhiannon had been oddly familiar, though she'd never met Cael before that day, fresh from her tumbril.

Nay, he would never hurt her.

She sensed that truth deep in her soul.

Somehow, she'd always trusted that Cael would defend her, despite everything.

She felt his chest expand with a contented sigh as he pulled the edge of the cloak over her face, taking care to keep the rain from her, and Rhiannon lost the battle to stay awake. They'd been traveling too long now, with her nerves on edge, and now that she was in her husband's arms, she hadn't any spirit left to muster. Closing her eyes, she rested her cheek against his leathered chest, and slept like a newborn babe. When she reopened her eyes again, the first blushing of morning light had begun to unfurl.

"Wake up," said Cael. "Rhiannon!"

Her head shot up, as she heard bellowing.

The morning sky was a watery rose as they ventured onto Amdel's parklands, and though the rain had stopped, the entire landscape was a muddy brown.

Looking far more like a pile of stones against the dusky horizon, Amdel castle lay shrouded in a thick morning mist, its aura black as pitch.

"Tell him to come out, treat like a man!" shouted one of two fellows standing in the middle of a muddy field—one mounted, one not.

The one doing the bargaining stood, arms akimbo.

Reining in their mounts, the entire cavalcade stopped to assess the situation.

Rubbing the sleep from her eyes, Rhiannon righted herself in the saddle.

Marcella patted her mare's neck, whispering gently to the beast to keep her calm.

Jack reined in as well, tightening the lead rope to Rhiannon's riderless horse, bringing it close.

Even the wolfhound stood silent, perhaps evaluating the level of danger. Although Rhiannon half expected the animal to growl or to leap at the pair of warriors standing in a watery field, he remained close by their side.

Before them, Amdel Castle rose from rich, black loam, looking like a debased tomb, with its half-finished stone wall nearly gone to rubble.

It was, as though, she thought... the lord of this place had begun to construct a bastion, only to be thwarted by his coffers, or perhaps even a king's mandate.

There were many adulterine castles built after

King Henry's death—over a thousand, so she'd heard. So long as their lords bent the knee, the Usurper had allowed many to remain, far too many, his barons would say.

Only naturally, Stephen would respect a man who took what he wanted per force. After all, hadn't he done the same?

Still, it was impossible to say if this castle might be among the ones he did not approve. For whatever reason, the construction had been forestalled long, long ago. And even so, its aura gave Rhiannon the distinct impression that it had only been recently abandoned. It filled her with a strange sense of presentiment. Even the air itself held the faintest whiff of death. But she sensed heart flames within, so the castle wasn't entirely abandoned. More proof of that stood upon the parapet... one man with arms akimbo, though Rhiannon could spy others hidden behind the *meutriers*, bows knocked and arrows ready to loose.

"He'll not treat with the likes of you!" he shouted. "Get ye gone, else we'll loose another volley!"

The two men standing before the barbican stood far enough away that the first round of missiles had embedded themselves harmlessly at their feet. At least half a dozen stood planted in the sodden ground.

"Cael?" said Marcella. "I believe that's...

"Giles," he said.

Rhiannon perked over hearing that name.

Her sister's husband?

What were the odds?

Small, in truth, lest the fates be bound.

Rhiannon recognized him as well, despite that

she'd only seen him once in a vision—more than four years ago when he'd first encountered her sister en route to Aldergh... before their mother placed her in shackles.

"God's bones," said Cael. "It is him."

So far, neither man on the ground had any sense of their presence, so preoccupied were they with the soldiers on the wall. And yet, the man on the wall did note them. His hands fell from his hips, and he retreated a few steps, then returned. Rhiannon could see the color of fear rising in his aura, even from this distance—brown as the loamy fields stretching before the castle.

"I must speak to him," said Rhiannon, as she rushed to dismount.

"Nay," said Cael, restraining her with a hand to her breast.

"Please!" she begged.

"Nay," he said, and before she could protest, Rhiannon suffered another vision—the first since removing her shackles. The intensity of it dizzied her, and any complaint she might have uttered died in her throat. It was no more than a fleeting glance, but when it was gone, she suddenly understood... and swallowed, hard.

This was the place...

Here.

This was where they would face Morwen—this monstrosity of construction, with its melancholy spirit and cadaverous stench.

"I'll go," offered Jack.

"Nay," said Marcella. "I will go."

And before anyone could stop her, she spurred her mount ahead, covering the distance quickly, her dark hair sweeping her back as she shouted in greeting.

"Hail, brother!" she said, waving in greeting.

Both men spun about, drawing swords. Giles froze when he saw her—thank God. They were far enough away that no one could intervene if he meant to cut her down.

To everyone's relief, both men re-sheathed their weapons, and Marcella stood speaking to them a long moment, then she waved the rest of them forward as she dismounted.

Jack complied at once.

Only Cael hesitated. "Until I know what they're doing here, say nothing, Rhiannon."

"He's my brother by law," she argued. "Why would you believe he would do me harm?"

Silence was Cael's response, but he nudged his destrier forward.

Rhiannon persisted. "We are en route to Warkworth, where you wouldst seek the man's aid. Why does it matter *where* he is? Inexplicably, he's here, when we need him most. I call it a gift from the Goddess."

"Rather convenient, don't you think?"

"She works in mysterious ways," apprised Rhiannon.

"Aye well, you'd do well to remember that your mother is a child of the Goddess, as well."

No doubt that was true, but Rhiannon also had *dewine* blood in her veins. She spoke her true heart and found lies distasteful. No one knew this more than Cael.

How many times had he begged her to pretend? All Rhiannon ever had to do was to marry him and bow to her mother, and never could she allow herself to do so.

In all her life she'd only spoken one lie—one—and that was the night she'd convinced Elspeth to escape Llanthony. She'd told all her sisters that she'd envisaged the future and that Cael would never have her. But even then, she'd known that wasn't true. The lord of Blackwood would have wed himself to a leper for the promise of Wales.

In part, Rhiannon had lied because she knew it was her sister's destiny to wed Malcom Scott, but there was yet another reason she'd done so: Some part of her woman's heart had admired Lord Blackwood even then.

He was her soul's mate.

Even now, she longed for his kisses.

De Vere," he said in greeting as they approached the gathering in the muddy field.

"D'Lucy," answered Giles with a half-hearted smile.

Clearly, they knew each other well enough to use given names. But then, again, why shouldn't they be well acquainted? They were cohorts, after all.

Only the bigger man seemed utterly confused. "What goes here?" he said.

All the while they approached, Giles de Vere had locked gazes with Rhiannon and then seemed unwilling or unable to take his eyes off her. Sensing he recognized the familial resemblance, Rhiannon dared to *mindspeak.*

"My lord Warkworth, we meet at last."

"Giles?"

Giles De Vere blinked, peering up at Marcella, and shaking his head, and Rhiannon understood that he must be confused by the voice in his head, although not entirely surprised.

For a moment, he tore his gaze away from Rhiannon, perhaps doubting his sanity. He nodded toward the castle. "Eustace is inside," he said.

"The King's son?"

Giles nodded. "So, his men have said."

The bigger man spoke now, his brow creased more with anger than concern. "I'll warrant the sorry bastard knows I'm ready to break his neck."

Giles cut the bigger man a quelling glance, then beamed at the young paladin in their company. "Jack," he said warmly, and suddenly the bigger man's face erupted with a grin.

"Jack!" he exclaimed as he rushed to the young man's side, reaching up to offer a hand in greeting.

Jack grinned. "Thought ye were rid o' me, di' ye?"

"You've grown whiskers," the bigger man said, rubbing his own face. "I scarcely recognized you." And then he tugged Jack down from the saddle, as though he were just a wee boy, dragging the apprentice into his burly arms, then clapping him hard on the back. He said fondly, "'Tis been too long!"

For his part, Jack could scarcely respond for the force of the hug. "You'll be the death of me yet, if you don't release me, old man," he complained.

The giant released him, and Giles said at large, though he once again settled his gaze upon Rhiannon, "This is my brother, Wilhelm Fitz Richard."

Rhiannon's gaze shifted to the brother, realizing only belatedly that she was face to face with not one, but two of her sisters' champions. Wilhelm was Seren's husband.

"So, what's it going to be?" shouted the man on

the parapet, rudely interrupting their reunion. "Will you leave peaceably, or must we fill you with holes?"

Brave words, said with less conviction than he'd spoken only moments before, but his warning effectively cut their greetings short. Whatever more need be said must wait until they dealt with the rogue prince and the adulterine castle he'd squatted upon.

Giles offered them a quick detail: They'd tracked Eustace to Amdel, after chasing him from Bury St. Edmunds. According to his men—those on the parapet—he was inside now, though he'd yet to show his face.

"How many are there?"

"No more than four on the parapet," said Giles. "No telling how many more within, but evidently they aren't concerned enough by our presence to provide a show of force."

"'Tis been these same four men on that wall," explained Wilhelm. "Only one of them speaking for the rest."

"There's only one inside," said Rhiannon.

Every pair of eyes slid to her, where she sat before Cael in the saddle.

"How can you know?" asked Wilhelm.

Rhiannon's eyes met Wilhelm's and she held his gaze. "Because... I feel his heart flame."

The behemoth narrowed his eyes.

Undaunted, she continued. "There are four on the ramparts, one elsewhere on the premises, and I presume he must be hiding inside the keep."

"Like as not drunk and lamenting his fate," agreed Giles.

"Quite likely," agreed Marcella. "We heard the cur

was dispossessed and that Stephen intends to cede his throne to Duke Henry."

Giles nodded affirmation. "Indeed, that's the plan," he said. "However, after I left, Eustace accused his father of ruining his life. He took a contingent of his own men—more than he has here, I presume, but I believe he lost them all after looting Bury St. Edmunds."

"Idiots," said Cael.

"Anyone of note on the ramparts?" asked Marcella.

Giles shook his head. "I don't believe so." He shook his head again. "Only a handful of dafties who believe the King's son has some chance with Morwen's intervention."

A prickle of fear raced down Rhiannon's spine at the mention of her mother. Instinctively, she peered up at the skies, searching for ravens. None were yet to be found.

And yet, even so, she understood with conviction that there were no coincidences. The Mother Goddess provided, if only one listened, and there must be some reason Wilhelm and Giles were already here.

There was a good reason they'd happened upon the King's son as well.

Whether or not they were aligned, their fates certainly were.

"We're pleased to see you," said Giles. "Now mayhap, we'll root out the bastard and set off to Warkworth together."

"We won't be traveling on to Warkworth," said Rhiannon. "I'm afraid this is where we must make our stand."

"Impossible!" declared Marcella.

"We haven't the men or resources," said Giles. "Warkworth is where they will send reinforcements."

"What goes here?" asked Wilhelm, frowning, perhaps slow to realize who Rhiannon was, since they had never laid eyes upon each other before now.

Rhiannon closed her eyes, inhaling a breath, communing with the *aether*, if only to be certain. When she opened her eyes again, she was sure and she met Marcella's gaze, pleading with the paladin to keep faith. Out of everyone standing here, Marcella was the one person who might fully understand. "And nevertheless, this is where we must remain," she said.

"God's bones!" erupted Wilhelm. "Who the hell is this woman to tell us what to do?"

Very somberly, Giles clapped a hand to his brother's shoulder, and said, "You of all people... can't you see the familial resemblance? She's Rhiannon Pendragon."

TWENTY-EIGHT

Like Warkworth, so many new castles were being designed with an eye toward safeguarding against fire. The brothers had learned the hard way how devastating such a happenstance could be. Five years ago, at Morwen's behest, Warkworth was put to the torch, on the command of the man who now lay hidden within this very fortress.

It was Wilhelm Fitz Richard who proposed sending a few, well-placed missiles onto the ramparts — "An eye for an eye," he said. Positioned right, those arrows could very well ignite the entire edifice, especially if those dull wits atop the barbican were keeping barrels of pitch over the gates, ready to boil and turn. If those should happen to catch fire, the parapet would ignite and burn swiftly.

As with Warkworth, there were two curtain walls, one defending an already compromised outer bailey and a smaller, stone wall surrounding the keep.

Only part of the outer wall was made of stone, and the wood they'd used to bolster it was dry and ready to burn, even despite the deluge they'd received last night.

Additionally, the ground, though puddled, was baked, signifying an overall lack of rain.

All things considered, they decided it would be simple enough to take out the outer wall without compromising the inner wall. Worst case, if the arrows didn't catch, they would create a suitable distraction, and Giles and Wilhelm could approach the gates to set fire to the doors.

Rhiannon thought it was a terrible plan, even if it was the only one they had. There was simply no way to know if there were barrels of pitch stored up on the ramparts, much less be sure where to find them. Simply because they employed such tactics at Warkworth did not mean the lord of this demesne would know to do the same. Clearly, though Beauchamp had had plans for his castle, he hadn't found the funds to complete it, much less defend it.

There were but four men, though unless they caught a pitch barrel, the flames could be easily extinguished, and quickly.

Moreover, they could run a torch to the gate and set it to burn, but only if they could get close enough for long enough to nurture a blaze, without acquiring an arrow through the skull. In the end, there was naught to ensure those flames would catch in time.

Frowning as the men prepared arrows, Rhiannon stared at the castle, a feeling of intense unease growing inside her.

Time was of the essence...

They *must* breach these walls and get within to fortify the castle's defenses, but not at the expense of anyone's lives—at least none of their side.

They had only six altogether, and on the other hand, Morwen had an entire army ready and willing to die for her cause.

Peering up, she spied a lone bird circling overhead—a reminder of how little time was left to be wasted.

Panic welled within her as everyone prepared to engage.

"Is there any reason you might wish to recruit any of those bowmen?" she asked, referring to the men inside.

Marcella shook her head adamantly. "Nay," she said. "Those idiots would betray us."

Giles added, "I agree; if anything, they'll be emboldened by the witch's presence."

"Let's burn them all," declared Wilhelm.

Rhiannon swallowed her fear, knowing intuitively that the moment they'd all dreaded had arrived.

So, it seemed, they would face her mother, with very few supplies, no soldiers to speak of. Their chances seemed grim, and it was imperative they enter the fortification as quickly as possible to begin warding the premises and to search for more supplies.

Unfortunately, without the *grimoire*, her efforts would be entirely instinctual, and there was no surety any of it would work. No matter that she liked to imagine herself a powerful *dewine*, she was as much a novice as her sisters.

But this much gave her hope: *Now* was the moment she had prepared for her entire life.

Now was the time she would be tested.

This, indeed, was the reason she had defied Elspeth at every turn, because Rhiannon had always known this moment was fated. She might not be Regnant, in truth, but she could not allow her grandmother's gifts to lie fallow.

At any rate, Seren was not here, neither was Ellie, nor Rose. As she had always feared it would be, Rhiannon was the one who must rise to the occasion.

"So be it," she said, and without further ado, before anyone could make her reconsider, she cast her thoughts in the direction of the ramparts and summoned a flame—not the same sort of flame as *witchfire*, but the conflagration was sudden and fierce. The gate erupted first, sending its torrent along the outer wall—the pier and beam floors, all the wooden accoutrements, as well as the gate itself. The edifice lit like a peat-covered torch.

Shouts resounded within. Men screamed as they burned, two cast themselves over the parapet, into an empty motte. The others shouted like banshees until they were consumed.

"Goddess alive!" exclaimed Marcella, with the firelight reflected in the pupils of her eyes. "Like mother, like daughter," she said, although there wasn't any indication of condemnation in her tone; rather, there was admiration.

"Bloody hell," said Giles.

Her husband said nothing, though his gaze traveled slowly from Rhiannon to the castle and then back.

Rhiannon averted her gaze, unwilling to look into his eyes, lest she spy contempt or revulsion for the sin she'd just committed against life. No doubt the Goddess would require she atone for those lives. Threefold their deaths would return to haunt her. And Cael... he might, indeed, say he understood, and he might have once aligned himself with her mother, but she had lived too many years spying revulsion and fear in the eyes of others. It was one thing to know what she was, and another to witness it.

Simply because she must, she hardened her heart.

This was war, she told herself, and those men on the parapet had cast in their lot with Morwen.

It was only Jack she was concerned about now, remembering only belatedly that he had been a witness to his father's demise. The young man stood, staring into the raging flames, his face pallid and his blue eyes wide as saucers. He grimaced as the last of the bowmen cast himself over the wall.

"Blast and damn," said Wilhelm, with a note of exultation.

Alas, Rhiannon daren't look directly into anyone's eyes. She watched the ramparts burn until every inch of wood was consumed and then finally extinguished. It happened swiftly, like a pile of old dry leaves put to a flame.

"Remind me to never anger you," jested Cael, and Rhiannon felt the heat of his gaze. Even so, she daren't face him—not yet... because... she didn't want anyone to see the uncertainty that must be emblazoned upon her face.

Uncertainty was weakness.

This was no time to be weak.

And worse—she must confess—there was a hint of rapture in her heart. She might not be too proud to have ended those lives, and yet... and yet... she had, indeed, thrilled over the return of her *magik*—the song in her veins longing to be sung. Even now, her body thrummed with energy and the hair on her head stood on end as she thought about her mother. *I will end you,* she thought silently.

I promised retribution, and I will give it.

Finally, at last, she would put an end to the woman who gave her life. Her mind whirring with thoughts of vengeance, she stood back and watched as the gate was completely consumed, leaving only a dark smoldering crater in a blackened wall.

When the smoke cleared, altogether they mounted their horses, and one after the other, marched into the castle, as that same, white-necked raven soared overhead.

TWENTY-NINE

ierce and beautiful.

His wife reminded him of the warrior queen Boudicca. Although she was long gone before his time, his father used to recount her tale to him as a boy: A noblewoman by birth, her lands were seized by the Romans. She and her daughters were flogged and defiled. In retribution, Boudicca raised an army and crossed the nation to challenge the governor in Anglesey, putting to shame the hearts of men who'd so willingly prostrated themselves for greed. Hers was the voice in his ear that had given him so much ambivalence throughout his life—on the one hand enjoying the fruits of his associations with Rome. On the other, shamed by the demise of the Old Ways.

Seduced by power and gold, he was as responsible as any, and for so long, he'd been a man confused; today he was not.

He was fiercely proud of his Welsh bride.

She was wise beyond her years and ruthless as she must be to deal with the Witch Queen.

Standing there, with her deep, copper hair and

her bright blue eyes, she'd cast a judgment upon the Prince and his men, ending all discourse over their fates as swiftly and easily as one doused a candle's flame.

God only knew, he pitied those men their final moments, even as he understood it was the right thing to do.

Wilhelm Fitz Richard was right. Given the opportunity, they would have aided and abetted Morwen in the coming battle; this was no time for mercy.

Familial pride lifted his shoulders as he cantered up alongside Rhiannon, waiting patiently as she refused to meet his gaze. Finally, when she dared to look at him, her eyes were bright with unshed tears.

Clearly, she wasn't so hard-hearted as she wanted people to believe—fortunately for him, else she would never have come to love him. Only now he knew she did, despite that she'd yet to say those three precious little words.

"You did what you had to do," he told her gently. "They would have proven to be disadvantages. I know how difficult it is to resist your mother's call."

"And yet... you did?" She furrowed her brows. "Did you not?"

The breath caught in his lungs. How to properly address this—and should he do it right now?

"Alas, I must confess, even now 'tis not so easily done."

"I see," she said, with a note of discord, her voice turning icy. "So, then, what keeps you by my side, Lord Blackwood?"

Love, he thought.

Pure and simple.

Love so impassioned, he longed to fall to his

knees and kiss her feet. "I spoke true. I'm here for you."

He recognized the storm brewing in her eyes.

It raged within him as well.

"What now if she tests you? Who wins?"

Even through her sarcasm, he heard uncertainty in her voice and it was nearly his undoing.

What, indeed, would he do?

It was an honest question and deserving of an honest answer, but Cael frowned, averting his gaze, because he didn't know how to reply.

In the end, defying Morwen could cost him his life—or, at the very least, his soul.

And yet, did he still have a soul in his body?

How did one extricate the essence of one's being and wholly unite it again? After all, one did not simply dismantle a dog as one did a plough.

Admittedly, he oft felt cold inside—ravaged, wasted, little remaining but an empty carcass.

Were it not for one thing... this small thing... he might think himself already spent. That one small thing was the spark of his heart flame reignited by Rhiannon—and would that be enough when faced with the end, as it naturally must come?

Would he truly be strong enough to die for what he loved... *this time?*

Alas, though he had the reliquaries in his possession, he was still ignorant of their power, and if Morwen should wield them against him, would his resolve crumple like a decrepit auld cairn?

When it mattered most, would he choose love over life?

Or life over love?

Cael liked to believe he had a definitive answer...

But did he?

Truly?

It was easy enough to speak what he knew in his heart to be the right and honorable thing to do under these circumstances, but would he act upon his words?

And this was the thing that haunted him most... all those many moons ago, when Nesta begged him to allow her to sacrifice herself to save his life... he'd let her.

Instead, he should have denied her and allowed her to live out her life in peace... without him. He should have closed his eyes evermore, and let it be so.

But nay, he had not. He'd given her assent.

Delirious or nay, he'd made a choice. And perhaps he'd hoped it wouldn't cost her life, but she did say it would, had she not?

Only speak the word, and I shall gift you my life!

Aye, he had said, and so she had... and here he was.

And then, when he'd sworn to honor her memory forever, what had he gone and done? He promptly forgot her and gave his heart to another.

He'd given it to Rhiannon.

But... was he truly capable of the selfless love Nesta had displayed? Or, when push came to shove, would he betray his own heart? And this time, if he failed, he'd never find comfort in vengeance...

This time if he failed, he would long for death.

They breached the gate without contest and Rhiannon averted her gaze.

"Forgive me," he begged.

"For what?"

"For everything I have done," he said, and once

again, his wife dared to look at him, her demeanor hardened again.

"What about for the things you did not do?" she asked, and gone was the soft, sweet young woman who'd slept so peacefully in his arms.

Cael swallowed, tormented.

Why, indeed, had he not set her free?

Because he was afraid she would leave.

Because he was afraid to die.

Because he was a greedy bastard intent on revenge.

More than anything, he longed to pull her into his arms, and kiss her desperately, tell her again and again that he loved her—as he knew, he should have long ago.

She was, he feared, much like a cat, nearly gone feral—one instant curious and longing, the next ferocious and distant. "Ask me no promises, I'll give you no lies," she said, tossing his own words back at him. God's truth, it was nothing less than he should expect from the defiant woman he'd come to know and adore. And nevertheless, it struck him a doubly painful blow, because, in truth, he didn't deserve anyone's forgiveness, much less hers.

Nor was he entirely certain he would ever earn it.

In the end, he decided, this was not the time for a heartfelt discussion, not with so many curious ears. So, he let it go, leaving her question to linger between them.

What now if she tests you?

THIRTY

Dismounting in the courtyard, the entire entourage approached the keep together.

No groomsmen came running, nor did any sign of life catch anyone's eye, save for one lone cock pecking about a garner.

Cael commanded the wolfhound to stay, and the solemn beast lay down beside the horses to wait.

Inside the castle, it was equally as dismal.

Amdel's hall was dark, its walls covered with smoke-stained, sagging tapestries. The sour scent of spoilt rushes made Cael's nostrils flare as their boots clicked along rough stone tile. Following the light of a lone, flickering torch illuminating the recesses of the great hall, they entered to the resounding boom of a clap. Thunderous against the silence, it cut through the room, echoing harshly against bare stone walls.

Clap. Clap. Clap.

There, they discovered the brat prince seated atop the lord's dais, hunkered down in his chair, drunk and belligerent, his eyes bloodshot and angry as he glared at both Warkworth brothers, leading the way into the hall. "Lauds!" he shouted. "Lauds!" And then he laughed maniacally. "Shall we toast to your perseverance, my lords?" He clapped again, and this time the sound was hysterical.

"Guards!" he called. "To me! To me!" But no one came.

No. One. Came.

The hall remained empty of footfalls, except for their own, until all who were present came to a wary halt before the littered dais.

The Warkworth brothers immediately moved to one side, Jack and Marcella to the other, just in case Eustace attempted to run, though he scarcely wiggled a toe. In fact, his gaze followed Giles and Wilhelm as he sank further into his chair, and said, wiggling a cup, "Drinks, anyone?"

"You're a sot," said Giles.

"And you, my lord de Vere! You're but a lackey, though you believe you're a very wise man. My auntie Matilda keeps you by the short hairs of your cock."

Giles unsheathed his sword.

Cael knew the brothers longed to silence him forever for his sins against Warkworth, and, in truth, he would like to hand them both a torch. The King's son was a waste of human flesh—a bag of bones with no redeeming qualities aside from the potential enrichment of good soil.

"You're all so pathetic!" said Eustace. "Look at you!" He laughed, and then, his gaze fell upon Rhiannon, his eyes narrowing as he scoffed, "At long last! The proud, prodigal daughter emerges. Has anyone ever told you that you look precisely like your mother, dear? Alas, I warrant you've not half the wits she has. Too bad."

Smiling thinly, he then turned to Cael, and said,

"And you! Traitor! Your lips speak words—" He made a kneading motion with his hands to simulate froth at his mouth. "But 'tis little more than scum of the mouth. You are no better than Morwen's ungrateful daughters. Oh, but I warrant she'll see you pay for your faithlessness—every one of you!"

He pointed to each of them in turn, stabbing at the air. "You. And you. And you. And you. You. And you!"

His gaze returned to Rhiannon then, and he said, "There's nothing you can do to stop her, witchling!"

It was Marcella who spoke next, her voice resounding throughout the empty hall. "And yet, Prince Eustace, 'tis you who sits alone in the shadows of an abandoned castle, drowning your sorrows with sour *vin*! I warrant 'tis you who is the fool—you and those poor dafties who were stupid enough to follow a worthless, would-be king."

Eustace's gaze shot to Marcella, his gray eyes burning with loathing. "I may yet show you how ineffectual I am, you black-eyed cunt." His hand moved to grasp the area of his genitals, and he squeezed furiously.

Marcella drew her sword and rushed the dais. Cael intercepted her, throwing an arm about her waist and drawing her back to a safer distance, even as the brothers advanced upon the dais.

"You'll die poorly," promised Marcella, even as she allowed herself to be restrained.

"Not yet," said Cael. "As it stands, he's one more bargaining chip in our favor. We'll make good use of him. Seize him," he said to the Warkworth brothers, and both men rushed the lord's chair, dragging the prince up by his skinny arms.

No more than a lanky boy, he stumbled as they tossed him roughly toward the steps. But, emboldened by the realization that he would be spared—for the moment—the relief in his eyes was evident. His gaze narrowed malevolently. "You haven't the first hope to defeat her!" he screamed. "Hail the Witch Goddess!"

And then he roared, "England will fall, and then rise again from its ashes! 'Tis I who will rule in the end! Damned be my father and to hell with Duke Henry!"

"You're a fool," said Rhiannon. "My mother will give you nothing. She'll take whatsoever she pleases, including your seat on the throne, and in the end, no one will remember your name."

Cael frowned at the disheveled prince being led off the dais, feeling a twinge of regret for what they were forced to do, if only in part because the lad was the same age his own son had been when Uther murdered him. "I'm certain Beauchamp kept an oubliette," he suggested. "Find it and put the prince there."

"Gladly!" said Wilhelm.

"He's all yours when the time is right," said Giles. "Don't harm him yet."

"Guard him as though your life depends upon it," added Marcella.

"Because it does," agreed Cael.

Once the prince was led from the hall, the remainder of the party dispersed, Giles to search for supplies and Cael to look for signs of life.

Rhiannon and Marcella worked together to safeguard the castle with warding spells and the remainder of Marcella's philters. But the castle was a poor refuge as it stood.

The outer gate was destroyed.

The ramparts were still smoldering.

Whatever protection the outer bailey had afforded them, it was gone.

Alas, there wasn't time to rebuild. Between now and such time as Morwen descended upon them—whenever that might be—they must find some way to secure the stronghold as best they could. Unfortunately, the prospects were grim—two women, one dog and four men against whatever army Morwen was rousing. Consequently, before setting out to inspect the grounds, Cael did something he hadn't done since his time in the monastery. He searched for and found Amdel's chapel—hidden as it was at the back of the bailey behind a savage little garden. He shoved open the door, revealing a dusty and cob-webbed interior, and made his way down the aisle toward the nave. Then, he knelt before the altar and prayed.

Macbeth, William Shakespeare

Our reunion is bittersweet. In your belly, swollen with promise, I made the tricksy *fae*. Within your bowels I wrought the future. With your brew I'll change the fates.

Very soon, when the light of this world has been doused like the flames of a hundred thousand dying stars... here, I'll remain. "With you, my sweet..."

D'Lucy will pay.

Rhiannon will pay.

Stephen will pay.

The years have been long, and my body left wanting—too long without a lover's touch.

The last I had in my bed was no more than a selfish little twat with dreams of wearing his father's crown.

"Marcella," I hiss. *You'll pay most of all, because you knew me when my heart was tender with pain... because when I revealed unto you the deepest, darkest place in my soul, still you held me and sang to me in the crook of your arm.* "Deceiving little witch."

How easily you plotted and schemed to steal away my daughter. How easily you betray me.

"Fire burn and caldron bubble," I say, coaxing a flame about the fertile belly of my grail. And then, for a moment, I watch, fiddling with my ring. After a moment, I open the hidden compartment, then turn the contents into the kettle: Newts. Moon snails. A touch of human remnants. A pinch of bloodroot and hemlock, only for good measure.

Stirring the pot with the tempest of my thoughts, I stand and stare into the silvery solution, once again mourning the loss of my scrying stone—that heirloom of my destruction that was stolen from me, along with my cauldron and my children. I suffered Taliesin to live and he repaid me by conspiring with my enemies.

Creirwy, you fool. Did you believe there would be no reckoning? Did you not know I'd suck the breath from your lungs? Did you think I would allow you to grow old and die here in this wretched pile of stones, keeping from me my *grimoire* and my grail? *Nay.*

Arrogant, faithless, ungrateful daughters.

Every one of you—*Creirwy, Elspeth, Rhiannon, Seren, Arwyn and Rosalynde.*

I brush a finger across the lip of my cauldron as Mordecai appears before me in the courtyard, his dark form silhouetted by the shifting dawn.

"Where are they?"

"Amdel."

"Not so far," I say.

And yet, not close enough.

"How many travel with them?"

"Six, including Marcella and Lord Blackwood."

Cael, you fool! I told you not to lose your heart to my daughter, and what did you go and do?

My gaze moves slowly to Mordecai. "Do *not* call him thus in my presence ever again. Blackwood is mine. I am done with pretense."

"As you wish, *meistres.*"

"What of the lords you roused from slumber? How many will pledge their armies?"

"*All* are persuaded."

"Good," I say. "Send my ravens. You and I will await our travel companions."

"Aye, *meistres.*"

"Go now," I say, anger darkening my tone—a fury not unlike that day so many ages thence when I last faced my makers, and they exiled me for my "tantrum." And yet, they did send me to rule the realms of men, and this I will do.

Damned be their prophecy!

Damn be the words written in the grimoire!

I will not return to a watery grave!

Ego Draconis,

Natus Sylph

A capite ad calcem, igneus et fortes.

. . .

I AM THE DRAGON.
   Born Sylph,
   From head to toe, fiery and strong.

THIRTY-ONE

They found the oubliette in, of all places, the evening shadow of the church, constructed so that the spire, with its swordlike crucifix, might cast its long, punitive shadow into the rat-infested pit—a daily reminder to repent.

Clearly, the Prince hadn't any compunction over his sins. He spat at Wilhelm before entering the pit. "My only regret was that you were not there when Warkworth burned," he said, and Wilhelm reared back, and punched the man, breaking his nose, drawing blood. The Prince squealed indignantly, bringing a hand to his face to catch the blood. "Do you know who I am!" he railed. "Do you know who I am?"

With something like a snarl, Wilhelm pushed the man backward, not bothering to afford him a ladder or rope. He plummeted downward, landing with a thud and a crack.

Rhiannon was close enough to hear the exchange, but not close enough to know whether he was injured—clearly, not badly, because she could still sense his heart flame strong, and he continued to shout so loudly that his voice carried all throughout the bailey.

She could still hear him, even as she searched the garden, hoping to find ingredients for a good meal.

Although there was little to celebrate, they would need their strength over these coming days, and Rhiannon hoped there might be enough vittles to provide them all sustenance after a *sennight* of travel.

Unfortunately, *magik* could not produce food from thin air. That's simply not the way it worked. It was only possible to manipulate the *aether* in ways that did not violate the laws of nature.

Fortunately, there were still several chickens living and thriving, nourished by the remnants in the garner. She counted more than a dozen hens and two healthy cocks pecking around the yard. Without delay, she and Marcella collected two of those hens, then found the kitchen to clean and prepare their prizes, then Rhiannon returned to the garden to see what else she could find.

At one time, these raised beds must have been well-cared-for. But they had gone wild during these past few months while the castle sat empty—not more than two or three, she thought. She was heartened to find radishes, peas, parsnips and leeks, as well as carrots.

However, whilst she was exploring, she caught an image as she passed... It was her sister Elspeth, kneeling with a lovely young woman next to a bit of bedstraw, both tugging at weeds. It was no more than a glimpse, but she knew intuitively it was a look into the past, and she fell to her knees where her sister had once knelt, missing Elspeth so dearly that she feared she might weep.

Five years.

Five long years since she'd last seen any of her sisters, except through visions and dreams...

"Soon," she whispered. "Soon."

For better or worse.

She thrust a hand into the cool, damp earth, and just as surely as she could feel it fill the palm of her hand, she knew she would see her sisters again...

It was a feeling she couldn't explain, but it was strong now... strong enough to squeeze her heart.

Ellie had been here... right here, in this very garden... perhaps en route to Aldergh...

Perhaps, in truth, this was where Malcom had left her that day when he'd returned to Wales to find Rhiannon.

Smiling over the memory of Malcom Scott approaching her tumbril, she sprinkled the soil back into the bed.

She knew who he was the instant she saw him. Tall, with a great bearing and a face that no doubt made women swoon, he'd approached her tumbril with a sense of purpose and she'd had little doubt he would draw his sword and fell every guard assigned to her travels.

She wouldn't allow it.

Affecting a pretense so that her guards wouldn't realize she was *mindspeaking* with him, she'd shouted obscenities at Lord Aldergh and tossed a makeshift *grimoire* at his head. She felt badly about that now, but a sense of panic had come over her when she'd realized he meant to free her.

I go where I need to go, she'd said.

Straight to her destiny...

Straight to Cael.

~

DURING A THOROUGH SEARCH of the premises, Giles and Wilhelm discovered a well-equipped armory. Unfortunately, most of the weapons had already been confiscated. Still, there remained an anvil and forge, and more than enough tools and scraps to effect repairs. Therefore, while Giles assisted, Wilhelm put to use his modest skills, honing all their weapons in preparation for the struggle to come.

Marcella made use of the kitchens to brew more philters, and meanwhile she cooked up a few hens.

Cael inventoried supplies, then devised a plan for defense.

It was to be expected, perhaps, that, after Beauchamp's death, someone—likely the King's men—would have swept through these grounds and seized most of the dead lord's valuables. In fact, it could be that Beauchamp's sister, now wed to Blaec d'Lucy, had appropriated what she could. But Cael suspected it was Eustace who'd laid the castle bare, stripping even the walls of its tapestries, if only to sell.

Surprisingly, they found no evidence of plunder on the premises—not until they discovered a small room adjacent to the lord's chamber, which, in fact, did contain some of the relics belonging to Bury St. Edmunds.

Here, the King's son had evidently begun to store his treasures, perhaps having seized upon Amdel as a base from which he'd intended to mount a coup against his father.

In support of this conjecture, they found evidence to that effect within the lord's chamber, including a list of barons who might be persuaded to rally to his cause.

They also discovered maps of Winchester and the treasury at Flint Tower. More documents like these were littered about the lord's bower. Cael gathered them all together and took everything to Giles, leaving Rhiannon to further investigate the room. It was a mess, littered with sour-smelling cups, and items of note that probably belonged to Eustace—a fine sword, a golden scabbard, a nice bow with fletching, a very nice set of ringmail armor, with all the necessary bits, all in very good shape. As it so happened, because Eustace was slight of figure, it also fit Rhiannon, so she put it aside.

The room itself smelt of spew and piss.

Evidently, Eustace had also discovered a store full of ale, and perhaps consumed every drop, judging by the horrid state of his room. It was no wonder he did not join his men on the wall; his pores had also reeked of alcohol—easy to scent at twenty paces, and more.

Evidently, he was sulking, and furious over his dispossession—a manner of depression that manifested itself with a terrible stink that he never bothered to dispel, even despite having the use of a large, ornate tub.

In fact, no one had used that tub in quite some time, Rhiannon surmised, evident by a thick layer of dust inside. She longed to fill it and bathe, because, in truth, except for a few sponge baths, she'd not even done so on the night of her nuptials. She'd donned that beautiful wedding dress with a week's worth of grime on her person. And so, it seemed, she might yet get the chance, because when everyone claimed a room, they conveniently left the lord's chamber for the "newly wedded couple."

Rhiannon was quite sure it wasn't entirely charitable; the stench of the room was difficult to bear. Therefore, after she finished placing a few more wards about the inner bailey, she mounted the stairs again to begin repairing the room as best she could.

Really, considering what they were about to face, it was perhaps of little consequence, but some small part of her longed to spend at least one night with her husband that was... special—not that she would live to remember it, mind you, but it was important to her that she at least have one moment of joy to cherish.

Indeed, she still had cause to be vexed with Cael, but the time for petty grievances was over. He was here, with her, and he had, indeed, confessed his love.

Sadly, they were not even promised one evening together, much less the morrow. Therefore, if they were still alive and breathing after the Golden Hour— which she knew intuitively would be their greatest hour of peril—she intended to make the most of her time with Cael.

At any rate, ever since her conversation with Marcella about the particulars of congress, she very much longed to... *explore*.

To that end, she found a lovely, but scandalously diaphanous shift hidden away in a wooden coffer that appeared as though it might be part of a bride's trousseau. The contents were musty, but everything inside the chest was of the utmost quality—all women's garments.

There was also a small armoire in the room with the remnants of a man's wardrobe. Most of what it once contained was gone. Within it she discovered a single *sherte*, one pair of very pointy shoes, and a rich, blue velvet surcoat that was heavy with dust.

Such as it was, there were no other signs of a woman's touch in these quarters. The coffer, she surmised, must have been a gift in wait for a bride—very convenient, she decided, considering that she herself was a newly wedded bride.

In fact, she might have presumed this one was meant for the lord's sister, since Cael had said she was recently wed, but the garments were not at all what Rhiannon would suppose a brother would provide for a sister.

For example: The *chainse* was as sheer as a woodland mist, and there were gowns inside that trousseau that revealed more than was prudent, or even acceptable.

To be sure, there were some women at court who dressed so outrageously, but not even Morwen had dared.

Rhiannon hadn't any interest in those, but she did intend to make use of the *sherte*, exchanging it for the smelly tunic Marcella had given her. She no longer needed the masking philter, and though it was a little too big, she could easily tuck the *sherte* into her breeches, at least until she could wash the tunic she was given. She couldn't very well wear some silly gown whilst wielding a sword, nor could she use the ringmail without some protection for her skin.

It was easy to imagine why Marcella wore such garb. No gown was suitable for warfare. She could easily trip over the hem and injure herself, and Rhiannon didn't intend to unintentionally aid her mother's cause. They would need every sword arm they had to bear, even if Rhiannon's was less than able.

But at least she had her *magik*, which was growing stronger and stronger by the hour.

She found a set of clean bedsheets in a storeroom, and after changing the bedding, she put the delicate *chainse* on the bed, turning her attention to the remainder of the room.

By the time she was finished cleaning, the sun was already lowering to the west—a beautiful view from the lord's window, where she could peruse the outer bailey and the parklands beyond.

For the time being, the tree line in the distance revealed no sign of movement and neither was there any sign of Morwen's birds, except for that one. For this, Rhiannon breathed a sigh of relief. Perhaps they would be spared tonight—she hoped. She had a strong intuition for which there were no promises. Still, though she felt a terrible ramping of tensions in her soul, the moment right now was serene. The sky was beautiful, with shades of lavender, peach and pink, and she sighed wistfully, considering the beauty of the moment. It was no wonder these were called the Golden Hours. It was a time of limitless possibility if only one had the will to open their hearts. Here and now, it was impossible to believe that somewhere out there her mother was preparing to butcher them. And yet, Rhiannon knew it was true. There was no way that Morwen would let this be; she was like a wounded beast no longer caged.

Hic est Draco...
Here be the dragon.

Only now she truly understood what that meant —the inscription writ upon her bracelets...

In their purest forms, the *Sylphkind* were winged creatures, like dragons, both beautiful and terrifying at once. For love of these famed creatures, the kings of Wales had all named themselves the Dragon's Disciples, and it was for the *Sylphkind* they'd decorated their banners.

Hic est Draco...

Rhiannon herself was a Pendragon, named for Uther, whose pennants he stole from the true Dragon Lord. Anglesey was said to be the cradle of Wales. *Ynys Dywyll*, as her people once called it—the Dark Isle. And *Môn Mam Cymru*—Mother of Wales. Rhiannon had never been there, but she'd been told much about this sister isle to Avalon. It was said to be riddled with *menhirs*—the standing stones of the gods. These days it was Owain Gwynedd who raised the dragon pennant, but Rhiannon knew by the way he spoke of it that her husband had bartered his fealty for the payment of this county in Wales. *He* longed to have and hold the Dark Isle.

Hic est Draco...

If, indeed, Morwen was Cerridwen, then *she* was the true mother of Wales, and all its people—Cael included—were honor-bound to rise to her defense.

Was this, then, the crux of Marcella's story?

Was this her dire warning?

Was it from Cael and not her sisters that she must be wary of betrayal? She thought about that as she filled the tub—an easy enough endeavor with her strengthening *magik*. There was so much moisture on the ground after last night's deluge, even after a full day in the sun, that it took little effort to gather the moisture into droplets and the droplets into a lovely shower. She stood inside the tub, naked as the day she was born, allowing herself to be showered by the gifts of the Mother, feeling anew the thrill of *magik* hum through her veins and the gentle downpour of cleansing water rushing over her face.

This was what she was made for!

These were the moments when she felt whole!

It could be, in truth, that her husband was still her enemy, but for this one night alone, he would be her lover. This, she knew in her woman's heart. For better or worse, tonight... they would consummate their vows.

CHAPTER

THIRTY-TWO

Cael froze, stunned by the vision that greeted him upon entering the lord's chamber—the sight both startling and surreal. Never in his wildest dreams could he have conjured an image so fine as the one he saw before him.

Rhiannon.

But Rhiannon as he had never witnessed her before. Gloriously made, unashamed, reveling in the pagan *magik* that fed her soul.

The soft curves of her woman's body were masterfully formed—breasts high, taut and round.

Revealed to him fully, her mons was as dark a copper as the hair on her head.

She stood with palms turned up inside the downpour, eyes closed, while a soft cascade of rain fell over her and *only* her, showering her where she stood *inside* the tub.

It straightened the curls of her glorious tresses, so it fell like copper satin against her face and proud shoulders, diverting water so it cascaded like a fountain over her breasts, teasing her nipples till they pebbled with pleasure.

330

Cael's response was visceral; his body reacted at once, hardening to its full length, unyielding as stone and throbbing for a release long denied.

He wanted nothing more in that instant than to go to her and open his mouth to receive the blessing of water from her bountiful breasts.

"Rhiannon," he said hoarsely.

Very slowly, she opened her eyes, though if he feared she would conceal herself from his greedy eyes, he feared for naught. Immodesty was her cloak this eve and her ice-blue eyes were feral, her lips curved ever so gently at the corners, into that wicked little smile that set fire to his blood—entirely reminiscent of the smiles she used to give him when she defeated him at Queen's Chess. And now, even as then, he would gladly lose, with grace, and cede all he owned but for the promise of a kiss from her lush, beautiful lips.

He was a man lost, besotted by his wife. No other woman in his long, strange life had ever put such a flame in his heart.

Only belatedly, he closed the door, hoping to God that no one had been hiding in the shadows of the hall, because, in a fit of jealousy, he thought he might pluck out a man's eyes only for having taken the liberty of ogling his wife.

His wife.

His.

Wife.

A primitive and fiercely proprietorial instinct swept over him in that instant and he knew that he would kill any man—or woman—if they so much as dared to harm a hair on her head...

His wife.

All memory of the women who came before her vanished from his heart and mind as his feet moved of their own accord. He swallowed with difficulty, but never dared avert his gaze.

As he had for so long, Cael yearned to possess this woman, body and soul, and, at the moment, he was entirely too aware of how long it had been since he'd lain with a woman—years and years and years. Even now, his cock was hard as stone, hot and throbbing.

"Husband," she said softly, warmly, and the single, softly spoken word struck him no less violently than a hammer.

It shook him to his bones.

She crooked a finger at him, and Cael crossed the room like a man enslaved, wanting nothing more than to take this nymph into his arms and whisk her to the bed—at least he hoped there was a bed, because his eyes were blind to all but Rhiannon...

MARVELING OVER the look of appreciation on her husband's face, Rhiannon beckoned him forward, feeling more emboldened than she had in all her given years.

She did not feel afflicted, nor plain, nor ugly when he looked at her just so. In fact, he appeared to her as though he might sink to his knees at any instant to worship her where she stood. A sense of empowerment came over her at the realization—a feeling quite unlike anything even her *magik* had ever provided. It was as though her husband's admiration lifted her up and proclaimed her a goddess, and she had never, ever felt so beautiful as she did in that moment.

Sweet fates.

This was not what she had intended.

She had meant to dress and present herself to her husband clean, with freshly plaited hair, wearing that beautiful diaphanous *chainse*. But she had been carried away by the moment, and now, seeing him standing before her, sweat beaded upon his achingly beautiful brow, and his tunic sodden with perspiration, she wanted nothing more than to gift him with the same joyous experience she'd given herself—a shower courtesy of the *aether*.

She reached out for him, luring him inside the tub. And then, once he was there, she tugged at his clothes, helping him disrobe. One by one, his garments found the floor.

Only once his chest was bare, she eagerly reached for the twin reliquaries; he reacted swiftly, pinning her hand to his chest, cutting her with a warning glare.

But then, just as swiftly, he seemed to reconsider, grasping both reliquaries in one hand, and removing them himself, discarding them into the folds of his tunic, before giving Rhiannon a long, hard glance...

Curious though she was, Rhiannon hadn't any true interest in his baubles now. She was far more concerned about what else remained to be unveiled...

Once his hands moved to his trews, she stood back, watching breathlessly, eyes wide as he loosened his ties.

She swallowed convulsively as his breeches fell away and he shrugged them off, revealing himself fully to her wide, greedy eyes.

Sweet fates... he was truly magnificent—like a god—perfectly formed. His shoulders were broad, his chest lightly flecked, and his manhood fully and frighteningly erect.

She did, indeed, want to lower her gaze—and did only for an instant—but then she lost her nerve and, instead, met his deep, dark eyes.

Now it was his turn to smile—a small, knowing, satisfied male smile that sent a frisson down Rhiannon's spine. And yet it wasn't fear. Because she wasn't afraid. It was anticipation. She wanted this more than anything in life. Tomorrow would be soon enough to remember all that was at stake.

Tonight, he was her husband.

Tonight, she was his wife.

This moment a gift from the Goddess...

THIRTY-THREE

The casting of *magik* required intense concentration.

It was a long, muddled moment before Rhiannon could remember herself well enough to resume the shower, and then, once she did, still another before she could remember what else she was supposed to do—lave him, she supposed.

In that instant, all pretense of self-assurance fled, and she was left only with a virgin's uncertainty.

Mercifully, Cael didn't wait to see what she would do. His arms slid about her waist, embracing her and pulling her close. His lips claimed hers, hot and insistent, and Rhiannon could only whimper with pleasure as his lips melded with her own, hard and unyielding, coaxing her to open for him.

And then, before she could respond, his tongue swept between her trembling lips, taking and plundering the depths of her mouth, his tongue lapping her teeth, exploring, sparring with her own, only this time with a hunger she hadn't known before.

Sweet fates.

She could *taste* his ardor, *smell* his arousal—the

faintest trace of pollen, that made her ache deep down.

Freely choose, or choose to be free...

Unbidden, she heard the words like a whisper in her head, and despite that she'd already spoken her vows before a priest, she knew it was a plea from the Goddess for Rhiannon to speak now or forever hold her peace.

"I choose you," she said breathlessly, and heard an answering whisper...

Bound by destiny, to destiny bound,
Another to one, and one to another.

"Rhiannon," he cried softly, perhaps oblivious to the words of the Goddess, and Rhiannon melted against him, her breasts hardening against the tiny hairs of his chest.

Instinctively, she arched backward, supported by the strength of his arms, as he trailed soft, little kisses from her lips to her chin, down her neck, and down through the valley of her breasts. When his mouth closed, hot and insistent, over one nipple, she moaned softly with terrible longing.

This was everything she had ever desired and yet nothing she had ever anticipated. Even as he suckled, Rhiannon felt a delicious tug at her womb, and a dampness creep between her thighs.

And then... sweet Goddess... he lowered himself again, kneeling at her feet, and lifted his face to her mons.

His tongue struck out, boldly sweeping between her woman's flower, pressing high against her bud, the sensation warm and delicious in contrast with the cool water cascading over their bodies. And suddenly, she lost the thread of her *magik* completely, leaving the water to trickle over them in spurts that mirrored each foray of his tongue.

"Cael," she cried out, her fingers weaving themselves into his thick, black hair, groping desperately as he drank from her, rewarding her with a first taste of animal pleasure; it washed over her in waves, wracking her body with shivers. And then he rose again to offer her his tongue and Rhiannon was shocked to find the taste of her body lingered.

Bold. Shocking. Delicious.

If she'd thought herself intrepid, this only inspired her sense of daring. She accepted the gift, a pleasant tang that she would never have been audacious enough to explore on her own. Her body began to convulse in the most private of places, and she longed desperately to be filled—intuitively, knowing it could only be Cael.

"I'd lay beneath you," she said, shivering in his arms.

He smiled gently. "I'd have you lay beside me instead."

She nodded, understanding, and lowered a hand to his manhood, touching it tentatively.

"Art certain?" he asked.

"I'm your wife," she said.

THAT WAS all Cael needed to hear.

Merely hearing those heartfelt words nearly unmanned him where he stood.

He could barely restrain himself. She was perfect, a blend of innocence and daring that fueled his jaded imagination. He could think of a million ways he longed to have her, but realizing this would be her first coupling, he intended to prepare her as best as he could. If, indeed, his time in this realm was nearing an end, he would die contentedly, knowing he had, at long last, found the light of his heart. As it so happened she was Uther's heir.

Morwen's daughter.

Yet none of that mattered.

Not right now.

Burying the tips of his fingers into her silky mons, he continued to kiss her mouth, mimicking with his tongue the rhythm he longed to follow with his hips.

She tasted sweet, like honeysuckles, sex and rain —the odd combination like manna from Heaven. This night would be theirs, he vowed—even if on the morrow the fires of hell rose to destroy him. Nothing, no one, could keep him from claiming his wife...

Bound by destiny, to destiny bound,
Another to one, one to another.

Strange whispers in his ears, from a voice he didn't know. But he needn't a word of encouragement.

He bent to sweep Rhiannon into his arms, and carried her to the bed, laying her down very gently, unconcerned that they would dampen the bedding. Now, he longed to drown in the love she so willingly gave, and not even the fact that he was parted from his reliquaries occurred to him.

"Rhiannon," he said, as he caressed her face, and then he covered her body with his own, pressing her down into the bedding, giving her only half his weight, his hips already moving of their own accord, seeking and begging entrance to the temple of her body.

"I love you," she said, startling him with the declaration, and his heart sang with a chorus of joy. Still, he was determined to afford Rhiannon the same pleasure she gave him.

"Spread your thighs," he demanded. And then, once again, he shimmied down her body, kissing and lapping at the valley between her breasts, suckling each nipple in turn, before moving down to kiss her belly and mons. And there, again, he sent his tongue to coax the wetness from the font of her womanhood, knowing intuitively that this would make her first time easier to bear. Rhiannon moaned and he reveled in the sound, lapping hungrily and suckling her silken petals. When he was certain she was ready for him, he lifted himself to look into her eyes and said slowly, clearly, lest a word be mistaken. "Live or die, I will do so for you, my love. I love you, and only you, Rhiannon Pendragon."

And then, he positioned himself between her thighs, nesting himself there, as he pushed himself inside her. He entered slowly, then paused for an instant to savor the silky heat of her body. But her eagerness was, again, his undoing. Undulating beneath him, she lifted her hips to welcome him, and he gave her what she sought. Feeling her maidenhead rupture, he bent to swallow her soft cries with his hungry mouth, offering his heart, his body, and soul, and finally, his seed—though not until she cried out one last time, so intensely that he momentarily feared he had harmed her. He felt her body stiffen and knew instinctively she'd found release. That carnal knowledge set free the beast within, and he filled her desperately, sweat dripping from his temples as he worked for his pleasure, until he cried out with sweet release, then collapsed atop her with a heart filled with joy, and his cock still throbbing violently.

Unwilling to withdraw even then, he grasped her by the arse and turned them both so she held his cock inside her, both their bodies pulsing with pleasure.

"Christ have mercy," he said.

And this was, perhaps, the wrong thing to say, because his impish wife grinned sportingly, and said, "Oh, my dear husband... God may, indeed, provide you mercy, but I will not."

And then she smiled a secret smile, and again began to undulate atop him, her hips rocking him ever so maddeningly, slowly, slowly, coaxing, coaxing... coaxing.

Inconceivably, he found himself hard as stone once more, and ready to be ridden. Of their own accord, his hands found her hips, prepared to guide her, but then he felt her tighten about him, and he nearly died with pleasure. Submitting entirely to her will, he let his hands ride the silken curve of her hips, giving Rhiannon complete control over their loving.

Five.

These were the number of years Rhiannon had dreamt of this moment—ever since she'd spied this glorious man in her vision. Goddess ordained, he was her husband, and all the *Sylphs* in Heaven and all the dragons on deep couldn't keep her from taking her fill of him.

Here and now, this very instant, she confessed, if only to herself, she would have moved Heaven and earth on that day she'd helped Elspeth escape, to keep her sister from this glorious man who was destined to be hers. It was in some ways the most selfish act of her life, and would she have coveted him if he were not Goddess sent?

Yes, she thought. *Yessss...*

With the greatest satisfaction, she rode him fiercely, like a primal queen atop her cherished steed, eternally grateful for Marcella's advice, because even as she watched, his eyes rolled back into his head and she knew the instant he submitted to her pleasure.

Bound by destiny, to destiny bound,
Another to one, one to another.
Here now and forever.

THE SKY outside her window was a cloudless blue.

Rhiannon laid her head atop her husband's arm. His free hand cupped her bottom, and when she stirred, he sleepily drew her close.

"Good morning," she said, when he opened his eyes. This near, they were so deep and dark they appeared fathomless, and she could peer into them evermore.

He slapped her bottom gently. "Good morning, wife."

Rhiannon smirked. "No regrets for having wed a witch?"

"None at all," he said, lazily caressing the sting from her flesh. It was only then that she realized that, sometime during the night, he'd risen to retrieve his reliquaries. He was naked still, but for those twin chains, and the reliquaries they were bound to. Both fell heavily between them and she dared to lift one up to better inspect it.

"One belongs to me," he said. "The other to your mother."

"So, you said. What are they?"

"*Grisial huds*, so I'm told."

Magik crystals—but to what purpose?

Rhiannon thumbed one of the crystals, brushing it thoughtfully.

SHE REALLY DIDN'T KNOW, Cael realized, thinking back to his conversation with Marcella.

Of course, he didn't say it then, nor had Marcella asked. Alas, though, he realized he couldn't keep the truth from his wife. Reaching out for the chain in her hand, he explained the reliquary's purpose, waiting to see disgust in her eyes.

"Shadow *magik*," she whispered.

Cael's soul was bound to the reliquary, his body borrowed—usurped from a man he'd never met, save through the intricacies of his body. He'd assumed a dead man's name instead of his own after Morwen summoned him back to this realm. Unfortunately, he'd always known she could and would return him from whence he came.

"So then... d'Lucy is not your true name?"

"Nay," he said.

"What, then?"

Cael shook his head, unable to speak the rest of his truth.

God's blood, what could he say? He was born before she was ever a thought in her mother's head? That her great, great, great, grandsire was his foe? That he was murdered six hundred years before she was born?

Nay.

It was inconceivable. The very thought of speaking those words made him feel like a madman... except that... it was all true.

He could offer a partial truth.

"What Mordecai is, that's what I am, too."

"A... Shadow Beast?"

There was contempt in her voice. Cael tugged his reliquary from her hand and let it drop between them. "If that's the name I must bear."

"Nay," she said. "You are not what he is! I know that in my heart!"

And yet, he was...

"Oh, my love," she said gently, catching his cheek in her palm. "A man is not the sum of his body parts, but rather, the sum of his deeds." Very gently, she moved her hand to his chest, laying it atop his beating heart. "I know you! You are not the same as Mordecai."

Cael swallowed whatever words he'd been about to say.

He wanted desperately to believe she spoke true... wanted to see himself through her eyes—not as the shell of a man he'd become. Later, he decided. Later was soon enough to reveal the rest—later when he hadn't any choice.

Right now, bathed in the light of his wife's love and adoration, he couldn't bear it if she turned away. One last time before they rose, he longed to taste the sweet nectar of her body and revel in the warmth of her touch. Forgoing any more words, he rolled atop her, lifting himself up and taking his cock into his hand, he gave her a lazy smile...

THIRTY-FOUR

Morwen did not appear that day, nor the next, nor the next.

Every moment that passed stretched by as taut as the string of a bow; something terrible was looming, no doubt.

Even the air began to thicken like a mire.

Anticipation bubbled like a yeasty brew.

Outside the castle, a few common black crows had begun to congregate, perching in nearby trees like an infestation of fleas.

Knowing intuitively that six alone could never defend against Morwen, they dispatched Jack to Drakewich to engage d'Lucy's cousins. Cael wasn't entirely certain they would feel compelled to make this fight their own, but, if indeed, Morwen should descend upon these parts with an army of Welshmen, Drakewich was too close not to be warned. At the very least, they should be armed with information and be allowed to choose a side—not that Cael had any delusions that his "cousins" had any true regard for him. They'd met but thrice, and despite that Cael did hold

Blaec with the utmost respect, they were hardly close. They were cousins in name only. Pressed about the details of their affiliation, Cael would surely fail such a test.

And yet, what was there to apologize for? He was not the one who chose this man's body. He was simply the one forced to occupy it. Whether the true d'Lucy lord was kind or cruel, Cael hadn't a bloody clue.

Such as it was, no matter what happened here in these parklands over the following weeks, and no matter whether he confessed himself to Rhiannon, the lords of Drakewich would never hear the truth from him.

In spirit and mind, they were aligned.

Rhiannon found him poring over the reliquaries late one afternoon, trying to determine how best to employ them. If only he could determine which was his, beyond doubt, he could destroy the other.

And yet, he wasn't even certain that would have any bearing on Morwen's presence in this realm. It was a crystal, no more, and her soul was already bound to the body she'd appropriated.

Well, at least hers bore the same blood in her veins.

He was someone else, and his true self was a man long forgotten.

Worse yet, Rhiannon did not fully grasp the truth. In Mordecai's case, he, too, was returned to his own body.

Conversely, Cael was not who Rhiannon believed him to be.

She leaned over his shoulder, examining the reliquary in his hand, watching him fiddle with the crystal, poking at the place where it sat mounted —seamless.

"Even diamonds can be destroyed," she said. "They crack when struck. Have you tried?"

Cael nodded solemnly. "I have," he lied.

"Have you tried burning them? Even the strongest of metals will melt given the proper degree of heat."

Cael sighed, and shook his head, ashamed to say that he had, in fact, never intended to destroy his. Only once, in his anger, had he ever attempted to crush the stone, and he was heartily relieved when it refused to break.

She slid her arms about his neck, leaning close so he could feel her warm lips on his cheek. "You know... I once saw my sister battle a Shadow Beast..." She peered at him, offering a smile, and teased, "Perhaps you can shift shapes, as Mordecai can?"

Her jovial tone intimated she didn't believe it. But it wasn't particularly amusing, and Cael did not laugh. "'Tis not an art your mother ever taught me."

"Of course not," she said, withdrawing, but leaving a hand on his shoulder. "Why would she share anything with anyone?"

She still didn't understand, he realized. He sensed she understood that he was bound *by* the reliquary, but not *how* he was bound to it. He longed to say more... ached to find the words to tell her the truth —everything.

Fear caught and held his tongue.

"At any rate," she said. "My sister spoke words to bind the Shadow Beast to his body. That alone was not meant to destroy him, only to keep him from shift—"

A solid horn blast erupted from the ramparts.

At this point, they had bolstered their defenses as best they could. At least one person was always assigned to man the wall. Right now, it was Marcella's turn. Seizing both reliquaries, Cael looped them about his neck and moved to the window. Rhiannon followed behind.

Away, in the distance, filtering from the trees, came a good-sized army—too big to belong to Drakewich, too small to belong to Morwen.

"Who is it?"

Cael narrowed his eyes, searching for banners, and once he spied one, he turned to Rhiannon and grinned.

"Come with me," he said, taking her by the hand.

~

It was a bittersweet reunion.

Five years since the sisters were all in the same room, and here they were, again, all together... without Arwyn.

The loss was felt no less keenly for the years gone by.

This evening, Amdel's hall resounded, though not with laughter, but quiet sobs.

There were tear-stained cheeks and tunics.

Embraces held too long.

On a bright note, they were six no more, but more than three hundred strong, with the Pendragon sisters all reunited and stronger for the power they wielded together.

And despite this, Morwen should never be underestimated. She was an ancient being, wielding all the power of her birthright. Maddeningly, all the while soldiers trickled into Amdel's bailey, crows and ravens continued to gather in the trees of the surrounding forest, their numbers so great that they burdened the trees with their weight—a reminder that this was no reunion for pleasure and their time now was growing short. Once all their greetings were made, everyone attended an emergency council in the great hall: Giles with Rosalynde; Seren with Wilhelm; Elspeth stood with Marcella; and Edmund, Warkworth's seneschal, sat on a trestle table, his helm by his side, his face mottled from having worn the accoutrement so long. Arms crossed, Rhiannon stood beside her husband, his hand on her shoulder as they discussed matters at hand. The first question was posed to Elspeth. "What of Malcom? Will he join us?"

Elspeth nodded, though solemnly, her response somewhat less than affirmative. "*If* my message reaches him, I warrant not even his king will keep him from it."

Giles tore his gaze away from Rosalynde, a muscle ticking at his jaw. "What of the Scots King?"

Elspeth shrugged. "Your guess is good as mine," she said. "Already, I have appealed to him twice, and twice he has answered when he did not have to. I only hope he values my husband well enough to support him."

"Is this not Duke Henry's war as well?" asked Wilhelm tersely. "Why is that pup not here?"

Giles appealed to his wife, and she gave him a subtle nod, then said, "His mother will rally forces, so I'm told. But they were due at Warkworth, and the question remains if he will arrive in time."

"Unfortunately, ravens are not an option," said

Cael. "Save for a few stragglers, she commands them all."

"Pigeons neither," agreed Elspeth. "At this point, 'tis not entirely certain whether any winged creature can be trusted."

"I *am* certain," said Seren, rising from her chair to pace. "They cannot be trusted."

And this was perhaps the greatest shock to Rhiannon—to see her sister's altered appearance. Seren's hair had once been such a lovely shade of golden red; now it was silvery white. Her eyes, which were once blue, were the brightest amber—but they were not crossed, nor did her face reveal any of the haggardly lines of a woman with hair of that shade. Her skin was smooth as a baby's bottom, and pale—as though she'd never once enjoyed the sun. And yet, despite this, she was lovely, her appearance radiant and her presence ethereal. There was no doubt she had found her place in the service of the Goddess.

"Explain," said Giles.

"As many of you know by now, my mother is *Sylph*, aligned to *all* creatures of the air. Free will is, indeed, a gift from the gods, and yet, as 'tis well known... birds of a feather will flock together."

"*Sylph*?" asked Wilhelm, and Seren endeavored to explain, meeting Rhiannon's gaze at the end, if only for an instant. *I am sorry*, she said, mindspeaking. *I know you believed this to be your destiny.*

Rhiannon was quick to reassure her. *I am your servant, my sister. It matters not to me who should be Regnant, only that our mother is defeated. I am content enough with my lot. Do not fret for me.*

The sisters both shared a nod of solidarity.

This was no time for envy or discord.

All must work together to defeat Morwen, and not even Seren was capable alone.

Please, forgive me for what I must do, Seren said cryptically, and then, averting her gaze from Rhiannon, she gave a discreet nod to Warkworth's steward.

"Bring it," she said, and the seneschal departed the hall, only to return a moment later with a golden scabbard, revealing the shining hilt of a sword. Rhiannon's eyes widened, knowing intuitively what it was, although nothing could have prepared her for what transpired next.

Edmund handed Seren the sword.

Her sister turned to face Cael. "Dragon Lord!" she said, in a voice completely unrecognizable. Even her countenance seemed to change in that moment, the air about her shivering like steam from a kettle.

For his part, Cael appeared momentarily stunned, though Rhiannon was certain he'd understood the appellation.

"Dragon Lord," Seren called again, moving toward him. "I present you the key." She unsheathed the ancient sword from its scabbard, revealing it fully before them, and laid it upon her two hands.

THE SIGHT of it was momentarily blinding.

Cael blinked against the weapon once used against him.

The sword that took his life.

That same gift he was presented by Taliesin.

In all its silvered glory, it lay before him, presented in the very same manner it had been revealed to him on that fated night so long ago... lying atop open palms, so the inscription could easily be read. Etched in the most ancient of languages, lay inscribed and imbued, *"Take me, but turn the blade, and we will see."* Between the hilt was written: *Caledfwlch.*

After all these years, there it was... with its intricately crafted serpents entwined about the elegantly fashioned hilt...

Shaken by the sight of it, Cael's fingers ached to reach for it, but he met Seren's gaze, aware that his wife was watching him carefully.

This was not revealed to her yet... his relation to the sword. His relation to her kinsmen. His vow to kill everyone who bore Taliesin's blood. All his dark and terrible secrets. Even now the sword called to him, beguiling...

"All that you give you must give freely," said Seren. "Once again the sword has been imbued, so that he who wields it will not bleed. Even now my mother gathers the heirs to the twelve who conspired to betray you. She will give you all you seek, and more... wealth, power... Anglesey..."

Try though he might, Cael could not avert his gaze from that shining blade. "I... I don't want it," he said, not trusting himself to touch it. The temptation was all too real. With that sword, he could retake Wales.

He could rebuild his isle.

He could—

"Cael?" said Rhiannon, sounding bemused.

Seren waited.

It was his to take...

"Cael?"

"I... am... not... Cael," he said as he accepted the proffered sword. He lifted it high to inspect it, then brought it down with a confident swing, reveling in the feel of it.

"I am Maelgwn ap Cadwallon, true King of Gwynedd, Dragon Lord of Anglesey, firstborn son of Cadwallon Lawhir."

THIRTY-FIVE

Maelgwn would love to have imagined a collective gasp.

Alas, there was only one... the one emitted by his wife... the only person he did not wish to displease.

At least... this was not the way he'd wished to reveal himself.

And so, it seemed, the remainder of those gathered already knew who he was... and still they would grant him the sword.

For a long moment, that fact left him reeling, confused, though he'd reached for the sword anyway, the temptation too difficult to resist.

The very instant the cold steel had met his flesh—familiar even through the ages—it sent a sizzle through his veins, a surge of vigor and strength that hardened his cock where he stood. His breath halted over the feel of *Caledfwlch* in his hands, the fine way the pommel melded with his palm, the precisely honed steel crafted only for him... so long he'd coveted this weapon, even after it stole his life, and everything he'd loved...

Even now, he was a man possessed, willing to gamble for the sword, no matter the cost.

"Is it true?" asked his wife softly, her voice filled with pain.

She was astute enough to understand what was happening.

Rhiannon was no fool; she knew full well what things were possible through *magik*. Although she hadn't once suspected who he was, he knew she would know the truth when she heard it... and when he met her gaze, the look on her face filled him with dread. He responded instinctively, merely intending to remind her of her promises to him and her place by his side. The words came out harsher and less hospitable than he'd intended. "'Tis true," he said. "I *am* the Dragon Lord, and lest you forget, *you* are *my* wife!"

Rhiannon stood then, formidable as any woman could be. "Nay," she said. "Need I remind you, my lord? I am a Pendragon. I make up my own mind who I stand beside." And then, very swiftly gathering her skirts, she marched out of the hall, all three of her sisters filing out behind her.

"Rhiannon!" shouted Elspeth. "Wait!"

She was immediately followed by Rosalynde, but neither of her sisters could break her pace. Rhiannon disappeared from his sight, and Seren turned to give him a subtle smile, though her final words as she followed Rhiannon were not for her departing sister. She said quietly to Cael, "That sword is a gift, my lord. But so, it seems, you've not yet earned my sister's trust. Both are Goddess-given. One may provide you Wales, the other will gift your true heart's desire.

Choose wisely, Dragon Lord, or you may lose them both."

~

RHIANNON HAD KNOWN he was keeping secrets from her —something dark and dreadful. And yet, she would never have imagined it could be this—not *this*.

Sweet fates!

His life had been prolonged by blood *magik*. And though she didn't know precisely how that was done, she knew enough to know that to return to this realm, he must have been cauldron born, and bound to his summoner...

Morwen.

No wonder he did not kill her when he had the chance.

No wonder he did not turn away from her villainy.

No wonder he'd kept Rhiannon imprisoned far too long.

A shadow beast...

Bound to her mother.

Time and again, he had said quite plainly that his aim was Morwen's aim. Well, now she understood why. Only what, precisely, did it mean? Was he compelled by her mother? Did he possess free will? Was his life bound only to the Witch Queen? And now, if they killed Morwen, what did that mean for Cael?

All these questions formed a melee in her mind, though she found answers for not a one.

But worse! He was a sworn enemy to her family— a foe of the man who had, according to Marcella, slain

Maelgwn ap Cadwallon so long ago—six hundred years, to be precise.

Six hundred years!

And still... somehow, he was young and vibrant, with the vitality and passion of a flesh and blood man!

Sweet fates. She'd lain with him, and even so, she must confess: She did not regret it. Not for a moment. Even now, her heart ached for him, and some tender part of her soul mourned for the man he had been.

All those years ago, he had faced his own mortality, lost everything that was good and true in his life —his kingdom, his wife, his children and heirs...

The notion was too much to bear.

Marcella had warned her. In her own way, the paladin had revealed so many pieces of the puzzle— pieces Rhiannon hadn't had the wherewithal to comprehend.

And now she truly knew how arrogant she had been—to think she was so wise. Well, she was not.

Commiserating, she and her sisters ensconced themselves into what Elspeth claimed to be a women's solar, although the room was neither pleasant, nor comfortable, nor even well furnished. Spartan as it was, it was as barren as the womb of a crone. Verily, it appeared to Rhiannon that no woman had ever turned her hand to the chamber's good use, except for a broken-down, old loom. And yet, according to her sister, this was once the refuge of Dominique Beauchamp, the beautiful sister of Amdel's now dead lord, who was bride to Blaec d'Lucy.

Rhiannon wondered if the lord of Drakewich would bother to come. It would serve Cael right if he turned his nose at the request, and even so, they needed all the help they could get. She prayed to the gods that Jack would manage to persuade him. And then she wondered why she bothered to pray, because, in truth, her mother was a child of the Sylph, made by gods. How much good would it do?

Like Lucifer, she was cast down from the heavens. And therefore, it must be true: witches were angels, and demons were born by their whimsy—Cael himself was proof.

Her sisters gave her a long moment to grasp the import of her discoveries. And meanwhile, Rosalynde brushed a hand along her back, the gentility of her sister's sweet touch a comforting balm. It had been so long since she'd reveled in a sisterly touch, and it took every ounce of Rhiannon's strength not to cast herself into Rosalynde's loving arms and weep like a disconsolate child.

"So, I'm told, he swore to eradicate our blood from this realm," said Elspeth, with a note of bitterness. "Art certain you still trust him?"

Rhiannon shook her head, then nodded, and said with tears forming in her eyes, "He is my husband."

And yet, she feared; it was entirely possible they harbored an enemy in their midst, and hadn't Cael said so?

Hadn't he warned her endlessly over these past five years?

We are not aligned.

We are not aligned.

We are not aligned.

And still, he did leave Morwen at Blackwood, perhaps to die, and he came after Rhiannon to help defend her.

Or had he really?

She was so confused now.

What if, all along, he'd been doing her mother's bidding? What if he had brought them here to this godforsaken ruin instead of to Warkworth so they could be ambushed by her mother? For five long years, Warkworth had been preparing for this confrontation, and here they were... in a place and state of disrepair, with no chance to survive any siege and few allies to speak of—not to mention, they were ill-equipped to win a simple battle. If Morwen should descend upon them right now, whether alone, or with allies, they would be like lambs drawn to a slaughter.

"Listen to your heart," said Rosalynde sweetly. "As you know, I wedded a huntsman, Rhiannon. Like you, I should have never trusted Giles."

"And yet do you?"

Rosalynde nodded fervently. "Implicitly."

"What has he said?" pressed Elspeth, not so kindly.

We are not aligned.

We are not aligned.

We are not aligned.

"That is *not* the question to ask," reprimanded Seren, and then with a smile in her golden eyes, her middle sister knelt beside Rhiannon, placing a hand to Rhiannon's knee. Up close, Seren's skin was perfectly radiant. Her hair shone like filaments of light. "As you once told Arwyn—remember? —you must trust *your* heart."

Rhiannon blinked away a tear. "You were there?"

"Nay, I was not, my sister. And yet I have seen it." She sighed woefully, and said, "I have witnessed more than I ever cared to see. And still, I know what I know, and I do not know what I do not know."

"What does *that* mean?" snapped Elspeth. "Please, Seren! Do not confuse her with riddles. She has enough of a burden to bear."

"Goddess, alive! You might be eldest," argued Rosalynde. "But you are *not* all-knowing. Leave off with the tyranny, Elspeth!"

"Please, sisters," begged Seren. "This is not the time to battle amidst ourselves."

Rhiannon exhaled wearily.

So much had changed, and yet, so much remained the same. Elspeth was just as domineering as ever, only this time, it wasn't her eldest sister and her at odds. She smiled ruefully over that, amused despite the situation. In all her days, she would never have imagined Elspeth defending her... at least, not since they were children. And here she was, precisely doing that.

As usual, Seren's patience was heroic. "What I meant is this: I have seen the past, but the future is still to be written. I do not have the ability to see it. Rather..."

She turned to Rhiannon, *mindspeaking* her own words, and Rhiannon gave them voice. "Life is like a spider's web—so many threads flowing from its center, all leading to destinations unknown."

"Precisely," agreed Seren. "Such as it is, I cannot receive answers for which I do not know the questions."

Elspeth frowned. "Every day, you sound more and more like that crazy old bat, Isolde—riddle me this, riddle me that!"

"Isolde?" said Rhiannon, her attention piqued,

and Rosalynde explained about the old crone's visit to Warkworth, and all about the old crow that arrived at the same time. Remembering the crow perched on Marcella's shoulder, Rhiannon wondered... *could it be?*

Just in case, she told her sisters about the encounter, and all that Marcella had told her, including the tale of her mother's death, who was also, coincidentally, named Isolde.

"Isolde is dead?" asked Elspeth, confused.

"She died moons ago," said Rhiannon. "Marcella claimed it was the year she deposited us all at Llanthony."

"Hmm," said Elspeth, clearly disbelieving. "And what about Marcella? Do you believe we can trust her?"

"Aye," said Rhiannon, remembering the sword that the paladin placed between herself and Cael—or rather, between herself and Maelgwn.

Sweet fates, she was so confused.

"Indeed, you may trust me," said Marcella. She stood in the doorway, cocking a smile at all four sisters.

"How long have you been there?"

"Long enough," she said, before sauntering within. "If you do not mind, this is my story to tell." And true to form, she did not wait for permission. Without preamble, she confessed her story to the sisters—her love affair with Morwen, her departure from Blackwood after Ellie was born, as well as her very brief, but bittersweet betrothal to Cael.

Apparently, it was the real Cael d'Lucy who was once affianced to her, not Maelgwn ap Cadwallon. Ever-ready to use her minions to her own selfish purpose—even someone she claimed to love—Morwen had urged Marcella to play the part of d'Lucy's betrothed, only to claim Blackwood. If, indeed, those two had wed, and Morwen had managed to wrest Blackwood by another means, she would have forgotten all about her daughters. Originally, it was her plan to share it all with Marcella.

"D'Lucy was a fool," the paladin explained. "A poppet, too easily led." Unfortunately, or perhaps fortunately, as the case must be for Cael, Morwen discovered a *grisial hud*, like that one she kept around her neck. She performed the same blood rite that was performed to summon her return, though I do believe she anticipated it must be Taliesin's crystal, and she meant to end him once and for all." Marcella smiled benevolently at Rhiannon. "It wasn't, of course. The reliquary belonged to Maelgwn ap Cadwallon, and once he assumed d'Lucy's body, your mother had a change in plans."

"Please, do tell," said Elspeth, smartly.

Marcella eyed her cannily. "At first, she thought she might wed him herself, but he was never interested in the least. Oh, he gave her his fealty quick enough, as well as the use of his sword, but never his cock."

Rhiannon blushed hotly, feeling some measure of relief. She looked to see that her sisters' eyes widened over Marcella's crude language, but no one dared utter a word in rebuke, and Marcella continued. "Eventually she sent me *away* to spy on the Holy Roman Emperor, whilst she remained in England to press her wiles. I suppose I grew tired of her lies and found myself inspired by your sister Matilda."

Elspeth visibly softened, as she confessed, "She inspires me as well. I knew her to be driven, even as a young girl. When William died, I hoped my father would cede her his throne—and, of course, he did. But clearly this is not a woman's time to rule." Her tone sounded disappointed now, and she found even more cause to commune with Marcella.

"Alas, my friend, a woman's arse might not be allowed to warm a throne, but no good king ever reigned without a good woman at his side."

"Indeed," said Elspeth, as she nodded. "So, was it then you joined the Guard?"

Marcella nodded. "Indeed. And it was your sister who arranged it. I served as her personal guard for a long time, and then, when her husband died, and she was sent away, she made certain I was given an assignment with the Guard." She grinned then. "I was not entirely welcome."

The sisters all laughed, only imagining the first time Marcella had walked into their company.

"Marcella is a *dewine*," offered Rhiannon. "Aligned to earth, alchemy her calling."

"Is that true?" asked Elspeth. And then she put a hand to her breast. "I, too, am aligned to earth."

"Aye, so I am told," said the paladin. "We have this in common."

Only Seren seemed unsurprised by these revelations. Her sister sat quietly for a moment as they all discussed the potential applications for the pursuant battle.

Elspeth could help with a few more warding spells. She and Rosalynde had discovered some way to create *witchwater*, though not the type that needed summoning. With so much water lying about, it would be easy enough to gather it all into the motte.

Whatever became of anyone who fell into it was entirely up to the gods.

"That's a good idea," said Marcella. "I have herbs that could enhance the brew." But, really, it was only a half measure. The five of them alone, even working all together, wouldn't be any true match for Morwen and an entire army of her creatures. No doubt she was gathering all her sycophants, else she'd already have been here by now. What they really needed was aid from Scotia, Stephen and the Church.

"Speaking of which, I suppose I should say that Jack has joined the Guard as well."

"Jack?" the sisters, all but Rhiannon, asked in unison.

It was Rhiannon who nodded, and then explained. "He and Marcella escorted me from Blackwood together. He's gone to seek the aid of Cael's... *cousin...*"

Implicit in that disclosure was the truth of the matter: The lord of Drakewich was not her husband's cousin.

Would he ever be told the truth? And if so, what purpose would it serve? Not only was it inexplicable, but it was also far too fantastical to be believed: witches, demons, *Sylphs*, angels, gods and *magik*. And Cael—she did not know him as Maelgwn and refused to think of him thus—was for all intents and purposes, a demon, summoned by *hud du*. The very thought made Rhiannon's head hurt. Somehow, she, a daughter of the Goddess, was wedded to a Shadow Beast.

"What a tangled web," offered Seren, with a shrug.

~

Cael sat with his head in his hands.

He was not the man he used to be. That man was gone, dead and buried. *Quite literally.* If he ever chanced to locate where "Maelgwn ap Cadwallon" lay resting, he would unearth a pile of dirty bones.

Or would there be ash?

He didn't know.

All he knew for certes was this: He was monstrously ashamed of what he was, and what he'd done.

In the end, all he'd sought to achieve would amount to nothing without Rhiannon.

What, indeed, profiteth a man if he gained the entire world, but lost his soul?

Lifting both reliquaries from his tunic, he removed both chains from around his neck, placing them gingerly on the floor at his feet to study each in turn.

They were exactly alike—nothing to distinguish them at all.

He wished to Heaven he knew how they worked.

If it so happened that he destroyed the wrong one, he might leave Rhiannon to battle her mother alone.

Conversely, if he destroyed them both... he could save them all, but then he would be gone from this world, and his time with Rhiannon would be done.

But she would live, unburdened by a monster for a husband. She would find herself a better man, who could love her and keep her as she so deserved.

But God's blood! *He* wanted to be that man.

He wanted to wake each day to her sultry smile

until they were old and toothless—and he would love her even then.

To his dismay, the thought of another man touching her... loving her... filled him with white-hot rage.

Destroy the right one, and he might yet live the life he craved...

Destroy the wrong one and he would leave Rhiannon alone.

Destroy them both...

He swallowed convulsively, his hand reaching for the sword beside him on the bed.

Caledfwlch.

Even now, he sensed its innate power, and knew that, no matter how many times someone might attempt to destroy the *grisial huds*, they would fail immeasurably. Contrarily, this sword would do the job. Of that, he hadn't any doubt.

He could wait to face *her* in battle, and see which reliquary shone in her presence... and then, attempt to destroy the right one... but that may not work, he realized.

Even despite the sword's fabled blessing—that he who wielded it would not bleed—he couldn't be certain it was true. At least, not for him.

Neither was Morwen to be underestimated.

She was frighteningly powerful, even despite her recent misfortunes. If she should happen to take her own *grisial hud* back... if she destroyed his instead...

Running a hand across the stubble of his beard, he studied the crystals attached to each reliquary and chain.

Something in his gut told him that those crystals were profoundly important. Without them, the compartments they were attached to would be nothing but empty metal. They needed each other, and they needed to remain whole. The way he'd laid them across the floor... one good strike would destroy them both... and then come what may.

Lifting the sword, he fell to his knees, praying for the second time in as many days.

Making the sign of the cross, he kissed his thumb, then raised the sword aloft, taking it firmly with both hands as he continued to pray—not for his own soul, though he knew it to be in peril, but for Rhiannon and her sisters.

He prayed for England.

He prayed for forgiveness.

Most of all, he prayed for good aim.

And then he lowered the sword with a thunderous crack that resounded throughout the castle, smashing both crystals into smidirín.

THIRTY-SIX

The battle commenced without pomp or ceremony, signaling itself with a new influx of birds. More, and more, and more arrived, till the entire field before Amdel Castle appeared black with their numbers. Squawking noisily, crows and ravens quarreled amidst themselves, pecking and diving at one another as though vying for territory. And even as their numbers grew, so too did the cacophony, until the sound was maddening and the air held a note of menace.

Down in the yard, the wolfhound began to howl.

Presently, dark clouds rolled in, bearing with them the silent menace of lightning. Heavy with mist, the air held a wintry chill uncommon for the kalends of August.

Trying not to think about Cael, or his forced confession, Rhiannon shivered over the sight that greeted her as she arrived on the ramparts with her sisters. After the first inrush of birds, Warkworth's seneschal had come to retrieve them from the solar. At once, they'd equipped themselves for war and reconvened on the parapet, dressed in mail.

Morwen would strike at the most opportune time. For a *dewine*, this would be the Golden Hour—those delicate moments during which the Veil between worlds was at its thinnest and the *hud* was at its strongest. These twilight moments came twice every day with the gloaming. Some folks called the half-light a *witchlight* because it was during this time when otherworldly creatures drifted into the Realm of the Living: The *faefolk* danced through their sacred groves, changelings came to trade for babes, shapeshifters changed their forms, will-o'-the-wisps revealed themselves and banshees howled into the wind.

By now, both the inner and outer baileys had been warded, but it was difficult to say how effective those outer wards would be without walls to protect the circlet and spell.

Right now, those birds were well outside their periphery, but wards like these were easy to breach, and not even Elspeth knew for certain how to keep Morwen's ravens outside their proximity without help from the Goddess.

Like a pentagram, a circlet was only intended to harness *magik* into a specific area. It wasn't a deterrent to physical forms. In fact, it was quite easy to disarm a warding spell simply by stumbling over its lines.

Mercifully, Morwen herself could not enter the premises unbidden. But, to ban a person from entry, one must speak their name, and Morwen's soldiers were all nameless.

Warkworth's warriors came prepared; under the seneschal's direction, archers now formed a defensive line on the ramparts. Another defensive line two-men deep defended the inner bailey. Barrels of pitch were being boiled, poised to defend the gate. The postern door had also been warded and barred, and a handful of soldiers had been assigned to the gate.

However, there were not nearly enough men to defend the outer bailey, and slowly, slowly, slowly... the birds came closer and closer... alighting on the remnants of the burnt outer wall, breaching that barrier to amass in the outer bailey. Although, fortunately, as of yet, they had not come near the wards Elspeth had placed...

Because it was presumed that Morwen would attempt to barter for the things she most valued, Prince Eustace was dragged from the oubliette, hands bound, and brought to the ramparts. At the moment, he looked nothing at all like the arrogant bully who'd enjoyed picking on those less fortunate. Hungry, dirty and tired, he sat where they bade him to sit, and perhaps only bided his time, still hoping that Morwen would free him. With his head in his hands and his winter grey eyes so like his father's, he sat looking like the broken man he was.

Rhiannon didn't want to feel pity for him, and yet, she did.

She knew what it felt like to be discarded, and she knew what it felt like not to be valued. Only she would never have taken her fury out on others, as he had.

Sweet fates. What must it be like to feel so little compassion for human suffering, or the lives of others, that one would put an entire castle to the torch?

It was no wonder they kept Wilhelm from the King's son, because if that were Rhiannon's family murdered by his hand, she might, indeed, have killed him herself, pity bedamned.

Now, she watched from the ramparts, along with her sisters and Marcella as Morwen's birds transformed themselves into soldiers in the blink of an eye. It happened so swiftly, there wasn't a change to note. They were simply birds one instant, the next, black-clad soldiers, armed with glittering swords, exactly like those soldiers her sisters had encountered at the Widow's Tower. "She's here," announced Seren, rubbing her arms.

"Someone fetch Giles."

"I'll go," offered Edmund.

Giles and Wilhelm were both in the courtyard preparing their best line of defense, and if there was a bright side to be found, it was this: They wouldn't have to worry about any siege. But, alas, neither did they have the resources to win hand-to-hand. As it was, they hadn't even the numbers to hold the castle for long, nor enough missiles to keep Morwen's army at bay. Rhiannon begged the Goddess for mercy.

"I hope she's listening," said Rosalynde.

"What of Cael?" asked Elspeth. "Has he emerged yet?"

Rhiannon shook her head, even now dreading the sight of her husband as much as she dreaded the coming battle. Their time was up.

What would he say?

What could she say?

For all Rhiannon knew, he had already slipped away, and even now he was out there... *with* Morwen —his benefactress and mistress.

"Nay," said Seren, reading Rhiannon's mind, and Rhiannon frowned.

She had always been better at *mindspeaking* than any of her sisters. And, in fact, until now, she had been better at everything than everybody, except Morwen. It was wholly unnerving to discover that Seren was suddenly the better, stronger, wiser *dewine* —and neither was she accustomed to her sister's altered appearance, although for Wilhelm's part, he seemed unfazed by the changes in his wife, and if anything, he seemed relieved—as they should all be.

As the dark clouds grew darker, Rosalynde waved a hand, speaking softly to entreat the Goddess...

Goddess of light, protect us this night.
Ye who would harm, ye who would maim,
Proceed and face the same.
By all on high and law of three,
This is my will, so mote it be.

"Alas," said Marcella. "I fear it will not constrain her."

"It's something," said Ellie.

And then they waited. All together. All five *dewines* stood watching as the Golden Hour arrived, and the fields continued to pepper with soldiers, until every puddle bore boots.

An even colder mist crept out from the woodlands, crawling slowly toward the castle, frosting the air so that it was possible to spy one's breath. Rhiannon rubbed her arms vigorously, fear rising up her spine like an icy tide.

When finally, Morwen arrived, she came with reinforcements—Welsh standards raised high against the setting sun. But they did not rush the castle. Instead, they moved closer, and closer until the foreground was a crush of black and metal.

And then, suddenly, a sea of men parted before

the Witch Queen, as they had during the battle of the Tower, her soldiers standing quietly, allowing her to pass.

In she rode, astride some enormous black horse, her black hair plaited for war and her armor shining dully. And yet, though she was unmistakable, there was a horse and rider trailing behind her who wasn't immediately recognizable—not until she came closer.

Rhiannon gasped.

Marcella snarled.

"Christ!" said Giles.

Rhiannon's heart kicked violently against her ribs, as Giles immediately moved to restrain Marcella, who started screaming.

"Do not harm him, Morwen! Kill him and I will slay you myself!"

It was Jack.

Hands bound at his back, with a bloodied cloth shoved ruthlessly into his mouth, he was stripped of his armor, including his clothing. Naked as the day he was begot, he sat astride his courser, his wide blue eyes peering up into the ramparts, speaking words his mouth could not...

Do not treat with her, he said.

Rhiannon's heart gripped with fear.

Morwen halted outside missile range, tugging at Jack's lead rope, pulling his horse up beside her. "I've brought you a gift," she said sweetly, her voice echoing unnaturally across the misty, puddled field.

Poor, poor Jack!

Rhiannon attempted to connect with him and found his heart flame beating savagely.

Jack, she said. *Oh, my dear, sweet Jack.*

I am sorry, he said stoically.

We will trade for you! she said. *We have Eustace!*

Nay, my lady, do not. Do not treat with her, he said bravely, and even from this distance, Rhiannon could see that his shoulders lifted and his chin hitched defiantly.

Raucous laughter reached the ramparts. Clearly, having heard their *mindspoken* words, the Witch Goddess was heartily amused. And yet, Jack never once said from whence he'd come, Rhiannon realized. Had he somehow managed to keep that from Morwen?

Even now, could Drakewich's soldiers be en route?

Rhiannon prayed it was true.

"Let us treat!" demanded Morwen. "You have something that belongs to me. I wouldst have it returned. Moreover, as a sign of your enduring good will, I will require the traitors Cael d'Lucy and Marcella le Fae. Send both to me now, and I shall free this man-child and leave you in peace."

Behind her, her entire black-clad army shifted in preparation. At the flick of her fingers, all the Welsh bowmen in her company moved forward.

Do not treat with her, begged Jack desperately, shaking his head, and Morwen laughed. "Fool," she said, glancing at her defiant prisoner. "Do you not realize I can hear you?"

Go to hell, you spawn of the devil!

"Quite to the contrary," she said mirthfully, and tears pricked at Rhiannon's eyes because she understood what Jack was saying, and it was true. Whatever transpired, they should not barter with Morwen. And, to that end, he'd already decided he would die for this cause. And die he would, Rhiannon knew, and she swallowed the tears that rose to choke her. Her gaze sought Marcella, but Marcella's eyes were only for Jack.

Eyes burning, Rhiannon's gaze returned to Jack. Sadly, he would die without ever having told Marcella his true heart, and he would die before earning his sword.

Behind her, Giles seized the brat Prince by his hair and dragged him over onto the edge of the parapet. "You want the King's son, Morwen? Give us Jack and we'll give him to you," he offered. "If, indeed, you wish to rule, you will not do so without him."

"Rule?" said Morwen, laughing. "Rule!" She laughed to her leisure, then stopped, and then, again, when they believed she would speak, she laughed a moment longer, and finally declared, "What need have I for a poppet when I am already a queen?"

She waved a hand. "Do you not see who follows me, Prince of Paladins? Here, I have brought you Wales!" she exclaimed. "*I* am the Chosen One. I am the key to Heaven on Earth. What have you but a snotty little boy—the weakling son of a usurper, who, even now, slumps in his throne, heavy with defeat!"

A frisson of fear rushed down Rhiannon's spine as Giles held the King's son closer to the edge of the parapet, his temper rising. "P-Please d-don't!" whined the Prince. "P-Please! My father will treat with you. He'll give you aught you ask for. I will give you gold!"

Giles ignored him. "Neither have we any need for a sniveling fool, who cares more for his own turds than he does for his people!"

"Of that we are in accord," said Morwen evenly. She lifted a hand. "Therefore, let us be rid of the wretch!" she declared, and waved a hand, commanding her bowmen.

A host of arrows flew at the Prince's breast, every one finding its mark, narrowly missing Giles. Alas, their own bowmen could not answer in kind. The Welsh were famed for their precision; their arrows more deadly and their projection farther than England's. The impact gave the Prince's body a succession of violent twitches. Looking like a pinpush, he crumpled to his knees. Startled, Giles de Vere released him, and Eustace fell forward, tumbling lifelessly into the motte.

So swiftly the King's heir was gone.

So swiftly a father's legacy was done.

If, indeed, he'd meant to reconsider a treaty with Duke Henry, this would be the death of his waffling. And yet, Morwen was only toying with them as yet, perhaps realizing they hadn't proper numbers to fight her. First, she would have her fun, and then she would have her vengeance. Still, Giles insisted. "We'll not treat with you! Free the boy!"

Morwen shrugged. "I see no boy," she said. "I see a man, fledgling though he might be. A grown man with choices, and he made one. So mote it be." Without warning, she unsheathed her sword and turned to run it through Jack's heart.

Fight and prevail, said Jack, even as the blood gurgled into his throat, the fresh tide turning the cloth in his mouth even more crimson yet. He slumped forward in the saddle, and Morwen shoved his lifeless body off the horse, into the muck.

Seeing this, Marcella's scream rent the air; it was the beginning of chaos.

A bolt of lightning struck the keep behind them, the sound like a god's fury.

Morwen's soldiers silently marched forward, closing in on the castle, like mindless lemmings. The first line of defense fell into the motte, then turned upon their brethren, and seeing this unexpected sorcery, Morwen raged anew. Her scream sent forth a host of locusts swarming toward the castle, only to meet the sisters' wards and be thwarted.

Down in the field, the battle was fully engaged. Beguiled and confused, some of Morwen's soldiers fought each other, hand to hand. Up on the ramparts, Warkworth's archers waited for the seneschal's command. Knowing their missiles were scarce, he waited until the second line of Morwen's army was close enough, then shouted, "Loose!"

A flight of arrows whizzed through the air, and Seren waved a hand and said:

Fire in the air, fire on the ground!

The arrows erupted with *witchfire*, leaving smoke in their wake as they descended. Every mark they met igniting with searing blue flames. Men screamed, but those horrifying sounds that came from their mouths were akin to squawks.

Thunder cracked; the skies emptied. Lightning brightened the fields as a swarm of creatures launched into the air, bodies morphing from man to bird. Some flew away, some tested the wards, breaching their defense with little effort, only to dive upon their prey.

Elspeth hadn't the same level of skills as her sisters. She focused on the horses of those Welsh soldiers, commanding them all to unseat their riders. In answer, a wave of soldiers flew from their mounts, rolling into the muck, and she did it again, and again, until all Morwen's reinforcements were forced to fight afoot, slogging through boggy fields in the downpour.

Only Morwen's horse held its rider, but she struggled to retain it. "I should have snuffed your first breaths!" she raged, shaking her fist at the daughters.

Only now that her soldiers were grounded, Rosalynde focused on the fields, and all those remaining puddles, turning each one into quagmires, so that they sucked at the boots of passing soldiers, pulling them down into quicksand.

More screams and squawks rent the air. Swords clashed; metal rang. Somewhere down in the fray, Jack's body lay trampled.

The thought made Rhiannon's heart ache, but clearly not more than Marcella's. At one point during the melee, whilst everyone was otherwise engaged, Marcella flew down the stairs. Shouting vengefully, she cast open the gates. Sword in hand, the witch-paladin marched out from the inner bailey, straight toward her once beloved, intent upon doing what she knew best—wresting the head from Morwen's body. She might not have the same affinities as the Pendragon sisters, but she knew how to use a blade, and with deadly precision. As though called upon by her wrath, more soldiers arrived on the battlefield and Rhiannon feared the battle was done.

"D'Lucy!" shouted Wilhelm. "D'Lucy!"

Rhiannon's heart quivered, thinking that Cael had finally arrived to join them on the ramparts. But nay... nay... those were Drakewich's standards marching toward them—hundreds of men, all sporting a similar dragon banner as Cael's. And then, from the woodlands came yet another wave of reinforcements, all bearing Scotia's standard, with Malcom Scott at the helm.

Flanked between them, Morwen's soldiers crushed themselves together, pushing the first line into the motte as Marcella fought her way across the bridge, here and there shoving Morwen's soldiers into the motte. They emerged time and again, only to fall behind her, and by the time she'd made her way into the crush, their numbers had grown.

But it was not enough.

Like Jack, she would die if she dared to face Morwen alone, and foremost in Rhiannon's mind was the fear that now that the gates were open wide, their wards would all be breached. Once those circles were broken, the *magik* used to protect them would be useless.

She and her *dewine* sisters shared a look, and a shiver rushed up Rhiannon's spine as each of her sisters unsheathed a sword...

No time for kisses.

No time for embraces.

No time for good-byes.

No time for regrets.

No time for uncertainty.

It was impossible to say how many new warriors had joined the battle, but the match was still heavily skewed in Morwen's favor. One last look passed between the sisters as the battle entered their gates. And then, one by one they turned to engage, and Rhiannon hadn't any more time to wonder about Cael. She had a fleeting thought that his would not be the last arms she would fall upon, and then a dark shadow crossed the sky—a great, winged creature. A bird, no... an angel, descending from the heavens.

It did not alight on the ramparts. Rather, it flew over their heads, straight toward Morwen, landing at the Witch Queen's feet, standing tall amidst a fury of ringing swords.

Rhiannon blinked, then screamed, realizing who it was...

It was Cael.

THIRTY-SEVEN

Nothing else fazed her—not the dead lying at her feet, nor the battle engaged. Only now, her face twisted with fury at the sight of Cael, changed in form. "You fool!" she spat. "You've no idea what you have done!"

"Oh, I think I do," said Cael, stretching his feathered wings. Black as a raven's, they extended twice the length of his body—a dark angel in the flesh.

So, it appeared, destroying the crystals did not destroy the souls they were bound to.

Cael had been wrong: The *grisial hud* was *not* his sepulcher; it was a key. But simply destroying the crystal did not sprout him wings. Rather, it was a result of destroying the binding spell that Morwen had placed upon his *grisial hud*. Indeed, she had summoned him back to this world, but she had cast yet another spell with blood *magik* to ensure that he could not make use of the gifts he'd been given by virtue of Nesta's sacrifice. Rage unfurled his wings.

"Without it, your soul is bound to this realm," she said furiously. "Return me mine!" she demanded, thrusting out her hand.

Cael smiled coldly. "I'm afraid I can't do that," he said, and the two stood facing each other, one dark angel, one light. His key was to the dominion of the Horned God of Donn, the Dark One from the House of the Dead. She was a daughter of the Goddess, banished for her sins against man. Her body might now be consigned to this world, but her spirit had no refuge. At least he had his sanctuary with the Horned God. Truth was his guiding light now, banishing uncertainty from his heart and his brow. All things were revealed in the destruction of his *grisial hud*.

Morwen raged.

The sky exploded.

Thunder cracked.

Lightning forked.

The Witch Queen stood facing her equal and opposite, her fury so intense that it produced silvered wings. They unfurled to the breadth of his own. Beautiful and terrifying—as he must also be. Morwen's golden eyes radiated the light of ten suns. Her hair and brows silvered the shade of her wings... the color of Seren's hair.

She was *Sylphkind*, as was he. But though she was born with *Sylph* blood in her veins, Cael was made through grace. Nesta had given her life with love, paying his toll to the House of the Dead. Only this time, when he returned, he would remain forevermore, serving the Horned God beneath the Hill of Truth.

A dark figure emerged from the battlefield, rising to the aid of his mistress. Mordecai descended upon them, his face twisting and morphing, his features ebbing and flowing like smoke.

. . .

Slogging through the muck, Rhiannon rushed from the castle, Cael's wolfhound running behind her, and Morwen smiled gleefully.

"Here she comes," said the Witch Queen. "At long last she will see you for what you truly are—a servitor of death. How appropriate it was for you to serve as the King's executioner."

Breathless, terrified, Rhiannon stumbled after Marcella.

Waylaid by soldiers, the paladin paused only to fight.

Driven to reach Cael, Rhiannon fought her way past soldier after soldier, her limbs heavy with metal as rain seeped past the rings of her suit. Burdensome as it was, the sword in her hand threatened to slip from her grasp. When she stumbled into a puddle, she rose again to face one of Morwen's black-clad soldiers. Crying out in desperation, she responded with a swing of her sword. The clash of metal left her ears ringing and her hand numb. Dropping the sword, she bent to reach for it, slicing her hand in the process. If it weren't for Marcella coming to her rescue, Morwen's soldier would have taken her head where she knelt.

"Go!" said Marcella, reaching down to grasp the muddied sword and handing it back to Rhiannon. "Go," she said again, her stark green eyes commanding Rhiannon to rise.

Now is not the time for weakness.
Now is not the time to falter.

"Go!"

Summoning all her might and the last of her will,

Rhiannon rose again, and ran, her sides aching now. Somehow, she managed to evade more crossing swords, and made it past stumbling horses, men crawling from the muck, soldiers in the midst of combat...

"Spirit of vision, Spirit of night. Cast me a shadow to shield me from sight," she whispered desperately.

Do not see me!

Do not see me!

Do not see me!

Behind her, she knew that Marcella defended her back, but Rhiannon daren't look now to see how close. She could scarcely lift her own sword, dragging it after her, determined to reach Cael. Once more when she stumbled, she felt the wolfhound beside her, nudging her up, snarling and snapping at anyone who came near. Somehow, thanks to the hound, she discovered her feet again, and ran again, breathless and anguished.

How could they possibly defeat Morwen?

Here, amidst so many clashing swords, she felt outnumbered and hopeless.

This time when she stopped, the wolfhound stopped again by her side, snarling at the Shadow Beast.

Mordecai.

"Cael," she cried, stunned by the sight of him.

Crouched, preparing to pounce, the wolfhound growled.

Sweet fates! Cael was exactly as her mother was—both avenging angels. Larger than life, they stood facing one another, wings outstretched to catch silvery droplets of rain. The Goddess herself wept to see her children enraged.

Morwen turned to face her and the light from her eyes made Rhiannon shield her face. Her beauty was startling, her aura shining as brightly as the metal of the sword Cael had tucked behind his back...

Caledfwlch.

The Sword of Ages.

And her husband... his aura dark as a storm-ridden sky... dark as the specter of death... beautiful as well, though even more terrifying for the visage he wore.

What would he do?

Would he join Morwen?

What would he do?

There is one among us who could be swayed, Marcella had said...

It was Cael.

Alas, there was no time to consider her folly or faith.

In his Shadow Beast form, part serpent, part dragon, part raven, Mordecai faced Cael, his thick tail rising behind him, like a viper preparing to strike...

"Evil, conniving bitch!" screamed Marcella, reaching them at last, distracting everyone for the briefest instant—long enough for Rhiannon to leap at the Shadow Beast, taking him by the chain he wore about his neck.

The wolfhound pounced as well, sinking its teeth into Mordecai's leg but failing to find purchase. In the meantime, Marcella swung her sword, and Rhiannon summoned those words she remembered her sister speaking in the woodlot south of Whittlewood and Salcey...

I call the fifth to me!

Goddess, hear my plea!

Of smoke and mist you may be born.
But now I bind you here in mortal form.
"Now!" she screamed. "Do it now!" she demanded, and Cael wasted no time.

Advancing on Mordecai, he drew the ancient sword from its scabbard.

"I love you," she cried, releasing the shadow beast perforce and raising her own sword, preparing to join Marcella. But it was too late for the paladin. Even as they watched, Morwen grew a speared tail, whipping Marcella with it. The wolfhound snarled and leapt once more into the fray, but Morwen wrapped Marcella up, wresting her close. Then, with a cruel smile, she said, "Shall I say I once loved you, as well?"

"Go to hell!" hissed Marcella, blood seeping from the corners of her mouth.

It happened so quickly. Morwen tossed her away, hard, so easily. The witch-paladin's body landed with a sickening thud yards from where they stood. She didn't rise again.

Morwen turned to Rhiannon then, her smile cool as the mist now roiling about them. The wolfhound whimpered as she thrust out a hand and tossed him away, as well, then with a slam of her hand, she compelled Rhiannon to her knees.

Too late, Rhiannon heard her sisters' voices, searching.

Seren.

Rosalynde.

Elspeth.

Ignoring everyone, Morwen kept her attention on her second-eldest daughter. She raised a hand to her as though to strike, but she couldn't do so without gloating. "You thought you would be Regnant; look at you now—piteous and powerless!"

"Mercy for my husband!" Rhiannon begged, haplessly. "Mercy for my sisters!"

Morwen scoffed, until she heard Seren's voice.

"She might not be Regnant, but I am," said her sister, and Morwen turned to find Seren holding back her soldiers, her hand lifted so no one could pass.

"You?"

"Aye," said Seren, with a smirk. "Me."

"I'll deal with you in a moment," she said, her countenance darkening. She returned her attention to Rhiannon, stabbing a finger into the air, and Rhiannon shrieked in pain.

Behind Morwen, the Shadow Beast lost its head. Finally, it crumpled to the ground, its body withering where it lay. As it had once before, the wisp of Mordecai's soul returned to the *grisial hud* hanging around his neck. Even as they watched, it was all that remained—a tangle of silver with a darkened crystal, and Rhiannon gave her husband a tremulous smile.

"Leave her!" said Cael.

Morwen turned to him slowly, and said, "Lest you forget, she is mine, Dragon Lord! Born of my blood!" Without even looking her way, she spun a hand at Seren, and Seren found herself cocooned by a fine web of mist, and then Rhiannon as well, fine tendrils of mist coiling about her neck and tightening very slowly, leaving Rhiannon struggling to breathe.

Sweet fates, she couldn't even lift a hand to her throat to clear the way for a breath. Her face felt hot and engorged, her lips swollen and inflamed.

Air!

She needed air!

"You'll have to kill me first!" said Cael, as Rhiannon gasped for breath.

Her mother laughed, delighted. "So be it, Dragon Lord," she said with the silkiness of a cat, stretching her terrible silver wings.

Without warning, both dragon beasts erupted from the ground in a flurry of feathers, rising above the mist now grown so thick that Rhiannon could scarcely see. She tried to move but couldn't. She could only watch helplessly as Seren struggled to free herself, and then suddenly there was Elspeth.

"Rhiannon!"

Hands tugged at the bindings of her throat, loosening them so she could breathe again. More hands joined the struggle, but Rhiannon could only stare haplessly into the heavens as cold rain pelted her face, a downpour so violent it stung her cheeks.

"Cael," she whispered hoarsely, brokenly, but there was nothing she could do. Nothing she could say. No spell she could weave. No sword she could wield. The one she'd born in her hand now lay in the mud. Overhead, both dragon beasts vanished into the storm, and Rhiannon could see little as twilight turned to dusk, and the sound of thunder reverberated throughout.

Now they appeared, then disappeared, their tussling forms visible only in glimpses. Over and over the winged creatures spun and turned—one black, one silver—whirling about through the lowering skies, like a maelstrom.

Feigning, then advancing and parrying, they were half man, half beast, entirely mortal now without the crystals. At last, Morwen tumbled down, then surged up, lifting her sword with the speed of lightning, stabbing Cael with it as he fell into her, straight through his heart.

Roaring in pain, mortally injured, Cael somehow managed to raise his own sword and slashed it down across Morwen's throat, severing her head in one fell swoop.

Like Mordecai's, her soul withdrew from her body like smoke, then dissipated into the storm, and all at once, Cael's body plummeted to the ground.

The sound of fury died in that moment, and a rush of black wings darkened the sky as Morwen's birds took flight.

THIRTY-EIGHT

Rhiannon was the first to reach Cael.

Desperately, she knelt by his side, tears streaming down her cheeks as she scooped his bloodied head into her lap. "My sweet love," she said. "My dearest, sweet love."

He smiled weakly. "It's only a flesh wound," he said, and she nearly wept with joy, because, indeed, the spot on his tunic where Morwen had stabbed him was free of blood. His cheeks were still full of life, high with color. Retracting into his body, his wings had vanished by the time everyone else arrived. With Morwen's death, her soldiers fled. All her Welsh kings retreated into the woods. The mist vanished as well, and once the field was visible again in the waning daylight, only a few dozen bodies remained—mostly Welsh, though a number were allies. Their bodies lay twisted amidst a veritable sea of dead birds.

Later, they found Jack, trampled and dead.

Marcella was alive, though barely.

Rhiannon's sisters rushed the paladin into the castle, prepared to do what they must to save her life. Thankfully, everyone else survived.

Giles, unharmed.

Wilhelm, unharmed.

Edmund, unharmed.

The wolfhound, his left-back-leg injured, and limping, but healing.

And Rhiannon... only her heart ached... ached with love for the man who lay resting in her arms, his face so painfully lovely that it made her heart hurt only to see it. "You are *not* a Shadow Beast," she said, a hard lump forming in her throat.

His answering smile was as beauteously radiant as his face.

He was *Sylphkind*, pure and true.

A terrible, beautiful, fallen angel... like her mother.

Only better, kinder, stronger.

EPILOGUE
WINCHESTER CATHEDRAL, NOVEMBER
1153

Eustace of Blois died of mysterious circumstances. Some claimed the King's son was poisoned. Others said his heart had failed him, crushed by his father's betrayal. Still others claimed they'd caught a glimpse of the man as he was readied for interment, and his body was riddled with wormy holes. With concern for a plague, the Church remanded his body for burial, and not even his own father could see him in death. There was, however, a public funeral, open to the many, attended only by a few. Now, with the death of the King's eldest son and heir, Wallingford's treaty was ratified at last. Signed before witnesses by both the King and Duke Henry, it was agreed that, as his adopted son and successor, Henry Fitz Empress would assume England's throne on Stephen's death. In the meantime, though he would retain his royal authority, Stephen promised to heed all of Duke Henry's advice. Moreover, in exchange for promises of security for his lands, his youngest son, William, now Count of Boulogne and Earl of Surrey, agreed to do homage to Henry and renounce all claims to the throne.

Several strategic strongholds were held by guarantors on the Duke's behalf. All taxes were to be paid as usual, and all foreign mercenaries were demobilized and dispatched. Those who were exiled, including the Archbishop of Canterbury, returned with the King's blessings.

Stephen and Henry sealed their treaty with a kiss of peace at Winchester Cathedral, in a ceremony attended by his barons, and their wives. Thereafter, there was a feast held in the Duke's honor, with dignitaries from the Church in attendance.

Marcella recovered quickly enough to join her true mistress, the Empress, as a witness to the ceremony at Winchester. She remained thereafter as Matilda's personal guard.

Weary though he was, and resigned to the circumstances, the King himself remained in good spirits. But though he welcomed his barons in good standing, he ordered those who were not to be executed by his Rex Militum—one final mission for the sake of the realm.

Thereafter, "The Company" was formally disbanded, all its members dispatched to their holdings, and their names stricken from the royal archives.

As for the Papal Guard, if, indeed, it continued its commissions, no records remained, nor were any of its officers ever named.

At long last, the Witch Queen was defeated. No one knew precisely where she'd gone, though it mattered not at all—at least not to anyone who didn't know the truth.

Alas, Rhiannon and her sisters knew: Morwen was not dead.

In this world, all things were connected, living or dead. Her spirit was out there, somewhere, waiting for another opportunity to return...

And still, for the moment, there was peace.

To commemorate their victory over evil, the Church made yet another decree: The Pendragon name should be banned from further assumption. The dragon pennants were retired with Uther's son Arthur. And, furthermore, on pain of excommunication, no man could bear witness to the events that unfolded at Amdel. So far as all histories were concerned, no battle ever took place there. The Welsh kings were never present. Avalon did not exist. Wild Wales must now be tamed. *Magik* was no more than a dream.

Gathered outside Winchester Cathedral, Seren, Rose, Ellie and Rhiannon all stood saying their farewells to Marcella. The paladin's task before rejoining the Empress in Rouen, would be to visit Jack's mother in Calais... if for naught else, to give her sympathies, and to award the woman his effects, along with a generous stipend from the Church for his services.

Joined by their husbands, the sisters were summoned back inside the vestibule, and there, after all these long, long years, stood their half-sister, the Empress Matilda, along with her son, the future king of England. "I am told you are all to be commended," said the Empress, casting a brief glance toward Marcella le Fae. Her gaze fell first upon Elspeth, and she nodded her gratitude, grasping Elspeth's hand, and holding it delicately. "You above all, I must give my gratitude. We have endured," she said. "Against our enemies, and against the odds, we stand tall in the eyes of God." She patted Elspeth's hand. "Our father would be proud."

Elspeth inclined her head, and said, "We remain in your service, Your Eminence."

Rhiannon said nothing. She reached for the arm of her beloved and drew him back, letting her sisters enjoy Matilda's attention, because she and Matilda were not related by blood.

The Empress and her son exchanged pleasantries with her sisters and their husbands, laughing easily amidst themselves; the sight of them all together made Rhiannon's heart swell with pride. "England will never know how close it came to its doom," said Cael.

Rhiannon grinned up at her husband and said, "This I know."

"And you, my beauteous wife, you may never get your proper thanks, except from me." He bent to whisper into her ear. "But I vow I'll find new ways to express my undying love and gratitude for the rest of my days."

Fearing his whisper would carry in the vestibule, Rhiannon squeezed his arm to silence him, but he wouldn't be silenced. He pulled her aside, taking her into his arms. Haplessly, she gazed up at her beautiful, loyal husband, her dark angel, in truth. Though he might never again spread his wings on earth, she knew the truth—as all who were there to witness did as well: Angels did exist and walked amongst men.

But so, too, did witches.

"Rhiannon," said Matilda, her shrewd gaze finding Rhiannon's at last. And then, she and her son came to address her and Cael. "I am told you, in particular, are to be honored." As she had with Elspeth, she reached out to seize Rhiannon by the hand, patting it gently. "I only wish you to know that... *I know.*" She nodded very meaningfully, and said, "Your loyalty will be rewarded, my sister. And please, do remember, if ever you should find yourself in Rouen... my house is your house."

"Thank you, Empress," said Rhiannon graciously as Duke Henry insinuated himself into the conversation to kiss Cael upon both cheeks.

"Lord Blackwood," he said. "'Tis good to see you again. I trust you are enjoying your new commission?" *As Marcher Lord.*

"I am," said Cael. "I am grateful for the trust you've placed in me, my Prince, and I will endeavor to serve you well."

"I know you will," said Duke Henry, patting Cael's shoulder. "It was well deserved," he said with a wink, and then he reached over to tap his mother on the elbow, nodding toward his uncle to remind her of the procession still waiting to be greeted outside.

The Empress smiled fondly, and said to all, "Go with God, until we meet again."

"And you, as well," said the sisters in unison.

Together, they stood, watching with pride—and relief—as the Empress, along with Duke Henry, made their way out with King Stephen to greet the shouting masses.

High up on a narrow window, two black birds sat watching from a distance... two female crows, one bent-legged, one young with shining blue-black wings. Silent and watchful, they were joined by a third crow... this one a hefty young rook. As the guests turned to leave, it spoke a single discernible word: "Jaaack!"

Rhiannon turned to locate the creature, finding all three crows together, her gaze sought Seren's. Her sister nodded and winked.

"Jaaack!" said the crow. "Jaaack! Jaaack!"

AUTHOR'S NOTE

Dearest reader,

This series was crafted with love, interwoven with true historical events, with loving nods toward the Arthurian tales. Obviously, as fantastical as my story is, it's a figment of my imagination. However, I tried to stay true to those real-life characters and events I've included, weaving them into my story with the utmost respect.

Cerridwen, Taliesin and their brood are mostly taken from the Mabinogion, and early Welsh Folklore. Naturally, I've taken literary license to fashion Cerridwen as the Mother of Avalon, and attributed the legendary isle's demise to her as well.

Of course, no one knows whether Avalon truly existed and no record has ever been found of the mythical isle. Some sources claim ancient Glastonbury, completely surrounded by marshlands, is, in fact, the mythical isle. In Welsh, this island is called *Ynys Afallach*, which literally means the Island of Apples—probably because this fruit once grew there in abundance. Appropriate, in a way, if we consider

Avalon to be the original Garden of Eden, and this it would be, if Cerridwen were, in fact, an angel sent to guard the realms of men.

On the more Earthly side, Eustace of Blois was generally considered to be unfit to rule. He was a spoiled, greedy baron, often taxing his barons injuriously. He did, indeed, die during the Ides of August in 1153, shortly after storming out of his father's peace conference, and raiding and looting Bury St. Edmunds. The manner of his death has long been the subject of speculation, with many people claiming he was poisoned by his enemies to remove him from succession, probably so his father would finally agree to the proposed treaty with Duke Henry.

Of course, King Stephen did "steal" his uncle's throne, and he and the Empress Matilda engaged in a nearly twenty year battle to restore that throne to its rightful heirs. In the end, the Church backed Henry I's grandson, and so began the reign of the Plantagenets.

Maelgwn ap Cadwallon, also known as Maelgwn Gwynedd, was also a true historical figure. He was the Dragon Lord of Anglesey and he did inherit the dragon pennants from his father. Although little is known of him, precisely, I tried to remain true to what I learned. According to contemporary sources, he was actually an ally of Rome, and he fought many, many battles with them against invading Saxons. He did kill his uncle, and he did enter a monastery. He was also said to have died of a "Yellow Plague." One tale claims he was cursed by Taliesin, another claims he was cursed by a sword—perhaps Excalibur? According to some sources, he's buried at Llanrhos Church in Wales and to others, on Puffin Island.

Uther himself is a shadowy figure. What is known of him comes from fragments of literature in the Welsh Triads and various other epic poems, including a death song in the *Book of Taliesin*. His biography, as we know it, was first written by Geoffrey of Monmouth in his *Historia Regum Britanniae*. But, in fact, the name "Uther" has never appeared otherwise in contemporary records. Some historians believe that his name Uther is a descriptor, derived from Welsh uthr meaning "terrible" and that he was possibly a historical figure called Vortigern, who is sometimes named as King Arthur's father.

However, though much is written about King Arthur (generally speaking), and he doesn't live in my story, except as brief mentions, there's actually no proof that Arthur existed either.

As for Taliesin (also known as Merlin and Emrys throughout literature), he has many mentions throughout the Mabinogion, and there are intriguing new sources that give him an entirely new identity and history, placing him in Scotland. If you want to read more about that, you might enjoy *Finding Arthur* or *Finding Merlin* by Adam Ardrey.

Naturally, I took many liberties with all their stories in order to create a rich tapestry, and alternate history for you, one I hope will live in your hearts as much as it does in mine.

In the end, I very much feel these people could have lived in that time and place, and I'm sad to see this story end. But, as they say, all good things must come to an end, and so, with much love, until next time, I leave you with the immortal words of William Butler Yeats from *The Celtic Twilight*:

AUTHOR'S NOTE

*"I have desired, like every artist, to create
a little world out of the beautiful,
pleasant, and significant things of
this marred and clumsy world..."*

A Heartfelt Thank You!

Thank you from the bottom of my heart for reading Lord of Shadows. If you enjoyed this book, please consider posting a review. Reviews don't just help the author, they help other readers discover our books and, no matter how long or short, I sincerely appreciate every review.

Would you like to know when my next book is available? Sign up for my newsletter:

Also, please follow me on BookBub to be notified of deals and new releases.

Let's hang out! I have a Facebook group:

🖤 **Let's Hang Out!** 🖤

Thank you again for reading and for your support.

Tanya Anne Crosby

CONNECTED SERIES
SERIES BIBLIOGRAPHY

Have you also read the Highland Brides and the Guardians
of the Stone? While it's not necessary to read these series to
enjoy the Daughters of Avalon, all three series are related
with shared characters.

These books are ALSO AVAILABLE AS AUDIOBOOKS

THE HIGHLAND BRIDES

The MacKinnon's Bride

Lyon's Gift

On Bended Knee

Lion Heart

Highland Song

MacKinnon's Hope

GUARDIANS OF THE STONE

Once Upon a Highland Legend

Highland Fire

Highland Steel

Highland Storm

Maiden of the Mist

ALSO CONNECTED...

Angel of Fire

Once Upon a Kiss

DAUGHTERS OF AVALON

The King's Favorite

The Holly & the Ivy

A Winter's Rose

Fire Song

Lord of Shadows

ALSO BY TANYA ANNE CROSBY

THE GOLDENCHILD PROPHECY

The Cornish Princess

The Queen's Huntsman

The Forgotten Prince

ONE KNIGHT FOREVER SERIES

One Knight's Stand

DAUGHTERS OF AVALON

The King's Favorite

The Holly & the Ivy

A Winter's Rose

Fire Song

Lord of Shadows

THE PRINCE & THE IMPOSTOR

Seduced by a Prince

A Crown for a Lady

The Art of Kissing Beneath the Mistletoe

THE HIGHLAND BRIDES

The MacKinnon's Bride

Lyon's Gift

On Bended Knee

Lion Heart

Highland Song

MacKinnon's Hope

GUARDIANS OF THE STONE

Once Upon a Highland Legend

Highland Fire

Highland Steel

Highland Storm

Maiden of the Mist

THE MEDIEVAL HEROES

Once Upon a Kiss

Angel of Fire

Viking's Prize

REDEEMABLE ROGUES

Happily Ever After

Perfect In My Sight

McKenzie's Bride

Kissed by a Rogue

Thirty Ways to Leave a Duke

A Perfectly Scandalous Proposal

ANTHOLOGIES & NOVELLAS

Lady's Man

Married at Midnight

The Winter Stone

ROMANTIC SUSPENSE

Leave No Trace

Speak No Evil

Tell No Lies

MAINSTREAM FICTION

The Girl Who Stayed

The Things We Leave Behind

Redemption Song

Reprisal

Everyday Lies

ABOUT THE AUTHOR

Tanya Anne Crosby is the New York Times and USA Today bestselling author of thirty novels. She has been featured in magazines, such as People, Romantic Times and Publisher's Weekly, and her books have been translated into eight languages. Her first novel was published in 1992 by Avon Books, where Tanya was hailed as "one of Avon's fastest rising stars." Her fourth book was chosen to launch the company's Avon Romantic Treasure imprint.

Known for stories charged with emotion and humor and filled with flawed characters Tanya is an award-winning author, journalist, and editor, and her novels have garnered reader praise and glowing critical reviews. She and her writer husband split their time between Charleston, SC, where she was raised, and northern Michigan, where the couple make their home.

For more information
Website
Email

Newsletter

www.ingramcontent.com/pod-product-compliance
Lightning Source LLC
Chambersburg PA
CBHW011113100726
47898CB00011B/3063